STRANGE

Strange Alliance

PETER J. FOOT

UPFRONT PUBLISHING
LEICESTERSHIRE

Strange Alliance
Copyright © Peter J. Foot 2003

Also by Peter J. Foot
Oath of Allegiance

All rights reserved

ISBN 1-84426-160-3

First published 2003 by
UPFRONT PUBLISHING LTD
Leicestershire

Typeset in Bembo by
Bookcraft Ltd, Stroud, Gloucestershire
Printed by Lightning Source

*This book is dedicated to all Royal Marines
past, present and future*

Acknowledgements

I wish to acknowledge the assistance of my good friend Richard Riley in the editing of the rough drafts of this book, and to thank him for his enduring patience and good humour in the many hours this has taken.

Contents

Prologue

The dark satanic storm clouds of war, which were present in the skies of Europe, spread their evil influence to Asia and the Pacific towards the end of 1941.

In their frequent meetings, the War Cabinet in London were aware of the Japanese interest in Burma, Malaya and Indonesia. The engines of war demanded oil and rubber in large quantities. Malaya provided 40 per cent of the world's rubber and 60 per cent of its tin. Burma and Indonesia provided vast amounts of oil. These three countries, therefore, were prime targets for a Japanese invasion.

In Singapore, the so-called Island Fortress, few of the largely Chinese population took the threat of a Japanese attack seriously. The armies of Great Britain and the Commonwealth were there in great numbers. Singapore had huge guns to deter any assault from the sea. As for an attack on Malaya from the north, the country was covered in jungle for seven-eighths of its mass.

The Commander-in-Chief Far East, Air Chief Marshall Sir Robert Brooke-Popham, was concerned, however. Intelligence reports suggested that the Japanese were planning a seaborne assault on Thailand, to capture the seaports of Songkhla and Pattani and their respective airfields. This would enable them to launch a devastating attack on the north of Malaya and blast their way through the British defences at Jitra.

Sir Robert, despite this information, had great difficulty in persuading his army, navy and air force commanders to take this threat seriously. However, in the face of their reluctance, he produced a plan to frustrate the Japanese. It was to be code-named 'Matador'.

The basis of Matador was an advance into Thailand by the British forces and occupation of the ports of Songkhla and Pattani. It was considered that, with this achieved, the Japanese would abandon their plans to occupy Malaya.

The British had a treaty with Thailand at this time, which amounted to a non-aggression pact. Brooke-Popham thought he could negotiate this by claiming to be coming to the aid of a threatened friendly country. In London, the Foreign Office raised objections, but Churchill, by not rejecting the plan, stilled their voice.

The navy, conscious that their forces were 'light' in the Far East, dispatched the modern battleship HMS *Prince of Wales*, the older battlecruiser HMS *Repulse* and, to provide air cover for the ships, the aircraft carrier HMS *Indomitable*. 'Force Z', as it was called, suffered an immediate reverse when the *Indomitable* ran aground as it was leaving for the Far East. It had to go to the United States for repairs, leaving Force Z without air cover.

In November 1941, Brooke-Popham ordered his army commander to move his troops to Jitra ready for the advance into Thailand. Information had come from the Thai capital that General Pipul, who was Chief Minister, had said he would resist a British advance into his country, but not as forcefully as he would a Japanese invasion. With this indication of only a token defence against a British occupation Brooke-Popham thought his plan would succeed and he encouraged his army commanders to prepare.

For some reason the order was never given. Perhaps the Foreign Office persuaded Churchill and his War Cabinet to withhold their support. We shall never know, for Churchill ordered that these particular meetings should not be minuted. Without Churchill's support Brooke-Popham felt reluctant to order the advance into Thailand, although, as was pointed out later, he did have the authority to do so.

On the 6th of December, a Hudson aircraft patrolling the seas between Indo-China and the Thailand coast spotted a large number of troop transports and support ships. In response to this information, Headquarters in Singapore ordered that a further recognisance take place to confirm these sightings. The delay was fatal.

For Operation Matador to have succeeded it should have been launched not later than the 4th of December. It was now too late.

On the 8th of December, the Japanese landed at Songkhla and Pattani. Eighteen troop transports discharged the attacking army with little opposition, while a further landing took place on the northern coast of Malaya at Kota Bharu. The Japanese were now ashore in force. Their casualties were a mere twenty-seven killed or wounded.

In a different time zone, but at the same time, the Japanese bombed Pearl Harbor. America was now at war. Japanese bombers attacked Singapore and other targets on mainland Malaya. With the airfields now in their hands, the planes that had taken off from Indo-China could now land and refuel at these captured airfields.

Force Z now sailed from Singapore to prevent further landings on the east coast of Malaya. The ships had been promised air cover from the RAF bases in Malaya but, with these bases now under attack, that promise was never kept. At 1100 hours on the morning of the 10th of December, Force Z was attacked by torpedo bombers and within two hours the battleship *Prince of Wales* and the battlecruiser *Repulse* were sunk

Peter J. Foot

At Jitra, the army were preparing to halt the Japanese advance from prepared positions. General Percival ordered a battalion of infantry to seize a strategic position called 'The Ledge'. This was to the east of Jitra its capture would prevent the Japanese from outflanking the Jitra Line. However, due to the slowness of their advance, when they arrived at 'The Ledge' it was already in Japanese hands.

By the evening of the 13th of December 1941, the Japanese had overrun the British positions at Jitra and the troops of Great Britain, Australia and India were retreating from northern Malaya.

Within four weeks the Japanese had captured Kuala Lumpur and by the end of January 1942, the British forces had retreated across the causeway into Singapore. The Island Fortress had failed to live up to its name, despite having over a hundred thousand troops to defend it. On the 15th of February 1942, General Percival surrendered unconditionally to the Japanese.

Chapter 1

A dense pall of acrid smoke hung over the shattered ruins of Ipoh railway station. A few Malay railway workers were wearily fighting a losing battle against the many small fires the recent Japanese air raid had started. It was the 14th of December 1941, just six days after the first attack by Japan on the Malayan coast.

Outside the station, a hundred Royal Marines emerged from the deep monsoon ditches, which were a common feature of all the major roads in Malaya. They had arrived from Singapore just a few minutes before the air raid had started. Their train was now a twisted mass of metal; the engine lay on its side like a dying prehistoric creature.

The company commander of the marines, Maj. Mick Martin, called his sergeant major over to him.

'Get the men to rescue what they can from the train, then fall them in. I want a quick word before we move off.'

Sgt Maj. Rogers hastily summoned his senior and junior NCOs and quickly explained what was required. Within seconds the wrecked train was a hive of activity.

Ten minutes later the marines, having rescued what they could of their equipment from the train, were listening intently to what their company commander had to say. Maj. Martin looked at the mostly young faces assembled before him.

'We have been sent to deny the Japanese access to the road and rail bridge at Tanjung Rambutan, which is fifteen miles from here. In ten minutes we leave here to do just that. Your NCOs will tell you what equipment to take with you. The remaining kit is to be thrown on the fires, which the Japanese have so kindly provided. Sergeant Major, take over.'

Within the time prescribed the marines were on their way. Divided into subsections of ten, the company marched through the largely deserted streets of Ipoh. They were well spread out: five subsections on one side of the road and five on the other, with ten yards between each formation and two yards between each man. They were dressed in khaki drill shirts and trousers. Their boots were still shining, though not for much longer. All were rigged in full fighting order and they carried an assortment of weapons: Bren guns, Thompson sub-machine guns, rifles and four 2-inch mortars. Each man had three days' rations in his pack, four hand grenades, an appropriate supply of ammunition and a full water bottle.

Before they had left Singapore, Maj. Martin had obtained from the Australian army stores a bush hat for each man, but of course the Royal Marine cap badge was mounted just above the rim. They halted each hour for ten minutes. The heat was intense and all of the marines were drenched in sweat. Their NCOs made sure nobody overused their water bottles, at the same time being aware of the dangers of dehydration. As they marched through the small village of Tambun, the children there gave them chunks of fresh pineapple and followed them for a mile or so past the village.

Two hours latter they reached their objective and deployed in defensive positions either side of the road and rail bridge. One subsection moved a hundred yards further up the road to give an early warning of Japanese troops. An army brigadier at Kuala Lumpur railway station had briefed Maj. Martin and told him that all the army units had been moved north to try to halt the rapid Japanese advance.

'To be honest old boy, our communications are down and the buggers could be anywhere. Expect them any time.'

The tired and worried officer had then wished him luck and sent him on his way.

Maj. Martin looked around at his marines. They had been gathered in hastily from all over Singapore Island. Sixty had been borrowed from the marine detachments of the battleships *Prince of Wales* and *Repulse* and the others from the shore base. The marines from the sunken battleships had not been told of that particular disaster; no doubt in time they would find out.

For the rest of the day the marines improved their positions; they dug slit trenches in the soft earth and sited their various weapons to best effect. Using their rubber groundsheets they constructed 'bashas' (temporary shelters) and camouflaged them with the huge Atap palms, which were abundant in their location. It began to rain, gently at first, but in seconds it became torrential, painfully stinging their exposed skin. And it was cold. The rain felt as though it was melted ice. Then it stopped as suddenly as it had begun, the sun came out and within minutes they were almost dry.

They heard the sound of a truck approaching from the direction they had come. As it approached the bridge it ground to a halt just where the marines were stood to. An officer jumped out and Maj. Martin greeted him. After a short conversation a large number of ration boxes were unloaded and the truck turned around and sped off towards Ipoh. Suddenly there was the sound of aero-engines, which grew to a roar as six Japanese aircraft flew low over their position towards Ipoh. A few minutes later they heard the thud and rumble as the bombs exploded, adding to the destruction already caused in the previous raid.

Putting the raid on Ipoh out of their minds, the marines prepared a meal and settled down in their new surroundings, waiting for night to fall. As darkness came so did the mosquitoes. A relentless assault began on the marines. With no repellent to stave off the hordes of insects they spent a miserable, sleepless night. They were glad when the first sign of dawn touched the eastern sky, bringing with it some relief.

By noon that day their defensive positions were as good as they would ever be and passed the scrutiny of both the major and the sergeant major. Further rations arrived from the army base in Ipoh, including quinine tablets, mosquito repellent and water purification tablets. Also came the news that the army were withdrawing down the west coast to prepared positions north of Taiping.

The major looked at his map and shared the information with the sergeant major and the two young lieutenants.

'You realise that's less than forty miles from here. Within two days we could be fighting for our lives.'

Whether it was intended to or not, in a very short time the news of the Japanese advance was common knowledge in the company, which prompted a careful check of their weapons and ammunition. By nightfall they could hear in the distance the faint sound of heavy guns. It was apparent to them all they did not have to move, the war was coming to them.

With the mosquito repellent having some effect the marines spent a more comfortable night, but by dawn it was obvious the gunfire was appreciably nearer. At 0900 hours the supplies lorry from Ipoh dropped off an enormous pile of ration boxes.

The driver told the sergeant major, 'That's all you're going to get, we're withdrawing to KL today. You're on your own.'

Chapter 2

Marine Peter Blake made the final adjustments to the bipod of his Bren gun. It was now perfectly positioned on the grass mound in front of his slit trench. He had a clear view of the road ahead of him, giving a wide field of fire with little adjustment necessary to the gun's position. His number two, fellow marine Jim White, was on his right. Between them they had cleaned and refilled the twenty magazines, which were now covered with a groundsheet.

Blake was just nineteen and one of the youngest marines in the newly formed company. He had only been in the *Prince of Wales* Royal Marine detachment for a month when he had been told by his sergeant major that he had been 'kidnapped' by a Maj. Martin, for duties ashore in up-country Malaya. He had been told the day before that his ship had been sunk off Malaya's east coast. He found it hard to believe that the huge vessel was no more. He could not imagine it lying on the sea floor, his previous home full of seawater and his dead friends.

He had written to his parents to tell them of his new unit, but his Mum and Dad would assume he had been on the *Prince of Wales* when she had been sunk; letters were taking almost a month to get home. He thought of his home in Faversham, at the centre of the Kent hop fields, and of his girl friend Susie Howard. When he had told his best friend he was going out with Susie, his reply was 'You lucky bastard, she's got the best pair of tits in Kent!' Susie and 'the best pair of tits in Kent' were a long way off now.

The gunfire that they had heard yesterday was definitely nearer. A dispatch rider had left some new orders for the major, some suggestion of a new defence line south of the Slim River. Maj. Martin had told his two young officers and the sergeant major that they had been told to stay where they were and defend the road and rail bridge.

The sergeant major had suggested, 'Blow the fucking thing up.'

The major laughed. 'That's just what I said, but the brains at HQ said that we will need the bridges intact when we counter-attack.'

The sergeant major gave a snort of annoyance.

'The army is retreating so fast, what would we counter-attack with?'

The officers nodded their agreement.

By 1600 hours there was a steady stream of lorries passing the marines' position, all heading south filled with desperately tired soldiers, some of them clearly wounded. A few large guns went by, their towing trucks overloaded with men. One of their officers suggested the marines join them, but the major shook his head.

'We stay here', he said.

Just before dark, six Japanese planes flew over their position and dropped a stick of bombs a mile north of them.

Fifteen minutes later twenty soldiers ran towards them in the gathering dusk. Maj. Martin and the sergeant major managed to stop them and discovered that the men were the only survivors from ten lorries packed with troops, which the aircraft had bombed. It was pointless trying to detain the men, panic had set in. The major watched them run down the road in the direction of Ipoh.

That night was very quiet and the only attack came from the voracious mosquitoes, which appeared to have become immune to the liberal applications of insect repellent. The marines, being marines, were enjoying a good moan; chief source of their annoyance was the army. Marines had a low opinion of the navy, army and air force, but in this case the army was the cause of their complaints. 'Fucking useless' was one of the milder expressions used.

In Marine Blake's slit trench Cpl Hart was giving the other occupants the benefit of his vast experience with women.

'The secret of a good marriage', he said, 'is to keep her well fucked and poorly shod. Do that and she will never leave you.'

The two young marines digested these pearls of wisdom. Blake thought on what the corporal had said.

'I thought you said you was divorced, Corp.'

Hart grunted, 'Aye, she just wasn't right lad.'

At dawn the marines stood to. They all had the feeling that today the Japanese would come down the road and their mettle would be tested. Maj. Martin was of the same opinion, and he decided to send half a dozen men and a sergeant a couple of miles up the road to see what was going on. Peter Blake and his number two, Jim White, were among those selected. Well spaced out, they moved up the road. After ten minutes they came across the lorries that had been bombed the previous evening. Most of them had been burnt out and the bodies of the unfortunate soldiers had been evolved into a series of bizarre shapes by the fires. Several of the soldiers had already been wounded but had been left by their fellow soldiers. All were dead bar one, who lifted a hand to greet the marines. Blake gave the wounded man a drink of water.

'You Aussies?' asked the soldier.

'No', said Blake. 'Royal Marines. We'll pick you up on the way back.'

The marines moved further up the road. Still no sign of the advancing Japanese. It was eerily quiet. After another mile the sergeant in charge told them to take a ten-minute break, then they would go back.

As the marines made their way back down the road, they heard the sound of aircraft engines. Quickly they moved out of sight into the long grass at the side of the road. Three Japanese planes flew overhead in a 'V' formation. As the planes disappeared they resumed their journey back to their bridge positions.

When they reached the burnt out lorries, the wounded soldier they were going to pick up was dead. Flies were beginning to occupy the still moist passages of his mouth and nose. They hurried on, anxious to put some distance between themselves and the sweet sickly odour of the already rotting corpses; in the tropics twenty-four hours is a long time to be dead.

When they reached their company's position it was a scene of frantic activity. The major had sent a small patrol down the road towards Tambun and they had spotted some Japanese troops coming up the road towards them. Quickly the marines adjusted their firing positions and awaited the arrival of their enemy.

After about ten minutes the enemy troops came into sight. They were not the impressive sight the marines had expected. About twenty strong, they were dressed in a variety of uniforms and some were wheeling bicycles with their weapons tied to the crossbar. The marines could not believe their eyes. How could this ragtag army defeat their well-trained troops? As the marines waited for them to walk into their ambush, the Japanese suddenly stopped. An order was given and in seconds they were in the undergrowth on each side of the road. The marines quickly realised that, despite their appearance, the Japanese were also very well-trained troops.

Peter Blake sighted his Bren gun on a spot five or so yards from where the enemy troops had melted into the roadside cover. Suddenly, half a dozen Japanese reappeared and cautiously made their way towards the road bridge. They came level with the marines, sniffing the air like gun dogs. An order was given and a blast of fire swept their bodies off the road like a giant broom.

Silence. Not a movement from where the marines knew the rest of the Japanese were. Then they struck, a sudden rush from their right, a burst of fire and the Japanese were almost into the marines' slit trenches. Blake tried to move his Bren gun to the opposite side of his trench but he was too late. A screaming Japanese soldier thrust at him with his bayonet. He twisted his body to one side and it missed him by a matter of inches.

As the soldier fell against him, Blake seized a spare magazine and crashed it against the side of his attacker's head. Twice more he stuck. The magazine, slippery with blood, flew from his hand as he attempted a fourth blow. The soldier fell into the bottom of the slit trench. Blake crashed his booted foot down on the soldier's unprotected throat.

He grabbed his Bren gun and greeted another attacker with a burst of fire across the man's chest. He was conscious of firing all around him, then it went silent once more.

Blake could see several bodies lying in front of the marines' trenches. Where was his number two? Then he saw him. Jim White was sitting in the bottom of the trench with his eyes and mouth wide open. One of the sergeants came across to Blake's trench.

'You OK, son?' he asked.

Blake nodded towards the body of his friend.

'Shit!' said the sergeant and together they dragged the body of Marine White onto the parapet of the trench. Blake could see that his friend had been hit by a single round just above his ear and would have died instantly.

The enemy soldier was also removed from the trench, his neck clearly broken by Blake's frantic stamp. After about ten minutes the marines had cleared the Japanese dead from their position and were taking stock of their situation.

They had counted eighteen dead Japanese soldiers. Two must have got away. The marines had four dead and two wounded, one in a serious condition. Maj. Martin decided to split his force in two for the night and move two hundred yards either side of the bridge. Within thirty minutes they were in their new positions and making the best of their situation.

Suddenly, a Japanese plane flew overhead. It turned and dived on their previous position and dropped two bombs. It then returned and machine-gunned the ground around the bridge. When the plane had left, some of the marines inspected the damage the bombs had created. The bridge had collapsed onto the railway line and their reason for being there was now gone.

The marines spent the rest of the daylight remaining in putting their dead to rest. Maj. Martin made a careful note of where the bodies were buried. The Japanese dead were placed in one of the bomb craters and covered over with the loose soil there.

Chapter 3

Despite the attentions of the night-time insects, when it was Blake's turn to sleep he dozed off quite quickly. It was not a trouble-free dreamless sleep. His body twitched and shook as he relived, in his unconscious state, the horrific events of the previous day. In his dream, his friend Jim White was a charred twisted figure who held out his hand to Blake. When the hand was grasped it came away from his arm and reshaped to become a Japanese bayonet that pursued Blake around his small trench, stabbing at his eyes. He came abruptly awake as a sudden downpour of rain ran off his groundsheet and onto his face. Cpl Hart, who was sharing his trench with him, gave him a reassuring touch on the shoulder and he was able to relax.

It was a relief to them all when morning came, and the hot sun dried out their clothes and trench. They began to appreciate what the army had had to endure in the retreat south, with confusing orders or none at all. The marines revised their previous opinion of the soldiers. They weren't useless, but had done their best in the circumstances in which they had found themselves. It was not the British soldiers' fault that the generals had underestimated the Japanese.

During the morning Maj. Martin sent the sergeant major and six marines, including Blake, to recce the road back into Ipoh. With some caution, they moved back down the road they had marched up just a few days earlier. As they made their way through the village of Tambun, a few frightened faces were seen following their progress. There was no sign of any Japanese, just a few abandoned vehicles, some of which appeared undamaged. An hour later they were on the outskirts of Ipoh. To their surprise an English voice called out to them from the ground floor of a large house.

A British officer appeared. He was a lieutenant colonel.

'And where are you chaps off to?' he said.

The sergeant major saluted the officer and the two were soon deep in conversation. The colonel told him Japanese troops had landed on the coast west of Ipoh in the early hours of the previous day and were about a thousand strong. The Japanese had split into four groups. One had moved due north, another due south, and the other two had moved towards Ipoh, but had split one to the north of the town and one to the south. The British troops still in Ipoh had resisted the Japanese advance and had inflicted heavy casualties on them. The attack on the marines the previous afternoon had been the remnants of the group that had gone to the north of Ipoh.

The colonel informed the sergeant major that there were still two battalions of Allied troops in the Ipoh area, one British, the other Australian. As he was the senior British officer, he gave the sergeant major fresh orders for Maj. Martin.

'Ask him to move back to Tambun and dig in on the north side of the village. I'll get some more supplies up to him this afternoon.'

The marines retraced their footsteps and ninety minutes later were back with their fellow marines. After digesting the sergeant major's fresh orders, the major moved the company back to the northern side of Tambun village. They spent the next two hours digging in on either side of the road, this time making sure they had a clear field of fire to their rear as well as their front.

Marine Peter Blake and Cpl Hart were fascinated by the huge limestone outcrops that ran for several miles a few hundred yards from their position. Some were almost six hundred feet high, the smallest at least three hundred feet. The Malay name for them was 'gunungs'. Blake could see they were a maze of gullies and caves. He turned to Cpl Hart.

'We could hide in them for years, Corp. The Japs would never find us.'

Hart grunted, 'If we had a couple of women with us I might consider it, but you are hardly attractive company for a long stay.'

Later that afternoon a lorry drove slowly up to the marines' position. The colonel had brought their food supplies and a fair amount of ammunition. He and Maj. Martin were old friends and spent an hour discussing the situation. At last they shook hands and the colonel left. The major briefed his two young officers and the sergeant major. They in turn passed on the information to the rest of the marines. In short, they were to hold their position for as long as they could, then move back in a southeasterly route away from the major roads.

As night fell they could hear the sound of heavy gunfire from the south; Ipoh was under attack. They stood to most of the night and by dawn the heavy explosions had given way to machine-gun fire. During the morning the gunfire lost its intensity, with just a few outbreaks of fire. The battle for Ipoh had either been won or lost.

At about 1100 hours the marines heard the sound of an approaching vehicle. It did not sound like a military engine.

Cpl Hart turned to Blake and said, 'That sounds like an old Austin Seven.'

Hart was right. Into view came a battered old black Austin. The front tyres were both flat and both wheels were running on the rims. Several marines moved out of their slit trenches

13

and into the road to stop the car. It ground to a halt, its engine sounding if it was on its last legs. The occupants emerged, two young white women and a middle-aged Malay.

Chapter 4

The army doctor listened to the sound of small arms fire coming from the direction of the bridge over the Sungei (River) Kinta, the only crossing in the town of Ipoh. The British and Australian troops had fought hard to keep the Japanese at bay, but had been outflanked by enemy troops crossing the river to their north and south.

Capt. Healy was the Senior Medical Officer. In fact, he was the only medical officer left in Ipoh. His makeshift hospital contained sixty or so seriously wounded soldiers, few were expected to survive. The day before he had managed to evacuate a hundred stretcher cases in the last train to leave Ipoh for the south, the wounded lying on open flat bed rolling stock. He had as his staff two British nurses and some Malay orderlies.

The two young nurses were the last to escape from the Taiping military hospital just ahead of the Japanese advance. Healy knew he must get them to safety; what the victorious Japanese troops would do if these two pretty young girls fell into their hands did not bare thinking about. The captain knew that there were some Royal Marines just north of Tambun and that the Japanese were already south of Ipoh and had captured Batu Gajah. He called over his senior Malay orderly and told him what he wanted him to do. Hari Khah was a loyal friend, in his early forties, and was clearly reluctant to leave, but agreed to do what the captain wished. The officer then called over the two nurses and told them to collect their things and two medical packs and go with Hari Khah. He watched as the three got into his old Austin Seven and drove out of the compound with a final wave.

Jan Riley and Joyce Hammond knew why they had been sent away from Ipoh; they were both terrified of being taken by the Japanese. As the car slowly made its way through the outskirts of Ipoh, they saw the effects of the recent bombing. Many of the houses were still smouldering from the countless fires that had been started. Bodies lay in the road and Hari Khah had to drive carefully around them.

Suddenly, ahead of them they could see some troops sitting by the side of the road; they were Japanese. Hari told the girls to lie down in the back of the car out of sight, and he drove towards the soldiers without slowing down. As he reached them he raised his hand in greeting. To his amazement one or two waved back, and no attempt was made to stop him. The two nurses stayed on the floor of the car; they could hardly credit their lucky escape.

A mile further on they saw some more Japanese soldiers in the road. As they drew near Hari tried the same tactic. This time they were unlucky and the soldiers indicated they should stop. Hari slowed down, then as he reached them he accelerated away, his foot pressing the pedal to the floor. Shots were fired and the car lurched as both front wheels were hit, but they kept going and five minutes later they reached the village of Tambun. They drove slowly through the almost deserted main street, looking for the marines. As they left the village, some troops appeared from the sides of the road a few hundred yards in front of them. As they drew near, they saw with relief that the soldiers were Royal Marines.

As the car came to a stop they all got out. The surprise the marines had shown, when it became obvious that two of the occupants were female, almost brought a smile to the girls' faces, but they were still shaken by their narrow escape.

Maj. Martin and the sergeant major were the first to greet them. The girls explained about the Japanese just down the road. Orders were given and their car was pushed out of sight into the long grass just off the road. The marines returned to their defensive positions and the two nurses and Hari Khah were escorted to the safety of a nearby trench.

The appearance of the two attractive nurses was a great morale boost to the marines. Cpl Hart was moved to say he was the obvious choice as personal escort to the nurses because he understood the needs of a woman.

The sergeant major on hearing this said, 'Cpl Hart, you have bollocks for brains. I wouldn't trust you within a mile of these innocents.'

The two nurses smiled; it was the type of conversation they were familiar with.

Ten minutes later the marines stood to, as the column of advancing Japanese came into sight. The marines let them come within sixty yards of their position before they opened fire. About ten of the advancing soldiers fell in the first burst of fire, then the Japanese were off the road and moving through the undergrowth to the right of the marines' position. A few minutes later the Japanese attacked again; this time a concerted rush from the right and from the north. It was only partly repelled, with the loss of two of the marines' slit trenches on their northern perimeter. Maj. Martin ordered that the two trenches be retaken and a short bloody skirmish ensued, with the marines being successful with the use of grenades and bayonet. It was obvious to all the Royal Marines that they were outnumbered and it was just a matter of time before they were overrun.

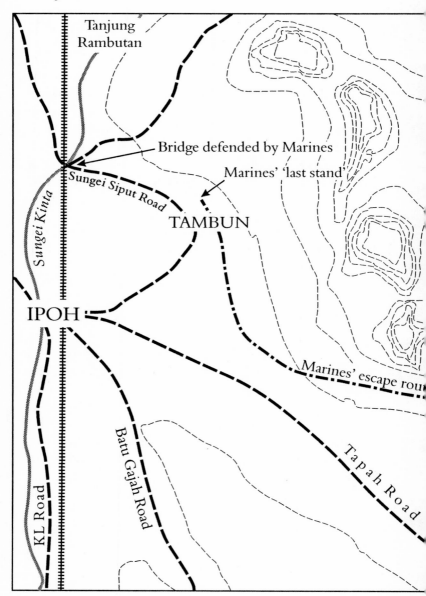

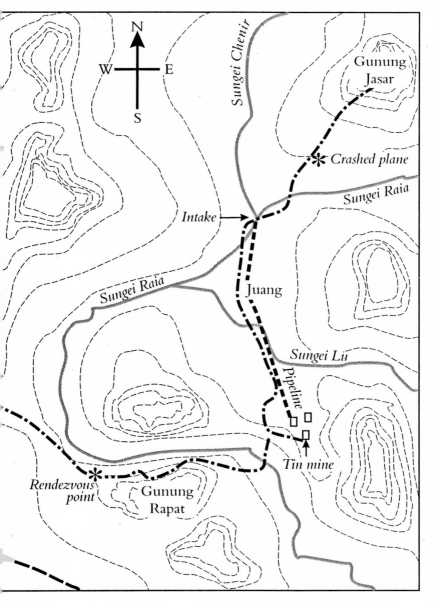

It was now 1700 hours. Maj. Martin knew a night attack was likely from more than one direction. In the confusion there would be an opportunity to withdraw to the southeast, but first he needed to get the two girls and the Malay on their way in that direction. He discussed a plan with the sergeant major and a decision was made. The oldest sergeant in the company was Jim Muir, a Scot, hard as nails and totally reliable. He would take the two girls and the Malay, plus another marine, to a position Maj. Martin had chosen as a rendezvous for the company survivors to make for after the coming battle. Martin called Sgt Muir over to his trench and briefed him. Muir was not keen to leave but accepted the situation. He was told he could choose which of the marines he would take with him.

'I'll take young Blake, Sir. He's a good lad and he can handle himself just fine.'

As dusk fell, the escape group, after a final word from Maj. Martin, quietly slid away from the company position. They were all loaded with supplies to last them a few days. Sgt Muir was carrying a Thompson sub-machine gun, as were the two girls. They had been shown how to load and fire the weapons. Blake carried his Bren gun and between him and Hari Khah they had a total of twenty full magazines. With Sgt Muir leading and Blake bringing up the rear they headed southeast, keeping close in to the gunungs on their left. They had a distance of about ten miles to cover to reach the major's rendezvous. Sgt Muir wanted to be there by daybreak.

They had been on the move for about thirty minutes when a fierce exchange of fire broke out from the marines' position. It lasted, on and off, for about fifteen minutes, then all went quiet. Blake had mixed feelings about leaving his friends but an order was an order. You just got on with it.

They had now been on the move for four hours. The girls were not used to this kind of activity so Sgt Muir gave them a ten-minute rest every hour. He thought they had covered between five and six miles and he decided to let the girls rest for thirty minutes on their next break.

Jan and Joyce were near exhaustion when he told them they could now have a rest. As they sat down, a prolonged and heavy burst of firing came faintly from the direction of the marines' trenches. Peter Blake helped Joyce Hammond off with her pack and checked that her Thompson was on safety. Sgt Muir did the same for Jan Riley. Hari Khah lay there and said nothing, his mind in turmoil.

When they resumed their march the girls felt worse than ever as they had stiffened up, but ten minutes later they were back in their stride. They had one scare when they disturbed a couple of wild pigs that crashed off into the thick undergrowth squealing loudly. At last there was a slight lightening of the sky to the east and Sgt Muir could make out, a mile or so away, the distinctive shape of the two gunungs that marked the entrance to the Sungei Raia Gorge. An hour later they had reached their objective and the two marines selected a sound defensive position thirty yards up a jungle-covered gully. Peter Blake stood watch while the rest of the group under Sgt Muir's firm hand set up a small camp. Twenty minutes later Joyce Hammond handed him a mug of hot sweet tea and some biscuits and corned beef.

From where he sat Blake had a good view of the ground they had covered in the final stages of their march. If anyone approached they would have ample warning. After an hour Sgt Muir relieved him and he moved further up the gully to where the others were resting. Jan and Hari were asleep, but Joyce was still awake and smiled as he sat down near her. A few minutes later she too was asleep. Blake watched her well-formed breasts rising and falling as she fell into the rhythm of sleep.

'Christ!' he thought. 'I'm getting a hard-on watching her.'

He turned his mind to other things, then fell into a deep sleep.

Blake awoke with a start. Sgt Muir was asleep just a few yards from him. Who was on watch? Grabbing his Bren he went down the gully. The two girls looked round as he reached them. They both smiled. He had a strange feeling and a tingling in his genital area.

'It's OK, Peter. Sgt Muir said to wake you in two hours. We are doing a two-hour stint together.'

Blake smiled and said, 'That's fine, I'll go back to sleep then.'

As he left, the two girls looked at one another and shared a secret smile.

Chapter 5

At 1400 hours Joyce woke Blake.

'It's all quiet, Peter, nobody in sight. Hari has woven some Atap palm leaves and made a good basha at the sentry post.'

As Blake got to his feet she added, 'Jan and I need to use a toilet, where shall we go?'

The gully was about fifteen yards wide, with many crevices in its sides.

Blake indicated a wide crevice over to the right, saying, 'Use that. With all those ferns around it's quite private.'

He went on down to the sentry post and sent Jan back to join Joyce. Hari Khah was sitting looking out over flat ground to their front. He turned and smiled as Blake sat down. Blake spent the next two hours explaining quietly to Hari how the Bren gun worked. He was a willing pupil and would make an admirable number two. Just as Sgt Muir came down to relieve Blake it started to rain. They sat under the palm shelter, remaining pretty dry. The rain became torrential for a few minutes then suddenly stopped. As the sun broke through their visibility was restored and about three hundred yards away they saw two figures staggering towards them.

'It's the major, Sarge', said Blake. 'They look in a bad way.'

Sgt Muir told Blake to cover them and he and Hari Khah made their way down the gully and out to meet the two men. Ten minutes later they returned to the entrance to the gully. Hari Khah was helping Maj. Martin; Sgt Muir had slung the other figure over his shoulder. As they climbed up to where Blake was, the two girls came down and lent a hand with the two survivors. The man Sgt Muir was carrying was the sergeant major. He was unconscious and looked badly hurt.

Blake remained at the sentry post while the two nurses went to work on the sergeant major. QMS Rogers had two gun shot wounds, one in his shoulder and one in his leg, from which he had lost a lot of blood. But his worst injuries were two bayonet wounds in the stomach. The two girls were doing what they could in a very professional way. The shoulder and leg wounds were soon treated, but the deep stomach wounds were past even the attentions of a skilled surgeon.

As daylight faded the group made some tea and shared out some corned beef and biscuits. Maj. Martin fell asleep; he was exhausted. They made the sergeant major as comfortable as possible.

Night fell and Sgt Muir and Blake shared the night watches together. At dawn a light misty rain set in. Muir sent Blake back up the gully to make some tea. Joyce was wiping the sergeant major's face. His eyes were open and when he saw Blake he held out his hand and smiled.

'Hello son', he said, as Blake took the outstretched hand in his grasp.

The sergeant major's eyes closed and he died. Blake's eyes filled with tears and he lowered the hand back onto the dead man's chest. Joyce saw the grief in his eyes and put her arms around him. They stood together for a few moments. He then went over to the small cooker and made some tea.

Later that morning they carried the sergeant major's body down to bottom of the gully. There was a small cave there, almost hidden by the thick foliage. They covered the body with stones and sealed the entrance with palm fronds. By midday the sun was out and it was very hot even in the sheltered gully. Typical of the Malayan weather, a torrential rainstorm set in at about 1500 hours. They were able to fill their water bottles from the little rock gullies that ran down the side of the main gully. The two girls managed to have a good wash in the rain, the marines discreetly looking away, despite the temptation to peep.

Towards evening Maj. Martin told them of the final Japanese attack on their Tambun position. They had repelled two attacks during the night and inflicted heavy losses on the attackers. At dawn the marines only had about twenty men still alive. The major had drawn them into a tight semicircle. He told them, after this last attack, that those who were still able were to head for the rendezvous at Gunung Rapat. The Japanese launched a fierce assault and it was repelled, but they came again. Out of ammunition, the marines fought with rifle butts and bayonets. At last the Japanese withdrew to re-form for a final assault. Then there was a torrential rainstorm and the five marines who were left alive withdrew and headed for the safety of the jungle. The major went on to say that he and the badly wounded QMS Rogers had sent the remaining three marines on ahead. They never saw them again.

The next day Maj. Martin told them they would stay in the gully till nightfall, just in case the three marines managed to find them. They would then move through the Sungei Raia Gorge, head into the jungle and make for a small village called Juang. The village was situated at the head of the water pipeline that serviced the local tin mine. All that day they made their preparations for the move. They checked their food and ammunition. With no sign of the missing three marines, they set off at dusk. With Sgt Muir leading and Maj. Martin behind him, the survivors made their way to their next destination.

There was a well-used track alongside the Sungei Raia and they made good progress through the gorge. After an hour they stopped and rested for ten minutes. It was a clear night and the moon was almost full, which enabled them to make good progress. They had one scare when another wild pig was disturbed and dashed across the track in front of them. It took them just over two hours to negotiate the gorge. The high limestone sides created a sinister effect in the half-light. Ahead of them was an area of lalang (or elephant grass as some people called it) between four and six feet high. Beyond that, jungle-covered slopes rose away into the distance.

Maj. Martin was concerned that their track through the lalang would be easy to follow. The alternative would be to wade along the Sungei Raia shallows, but that would be too noisy, so they stuck to the lalang. By 0400 hours they were almost out of the lalang, with the jungle-covered slopes just a couple of hundred yards away.

Hari Khah had told the major there was a tin mine about a mile over to their right. It was run by a European couple who might be still there and could give them some food. Maj. Martin decided it was worth a look, so as soon as they reached the edge of the slopes, he told Sgt Muir to stay with the two nurses whilst he, Blake and Hari Khah had a look at the tin mine.

With Hari Khah leading it took them about twenty minutes to reach a spot where they could observe the tin mine compound. It appeared to be deserted, but just in case there were Japanese troops there, Hari volunteered to have a look. If challenged he would say he was a pipeline worker from Juang. They watched as he made his way quietly, but openly, down to the mine. In the improving light (it was almost dawn) he reached the main house and disappeared from view. Maj. Martin and Blake waited with baited breath for him to reappear. At last he came back into sight and raised his hand, his right hand. The arrangement had been 'raise your left hand if the Japanese are there'. Together the major and Blake walked down to the mine, somewhat relaxed but still alert.

Hari met them at the manager's house.

'It's deserted, they must have left in a hurry', he said.

They made their way into the house.

'We want food, medical supplies and, bearing mind it's got to be carried, anything you think will be of use to us in the jungle', instructed Maj. Martin.

After a good look round, they had found some rice, about 28 lb, tinned milk, tea and sugar, some assorted tins of fish and meat, salt and two bottles of rum. Blake had also found some quinine and a roll of mosquito netting.

They left the place as they had found it and, with their plunder secured in three sacks, made their way back to the nurses and Sgt Muir. The loads were evened out and they set off again up the jungle-covered slope to find the pipeline that was marked on the map. It took them an hour of hard slog to climb the steadily rising ground to the pipeline. Here, the major decided, was a good place to rest and have breakfast. Using the little stove, Hari Khah soon made some tea and they opened a small tin of jam to put on their biscuits. It was plain to them all that Hari was in charge of catering.

They were about to leave when Joyce gave a subdued cry and pulled down her khaki drill trousers. Fastened to the inside of her thigh was a blood-gorged leech. Blake rushed to help, stirred by the sight of the soft white flesh, but Jan beat him to it and lighting a cigarette she applied the glowing end to the leech, which dropped off Joyce's leg. They all then checked themselves for leeches; those that were found quickly dropped off when heat was applied.

Panic over, they slowly made their way along the pipeline which gradually climbed towards Juang. Just before noon they caught sight of the village; it was deserted. To call it a village was an exaggeration. There were four small huts holding at most a dozen people. Hari explained that the river ran into the pipeline here, providing enough pressure to force the water along the pipeline to the tin mine.

The small concrete funnel, which diverted some of the river's water into the pipeline, had a steel mesh guard over the entrance to prevent anything larger than two inches in size from entering it. It was the principal duty of the pipeline workers to keep this mesh clear and prevent a blockage from the debris washed down river in the monsoon season.

Chapter 6

Maj. Martin was not anxious to stay in the village long, for if any of the villagers returned and saw them this information might well get back to the Japanese. So, after a fifteen-minute break they moved off. To start with they waded north through the water of the Sungei Raia, which was only two feet deep at the edge. In this way they would not leave any tracks.

After a hundred yards they left the river and moved inland, moving due east towards the slopes of Gunung Jasar, which according to the map was about five miles from Juang. The gunung was about four thousand feet high and Maj. Martin had planned to make semi-permanent camp there. In places the ground rose quite sharply. The jungle was not that thick and as the height of the trees increased, the thick ground cover decreased. After an hour they took a thirty-minute break. The two nurses were doing better than expected, despite the extra loads they were carrying.

As they rested Mick Martin looked around his small band. Sgt Muir was about thirty-five, six feet tall and well built. He was a tough rough Scot, unmarried and totally reliable. Marine Blake, young, about nineteen, was just under six foot, fair-haired and strongly built. His first taste of action had been at the railway bridge, where he had acquitted himself well in the hand-to-hand struggle. Hari Khah, at just over forty, was the oldest member of the group. He seemed reliable but Martin was not too sure where his loyalties lay. However, the girls seemed to trust him and they knew him best.

Then the two nurses were pretty by any standards. They were both about twenty, slim and about five feet five tall, but not soft and, judging by the way they had nursed QMS Rogers, extremely competent. Martin then thought of his own wife and two children and their pleasant cottage in Blandford. Would he ever see them again? He decided it was time to move on.

'I'm lucky', he thought. 'I've got a nice little band of freedom fighters here, though of course they don't know it yet.'

That day they made good progress, despite the difficult terrain. At 1600 hours the major decided they had done enough for the day and should make camp for the night. They constructed one shelter using the six rubber groundsheets. Hari covered the ends with woven Atap palm, which looked sound and was, hopefully, waterproof.

Hari said he would provide a meal for them all and, despite the limitations of the one small cooker, he produced a corned beef curry and rice, with tea to follow. Maj. Martin decided on the pairings for the night's watches: Blake and Joyce, Muir and Jan and Hari Khah and himself, two hours on and four hours off. He could tell this was popular with all concerned, for various reasons of course.

Peter Blake and Joyce Hammond took the first two-hour watch. They sat side-by-side under the Atap palm basha Hari had constructed. It started to rain. A few drops to start with, then it poured down for about twenty minutes. Blake was conscious of how close Joyce was to him. Jesus Christ! Her leg was touching his.

She was well aware of the effect her closeness was having and moved slightly away from the young marine. At last it was time to hand over to Jan and Sgt Muir. As they changed places Muir asked Blake if he had anything to report.

'Yes, Sarge', said Blake. 'I've just had a hard-on for the last two hours, and no sign of relief.'

Muir smiled to himself, 'Ah, the impatience of youth', then settled down for two hours with the very nice Jan Riley.

When dawn came, despite only four hours of uninterrupted rest between watches, they all felt in good spirits. After a breakfast of cheese, hard biscuits and a mug of tea, they broke camp. They took great trouble to try and hide any evidence of their night's stay, unplaiting the palm fronds and burying any tins and paper. At 0800 hours they moved off, with Sgt Muir leading. Hari Khah followed him with the machete ready to cut a path, if required. The hill slopes of Gunung Jasar were not a gradual incline; at times they descended into steep valleys, which meant an even steeper climb out.

By noon Maj. Martin had expected to be three-quarters up the east face of the gunung, but they were not even halfway; the maps did not show all of the dead ground. They took a break of thirty minutes and had some water with four squares of chocolate each. Blake exchanged weapons with Sgt Muir and took the lead. The track was getting very rocky, with little streams flowing down the side of the rising ground. They began to descend into another crevasse; it got very steep. Blake could smell something unjunglelike, and he stopped and called Maj. Martin to the front.

'It smells like petrol to me', said the major.

Blake agreed and suggested he should go forward on his own and investigate. The major agreed. He told the others to take a break but to be ready to move instantly. Blake made his way to the bottom of the crevasse. The smell was stronger here. He moved carefully to his right and followed the rising ground. Then he saw what was causing the vaporous smell; it was a wrecked aircraft. He moved towards it. Its wings had almost been folded back by the impact and the nose was compacted up to the flight deck. Blake recognised it as a Dakota transport aircraft. He made his way back up to Maj. Martin and told him what he had found. The others were informed and the whole party moved towards the crash site.

With the two nurses keeping watch, the others carried out a careful check of the plane. Blake climbed up level with the flight deck and he glanced inside the broken windows. He could see three bodies. It was obvious they had been killed instantly, partly by the impact as the plane had struck the rocky hillside, and partly by the cargo moving forward and crushing them.

They managed to open the aircraft's side doors. The sight that greeted them was like entering an Aladdin's cave. The aircraft was packed with supplies. Boxes of rations were piled from the floor to the roof, along with many other packs of stores. It was plain to see they would not know what they had here until everything was unloaded from the aircraft. It was not too pleasant a place to stay for very long; apart from the smell of fuel there was also the smell of death. The bodies of the crew members had been here at least three or four days, and in the moist heat they were beginning to decay. The jungle was also recovering from the plane's impact, vines and creepers rapidly covering evidence of the crash site.

Maj. Martin decided to leave the aircraft for now and push on up the steep slope to find a suitable campsite, which would serve as their major base. Twenty minutes later they broke clear of the thickest undergrowth and could see the almost sheer side of Gunung Jasar; its limestone sides were full of gullies and small caves. There was still tree cover leading right up to the steep face and there in front of them was a cave entrance, which seemed to draw them toward it. It led back twenty feet, then the roof rose from ten to fifteen feet; the width was treble that of the entrance. At the back of the cave were several passages.

'God knows where they lead to', Blake thought, 'but what a place to camp.'

It was almost 1600 hours, so it was decided to set up camp in the cave. The two nurses were stationed on one side of the cave and the four men on the other. While Hari prepared a meal for them all, Blake stood watch just inside the cave entrance and the other two marines explored the back of the cave. Blake could hear running water. He looked for the source and found it was just outside the cave to the right; a steady stream of water running down a small crevasse in the face of the gunung. After he had been there for nearly an hour, Joyce appeared carrying their mess tins. They sat there together eating Hari's 'special', Irish stew and rice. To be fair to Hari, the ration packs they had comprised only of Corned Beef (Type A), Irish Stew (Type B) or Herrings in Tomato Sauce (Type C), but it was Hari's treatment of the rice that made the difference.

As it got dark they all noticed how cool it was compared to where they had spent the previous night. Maj. Martin pointed out they were at least a thousand feet above sea level.

At about midnight, there was a thunderstorm, torrential rain and, for a while, strong winds. However, the cave was as dry as a bone and mosquito free. Apart from the storm, the night passed peacefully and it was cool enough to require them to cover themselves with their groundsheets. Blake looked enviously at the two girls huddled together on the other side of the cave.

After breakfast, leaving their packs behind, they all made their way back towards the crashed plane. They removed twenty wooden boxes of rations; each box contained ten one-man ration packs. The marines could carry one box each, but the girls only one box between the two of them. They made numerous journeys up to the cave and back. They installed Hari back in the cave to open the boxes and sort out the rations. By noon they had recovered the twenty boxes.

After a mug of tea and some biscuits with jam, they went back to the plane for more plunder and another twenty boxes of rations were moved up to the cave. Maj. Martin, before their final journey of the day, looked into the plane to see what remained. He counted at least another ten ration boxes and then what looked like ammunition and bales of something.

They got back to the cave with their final loads as the light began to fail. Hari had prepared curried herrings in tomato sauce and rice, which tasted better than it looked. They were all exhausted from their efforts and Maj. Martin decided to give the nurses the night off. The three marines and Hari did an hour each on watch. The night passed peacefully and quickly.

All the next morning they moved more supplies from the aircraft. Two of the bales they had seen were blankets, twenty to each bale. There was quite a lot of ammunition: five thousand rounds of .303, about the same in .45 for the Thompson sub-machine guns, five boxes of hand grenades and their detonators in separate red tins. The last haul, before a lunch-break, comprised of two 2-inch mortars, fifty high explosives and ten smoke bombs. Maj. Martin looked at what was left in the aircraft. He calculated that a couple of hours in the afternoon would see the plane completely empty.

In two hours all of the rest of the contents were safely in the cave. Four 28 lb bags of rice were found jammed up against the back of the pilot's seat; another sack contained about thirty jungle green shirts and trousers. Two cardboard containers marked medical supplies were given to the two nurses to sort out. Two wooden crates contained a field radio and batteries and a small hand generator. The last item to be moved was a long wooden box, inside which were two brand new Bren guns.

Chapter 7

The three bodies were left where they were. All traces of the removal of the cargo were wiped away and the plane's exit doors were closed. If the Japanese discovered the plane they would think it had been empty when it crashed. The area below the aircraft doors, which had borne the brunt of their frequent comings and goings, was raked over. With the jungle growth being so rapid in the moist warm conditions, three days would see all evidence of their presence obscured.

Back in the cave, Hari Khah had done a marvellous job in stowing and sorting out the supplies. All the ration boxes were stacked neatly in piles, As, Bs, Cs and Ds. They all knew what A, B, C were, but D? The problem was solved that evening when Hari gave them boiled rice and pressed tongue, the mystery content of ration box D.

The medical containers Jan and Joyce had sorted out had the usual contents of shell and small field dressings. These included Mepecrin tablets, which were the new anti-malaria drug, anti-septic ointments, various tablets to treat a variety of conditions and two cardboard boxes containing two hundred French letters. The two nurses gave one of the boxes to Peter Blake to open.

Feigning innocence, they said, 'What's in that one, Peter?'

He opened the box and his face went scarlet with embarrassment. With the nurses' laughter ringing his ears, a still red-faced Blake relieved a surprised Sgt Muir thirty minutes early for his watch.

At midnight, Blake and Joyce began their two-hour watch together.

She said, 'Sorry for this afternoon, Peter. That was cruel', and kissed him on the cheek.

She added, 'My close friends call me Joy and I would like you to do the same.'

Blake thought the two hours went too quickly for him to make any further progress in this new relationship, but it was a good start.

Maj. Martin had issued them with four new blankets each. They lay on three and covered up with one and they all had their best night's sleep yet. When morning came, Mick Martin decided to talk over their situation with them. It was also New Year's Day, the 1st of January 1942.

The major gave them his assessment of the situation. He thought they were at least fifty miles from any friendly forces, perhaps even further. They had enough supplies to last them in excess of six months, they were all fit and had enough fire power to deter a limited enemy attack. He proposed to stay where they were for the next month at least, to improve their camp and complete a through exploration of their cave and its surroundings. The two nurses were to be given as much privacy in their accommodation as was practical.

He added, 'The chain of command is myself, Sgt Muir and Marine Blake; that is not negotiable.'

Sgt Muir and Peter Blake were sent to check the ground either side of the cave entrance. At first they moved round to the right covering about a hundred yards. The face of the gunung was almost sheer, but there were numerous crevices, all just a few inches across. As they reached the extent of their search they saw a small cave entrance about twenty feet up the face. With some difficulty, they climbed up to it. The entrance was about four feet high, but as they moved into the cave they could see it went back quite a long way. They moved further in and, as their eyes became accustomed to the dark, saw that the path split into two, one passage leading up, the other leading down. They followed the downward passage, which bent round to the left and levelled out. It seemed a little lighter here and the ground began to rise gradually. Sgt Muir, who was leading, suddenly stopped.

'I can hear fucking voices', he said.

They moved on. Some light appeared faintly on the left-hand side of the passage and as they drew level with it they heard more voices; they were female. A large crack in the side of the passage was the source of the light and the voices. They looked through. Six feet below them were the two nurses. Both were clad only in their underwear, and it appeared they were about to go further. The two marines looked on in appreciation.

Sgt Muir solved the problem by calling out.

'Don't be frightened girls, it's only us.'

A startled gasp came from the nurses and they hurried to cover up their near nakedness. Sgt Muir and Blake slid sideways through the tunnel side and dropped down onto the main cave floor.

Having convinced the girls they had not planned to spy on them, they reported to Maj. Martin. He told them to follow on from the crevice at the back of the cave and see where it led. They followed the passage; at times it was almost pitch black, but then a little light would filter in from some fissure in the limestone. After ten minutes they could see some light at the passage end. As they carefully made for the daylight, they considered they had travelled about a hundred yards. They reached the end and looked out; jungle-covered hills stretched as far as the eye could see. A steep slope led from the small cave exit to the first line of small trees. They had their emergency exit.

Later that afternoon they explored the other fork in the original passage, the one that led upwards. At times it was quite steep and narrow. Then it descended abruptly. More light appeared and the passage ended with an exit four feet high and eighteen inches wide and about twenty feet above the tree line on the south side of the gunung. They now had two exits, one to the east and one to the south. They reported this to Maj. Martin. He seemed delighted and told them that all of the party should be shown both passages and exits the next day.

Hari Khah had proved to be as competent with the radio as he was with the cooking. He had managed to tune in to Radio Singapore, but the news was far from good. The announcer said that the Japanese were being held at the Slim River, but landings were being made to the south of the Allied positions and lines of communication were being cut. On the major's instruction he trawled the net until he found some military traffic. Clearly many call signs were not responding, adding to the confusion. Rather than waste the batteries, they tried it on the small hand generator and found it worked perfectly.

They rearranged the sleeping positions to the back of the cave. Each person now had six ration boxes between him and the next person. They looked like a line of cubicles and they gave each person some privacy. Mick Martin had intended the arrangement to be just for the two nurses, but it was less obvious if it applied to them all. Another decision he had made was to have only one person on watch at night. The two girls and Hari had shown they were completely reliable, and it gave them all extra sleep. That night they had a stew with three packets of hard biscuits put into the mixture just before serving, which almost tasted like dumplings, but not quite.

The next day, Maj. Martin and Blake, carrying a tommy-gun each, explored the ground to the south. It was tough going, with thick jungle and no signs of any tracks. For three hours they pressed on, at times losing sight of their gunung home. At last they came to a track used by woodcutters, but not recently. They rested up for thirty minutes. They had consumed most of their water in the intense heat. They returned by a different route, moving due east for an hour than swung to the north. They crossed two streams, refilling their water bottles, and cooled off by sitting up to their necks in the deeper places. At last they could see their limestone home. They re-entered their cave by the eastern entrance, no easy matter up the steep slope. To avoid alarming the rest of the party they called out as they came to the end of the passage. Judging by the welcoming smiles, the others were pleased to see them back.

To make everyone familiar with the area, the next day Sgt Muir and Blake were told to take the two nurses out of the southern cave exit and to patrol southeast for two hours, then swing back north, before turning west back to the base camp. The nurses thought this was a great adventure, but realized the serious intention of making themselves familiar with the area in case of attack. On the return journey they crossed the stream Blake had encountered the day before. With the two marines keeping watch, the two nurses stripped off and bathed in the cool water. Peter Blake found it hard to avert his eyes from the two naked bodies. The girls were not the least worried by the obvious glances the marines were making in their direction. When they had finished, it was the marines' turn. With the two nurses keeping a careful watch, Jim Muir and Peter Blake enjoyed the refreshing cold water, with the girls being just as obser-vant as the marines had been.

The next day it was Hari Khah's turn for some exercise, and he joined the major and Sgt Muir as they headed due east to cover that area, returning from a northeasterly direction. It became obvious to them all that the area they were in was pretty isolated, and as that meant safety they all slept the better for it. That night there was a tremendous storm with thunder and lightning. Peter Blake was on watch and woke Joy who was down to relieve him; as she was a bit nervous he stayed up with her. His gesture was not without its reward, as she gave him a kiss full on the lips. He pulled her close to him and dropped his hands to her bottom.

She pulled away, saying, 'Not yet, Peter.'

For the rest of her watch they sat close together. Blake thought he was making progress in their relationship and was anxious not to spoil his chances by coming on too strong.

They spent the next day within the confines of their cave complex. Maj. Martin was very interested in some of the radio traffic they were picking up. The news seemed to be about withdrawing to fresh positions, with no indication that any counter-attack was underway to drive the Japanese back up north. They all began to realise that they were safe where they were up to a point. The Japanese were not likely to put patrols deep into the jungle without good reason. Their priority was the capture of Singapore, and that was where their best troops were heading. The supplies they had would last them at least six months, which was Maj. Martin's first calculation. He now realised that, with a few amendments to their diet, he could stretch them a further month at least. Hari Khah, who was in charge of catering, agreed. He was now aware of their appetites and cooked just sufficient to fulfil their needs.

Chapter 8

Blake felt the pressure of small soft hands busy on the waistband of his trousers. One by one the buttons were undone. He felt the cool of the night air on his stomach, as the last button was released. His hard and excited penis sprang out. Joy gasped and bent over him, undoing her shirtfront. Her shapely, slightly upturned breasts moved closer to his penis. Blake could hardly contain himself. One of Joy's nipples, like a firm black grape, touched the end of his penis. His control vanished and his pent-up semen spurted over her breasts.

He woke up with a groan. It was still dark and his groin area wet as a result of his 'dream fantasy'. He made his way to the passage at the side of the main cave. This was their toilet area and a blanket was hung there. If it was closed it was in use. It was open. He urinated then using a couple of brown square sheets of toilet paper, wiped the evidence from the inside of his trousers. Water ran down the side of the passage wall and he washed his hands in the cool flow, then made his way back to his bed.

In the morning, after breakfast, Maj. Martin called them all together. He explained what he intended to do. He would take Sgt Muir and Marine Blake and return to the road south of Ipoh to see what was going on in terms of Japanese troop movements. Hari Khah and the two nurses digested the news with some misgivings. What would they do if the marines failed to return? Maj. Martin smiled.

'I promise you, the way I intend to operate one of us will always be able to return.'

He told them they would be away not more than four days and they would carry just three days' rations. Blake would carry the Bren gun and he and Sgt Muir would take their Thompson sub-machine guns. For the rest of the morning they made their preparations and after some tea and biscuits with cheese, the marines set off, leaving by their southern exit.

They headed southwest to bring them out of the jungle near the tin mine they had looted on their way in. By 1700 hours they had the mine in sight and decided to spend the night in the jungle edge. They made camp. Their three groundsheets making an adequate shelter, they made some tea, but ate cold corned beef and a few biscuits. As darkness fell, mosquitoes assaulted them. They applied the repellent but with limited success. Their time in the high cave had made them forget the misery of an insect attack and they were relieved when dawn arrived. After breakfast they broke camp and moved out of the jungle towards the tin mine. Two hundred yards short of the building they stopped and Maj. Martin went forward to see if it was still deserted. It was.

The inside of the house was as they had left it. They took the opportunity to remove most of the food supplies that were left and placed them under cover at the jungle's edge. They would collect them on the way back. Carefully, keeping in close to the jungle edge, they moved further towards where the road to Tapah should be. It took them another two hours to reach the road where they found a good observation spot in long grass overlooking the road. Just two army lorries passed them during the rest of the day and as the light began to fail they moved back into the jungle to spend the night.

They had just erected their shelter when it began to rain, It continued all night and when dawn broke a misty rain was still falling. Moving back to their observation position of the previous day, they watched as four lorries of Japanese troops passed by. This was the only traffic for five hours, and then a column of troops went by in single file either side of the road. They counted four hundred men, carrying a variety of weapons. They wore a mixture of khaki, gray and dark green uniforms; some had boots, others wore rubber gym shoes. Not very impressive, but as the marines knew to their cost, they were very determined soldiers.

As the day came to an end, they withdrew to the campsite of the last evening. They cooked some rice and made tea and as it began to rain again they were thankful for a dry shelter. They spent a quiet night. The rain seemed to deter the mosquitoes and, apart from being woken to keep watch, they had sufficient rest by morning. They started to move back towards the tin mine, this time by a slightly different route to avoid leaving an obvious track. Maj. Martin told them he wanted to approach the cave on Gunung Jasar from the southeast, so they aimed their march to enter the jungle well to the south of the tin mine. They diverted to pick up the food they had taken from the house. The jungle was denser here than further north, and their progress was slower, but they pressed on and by time it came to settle for the night they were within three hours of the cave.

When morning came they ate a hasty breakfast, broke camp and moved off, hoping to reach the cave by noon. They made one stop of ten minutes to fill their water bottles and soon they were on the slopes of Gunung Jasar, where they made their way to the southern entrance. As they climbed up to the small cave all was quiet. They moved wearily along the cool tunnel, which would give them access to the larger cave. They could hear voices; they were not those of Hari or the two nurses. With Maj. Martin leading they crept up to the slit in the cave face and looked down. The two nurses were standing with their backs to the marines. Hari was to their right. They had their machine-guns in their hands. In front of them stood two men, both Chinese, their weapons pointing at the nurses and Hari. One was speaking in English. He was telling them they were his prisoners, but he would treat them well and hand them over to the Japanese who would reward him. The other man made a lewd gesture to the girls. He said, 'Japanese give you plenty fuck, fuck', and laughed.

Maj. Martin whispered to Sgt Muir and they took aim together and fired. The two Chinese were hurled backwards by the .45 bullets, and within seconds the three marines had bounded down into the cave. The two girls were shaking with fear, but as Muir and Blake ran to comfort them they quickly recovered. The major asked Hari Khah if there were any more of these men about.

He said, 'No, they are bandits who have been looking for British soldiers. They hand them over to the Japanese for money. They walked up to the cave entrance fifteen minutes ago, saying they were friends.' Sgt Muir and Blake went to the entrance and looked out; there was nobody in sight. Blake stayed there and the major and Sgt Muir dragged the two bodies out. There was a deep gully some hundred yards to the right and, after going through the clothing of the two men, they dropped their bodies into the gully. They made a satisfying thud as they eventually hit the bottom.

Back in the cave, Maj. Martin spoke to the two girls and Hari Khah.

'I understand your reluctance to shoot these two men, but you see the position it left you in. They would have murdered Hari, enjoyed themselves with you both, then handed you over to the Japanese for more of the same. Be ruthless, it's the only way to survive.'

The two girls, still pale from their fright, nodded their heads in agreement. For the rest of the day the atmosphere in the cave reflected the shock Hari and the girls had felt. The three marines attempted to lighten the gloom, but it would take time. After cleaning their weapons, the marines had a wash down in the toilet passage; after the recent rain a good flow of water ran down the crevice.

To celebrate their return Hari cooked a corned beef curry and rice. It was delicious, and with good food inside of them their good humour returned. At midnight, Blake was woken by Hari. It was time for his watch.

After about ten minutes he heard a sound. He moved slightly back into the cave and listened. He heard two people whispering. One was Jan Riley; the other was Jim Muir. He heard the rustle of clothing, then the sound of lips on flesh. After more rustling, the sound of moving bodies, a grunt followed by an 'Ah' and a rhythm was soon established. 'Urg—Ah—Urg—Ah—Urg—Ah', then 'Ahhhh'.

'That dirty bastard is fucking Jan', thought Blake. 'Dirty, lucky bastard!'

When it was time to wake Joy his mind was still in turmoil. When she came to relieve him, he was about to say something then changed his mind. She gave him a kiss on the cheek and he went back to his bed.

The following day, Blake and Sgt Muir were sent down to see if the two bandits had left any trail to the cave. They found their camp. It was just a piece of canvas, fastened between two pieces of bamboo, in which was a small pack with some rice and dried fish. Also in the pack was a pass of sorts written in Japanese. They took a break.

'Sarge?' said Blake.

'Call me Jim', said Muir.

'I heard you fucking Jan last night', said Blake.

Jim Muir laughed, 'Now listen to me Peter lad, Jan and I have an understanding. She wanted it as much as me and when all this is over, we might even marry, if that's what she wants. You look after Joy and I'll look after Jan, OK?'

Blake nodded; it sounded like a good arrangement.

Having completed a thorough search of the ground around the small shelter, they were confident there was no obvious track left by the two bandits for anyone else to follow. They made their way back to the cave and reported this to the major.

Peter Blake spent most of the rest of the day cleaning their three Bren guns and unloading the twenty magazines. He then reloaded their spare magazines. It was important to let the springs of the magazines recover after being fully charged for three days. He had woken up that morning with a slight headache and after he had returned from the patrol with Sgt Muir it got progressively worse. He finished reloading the Bren magazines. He sat on his bed, but he needed some fresh air, so he got up and walked to the mouth of the cave.

Maj. Martin was sitting there talking to Jan Riley. They looked at Blake as he reached them. They said something to him but the sound seemed to take a long time to reach him. He saw the major stand up and move towards him, concern on his face. The ground seemed to leap up at him and his legs dissolved like water. He fell into what seemed to be a deep dark pit with no bottom.

Maj. Martin just managed to catch Blake as he fell. He told Jan to fetch Sgt Muir, and when he arrived they carried Blake back to his bed. The two nurses examined the young marine. He was unconscious and drenched in sweat. Joy took his temperature from his armpit; it was 103 degrees. Hari Khah examined Blake. The two girls valued his experience.

'I don't think it's malaria', he said. 'It's more like scrub typhus. His glands are swollen and I know he has taken his anti-malaria tablets each day.'

The two girls took it in turns to stay with Blake. They stripped him and washed him down with cold water, then covered his naked body with a blanket. They managed to get some water and medication down his throat, but he was strong and fit and it was just a matter of time. By 2200 hours he had stopped sweating and his body was consumed by a dry fever. The two nurses spent the night at his side, taking it in turns to wipe him down with wet cloths. By dawn his fever was down and he was sleeping peacefully. Both the major and Sgt Muir had been frequent visitors and shared the nurses' anxiety over their fellow marine's condition. Hari Khah insisted the two girls got some rest; he would attend to the patient.

'The worst is over', he said. 'I will stay with him. I'll get some warm tea down him.'

For two days Blake drifted in and out of consciousness. He dreamed some amazing dreams, nightmares and beautiful fantasies in equal measure. In one strange sequence his legs were twenty feet long and his mother had said, 'Now you can run', but he could not stand up. In another he was running towards Joy Hammond who was calling, 'Help me, Peter', but as fast as he ran the distance between them stayed the same. On the third morning he woke. He was feeling weak but, apart from a raging thirst, was much better. Joy was lying asleep next to him. As he moved she awoke. Seeing he was better, she hugged him to her. He felt her breasts against his face and thought out loud, 'I've died and gone to heaven!'

They were all pleased that he had made a good recovery. Blake made it his business to thank them all for the care they had shown, in particular the two nurses. Jan told him the best bit was stripping him naked and washing him.

'I let Joy do the bottom half though, she enjoyed that.'

On the fourth day, the major let him resume light duties, day watches only. Within a further two days he was back to his normal self. His pleasure at regaining full fitness was tempered by the news from Singapore. It was the 15th of February 1942 and when they tuned into the English-speaking station it was only to hear Singapore had surrendered.

The news hit them hard. They had thought about their future but always assumed that somehow the Allied forces would counter-attack and regain Malaya. Now what could they do? For them to give themselves up was out of the question. They were safe where they were, but their food would not last forever. How long would it take for the war to end? Moreover, who would win? The major thought, with the Americans now in the war, that within two years the Japanese would be beaten. Sgt Muir thought longer.

Chapter 9

Maj. Martin thought they should go on the offensive. He discussed it with the two marines and they began to think up plans. Any excursion away from the camp was, as its first consideration, to bring back food and not put the safety of their camp in jeopardy. If these criteria were met, then they would be free to hurt the Japanese. The major also decided that one of the marines would always be left in the camp. Hari Khah was asked if he would be the patrol's third man. Hari was delighted to agree.

The major left next day with Sgt Muir and Hari Khah. They carried a Thompson each, three days' rations and the 2-inch mortar with six high explosive bombs. They made for a point south of Juang. By the first night they were at the jungle's edge, overlooking the tin mine where they made camp for the night. The next morning, before it was fully light, they went to the mine. It was still deserted. They followed the track along the Sungei Raia, past where their rendezvous camp had been, and headed towards the small village of Ampang.

When it was dark Hari Khah made his way into the village. He had known some people there before the war. He was gone several hours, and Maj. Martin and Sgt Muir were beginning to get worried when at last he returned. The news was not good. The Japanese were rationing rice and you had to register in Ipoh for your ration card. There was also a dusk to dawn curfew, but a few Japanese soldiers were about at night. Maj. Martin decided they would move off towards the main road while it was still dark. As they made their way towards it, they could hear the sound of lorries; it was being well used by the Japanese.

Hari Khah and the two marines lay in the grass as several lorries passed within feet of them. One stopped and the driver, who was alone in the vehicle, got out and walked over to where they lay. The soldier undid his flies and urinated into the grass. He was so close it splashed over Hari's face. The soldier farted loudly and started to walk away. Sgt Muir rose to his feet and crashed his weapon's butt with sickening force on the back of the soldier's head. The Japanese fell to the ground without a sound. The ambush party made their way to the lorry, dragging the soldier with them. They pushed his lifeless body into the back of the truck and all three climbed into the front. Hari started the vehicle up and drove down the road. The major told him that according to the map there was a track on his left about two miles up the road. Five minutes later they turned left off the main road and a hundred yards in they stopped under some trees.

The two marines climbed into the back of the lorry to check its cargo. It was half full of British ration boxes, rice, bananas and pineapples. Maj. Martin thought the track they were on led to the tin mine and instructed Hari to drive in that direction.

Dawn was just breaking when they drove up to the still deserted buildings. They parked the lorry out of sight in one of the sheds and offloaded its cargo. They then made their way to the jungle's edge and settled down to rest until it was dark.

Back at the cave, Blake was in his element. He felt fit and strong and had the company of two attractive girls. When it got dark he was relieved on watch by Jan. He made his way to where Joy slept; she wasn't there. When he got to his own bed space, he noticed a figure under his blanket. He lifted it, revealing the naked body of Joy Hammond. She reached out and pulled him down beside her. He removed his shirt and trousers and placed his now naked body next to hers. They embraced. Her lips opened and he thrust his tongue deep into her mouth. His hand moved over her breasts, her nipples hardening to his touch. Her hands were also busy and were moving up his rampant penis. He slipped his hand down between her legs. They parted and his finger sought and found their target.

Joy whispered, 'Put this on, Peter', and handed him a French letter.

He slid the latex sheath over his penis and Joy moved over onto her back. As he moved on top of her, she parted her legs and guided him into her. She gasped as he entered her. Gently at first, then more firmly, he moved in and out of her body. As he pushed deeply into her she returned his thrusts and the pace of their lovemaking increased. It became frantic and they climaxed with great gasps of pleasure. At the cave entrance Jan was listening to the frantic noises. She smiled and thought, 'Bloody hell, I hope Jim and I are not as loud as that!'

As the light faded Maj. Martin led the others back to the tin mine. The first priority was to get rid of the lorry and its driver. A hundred yards from the manager's house was a large, water-filled crater, almost the size of a lake, the result of the mining of the tin bearing sand.

Hari said it was about thirty feet deep. They drove the lorry almost to the edge, put the body of the driver behind the wheel and pushed it over the edge into the water. As it hit the water it righted itself and floated towards the centre of the pond. Gradually it began to sink, finally disappearing from view in the deepest part.

They spent the rest of the night moving the ration boxes to the jungle's edge, concealing them in the dense undergrowth. They had fifteen boxes of rations, some rice and fresh fruit. They rested until it was light, then began the task of moving the boxes further into the jungle. Taking a box each, they moved another three hundred yards in and found a spot near a stream as a semi-permanent dump. Hari constructed a living shelter of Atap palm and creepers, which would cover their hoard until it could be recovered. All day they moved the rations, not using the same way more than once, to avoid leaving an obvious track. By nightfall it was completed. Hari cooked some rice and corned beef and, as a special treat, they each had a banana.

Once they had finished breakfast, with Sgt Muir leading they started their journey back to the cave. The two marines carried a box of rations each, while Hari Khah carried a bag of rice and some fruit and had the 2-inch mortar slung over his shoulder. They made slow progress and it was obvious they would not get back to the cave by nightfall. Maj. Martin thought it would take five trips to move their 'booty' back to the cave.

They had several breaks and by dusk they still had some way to go. It rained heavily during the night, but due to Hari's expertise they kept dry. However, they were sorely troubled by the mosquitoes again. After some hot tea and some biscuits they resumed their journey and by midday they had the cave in sight. Blake was on watch and saw them climbing up the slope. He called the girls, who went to meet them and helped carry some of their loads into the cave. The three all looked exhausted. After they had washed down, they had something to eat before going to their beds where they slept till dusk.

Blake and the two girls offered to do all the night watches, but the others would not hear of it and insisted in taking their turn.

During the evening Maj. Martin tuned in to Radio Singapore. The Japanese were appealing in English for any soldiers still at large to give themselves up.

'You will be well treated. We Japanese honour brave soldiers such as you. Give yourselves up by coming into the nearest town or village. A warm welcome awaits you.'

They listened in disbelief. They were all aware of what awaited them, especially the girls. As the major tried other wavelengths, they heard a very 'British' voice calling for supporters of 'Free Malaya' not to cooperate with the Japanese invaders. They all thought that was interesting. Perhaps there were others like themselves, still prepared to fight.

While Blake was on watch, he heard Jan and Jim Muir 'performing'. If he could hear, so could the major.

After breakfast the next morning, Maj. Martin took his two marines to one side. They sat at the back of the cave well away from the others. Mick Martin looked at them.

'I have a question for you both. I know you will be honest in your answers. Are you both "at it" with the two nurses?'

Sgt Muir said, 'I am having a relationship with Jan, Sir.'

Blake looked embarrassed and said, 'So am I, Sir, with Joy Hammond.'

The major sighed. 'Well I can hardly blame you, they are both very attractive, and I can't post you to another unit, so we shall have to set up some married quarters.'

So later on that morning, Blake moved his and Joy's bedding to the back of the cave's left-hand side and Jim Muir did the same with his bedding and Jan's to the right-hand side. Ration boxes provided some privacy. Maj. Martin and Hari Khah moved their bedding nearer to the front of the cave, one on either side. The matter was not raised again.

Both of the marines took full advantage of their 'married status'. The girls were not complaining, but were somewhat concerned that the latex sheaths would run out. The nurses solved this by washing out the items and re-powdering them.

Two days later Sgt Muir, Hari and Blake were sent to collect more rations from the food dump. They just took a ration pack each and a groundsheet, plus a Thompson sub-machine gun. That was as light as they could travel. They were instructed not to use the same track back as on the way out, otherwise the track from the food dump to the cave would soon become like a main road.

They made their way to the dump in quick time, but it was slow going on the return journey with two boxes and the other bag of rice. They stopped and made camp at 1600 hours. Hari made a fish curry, and they spent a reasonable night, despite the insects.

As they were about to have breakfast the next morning they heard voices, less than fifty yards away. Jim Muir and Blake crept towards the sound. They made their way up a small slope and peered over. Less than twenty yards from them, by the side of a small stream, sat eight people, two of whom were young women. All were Chinese except one, who was talking. He was English. They carried a variety of weapons, at least four shotguns, a Bren gun, some rifles and one Thompson sub-machine gun.

The marines lay there until the strangers moved off. They seemed quite relaxed and one of the girls seemed very friendly with the Englishman. They had no packs with them. Sgt Muir thought they must have a camp nearby, probably within a mile or so. The two marines went back to Hari and told him what they had seen. 'Perhaps they are resistance fighters. They're all Chinese, so they're most likely Communists', he said.

By late afternoon they arrived back at the cave and reported what they had seen to Maj. Martin. He questioned them both about the white officer.

'Did they have a radio?' he asked.

They hadn't seen one. 'We might go and have a look in that area tomorrow', he said.

As Joy and Blake settled down for the night, he put his arm around her.

'Not too tired?' she asked.

'Never', said Blake.

He eased her clothing to one side and slid his hand down inside her trousers. Within seconds they were both naked. Joy moved on top of him and guided his penis into her. She slowly moved up and down. Blake kissed her breasts, then her mouth. His hands were busy on her legs and bottom. She increased her movement and they thrust frantically at one another. One last thrust and they climaxed together. Ten minutes later Jan came across to them.

'If you can tear yourselves apart you are on watch in ten minutes, Peter.'

In the morning Maj. Martin decided to go and see if they could find the strangers' camp. He would only take Jim Muir with him. He told Blake, 'You are in charge. If we do not get back, act as you see fit, but the safety of the girls is your only priority.'

Blake would have liked to have gone with them, but it made sense for one of the marines to remain in camp. Jan was worried something would happen to Jim Muir and she spent most of the day near the cave entrance. Blake kept himself busy, cleaning weapons and making sure the cave was kept tidy. The day passed quietly, but they all were dreading the sound of firing. However, it stayed quiet. Hari cooked some of the tinned tongue with some curry powder and rice. They all thought it was good, but their minds were elsewhere.

By three in the afternoon, the major and Jim Muir were following the track the eight strangers had made. It ran alongside the small stream. The noise of the running water covered up any slight noise they made. They stopped at dusk and made themselves a shelter for the night. They did not cook but settled for biscuits, cheese and water. As night closed in they both felt they were fairly close to the Chinese camp.

It stayed dry throughout the night, so both of the marines got little rest from the insect swarms. Maj. Martin thought he could hear a radio at one stage, but he couldn't be sure. As it began to get light, they packed up their kit and moved further along the trail. After an hour they could hear voices and a woman laughing. They could also smell wood burning.

'Look for the sentry', ordered the major, as they moved slowly forward. In front of them was a clearing. Four Atap-covered huts were towards the back. Sitting in front of one of the huts were the seven Chinese and the Englishman.

Chapter 10

'Stay here', whispered the major to Sgt Muir. 'Cover me.' He stood up and called out, 'British officer.'

Seven weapons were turned in his direction. The English-looking person smiled and walked forward to greet him.

'And where', he said, 'did you spring from?'

The major turned and waved Jim Muir to come into the camp.

'We could ask the same question', he said.

The seven Chinese continued to view the two marines with suspicion, as Sgt Muir tried to engage them in conversation without success.

The Englishman introduced himself as Col Ralph Slater.

'I am one of five officers detailed as the "Stay Behind" group.'

He explained his job was to try and organise resistance to the Japanese among the Malay and Chinese communities. He had experienced some success with the Chinese, but they were mostly of Communist sympathy. However, this mattered little for the moment, as they hated the Japanese and that was the important thing. He went on to say this particular group was one of three he was involved with. They had twice ambushed Japanese lorries on the Tapah road and had moved into the jungle to wait until things cooled down.

Sgt Muir looked at the two attractive Chinese girls.

'You have all the comforts with you, Sir.'

The colonel laughed, 'You could not be more wrong, Sergeant. In these units that just does not happen. If a man and his wife volunteer to serve, they are placed in different groups. There is a strict moral code.'

The two officers sat down and talked for an hour. Sgt Muir passed the time with the Chinese. They offered him some coffee from a communal mug, which he took two sips from and passed on. He observed they did not seem to have much food.

The two officers finished their conversation, and Maj. Martin called Jim Muir over to him.

'This is only a temporary camp for these people. Their main base is about five miles south of here. I intend to give them a box of our rations; at least it will show goodwill. I want you to go to our temporary dump and bring back a box. Make it the fish.'

Sgt Muir agreed and set off. He reached the food dump in about ninety minutes, after which he took a ten-minute break before selecting a box containing 'Herrings in Tomato Sauce'. He then started the return journey, which, with the weight of the box, took him two hours to complete.

It was nearly 1500 hours went he arrived back at the Chinese camp. They all seemed friendlier now, and the major told him they would spend the night there. The Chinese did not set any guards, insisting that if the Japanese were in the area they would know.

They seemed to like the tinned herrings.

'I'm glad somebody does', thought Jim Muir, as he settled for some cheese and biscuits from his own rations. As soon as it was dark the Chinese settled down for the night, the two girls sleeping alongside the men. They were not shown any special favours, nor did they seek them.

After breakfast the next day, Maj. Martin told Jim Muir that one of the women would return to the cave with them and stay there for at least a month. He went on to say she would monitor the Japanese radio traffic on their set. Her name was Soo Lin and she was the group's second in command. They left the colonel and the Chinese with smiles and handshakes. Some trust had been established and the marines felt they were now once again part of the fight against the Japanese.

Soo Lin carried an automatic shotgun and little else. She had an army pack slung across her shoulders, which contained some spare ammunition and her very few personal effects. Dressed in the traditional black top and trousers, she could be mistaken for a rubber tapper, or a tin mine worker. They stopped each hour for ten minutes. Soo Lin thought it was for her benefit and was not necessary, but the marines explained it was their standard procedure.

After four hours they were approaching the southern side of Gunung Jasar, and thirty minutes later they entered the cave passage. Soo Lin's eyes were everywhere. As they neared the entrance to the back of the cave they called out. Blake gave an answering call, and they dropped down into the main cave.

The two nurses gave Soo Lin a tour of the cave, showing her the toilet arrangements and where they slept. The Chinese girl was not too impressed with the nurses sharing their beds with the two marines.

'Not proper', she said. 'I sleep near but not with your major.'

Maj. Martin showed her the radio and the hand generator, and this did impress her. She was amazed at the amount of food they had, as well as the guns and ammunition. She listened to the Japanese on the radio for two hours, writing down call signs and trying different wavelengths.

After her stint on the radio she shared her knowledge of the situation. She told them that many Japanese units were short of food and were existing on British army rations recovered from the Batu Cave supply dumps just outside Kuala Lumpur. There was a massive store there, which the British should have destroyed before their withdrawal south. This was now keeping the Japanese army from starving.

Hari Khah and Soo Lin did not like one another and barely spoke. She despised his acceptance of colonial rule.

'We fight for a free Malaya, governing ourselves', she said.

She went on to say she was a member of the Malayan People's Anti-Japanese Army. 'When Japan is defeated *we* will be in charge.'

Hari Khah snorted and said, 'You Communist. Your party was banned before the war, and will be when the war is finished.'

The major interrupted the argument saying, 'We do not talk politics until the Japanese are defeated. Is that clear to you both?'

Soo Lin seemed surprised but said, 'I agree', as did Hari.

Mick Martin was concerned that Soo Lin would turn out to be 'a cuckoo in the nest', but after a few days with them she had accepted their lifestyle and seemed to enjoy it. Blake and Sgt Muir, though still enjoying a physical relationship with the girls, kept things quieter, much to the major's relief.

Soo Lin began to tell them more of her small band's activities. She explained they had five camps where they could rest, from the Kinta Valley near Tanjung Rambutan to the south of Gunung Rapat. The colonel had two other groups under his leadership, which covered an area from Gunung Rapat to Tapah. These groups also had numerous camps but she did not know where these were.

'Good security not to know', she said.

In his talks with the colonel, Mick Martin had agreed to meet up with him again. The venue would be the pipeline intake above Juang and two dates had been decided, with the time set for midday. Both parties agreed to be there one hour before and to stay one hour after. Taking Blake and Soo Lin, they arrived at the spot and waited the prescribed time, but as there was no sign of the other party they abandoned the rendezvous for that day to return the same time the next day.

This time the colonel appeared. Soo Lin went to meet him and they conversed in Chinese. After a few minutes they came back to the major and Blake. The colonel shook them both by the hand.

'Soo Lin tells me you live in luxury and at first she did not understand your way of life, but she does now and hopes she can stay with you longer.' This brought smiles to the faces of the major and Blake.

'Of course she can, she is most welcome', said the major.

They then discussed a joint operation to blow up the railway bridge just south of Tanjung Rambutan.

'We know that place', said Mick Martin. 'We have some friends buried there.'

It was agreed to rendezvous a mile north of Tambun on the 6th of April, a week ahead. They said their goodbyes and went their separate ways, Soo Lin now very much at ease with the marines, and in particular Mick Martin. This had not gone unnoticed by Blake. Soo Lin was very attractive and, despite being married, the major was only flesh and blood. 'He might join us in the married quarters', thought Blake.

Over the next few days most of the group were detailed to retrieve the rest of the rations from the food dump. This took them two trips and Soo Lin insisted on carrying a box just like the others. She had even made an effort to improve her relationship with Hari Khah.

By way of the radio and Soo Lin's ability to understand some Japanese, they found out more of the deployment of the

Japanese forces in Malaya. In the small towns and larger villages they had a garrison of company strength, between sixty and ninety men. In the large towns, like Ipoh and Taiping, there was a battalion of around six to seven hundred men. In the major cities, such as Singapore and Kuala Lumpur, they were at brigade strength, four or five battalions.

It became obvious that the Japanese had no desire to try and patrol deep into the jungle, preferring to concentrate their resources on keeping the railway and roads open. Maj. Martin had always thought this likely, but Soo Lin's experience and the Japanese radio traffic confirmed it.

Mick Martin was becoming increasingly aware how attractive Soo Lin was. She had a devastating smile and he was frequently subjected to it. He wondered if Col Slater was responsible for the Chinese girl's warmer attitude. It was certainly having the desired effect.

Chapter 11

On the morning of the 5th of April, they began their journey to the rendezvous point, while Sgt Muir stayed in camp with the two nurses. Hari Khah had asked to go with them, arguing he knew someone in Tambun village who might be able to help them in the future with food, so he joined the excursion. When they passed the tin mine it was still deserted. As they made their way through the Sungei Raia Gorge they kept to the northern side of the river. By dusk on the 6th of April they were in the agreed position. This was only a few hundred yards away from the marines' last bitter encounter with Japanese, and Blake wondered what had happened to the bodies of his friends. Soo Lin had moved forward to look for Col Slater, and to their relief she returned with him a few minutes later.

The two groups moved carefully north to the bridge. Col Slater told them Japanese foot patrols had been seen there in the last two days. With the marines and some of the Chinese keeping guard, the others laid their charges under the bridge. The colonel was using some plastic explosive and gelignite, which was wired to some pencil fuses. A back-up detonator was positioned on top of the railway track.

The plan was for the colonel to wait until they could hear the train approaching, then when it was a few hundred yards away he would trigger the pencil fuses. The fuses they were using took one minute to ignite the charges, which would then blow the bridge just before the train reached it. This should cause the train to topple, with its carriages, into the river. If the pencil fuses failed, the back-up detonator on the railway track would detonate the explosives as the train ran over it. The engine would probably escape but not the carriages.

As they lay waiting for the train to come, Hari told the major that he had contacted his friend as they had passed Tambun and the man would like to help. However, he was scared of repercussions for his family if he were caught. The major told Hari to forget involving his friend. They would find other ways of getting food. In any case, they still had ample stocks in the cave.

Suddenly in the distance they heard the train. Col Slater went down and stood by the fuses, while the two groups were ready to open fire if the train contained troops. As it got nearer he snapped the fuses then ran back to the others. When the train was a hundred yards up the track the bridge blew. Immediately the train driver applied the emergency brakes. With its wheels locked the train slid towards the damaged bridge and stopped within a few feet of disaster in a shower of sparks and steam.

The marines and the Chinese opened up, raking the carriages with accurate bursts of Bren, tommy-gun and shotgun fire. Judging by the limited response, there could only be a few Japanese troops on the train, but the colonel ordered a withdrawal.

The two groups moved swiftly away from the scene, towards the Kinta Valley. As soon as they reached the river, the colonel's group crossed and made their way along its northern bank as previously planned. The major's group, in contrast, kept to the southern side, turning southeast after a mile, towards Gunung Jasar, resting after two hours. The major and his group were all disappointed with the operation.

They had expected to witness a dramatic train smash, but it was only the bridge that was damaged and, sadly, not that badly.

Putting their disappointment behind them, they carefully made their way through the dark jungle, the moon providing some welcome assistance. At 0200 hours thick cloud covered the moon and it began to rain heavily, so they were forced to stop again. They huddled together waiting for daylight. They all felt cold as the heat generated by their earlier rapid withdrawal was now lost.

As soon as it was light they resumed their journey, Soo Lin leading followed by the major, with Hari Khah and Blake bringing up the rear. The rain stopped at about 1000 hours and they took the opportunity to rest and made some tea. They shared out what rations they had left and ate some biscuits with cheese or jam. They were all carrying leeches on different parts of their bodies. They formed a circle and passed a lighted cigarette to each other as, with modesty forgotten, the leeches were removed. Soo Lin had several on her back and bottom and Blake removed them, marvelling in the softness of her skin.

The jungle was particularly dense and the going was slow. It was obvious they would not reach the cave by nightfall. They crossed two swollen streams, where they filled their water bottles, and carried on until the light began to fail. They made camp, Hari and Soo Lin quickly constructing a shelter for them all. They had some tea, sugar and tinned milk left, but no food, so they all enjoyed a mug of tea, then settled down for the night. Soo Lin slept between Blake and the major.

They each did an hour on watch. Blake was on his second hour when the sky began to lighten. With nothing left to eat they set off for the cave and just before 1100 hours they entered the eastern entrance. A few minutes later they had rejoined their friends.

Joy made a fuss of Blake, and helped him wash and change into clean clothes. Hari provided a meal of Irish stew Malay style and, watched by their three friends, the four returnees tucked in. They then cleaned their weapons and refilled their magazines, before all four fell asleep; they were all exhausted.

They slept for about four hours. Soo Lin was the first to wake and, with Sgt Muir cranking the hand generator, she listened to the Japanese radio traffic. When the major woke up she told him two companies of Japanese troops were searching the jungle east of Tanjung Rambutan. This was miles from them, and also a good way from the camp Col Slater had made for. The Japanese had some engineers repairing the bridge. From what she had heard the damage was not that bad. Mick Martin told them all that he would be meeting Ralph Slater at the Juang intake in one week to discuss further operations.

That night Joy and Peter Blake gently and quietly made love. She had been worried that he would not return and this added to the deep and satisfying encounter. They stood a two-hour watch together, and when they returned to their bed they made love again, this time more fiercely, she returning his thrusts with equal vigour. In the morning Jim Muir and Jan gave them a knowing look and both remarked on the ground shaking.

'Was it an earthquake?' they asked.

They stayed in the confines of the cave for the next two days, just in case the Japanese put up a spotter plane to try and locate them. Mick Martin was a little concerned that the two nurses were becoming cave-bound and not getting enough exercise. Jim Muir smiled at this, prompting the major to remark that he meant some jungle patrolling, not night-time frolics. It was decided that if they wanted to, the nurses could do a three-day patrol east of the cave with Sgt Muir and Blake. Joy and Jan jumped at the idea, and it was decided to make a dawn start the next day.

At 0600 hours they left the cave by the eastern entrance and by the time it was really light they were well into the jungle. They were all carrying the lighter Thompson sub-machine gun, as the nurses would not find these weapons too heavy or too cumbersome in the jungle.

By midday they had made good progress. It was sunny, but under the jungle canopy it was not too hot. They crossed quite a few streams, the girls taking advantage of the fresh water to wash the sweat from their faces. At 1600 hours they made camp, using their four groundsheets to make just one shelter. They made a corned beef hash, flavoured with an oxo cube, with a mug of strong sweet tea to finish. It rained heavily during the night, so mosquitoes did not trouble them unduly.

Sgt Muir and Blake knew that if they trekked due east they would enter the State of Pahang, the border of which was about another day's march away. As the jungle was dense all the way to the east coast, they would not know when they had crossed into Pahang, but this did not really matter.

Just before midday Sgt Muir changed the direction of their march to due south, and for two hours they kept to that direction. He then headed due west, to bring them back eventually to Gunung Jasar. It was important not to use their outward track as their route home in case of ambush. At 1630 hours they made camp for the night just above a small stream, constructing a similar shelter to the night before. They prepared a meal and settled down for the night, but at midnight there was a tremendous storm with thunder and lightning. Several trees were struck by lightning not far from their camp, causing them some concern for their safety.

By dawn the storm had passed, but the stream below their camp was now in full flood. The two marines cut some stout poles and used them to brace themselves and their partners against the swiftly flowing water, as they crossed in pairs. An hour later Blake, who was leading, came across a fresh track, which ran north to south across their path. It was very recent and some heel marks were still filling with water from the swampy ground. Jim Muir calculated about six people had recently used it, and they were heading south.

'We will follow their track for an hour and see where it goes', said Muir. So with the two marines in front they carefully followed the new track. After half an hour they could hear voices, some quite angry. Telling the two nurses to stay put, the two marines edged forward towards the sound. They saw, just ten yards in front of them, five Chinese and two figures who were tied together by their hands. It was Col Slater and the other woman in his group.

One of the Chinese was berating Slater and finished his tirade by punching him in the face. The woman spat in the man's direction, her spittle landing on his boot. Two of the Chinese grabbed her. Laughing, they lifted her shirt and fondled her breasts.

Jim Muir and Blake had seen enough and opened fire. They hit the two men closest to Slater and the girl. The other three grabbed their weapons and managed one burst, before they fell beneath a hail of fire from the marines. Blake and Muir moved swiftly into the clearing. One of the Chinese was still moving. Blake finished him with a shot to the head.

They released Slater and the girl, and checked the bodies of the Chinese. There were only four. A prolonged burst of fire came from where they had left the nurses. Blake raced back to them. The two nurses were standing over the body of the fifth man. They both smiled with relief when they saw Blake.

Col Slater was unhurt, but the Chinese girl with him had a wound to her arm. The two nurses took charge of the injured girl and had soon cleaned the wound and applied a field dressing. The bullet had passed through the flesh near the top of her arm and the wound was not serious. Ralph Slater was, of course, delighted to see them.

'What would have happened if you people had not turned up doesn't bear thinking about. We can't thank you enough.'

He told them he and Mai Peng were on their way to the Tapah area, when they bumped into the five Chinese bandits.

'They would have handed us over to the Japanese, but only after they had amused themselves with Mai Peng.'

Sgt Muir suggested they come back to the cave and rest up for a couple of days.

'It's only a few hours away, and the major will be glad to see you.' Slater agreed. Collecting the bandits' weapons, they slowly made their way to Gunung Jasar.

They entered the cave by the eastern entrance. Col Slater was most impressed, and even more so when he saw the cave proper. Maj. Martin was equally pleased to see him, and soon they were all sitting around drinking tea. Ralph Slater and Mick Martin talked long into the evening about future operations they would mount, either as a combined group or as two separate units. Slater was interested in doing several ambushes on the Tapah road, a couple in daylight and one at night. The Japanese were using the roads more because the railways were becoming a target all over Malaya. Slater thought that the Anti-Japanese Army was now close to a thousand strong, and with each success against the Japanese more recruits came forward. The majority of these were Chinese and this concerned him, as he was of the opinion that the aims of these freedom fighters went beyond the removal of the hated Japanese.

Blake and Joy were on watch together at midnight. Before that they had made love quietly and discreetly, so as not to upset their guests. Whilst on watch they heard the sounds of Jim Muir and Jan, gasping and groaning as they thrashed their way to a climax. In the morning Mai Peng gave the nurses a strange look. Later, when they changed her dressing she whispered, 'This good camp, everyone very happy, I like to stay. In my camp men fart and smell shitty.'

They passed this information on to Maj. Martin. He laughed, and said he would speak to Ralph Slater. Slater was not too happy to lose Mai Peng and suggested he lend her and borrow Hari Khah, in an effort to persuade more Malay's to join them. When this was put to Hari he reluctantly agreed, but asked that it would only be for a month.

Two days later Hari and Ralph Slater left the cave, loaded with rations. A joint operation had been agreed. This would be in a week's time and they would meet at the ten-mile stone marker on the Ipoh to Tapah road. They planned two road ambushes, five miles apart, on the same day. They would then withdraw a mile into the jungle and the following night meet at another milestone and do a combined ambush before returning to their 'safe' camps.

With Hari temporarily detached, Joy and Jan did the cooking. The major's sleeping arrangements were the cause of some amusement, as Soo Lin slept on one side of him and Mai Peng the other. When Muir and Blake asked if he was getting any sleep at all, he snapped, 'Don't be impertinent', but a slight smile as he turned away suggested he was flattered rather than offended.

Chapter 12

A few days later they left for the rendezvous. Jim Muir and Jan stayed behind to guard the cave. Blake carried the Bren gun, Soo Lin her shotgun, and the others all had Thompson sub-machine guns. It took them two days to reach the agreed meeting place. The weather had been appalling and the torrential rain and thunderstorms had turned the small streams into raging torrents.

Ralph Slater was already there. The two groups then moved two miles apart, one to the north and one to the south. They had been in position for about twenty minutes when three army lorries came down the road from Ipoh. When the lorries were level with them they opened fire. The leading lorry turned sharp right into a ditch as its driver died in the first burst of fire. The second braked hard and its two occupants jumped out, only to be cut down in a hail of bullets. The third lorry ran into the back of the second, but it contained at least ten Japanese soldiers who quickly returned some accurate fire at the ambushers. Blake threw two grenades, which exploded amongst the soldiers, and after a few more minutes of intensive fire the major instructed his party to withdraw.

He led the way to their holding position about a mile or so from the road. They had all escaped injury, but felt they had been very fortunate. They prepared a quick meal and some tea and then lay close together ready to take on any pursuers. It got dark quite quickly and it was still raining hard, but Mick

Martin didn't mind the rain as it would wash away their tracks.

They spent a peaceful but miserable night and dawn came as a relief to them all. After breakfast and a check of their weapons, they moved south to a position level with the next night's activities. Taking turns to keep watch, they all managed to make up some lost sleep from the previous night. At 1700 hours they moved back towards the road, and to the meeting place for the night ambush.

The weather had cleared, and as night came, so did the mosquitoes. Despite the application of the repellent, the insects were not to be denied.

A rustle came from their left. A challenge was made and answered, as the colonel's party joined them. An hour later they heard the sound of some lorries approaching. They had their lights full on and there seemed to be a lot of them. After a hasty consultation between the two officers it was agreed only to take on the last four lorries. The first lorry groaned its way past, then two, three, four, five, six, seven and eventually the eighth.

As the ninth lorry drew level they opened fire. Blake concentrated his fire on the last lorry, which had stopped as soon as the ambush had been sprung. Several of the ambushers threw grenades, which caused carnage as the Japanese soldiers ran to get to grips with their attackers. By the rising volume of fire coming their way, some of the eight lorries allowed to go through had stopped and their troops were joining in.

'Withdraw', called out the colonel.

The major's group, as arranged, began to move away, but as a last gesture they threw another four grenades before sliding down the bank and moving into the jungle. They headed northeast, knowing that Slater would head southeast. A few shots were fired over their heads as they swiftly sought the safety of the thicker jungle.

By midnight, despite it being a cloudy night, they had made good progress and were at least two miles from the Tapah road. They stopped for ten minutes and listened for the sound of pursuit. Apart from the usual jungle noises, they noticed nothing unusual. As they continued to move north-east, Blake led, followed by Joy, Soo Lin and Mai Peng, with the major bringing up the rear.

As dawn came, the major decided to rest for six hours. They made some tea and ate the hard ration biscuits with some jam. They put out one sentry twenty yards to their rear and, with an agreed one hour of duty each, settled down to get some sleep. Joy took the first watch, but after twenty minutes she was finding it hard to stay awake. By kneeling rather than sitting, she found the more uncomfortable position the best way to stay awake. After an hour she woke Mai Peng, who was next on. With some relief Joy lay down next to the sleeping Peter Blake.

Blake woke with a start. He shook himself to clear his sleep-fuddled brain. Something was wrong. A glance at his watch showed he should have been on watch an hour ago. Joy was asleep next to him. Soo Lin lay next to Mick Martin, but Mai Peng was missing. Blake quietly made his way to the sentry post. Mai Peng lay asleep, the shape of her small breasts rising and falling under her black tunic. He touched her shoulder. She awoke instantly, a look of horror on her face as she realised she had fallen asleep on guard.

Blake quietly told her to go and join the others, saying, 'This is our secret.'

She gave him a nervous look and left. An hour later Blake woke the others. Soo Lin and the major asked why he had not woken them up for their watches. Blake said he had toothache and couldn't sleep anyway. Joy gave him a strange look; Mai Peng a shy smile of gratitude.

With no sign of pursuit, they resumed their trek, this time due east. At 1700 hours they stopped for the night. They made camp and cooked a hasty meal. The major asked Blake how his toothache was.

'Oh, it's gone now, Sir', said Blake.

That night the watches went as scheduled. Blake followed Joy. Five minutes after he began his watch he was drenched in a sudden downpour. Mai Peng was next on and when Blake woke her he knew she wouldn't sleep on watch again.

The next day they made good progress, and shortly before 1630 hours they entered the cave by the southeast side. Jan and Jim were glad to see them, and while the ambush party cleaned their weapons, then washed, Jan cooked a delicious corned beef curry.

Chapter 13

That evening Maj. Martin and Soo Lin listened in to the radio. There was a mention of a sweep into the jungle following an attempted ambush in which several of the ambushers had been killed. They heard several Japanese units sending in situation reports; all reported negative contact. The major told them all they would not be going far over the next ten days, just a walk around Gunung Jasar for exercise. He saw Blake the next day and had a quiet word with him at the cave entrance.

'Mai Peng has told me what happened. She is deeply ashamed that she put our lives at risk. I told her she would have been shot if she was a Royal Marine. I have fined her ten dollars, which of course she doesn't have.'

He went on, 'Don't play the "White Knight" again young Blake. In this game you can't afford to be too nice, understood?'

Blake nodded. The major smiled and walked away.

Over the next week they gave the cave a good tidy up and changed all the Bren and Thompson magazines. Their boots were completely worn out with the soles hanging off; replacements were to be a top priority.

They took turns to do local patrols around their gunung, but saw and found nothing unusual. Ten days after the ambush, two welcome faces appeared at the cave, Col Slater and Hari Khah. The colonel had lost two men in the withdrawal from the night ambush; they had walked straight into a

Japanese patrol early the following morning. Ralph Slater wanted to have a go at the railway line again, just outside Ipoh on the north side, but only using the major's group. He and Mick Martin spent the rest of the day talking about this, and by evening they had agreed on a plan.

Col Slater and Hari left the cave after breakfast the next day. They were off to one of the colonel's camps to get some explosives. They said they would be gone three days, so Maj. Martin made sure they had some rations to last that period.

The two Chinese girls had settled in very well. They still insisted on sleeping either side of Mick Martin, which the others found hilarious. Joy told Blake she had seen Soo Lin kiss the major.

'Well why not?' said Blake. 'Look what we do.'

'But he's married', said Joy. Blake took her by the arms.

'Listen love, his wife will have been told that he's missing. By the time the war is over she may have remarried, think on that.'

Joy kissed him on the cheek.

'You're right, we must live for the moment. Who knows what tomorrow might bring.'

Maj. Martin spent most of his free time considering his situation. He was thirty-five and married with two children. His wife would have been informed he was missing. After a month, the War Department would revise this to missing, believed killed. With no way of informing the authorities that he was alive and active against the Japanese, his wife would accept that he was dead and her children fatherless. His mind turned to Soo Lin. She was quite beautiful, and clearly had feelings for him; she had kissed him the previous evening. It would have been easy for him to have gone further. He thought of the happy situation Sgt Muir and Marine Blake enjoyed. Joy and Jan had transformed a potentially unpleasant situation into one both those marines would be reluctant to change. Anyway, their next operation to blow up the railway line north of Ipoh could see them all killed. Perhaps he and Soo Lin should enjoy each other while they could.

That night Blake was relieved on watch by Mai Peng. As he settled down next to the sleeping Joy, he heard whispering coming from the major's bed space. A few minutes later he heard the familiar sound of one body moving against another with little gasps of pleasure accompanying the frenzied act. Blake moved closer to Joy. She no longer was asleep.

She whispered, 'Is that what I think it is?'

Blake kissed her and said, 'Yes.' Her hand moved to his erection.

'Time to join in then', she said.

Mai Peng, at the cave entrance, sighed. She was missing out on the fun. Perhaps Maj. Mick might have some energy left for her, though she knew Soo Lin would be reluctant to share.

Col Slater and Hari Khah arrived back at the cave late the next afternoon. They had with them about 30 lb of explosive. After the evening meal, the two officers sat down and began to complete their plan for destroying the railway line at Ipoh. By 2100 hours that night the plan was complete. The raiding party would consist of Slater, Martin, Blake, Hari Khah, Soo Lin and Mai Peng. Sgt Muir would be left in charge of the cave with the two nurses. They would leave the next morning at 0500 hours. By nightfall they should be at the tin mine. Under cover of darkness they would make for Gunung Rapat and hide out in one of the many gullies there until the next evening, when they would complete their trek to the railway line. Mick Martin briefed everyone involved, then they got as much rest as they could before their early morning departure.

After an early breakfast the next day, the party moved off with Blake leading. Before it was completely light they were well into the thick cover of the jungle. Despite some very heavy rain, they made good time and reached the tin mine ahead of schedule. They had a two-hour break and Hari and Mai Peng cooked a meal for them all.

As soon as it was dark they moved off to Gunung Rapat. They carefully made their way to the south of the feature and by 2300 hours they had found a good spot for the night in a narrow gully on the Ipoh side of the gunung. They made two lean-to shelters, which Blake shared with Hari and Mai Peng. They all did an hour on watch, making sure each got five hours' rest. They stayed in the gully all the next day until evening, but as soon as it was dark they moved down and out of the gully and headed for the railway line to the north of Ipoh.

They skirted any inhabited areas and did not see or hear any Japanese patrols. It took them four hours to reach the railway line. The major checked his watch; it was just before 2300 hours. Blake and Soo Lin kept watch to the south, Hari and Mai Peng to the north, while Ralph Slater and Mick Martin laid the charges. It was a good spot to sabotage, as two lots of points interrupted the railway line here and it would not be easy to repair. The charges would be set off by detonators laid on the railway track, so that the first train to pass over them would trigger the explosives. After Ralph Slater had made a final check they moved off north along the track, intending to turn east when they were level with the village of Tambun.

After ten minutes they heard the sound of a train leaving Ipoh station heading north. They stopped and waited to see the result of their labours. The ground suddenly shook as the explosives were detonated. A dazzling flash turned night into day and the noise of the explosion reverberated around the hills encircling Ipoh.

'Fuck shit!' said Blake.

Ralph Slater laughed, 'You marines say the strangest things, but I agree it was pretty dramatic.' Any further conversation was stopped by the sound of people running towards them from the north. They moved off the railway track into the undergrowth to the side.

'Nobody's to fire unless I do', said the colonel.

They waited with their weapons ready, safety catches off. About ten Japanese soldiers ran past, their sour body smell lingering in the still night air. As soon as they were past, the saboteurs, with Hari Khah leading, moved off towards Tambun. An hour later they skirted the village and headed for the Sungei Raia Gorge where they would hold up until the next evening.

It was almost a completely clear night. The clouds had made way for the full moon to bathe the track to Gunung Rapat in a clear light. They had spread out over about thirty yards and Blake had changed places with Hari and was now leading. Suddenly, to his front two figures moved out from the side of the road. He could see they were Japanese soldiers. They shouted a challenge in Japanese.

His answer was to fire two bursts from his Thompson sub-machine gun before he threw himself to his right, anticipating some return of fire. The rest of his colleagues dived off the track, ready to engage the enemy soldiers. It was completely quiet. Blake got to his feet and moved forward to where the soldiers had fallen. Two bodies lay there, their rifles lying a few feet from where their owners lay. Both appeared dead. Maj. Martin came up to his side. He glanced at the bodies and indicated they should push them into the undergrowth by the side of the track. They threw the rifles of the soldiers further into the undergrowth and then, with a great deal of caution, carried on. Two hours later they crossed the Sungei

Raia and hid themselves in one of Gunung Rapat's many gullies.

The two officers were concerned that the Japanese would soon find their two comrades and launch a full search of the area. It seemed strange that two Japanese soldiers were on their own on the remote track; it did not make any sense to deploy like that. Soo Lin thought there might be a more simple explanation. Perhaps the soldiers were on their way to a nearby kampong (small village) to look for women. Col Slater thought the idea made sense, the men were probably from a small unit on the Tapah road. But the firing might provoke some response. They made themselves as comfortable as they could in the gully and as soon as it was light they made breakfast. They had one meal left of their three days' rations. The colonel suggested to Maj. Martin they should stay in the gully till dusk, then head for the pipeline and the jungle.

During the day they heard several lorries using the track they had followed and, at 1600 hours, they saw about fifty soldiers in line abreast searching the undergrowth the other side of the Sungei Raia. As soon as it was dark, Mick Martin led them out of the gully towards the tin mine and the pipeline. They skirted the mine as they noticed there was several lights on in the building. By midnight they were well into the jungle. It began to rain and it was a very dark night. It was decided to stop for the night and rest up till morning and in a matter of minutes they had constructed two shelters. Blake shared with Mai Peng and Hari again.

They were all glad when morning came. They finished off what rations they had left and headed for Gunung Jasar. To avoid leaving a clear track they waded for about a mile along a streambed, which did not always go in the right direction, but it was good security. It took them most of the day to return to their cave home, and shortly before 1600 hours they were reunited with their friends.

They spent the next hour cleaning weapons and themselves. Ralph Slater and the major were listening carefully to the radio traffic, with Soo Lin translating. Jan and Joy prepared a meal and afterwards, they all sat together drinking tea as the colonel explained what they had heard from the radio. It was not all good news. The railway line was out of action, but 'only for a couple of days' said the Japanese.

'More like a week', said the colonel.

What did concern them was the news that the Japanese had arrested six men from Tambun village and had executed them for being responsible for the incident on the railway track and for the murder of two Japanese soldiers. Ralph Slater thought they should avoid any more operations in that area for a few months.

'We will concentrate further south for a while.'

That night Blake and Joy quietly enjoyed each other's bodies. After thirty minutes of teasing one another, they reached a satisfying climax in a more frantic two minutes. There was other activity going on in the cave, in at least two other places. In the morning Ralph Slater took Mick Martin to one side, and with a smile on his face said, 'How come a Royal Marines' barracks sounds like a brothel?'

'Because', said Martin, 'we are a very happy family!'

Ralph Slater stayed another two days, then left with Hari Khah and Mai Peng. He took all their boot sizes, promising to be back in about four or five days. Mai Peng told him she wanted to stay with the major's group. He said he would consider her request. Maj. Martin said they would do some two-day patrols to the north, avoiding the area to the west.

It was now July 1942 and one or two new voices were heard on the radio. A mention was made of 'Force Cobra' with instructions to contact them on certain wavelengths.

Blake and Jim Muir spent two days to the north and went as far as the Sungei Kinta, but they saw nothing untoward except a lot of leeches; the place was alive with them. Two days after their return, Ralph Slater reappeared with Hari and Mai Peng, and a sack full of new 'jungle boots'.

They were all fascinated by the new boots. Ralph Slater said they came from a factory in Kuala Lumpur, which had a contract to supply the Japanese with footwear suitable for the Malayan conditions. They were well constructed, with a canvas upper, which was of calf length, and a stout rubber sole with a deeply grooved pattern to provide purchase in the slippery ground. They each were given two pairs. Mick Martin thought each pair would last them about two months. Ralph Slater did not agree.

'I would not think a pair will last more than a month, but we will see.'

The colonel was very interested in the 'new' voices on the radio. He explained that they were indeed part of the new Force Cobra and that he understood some more British officers had landed on the west coast from a submarine to add to their numbers.

'We are receiving orders from Ceylon, which is the nearest Allied base', he added. 'The newly arrived officers should be joining up with other units of the Anti-Japanese Army to coordinate operations and to arrange for supply drops.'

He went on to tell them that, within the next two weeks, regular radio contact would be established between the larger groups and contact would be established with the British submarine by radio at certain times. Mick Martin asked if the details of his group could be passed to the submarine, so as to inform their relatives that they were alive and well. Ralph Slater thought it was possible, but suggested no names be sent, just their official numbers.

The next day they made contact with a group on one of the new wavelengths. This group called itself 'Doctor' and was in the Taiping area. The major said his group would be called 'Royal' for obvious reasons.

The morale was high in the cave that evening. For the first time since their escape from the Japanese at Tambun, they no longer felt alone. Mai Peng was also happy. Col Slater had agreed she and Soo Lin could stay with the major's group. This gave them a strength of eight, four men and four women.

Ralph Slater departed alone the next day; he was going to a camp near Tapah to try and organise another radio. He told them he intended to return in two weeks to discuss further operations.

Chapter 14

Back in Ipoh, the Japanese colonel in charge was dreading the arrival of a general from Headquarters in Kuala Lumpur. Col Sako was a long-serving army officer who had been decorated for his courage in the invasion of Indo-China. But the two serious sabotage acts on the railway between Ipoh and Tanjung Rambutan, along with the road ambushes on the Tapah road, had placed his future in jeopardy. He sat studying his map of the area. He had marked all the places his troops had searched after the recent attacks and no trace of those responsible had been found. Another problem he faced was the quality of his men. After the invasion of Malaya and the capture of Singapore, his best men had been sent north to fight and assist in the capture of Burma. His thoughts were interrupted by the arrival of Maj. Asana, who informed him that Gen. Ishinna's car had just driven into the compound.

The general had not been prepared to listen to any excuses. His face was white with anger and spittle flew everywhere as he berated the unfortunate Sako.

'Your men look and smell like shit. No wonder these renegades have been successful. You have one week to save your career, Colonel.'

As he left, he turned to the perspiring Sako.

'I will stay the night. After dinner have two young girls sent to my quarters. They must be Chinese.' Col Sako sat back down behind his desk as the general departed; his mind was in turmoil.

'I am a soldier not a pimp. I serve the Emperor not that fat pervert', he said to himself.

He stood up, re-buttoned his tunic and drew his pistol.

'I have my honour, my code', he said, and shot himself.

When he heard the shot, Maj. Asana rushed into his colonel's office. Satisfying himself that the colonel was dead, he gave orders for the mess to be cleared up. He reported the incident to the general, who nodded and said, 'You will assume command until further orders. Do not forget the two young girls; they must be Chinese.'

The major rushed off to make the arrangements for the general's entertainment, thinking to himself, 'I will be a colonel within the week.'

The weather over the next week was typical of the monsoon season, torrential rain and dramatic thunderstorms. At night the lightning flashes turned the darkest night into day. It was cosy in the cave, dry and safe from any lightning strike. They slept in four pairs now. Mai Peng slept alongside Hari Khah. Blake thought this was wonderful. He liked Hari and though he did not think he and Mai Peng were 'at it', they certainly were friendly. Soo Lin had asked Joy if there were some 'rubbers' she could have. Joy gave her a handful and told her to wash them out afterwards and re-powder them.

Joy's feelings for Blake were complex. They had been thrown together by fate. They were good together, but what would happen should the war end? Would he still want to be with her? She was reluctant to talk to him about their future, but resolved to raise it when the time seemed right, which was not now.

Mick Martin and Hari Khah were doing a careful check of their rations. It was working out pretty well. They were never hungry but they never wasted anything. As a result of their good housekeeping they had food for at least another two months. Hari thought another 28 lb of rice would add another three weeks to that figure.

Despite Ralph Slater stopping operations for the time being, Maj. Martin thought another raid on the Tapah road might help them restock their larder. He decided to give the colonel a few more days to return and then, if he had not shown, they would try for another food lorry.

Back at the Japanese Headquarters in Ipoh, Acting Col Asana was issuing his first orders. He was using two hundred of his men to sweep the area from the Tapah road to Tambun via the Gunung Rapat Gorge. The general had left that morning. He had thanked Asana for the entertainment of the night by saying, 'We warriors need to relax. You have done well Asana. Keep this up and I will confirm your promotion.'

The lifeless bodies of the two young girls on which the general had slaked his lust were driven to the nearby Sungei Kinta and thrown in. With the river in flood from the monsoon rain it would only be a few hours before they would be washed into the Straits of Malacca and lost forever.

Chapter 15

The following afternoon the figure of Col Slater was spotted climbing up the slope to the cave. It was still raining and he was exhausted, but after some hot food he quickly recovered. He had some interesting news and was clearly anxious to share it with them. He had been contacted by another officer further south, in the Kuala Lumpur area, and been given a code book. Also a wavelength had been allocated for the major's group. In two days' time they were to transmit on that wavelength to a submarine, which would surface in the Malacca Straits at 2300 hours. If there was no response they should try again the next night. In their message they should give a list of their group, not by name but by their service number. The other news that was vital to their survival was that once a month four transport Liberator aircraft would drop supplies at four points in Malaya. One of the dropping zones was the western slopes of Gunung Jasar. Mick Martin asked where the planes were flying from.

'Ceylon', said Ralph Slater. 'They are fitted with extra fuel tanks and have a range of nearly four thousand miles. It's about eighteen hundred miles from Ceylon, so they have a slight margin of safety.'

The news of the coming contact with the submarine and the possibility of airdrops raised their morale, not that it was that low in the first place. Ralph Slater and Mick Martin spent hours with the code book, which was pretty straight-forward despite first appearances. The alphabet was converted to numbers. To convert a letter, each group had to use a number allocated to their call sign. The major's group was call sign 'Royal' and had been given the number three. In addition, each day of the week had a number: Sunday one, Monday two and so on. The day of the month was the last element of the equation, with odd days numbered one and even days two. So, if the major's group transmitted a message on Monday the 12th, by adding all the elements together, page seven of the code book would be used to convert the code.

The night of the transmission came. At 2255 hours they switched the set on and at 2300 hours they started their transmission.

'Royal, this is Royal, how do you read. Over.'

To their delight, a very English voice answered.

'Loud and clear Royal, pass your message. Over.'

They gave their message in the numbers code, informing the submarine by their service numbers who they were. At the end of their message there was a brief acknowledgement: 'Message received. Out.' The significance to them all was clear. In a few days' time their next of kin would know they were alive and well.

The next milestone would be the airdrop in five days' time, between midnight and 0100 hours. A triangle of lights would signify the dropping zone. The lights fifty yards apart would consist of three torches, which the colonel had supplied. Over the next few days they spent several hours preparing the drop zone. The area selected was almost devoid of trees, just low scrub, which was all that would grow on the gunung's slopes. They carefully measured out the triangle, and placed a small pile of stones to mark the position for the torchbearers. Ralph Slater wanted to be there for the first drop, so he was to be their guest for a few days.

He wanted to see the crashed aircraft, so Blake took him to the wreck site. Time had already recovered the area. The bodies of the crew had little flesh left on them; they were almost skeletons dressed in flying suits. They did not stay long, and returned to the cave in near silence.

The colonel said, 'When the future is clearer, it might be possible to bury the remains of these men.' Blake agreed.

At last the night of the airdrop arrived. Joy and Jan stayed on guard in the cave mouth, while the others went through the cave passage to the eastern exit. The three Royal Marines made their way to the light markers. The others stayed by the cave exit; being hit by the descending supplies was not recommended.

A few minutes after midnight the sound of a plane was heard approaching from the south. They switched their torches on. The faint sound grew to a roar, then a massive shape passed overhead, disappearing to the north. Where were the supplies? Then the boxes, slowed by their parachutes, were hitting the ground all around them. The others joined them from the safety of the cave, and they began to recover the supplies.

It took them three hours to recover the eight parachute loads and get them to safety in the cave. There was a wide selection of rations; some were American in waxed cardboard boxes. They now had enough food for at least six months. Some plastic explosive had also been dropped, the red boxes being a clear indication of their contents.

As soon as they got to bed, at about 0300 hours, Blake made a grab for Joy. She pretended to resist, but they were soon out of their clothes. They made love quietly, then the tempo of their lovemaking became quite frantic and they climaxed together. They were not the only ones to celebrate the successful airdrop. After they had finished they heard Jan gasping and groaning as Jim Muir rode her to a finish.

In the morning the two officers finalised their plans for the next operation. It was to be a day ambush just north of Tapah. Whoever took part would be away from their camp for ten days. At the ambush, they intended to split the group over a hundred yards and take out as many vehicles as they could. Blake was to stay behind with the two nurses. He was disappointed not to be going, but the thought of having Joy almost to himself sugared the pill.

Two days later, just before it got light, the ambush party left the camp. By the time it was completely light they were off the slopes of the gunung and into the thick jungle. Despite the heavy loads they were carrying, they made good time, and by nightfall they were in the jungle's edge near Gunung Rapat. They made camp and prepared a meal, just in time, for it began to pour with rain. They had the unwelcome attentions of the mosquitoes to contend with. Dawn came bringing with it some relief.

They kept to the jungle edge and moved parallel to the Tapah road and by nightfall they were almost where they wanted to be. The next morning the colonel moved off on his own to contact his group. The major would stay where he was until Slater rejoined them. Just before nightfall he returned with his group of eight. They were in good spirits; they also had had a successful airdrop.

The two groups decided to stay together for the night and move to their likely ambush position at first light. Only the major's group kept one of their members alert during the night; the other group all slept, as was their custom, a sort of blind faith in the inability of the Japanese to track them down.

After a hurried breakfast, both groups made their way to the road. The site chosen for the ambush was ideal. There was a high bank on one side of the road and falling ground on the other. They spread themselves out over approximately one hundred yards, the major's group on the northern edge, the colonel's on the southern. Once they had sprung the ambush the decision to withdraw would be Slater's, his group heading southeast into the jungle, the major's group northeast. It was a bright, sunny and very hot day. After two hours only the odd vehicle had passed, but just before 1100 hours they could hear the sound of a considerable number of trucks approaching from the south.

At last they came into view. There were at least ten vehicles, only a few yards apart. They were all groaning along, belching smoke, a clear indication of poor maintenance. As the first truck drew level with the right-hand man of the ambush party they opened fire. The thirteen ambushers poured a torrent of fire into the vehicles. Bren, shotgun, Thompson and rifle fire ripped into the Japanese. The panic-stricken drivers either stalled or crashed their trucks into one another. Some of the vehicles contained troops, who began to recover from the initial shock and return fire. Two of the lorries were well alight and the smoke added to the confusion. The ambushers threw grenades into the chaotic scene, causing more confusion.

The colonel gave the signal to withdraw. They did not want to overstay their welcome and the returning fire was becoming more organised. Mick Martin's group of five moved as quickly as they could into the relative safety of the jungle. Hari Khah had his arm down by his side; it was dripping blood, and leaving a trail a blind man could follow.

The major stopped and, after urging the others on, quickly bound up the wound and put the arm in a sling. Then he and Hari followed the others into the thicker jungle. Jim Muir, who was leading, led them up the bed of a stream to try and confuse any pursuers. They kept up a good pace for almost an hour and then stopped and listened for any sound of pursuit. Mai Peng retied Hari's dressing, making it tighter. She also insisted on taking his Thompson to lighten his load. With no sound of any Japanese they continued their escape, planning to stop for thirty minutes after the next hour. It started to rain, lightly at first, then it became torrential. It was a blessing in disguise; though uncomfortable it would make tracking them more difficult.

The Japanese officer in charge of the convoy was incandescent with rage, screaming at his junior officers and NCOs to organise a pursuit of the 'terrorists'. At last he managed to send thirty men after the ambushers, telling them not to return without some bodies.

Four of his vehicles had burnt out; the other six had damage from gunfire. Only four were capable of moving. These would have to tow the others. His biggest fear was facing Acting Col Asana, who would take this ambush very badly indeed. The burnt out trucks were pushed off the road, and the rest of the depleted convoy slowly made its way to Ipoh and the waiting venomous Asana.

Mick Martin decided to make camp for the night at 1600 hours, a little earlier than usual. Hari was weak, as he had lost quite a lot of blood. Mai Peng followed Hari's instructions in dealing with the wound. The bullet had passed right through the upper arm but had broken the bone in the process.

They cooked a meal and drank some hot tea. For shelter they just covered themselves with their groundsheets, so that they could make a rapid departure should it be necessary. At first light, while the others had breakfast, Mick Martin and Soo Lin retraced their footsteps to listen for any sign of pursuit. They returned after thirty minutes, having heard nothing. When they had completed their breakfast, and after removing any trace of their stay, the group continued their escape.

Lt Matso, the officer leading the pursuit, had followed the blood trail as far he could, then the torrential rain had washed out the track he had been following. His men were not keen on going too far into the jungle. They were not hardened veterans of Indo-China, but replacements shipped in from Japan after a short period of training. The ambush had been their first taste of action and they had seen their friends' bodies ripped apart in the deadly hail of bullets; only a few of them had even returned fire. He allowed them four hours' rest during the night. They had little food and were hardly enthusiastic about further pursuit. He decided to split his force, sending his senior sergeant's group south. He would head north. He gave instructions that they would spend four hours in their respective directions, then head west for the road and on to Ipoh.

When Capt. Hora arrived in Ipoh, Acting Col Asana was waiting just inside the military compound. As the less damaged trucks passed him towing the more obvious bullet-ridden ones Asana's face took on a purple hue. When the unfortunate captain reported the ambush, Asana turned on his heel and waved Hora to follow him to his office. As soon as the door was shut Asana struck him across the face with his cane.

Hora gave an angry hiss at this indignity. Asana was unmoved by the junior officer's anger and screamed at him to explain himself. Hora told him that he had sent thirty of his soldiers in hot pursuit of the ambushers.

'I want some of them alive', said Asana. 'They will learn just how brutal we can be.'

Hora left the acting colonel's office with relief, vowing to repay Asana's insult in the due course of time.

Lt Matso spent another four hours searching the jungle before he turned and made his way to the Ipoh road. He was not surprised to find his senior sergeant already there. Together they made their way along the road to Ipoh.

It was midnight when they eventually reached the military compound. Matso dismissed his men and reported to Capt. Hora. His senior officer viewed his lack of success with gloom.

'That bastard Asana will flay us alive if we don't produce some prisoners. We leave at 0500 hours tomorrow to continue the search. Inform the men.'

Shortly after 0500 hours the next morning, Capt. Hora led his men through a rubber plantation to the edge of the jungle. He split his fifty-strong force in two. He headed northeast and instructed Lt Matso to search southeast.

'We meet back here at 1600 hours. Try and get a prisoner or two.'

The two officers were then quickly swallowed up as they entered the thicker jungle, with their less enthusiastic men close behind.

Mick Martin was concerned that the Japanese; faced with this latest affront, would put a determined pursuit in train. The last thing he wanted was to lead them to their cave hideout, so he decided to spend another day heading east before turning north to Gunung Jasar. Hari did not seem to be in any pain and the wound was clean thanks to the efforts of Mai Peng, who also carried some of Hari's equipment, despite his protests.

They stopped for an hour at noon. They had rations for one more day. While the others rested, the major and Jim Muir backtracked for fifteen minutes. They then sat silently listening for any signs of the pursuing Japanese, but everything remained quiet. It seemed they had eluded their enemies once again.

Lt Matso was about to change the direction of his march and head back to the road and rendezvous with Capt. Hora, when an excited young soldier informed him a group of people were just ahead of them. Matso quickly made his way to the front of the patrol. His sergeant, an experienced campaigner, whispered to him that voices could be heard ahead of them. Lt Matso halted his men and, together with the sergeant, made for the sound of the voices. He got within fifteen yards of Ralph Slater's group. He could see there were at least eight people sitting down near a small stream. Quickly he instructed his sergeant to deploy his men for a frontal attack. To his surprise, his soldiers moved almost silently into position and awaited his order to attack.

Ralph Slater was uneasy; he had wanted to be further into the jungle than he was. The problem with his group was that though they were happy to follow his plans, his hold on them in the jungle was not as he would have wished. They were not as disciplined as regular soldiers. They were brave and determined, but political rather than military. Suddenly there was a crashing noise to their right. He could see Japanese soldiers running towards them. To their credit his men reacted quickly and opened fire at the advancing troops. Slater fired one burst and then ran for it. His men and the one female in their group did the same. Six of them managed to escape, with only two of them slightly wounded. One of the men fell, hit in both legs, and the girl foolishly tried to help him. Both were caught as the Japanese swept through their position.

Col Slater ran for at least fifteen minutes, the others in his group a few yards behind. They were all shocked by the sudden attack and the realisation that two of their comrades had been killed or captured. The colonel hoped the two had been killed. The girl was new to the group. She was about nineteen, and he knew what she would face if she had been captured alive. Slater was not about to let their recent experience go without comment.

'Perhaps now you will realise how important placing out a sentry is. In future this will be done. Two of our friends are dead or captured. It must not happen again.'

He looked at them all. They hung their heads. The lesson had been learned, but at what cost.

Chapter 16

Lt Matso was delighted. He had two prisoners. One of his men had been killed, but he had two prisoners. The wounded Chinese looked terrified as his wounds were tightly bound. It was not a humanitarian gesture, just done to keep him alive for subsequent interrogation. The girl was unhurt and was hauled to her feet. The soldiers surrounded her, their hands everywhere. She knew what her fate would be as her tunic and trousers were ripped from her body. Naked, she was thrown to the ground. She attempted to get to her feet but the sergeant, who would be first to rape her, forced her back to the ground. He knelt between her legs, spreading them apart. Freeing his erect penis from his trousers he cruelly thrust it into her body. She cried out. Urged on by the waiting soldiers the sergeant slammed himself into the crying girl, finally climaxing with a last brutal thrust.

As he finished, the next soldier turned the girl onto her stomach and was about to penetrate her from behind, when Lt Matso intervened. He had watched the sergeant take the girl and knew he could allow that. Now, with his sergeant satisfied, he could rely on him to control the others. The soldiers were angry at being deprived of their fun, but the sergeant and the officer would not hesitate to shoot anyone who disobeyed. Lt Matso helped the girl to her feet; she gladly covered her body with her torn clothing, but she knew her fate was merely delayed.

Mick Martin heard the brief exchange of gunfire with concern. It was a good way off to the south, and it could only mean that Slater's group was involved. He decided to make directly for the cave now; the pursuers were not after him and he could try for radio contact at 2100 hours that evening.

With Jim Muir leading they made good progress. Their habit of following any stream that ran roughly in the right direction was a good ploy. Even in a slight flow of water, the bed of the stream quickly returned to its previous unmarked condition. After the recent tropical downpours this was even quicker.

They reached the southern entrance to the cave at about 1530 hours. They called out as they reached the back of the cave to warn Blake they were coming in. Peter Blake and the two nurses were very glad to see them. They had heard the faint sounds of gunfire and had been concerned. Hari was soon the centre of Joy and Jan's attention as his wound was carefully cleaned and the broken bone skilfully put into a light splint. Mai Peng looked on anxiously. Obviously Hari had an admirer. The two nurses told Mai Peng that Hari would be fine, largely due to her prompt and skilful first aid.

When Lt Matso met up with Capt. Hora on the Ipoh road, they were both in good spirits. They had two prisoners and this would appease Acting Col Asana. A few hours later they arrived at the military compound. Asana's face brightened when he saw the prisoners. He took the opportunity to address the returning men.

'You have almost redressed your failure of the previous day. These prisoners may well provide information vital for the safety of future convoys.' He then dismissed them.

Turning to Capt. Hora and Lt Matso, he said, 'We will interrogate the prisoners after dinner. Make sure the wounded one is kept alive till then.'

Later that evening the officers went to the interrogation room next to the guardroom. They had the wounded man brought in first. Asana took charge of the proceedings.

'If you answer our questions, you will be treated as a prisoner of war. If not, your legs will be broken one at a time, followed by your arms.'

The wounded man looked at the assembled Japanese impassively.

'Where is your camp?' said Asana.

The man spat on the acting colonel's leg. Asana nodded at the man's guards. A terrible scream cut through the night air as his leg was broken at the shin. The question was repeated. No reply. There was another scream as his other leg met the same fate. Asana was sweating now. He had thought it would be easier than this.

'Break his arm', he said. A sickening snap, no sound. The man had fainted.

Lt Matso had seen enough. He had just made the outside of the room when he parted with his dinner. Capt. Hora came out.

'He wants you back inside, he's about to start on the girl.'

With reluctance, both officers went back into the room. The girl was terrified. She had heard her friend screaming. As she was led into the room, Asana smiled at her.

'You are just a child. Answer my questions and you will be released to return to your family. Now, where is your main camp?'

The girl sobbed, 'I have only just joined the group. I have never seen their main camp, please believe me.'

Asana pointed to the table. The girl was bent over it and her torn trousers ripped off. One of the waiting Japanese soldiers eagerly undid his trousers and moved behind her. Asana moved round to where he could see her face. He raised his hand and the soldier thrust himself into the helpless girl. The girl cried out as she was savagely raped, the table moving across the floor with the violence of the act. After three more soldiers had taken their turn, Asana called a halt.

'We will continue this tomorrow', he said, and left the room.

Capt. Hora was disgusted. He felt his honour as a Japanese officer had been soiled by the senseless brutality and he was not prepared to allow this to continue. Lt Matso felt the same. He came from a long line of warriors, always faithful to the Emperor. He joined his captain in the guardroom. They took the keys from the sergeant in charge and unlocked the two cells. Hora shot the girl twice in the head, releasing her from her torment as she died instantly. Matso did the same for the man. As they walked back to their quarters, they both felt that they had regained some of their honour. But tomorrow they would face Asana.

Early the next morning Acting Col Asana had a phone call from Kuala Lumpur. It was Gen. Ishinna, who enquired how the interrogation had gone. Asana, who had been told by the guard commander that both the prisoners were dead, told the general they had died during questioning. He also told the general he wanted Hora and Matso charged with disobeying orders. The general told him, 'Be careful my friend. Hora and Matso have family connections at the highest level. Just send them both on frequent jungle patrols; with any luck they will get themselves killed.'

Patrol activity was increased on the Tapah road. Both Capt. Hora and Lt Matso spent six days out of seven patrolling the jungle parallel to the road. They knew that Asana wanted them out of the way and it amused them both when they were repeatedly sent to the same area. They called it the 'Hora–Matso Line'.

Ralph Slater had learned of the fate of his two former colleagues. An elderly Chinese woman was employed as a cleaner in the guardroom, and passed on the information. Slater was not surprised by the news that the two Japanese officers had put the two prisoners out of their misery. The Japanese Officer Corps, while ruthless in war, had high personal standards of conduct, although of course there were exceptions. Slater decided that should the opportunity present itself, he would like to assassinate Gen. Ishinna and Col Asana.

Chapter 17

Maj. Martin and his group had become fed up with the forced inactivity. They had cleaned their weapons, changed magazines and the cave was so tidy it would have passed any general's inspection. It was only the night-time sexual activity that kept them happy. Mai Peng and Hari were now lovers. His arm was mending nicely, and did not hinder his performance.

Mick Martin had doubts about the set-up, four men and four women. Apart from Hari, all were young. It was inevitable they would pair off, but it was not 'marine like'. After two weeks, Ralph Slater paid a visit. He told them what had happened to the man and girl after their capture and the two nurses listened in horror. Soo Lin and Mai Peng explained that they would kill themselves rather than be captured, and Joy and Jan should be prepared to do the same. The three marines knew the girls would never have to make that decision; they would do what was necessary.

A week later Col Slater contacted them again. Both groups would meet at the tin mine. Something special was on. Mick Martin decided to leave Hari and the two nurses at the cave and take his two marines plus Soo Lin and Mai Peng. They took three days' rations with them and they all carried Thompsons, except Blake who preferred the Bren gun.

They arrived at the rendezvous before the colonel, made some tea and rested. An hour late, Ralph Slater finally arrived. He had some interesting news. Tambun House, which was just a few hundred yards north of Tambun village, was being turned into a rest centre for Japanese officers. In two days' time Gen. Ishinna and Col Asana were going to visit and formerly open it.

As soon as it was dark the two groups made their way through the Sungei Raia Gorge. By dawn they were a mile from Tambun village. Keeping close to the gunungs opposite the village they pushed on until they could see Tambun House about a mile away. They had twenty-four hours to decide on their ambush site. The favourite place seemed to be a lalang-covered embankment almost opposite the house.

Col Asana was in a good mood, his promotion had been confirmed, and Gen. Ishinna was going to open his rest home. He had almost let Capt. Hora and Lt Matso have a day off from patrolling the Tapah road, but decided against it; he wanted the general to himself. The evening before, he had taken a personal phone call from the general. Ishinna had said he would spend the night at the new rest home and would the colonel arrange some entertainment for him. Asana knew what the general required: two young girls and they must be Chinese.

Col Asana had reviewed security for the visit. He would travel with the general in his staff car. Ahead would be their small armoured vehicle and bringing up the rear would be ten soldiers in a one-ton truck.

Ralph Slater had been informed of the travel arrangements, and the ambush was planned accordingly. They had split the two groups into three; each of the three smaller groups had a specific task. Group three would act first and take out the rear vehicle and the ten soldiers, group two would disable the general's car, and group one would take care of the armoured car with two explosive charges.

They approached the area while it was still dark. The general's convoy was due at noon. The plan was to take the general alive if possible. Both Ralph Slater and Mick Martin thought this unlikely, but it was worth a try. The main thing was to avenge their two comrades.

With everything planned, Maj. Martin and his group moved into their ambush positions before dawn. Slater had told Mick Martin it was his 'show' and he, the colonel, would be just a foot soldier. The final ambush position was an embankment, but further from Tambun House than originally planned. As arranged they had split into three groups. Blake was in the first group and would take out the lorry and the escorting soldiers, as his Bren gun was considered the best weapon for the job.

Back in Ipoh things had not gone completely to plan. The small armoured car had engine trouble and would not be available for the escort. In its place would be a 15-cwt truck with six soldiers as additional guards. After giving the general refreshments and assuring him that his evening's entertainment was arranged, Col Asana led the general to the staff car, and the journey began.

As they made their way out of Ipoh, the general asked what progress was being made against the Chinese terrorists. Asana told him of the daily patrols into the jungle at various points and that since these had started there had been no ambushes. Gen. Ishinna looked pleased.

'I have heard that British officers may be involved. An unlikely alliance, Capitalists and Communists, but we should take care.'

They were now driving through the small village of Tambun.

'Not far now', said Asana. 'The rest house is about a mile up the road.'

As he spoke they heard the sound of automatic fire coming from behind them. Asana looked round. The lorry that had been following them was off the road in a ditch, its occupants under heavy fire. The general screamed at their driver to drive faster. Suddenly, a burst of fire came from almost alongside them and the driver slumped to one side. The staff car ran off the road and up the embankment, before slowly turning over onto its roof.

Blake was halfway through his second magazine. He and his two companions, who had Thompson sub-machine guns, had poured a devastating volume of fire into the truck. No fire had been returned. Suddenly, three of its occupants ran from behind the crashed vehicle. Blake's group opened fire again and the figures sank to the ground.

Mick Martin, Mai Peng and Soo Lin slid down the embankment towards the overturned staff car. They could see the two figures in the back trying to force open the door. It was jammed. The other door was up against the embankment and could not be opened. They looked in at the two terrified Japanese officers. It was obvious who they were by their badges of rank. Soo Lin drew her knife and punctured the petrol tank and Mai Peng did the same. Soon petrol was pouring into the car over the two officers. The intention of the two girls was obvious. Maj. Martin was about to stop them when he remembered what had happened to the captured girl and man. He handed his box of matches to Soo Lin, who lit two together and tossed them onto the car. They sprang back as the petrol soaked car burst into flames.

Ishinna and Asana had been franticly trying to break open the door. They saw the two Chinese girls and the European looking at them. The officers' pistols had been on the seat next to the dead driver, now beyond their reach. They then smelt the petrol. It was soon running into the car and soaking their clothing. They saw the girl light the match. A flash, searing heat, and their world became a nightmare. Death for the two Japanese officers was not quick; their flesh erupted into blisters, their lungs were scorched and their eyeballs melted. Death dallied with them as if all the victims of the their previous cruelty were saying, 'Not yet, not yet'.

As the major and the two girls watched the officers' last moments, gunfire from the road ahead meant it was time to go. They took one last glance at the dead officers, their bodies contorting as their sinews tightened in the fire, then they moved off towards the gunungs and safety. The three groups soon met up, and delighted with their success, they stayed together until they reached Gunung Rapat. The colonel and his group headed south and the major's group northeast. By dusk both groups had made the safety of the jungle's edge. Mick Martin's group pushed on for another hour in the dark, before making camp for the night. After a cold meal they settled down, each taking their turn to do an hour's watch.

Capt. Hora and Lt Matso had returned from their regular patrol at 1700 hours. The camp sergeant major had greeted them with the news of the ambush and the death of the two officers. Hora and Matso managed to conceal their feelings until they reached the colonel's office, where they hugged one another with delight. When they had regained their composure, Capt. Hora said, 'I suppose I'm in command now. We must organise an urgent pursuit of these terrorists. When shall we start?'

Lt Matso grinned. 'How about the day after tomorrow?'

Capt. Hora laughed, 'I think we better start tomorrow, after breakfast. The terrorists should be well into the jungle by then.'

Chapter 18

Mick Martin and his group made good progress the next day. They used the now familiar tactic of following streambeds to avoid leaving an obvious trail. At times this diverted them from their line of march, but it made good sense, and was worth an extra hour or so on the journey.

By nightfall they were about two miles from the cave. They cooked the last of their rations, and settled down for the night. At about 2200 hours it started to rain heavily, but as their basha-building ability had reached a high level they remained dry and passed a comfortable night.

With only a hot mug of tea for breakfast they made a start for the cave as soon as it was light. In the interests of security, they went round to the west side of Gunung Jasar and were soon in the west passage. They called out as they neared the end of the passage and were relieved to hear an answering call from the two nurses. Joy and Jan made a fuss of Blake and Jim Muir. It did not go unnoticed that Mai Peng and Hari greeted each other shyly but with obvious pleasure.

Back in Ipoh, Capt. Hora and Lt Matso had returned empty handed after a day and a night searching the area around the tin mine at the end of the Sungei Raia Gorge. A Chinese manager was now in place at the tin mine, but tin production had not yet started because the skilled workforce had disappeared.

A new colonel had been appointed for the Ipoh district. He had been badly wounded in Burma, and was now unfit for front-line service. His name was Toshra and he had the nick-name Tora, which means Tiger. He was a decent and coura-geous man, and Hora and Matso knew him. They had both served under him in Indo-China and were looking forward to his arrival.

The first night back in the cave was eagerly awaited by them all, for obvious reasons. Peter Blake could hear whispering and little gasps of pleasure coming from three directions as he sat at the cave entrance with Joy. On completion of their two-hour watch they quickly got into their bed and removed their clothes. Blake covered Joy's body with kisses and spent some time teasing her nipples before working his way down between her legs. This he knew brought her to near climax. He could hold out no longer and she guided his penis deep into her. He thrust at her, her body pushing back frantically at him, and with one last grunting thrust they achieved satisfaction. As he lay by her side, both of them breathing heavily, he reached across and kissed her. She returned his kiss and they went to sleep with their arms around each other.

The next day, after a late breakfast, the major did a complete check on all their weapons and ammunition. They removed all the detonators from the grenades and after cleaning them put fresh fuses back in. They listened to the radio and Soo Lin told them the Japanese had announced that two officers had died in a car crash. This was obviously the general and Col Asana.

Later that evening there was a message for call sign Royal, stating 'Tileman' would call in the next two days. This meant Col Slater, as he was the only person who knew their location.

The following afternoon he arrived. He had brought them some more jungle boots. Much to their surprise, the boots were lasting longer than anticipated and this extra pair now gave them two spare pairs.

His main reason for his visit was to shift their operations further north, to the other side of Tanjung Rambutan, almost as far as Sungei Siput.

Col Tora Toshra invited his officers to join him for dinner. He had been pleased to see Hora and Matso and they had much to discuss. He told all his officers that they could not afford to antagonise the population, as more of the garrison of Malaya and Singapore would be taken to win the fight for Burma and India. He expected that within three months half of his command would be ordered north into Burma.

'We will need to make the most of our depleted forces, with more mobile patrols and less searching of the jungle', he told them.

He went on to say that all convoys would be heavily escorted, with mobile patrols searching likely ambush positions ahead of the main convoy.

He invited Hora and Matso to his quarters afterwards. He wanted to know what had gone on between Asana and the general. They talked until the early hours.

His last words to them when they left were, 'I will try and keep you here, but I anticipate that, despite my efforts, you will be in Burma within eight weeks.'

Over the next two weeks, Maj. Martin took his two marines plus Soo Lin and Mai Peng out from the cave with a box of rations each. They made a food dump two days away from the cave at the edge of the Kinta Valley. It was hard work, and after a week the two nurses joined in, leaving Hari Khah alone in the cave. Hari was not overjoyed at being left on his own, but his arm was not up to a jungle bash.

At last the dump was complete and well hidden. It would extend their patrolling range by at least five days. The Kinta Valley was its usual unfriendly self. Why there were so many leeches there was a mystery, but Mick Martin reasoned it was because this was the wettest area in the state of Perak.

Back in the UK, the Admiralty and the War Office had finally received the information regarding the missing nurses and Royal Marines. Of the five, Jim Muir was the only one without a next of kin; his parents had died some years ago and he had no brothers or sisters. The families of Joyce Hammond and Janet Riley were overjoyed to hear they were safe, but puzzled that it would not be possible to correspond with their daughters. The letter said the nurses were assisting in a jungle hospital and no contact was possible, but there would be monthly confirmation of their continued good health. Peter Blake's mother and father were surprised to be visited by a Royal Marine officer from Chatham. He explained that their son was active with a small group of Royal Marines deep in jungle held by the Japanese. Therefore it would be impossible for them to send or receive letters. He did tell them he would contact them each month to let them know of their son's well-being.

For Laura Martin, the news of her husband came as a shock. She was now living with a naval commander. She had not seen her husband for almost two years and as far as she was concerned the marriage had been over even before he had been reported missing, believed killed. She had told the two children, 'Daddy will not be coming home ever again', and she and the commander were even planning to get married.

In their jungle cave, the two nurses and the marines were unaware their loved ones had been informed; only Mick Martin had given the matter any thought. He knew his marriage was shaky and that his very attractive wife would not be short of male company. He thought that with him out of the way Cdr Jim Roberts would not be slow in taking advantage of the situation.

Ralph Slater was expected to contact them in the next few days. The decision to operate north of Tanjung Rambutan had been agreed. They would be away from the camp for two weeks and only the date needed to be confirmed. The major had decided to leave behind Hari and Mai Peng, and involve the two nurses in the operation. He rightly thought Blake and Jim Muir would prefer it that way, and the two nurses certainly would.

The Japanese in Ipoh had already lost a third of their strength to operations in Burma. Col Tora Toshra had been unable to retain Capt. Hora and Lt Matso; they had left a week ago. A few replacements had arrived, but they were all men who had been wounded in Burma, and were only fit for driving or deskwork.

The colonel knew the war was not going as the high command had predicted. With America now deeply involved, Japan was suffering setbacks not envisaged six months ago. His divisional commander had visited Ipoh the previous week. He and Toshra were old friends and the lieutenant general had told him in confidence that Japan was severely over stretched. They both knew the war was beginning to turn against them.

Mick Martin led his group to the rendezvous at the pipeline intake. Col Slater's group was already there. Together they made their way towards the Kinta Valley. They all were carrying extra rations, and would collect another two days' supplies at their new food dump.

The weather was foul, with heavy rain and even thunder and lightning. In the slippery conditions they were all concerned at the obvious track they were leaving. At 1600 hours they made camp, a circle of two-person bashas. Blake and Joy decided on a corned beef curry, and with just a handful of rice it made a substantial meal. They all took a turn at sentry duty. Even the colonel's group took a turn. The fate of their two comrades was still fresh in their minds. The night had been dry, but the mosquitoes were a constant menace. When dawn came they had a hasty breakfast and resumed their trek.

With the day being dry, they made better progress. It was almost like a Sunday afternoon stroll, but they knew danger might be close at hand. Just before noon, Jim Muir, who was leading, heard voices ahead. He and Mick Martin crept forward to investigate. It was a family of Sakai, the native Malay. There were six of them, but as Martin called softly to them they swiftly disappeared into the jungle.

They intended to make camp near their food dump. Just before 1600 hours they found it and thankfully it did not appear to have been disturbed. They collected two days' rations each, then they re-covered the site and moved a hundred yards further on and made camp.

After they had all had a meal, they settled down for the night. Blake and Joy made sure they applied lots of insect repellent to keep away the mosquitoes. As they lay close together Blake felt a hand at his trouser flies. He started to get an erection. Joy's hand released his erect penis and moved her hand up and down it. Suddenly it felt it was on fire! It was the insect repellent. In silent agony Blake grabbed his water bottle and washed his rapidly shrinking penis.

'Oh, the relief!' he thought.

Joy, realising what she had done, shook with laughter.

'Sorry, Peter', she whispered. 'I thought you would enjoy it.'

The next day they made an early start. After an hour they crossed the Sungei Kinta. It was in full flood after the recent heavy rain. They crossed in pairs, using bamboo poles to brace themselves against the swift-flowing river. At last they were all across, soaked to the skin, but in good spirits. As it was a typically hot day their clothes quickly dried out as they made the steep climb up to the ridge they were to follow.

At noon they stopped and made tea and ate some of their cheese and biscuits. Mick Martin and Blake led for the first hour after lunch. For most of their route the ridge ran in the direction they were required to go, but mid-afternoon they changed direction, leaving the high ground and following the valley floor.

The going here was difficult. The jungle was thick and they had to cut a path with their machetes; this slowed them down. Ralph Slater thought they were level with Tanjung Rambutan, but about a mile east, so at 1600 hours they made camp for the night. Just as they completed their shelters it began to rain, but they were all experienced in jungle conditions by now and, shrugging off the damp, all of the group were soon tucking in to a hot meal.

They spent a quiet night. After the previous night's performance, the mosquito repellent was treated with respect and Joy and Blake decided to leave their physical needs unfulfilled.

The Sungei Siput road ran in a northwesterly direction out of Tanjung Rambutan and to the best of Ralph Slater's knowledge no ambushes had taken place on it. As the two groups left the high ground of the Kinta hills it soon became apparent that the nearer they got to the road the less cover they would have.

The jungle now gave way to patchy scrub, then a small plantation of rubber trees led up to the road, and beyond that the railway line. They were about three miles northwest of Tanjung Rambutan and ten miles from Sungei Siput.

They made camp in the rubber plantation. The trees had not been tapped for some time; the last grooves in the trees were well healed. Mick and Ralph spent the rest of the day watching the road and the railway line. The road had little traffic, but the railway line was somewhat busier, with a train running either north or south on the single track every two hours.

The vigil continued all night, and by dawn the two officers had a good indication of the road and railway line's pattern of use. It was decided to lay charges on the line as soon as it was dark, then, if they managed to blow up a train, to wait and ambush any Japanese response.

They had given this a lot of thought, as it was potentially dangerous to hang around after such an act. However, the Japanese would not expect them to do this, and therein lay the astuteness of their plan. They spent the day cleaning their weapons and preparing the charges. Late in the afternoon they had a substantial meal, and by dusk they were packed and ready to move.

As soon as it was dark they moved off to the railway line. Col Slater and the three marines laid the charges. The detonators were placed on the top of the railway track. The two groups withdrew to the edge of the rubber plantation overlooking the road and waited in their ambush positions.

It was a clear night, with almost a full moon, and just before midnight they heard the sound of a train approaching from the south; it was going quite fast. They could see quite clearly in the moonlight that it consisted of five carriages, as it sped towards their explosive charges.

The engine appeared to pass unharmed over the detonators, but it was an illusion. With a satisfying 'crump' the rear of the engine was lifted and thrown off the line. With a tremendous noise of screeching metal, the carriages were flung on their sides and dragged a hundred yards along the track. Apart from escaping steam there was a momentary silence, then shouting came from the overturned carriages as soldiers began to drag themselves out of the debris. Both groups opened fire. Blake opened up with short bursts into the disorganised mass of soldiers. His Bren gun was the ideal weapon in this type of situation, taking a heavy toll.

After five minutes the return fire was becoming organised. It became obvious the train had contained a large number of troops. The ambushers began to withdraw, each group providing covering fire for the other.

They sped through the rubber plantation, bullets zipping through the trees above their heads. It took them twenty minutes to reach the jungle's edge and safety.

They took a short break and listened for sounds of pursuit. The only sound was gunfire from the troops at the railway line. Ralph Slater checked his group. All were accounted for. But Mick Martin knew something was amiss. Jim Muir and Jan were missing.

The Japanese soldiers who had survived the explosion and the ambush were bent on revenge. At least sixty of the three hundred aboard the train had been killed or seriously injured. A major, the senior officer on board, shouted to his senior NCOs to control the men who were about to take off in pursuit of the ambushers.

Gradually he regained control. Leaving his one remaining officer to do what he could to rescue and treat his wounded men, he took fifty soldiers and three experienced NCOs and began a pursuit. In extended line the Japanese troops moved through the rubber plantation. The moonlight hardly penetrated the canopy of the trees. He made them move slowly and together. If some got ahead of the others they would soon be firing at each other.

Jim Muir and Jan were huddled together at the edge of the rubber plantation. Jan had fallen heavily and feared her ankle was broken. She had begged Jim to leave her and catch up with the others.

'Leave you?' he had said. 'Never!'

He carried her to a clump of scrub, where they did their best to hide. Sgt Muir thought they would be safe until daylight, but if the Japanese were still searching by then they would most certainly be found.

He knew he could not allow the Japanese to take either of them alive. If he got down to his last two rounds of ammunition, one would be for Jan and the other for him. He could hear the Japanese coming through the rubber plantation. They were less than sixty yards away. The NCOs were shouting instructions, probably to keep them in a straight line.

Ralph Slater and Mick Martin had agreed on a rescue plan. The former would take his group back to the jungle's edge and fire into the rubber plantation. Hopefully, this would draw the troops towards them. They would then move north through the jungle taking the Japanese with them. The major could then retrace their route through the rubber and find the missing two.

As the colonel's group opened fire the effect was dramatic. The line of troops turned to face this new threat and began firing wildly. The Japanese officer and his NCOs tried to control the excited troops, but without success. Their troops on the right turned to face the threat and opened fire. All they succeeded in doing was to hit some of their own soldiers on the left, who then opened fire, a classic military nightmare, with troops on the same side attacking one another.

In the chaos, Jim Muir dragged Jan out of the scrub, and throwing her over his shoulder made for the jungle's edge.

He soon encountered Peter Blake, who was out in front of the major's group. Blake grabbed the two weapons Muir was carrying, and led him and Jan back to Mick Martin. The group, reunited once again, returned to the edge of the jungle and quickly moved deeper into safety.

Col Slater was delighted with the confusion he had caused and withdrew his group. Within a few minutes both parties were heading due east and well away from the confused Japanese soldiers. After fifteen minutes they stopped and Joy had a quick look at Jan's ankle. It was badly swollen and she suspected it might be broken, as it was turning a red-blue colour.

Joy applied a commonsense solution; if in doubt assume the worst scenario and treat it as broken.

She strapped it up, and Jim Muir gently picked Jan up and carried her piggyback style. Over the next two hours his strength became obvious. Blake tried to relieve him at one stage, but Muir shook his head.

'Thanks Peter, but I can manage.'

They decided to take a break, much to everyone's relief. They all took a long drink from their water bottles. The major and Blake went back down the track, but there was no sound of pursuit.

Chapter 19

The Japanese officer in charge at the railway line looked gloomily at the returning soldiers. It had been a complete shambles. They had killed five of their own men, and wounded ten others when they lost their discipline under fire. He would have to return to Ipoh and report to the colonel. He had heard he was a fair man, but he would demand an explanation.

Col Tora Toshra had already been informed of the derailing of the train. He knew the officer in charge would launch an attack on the ambushers, and hoped they had been successful. When the officer reported to him of the failure of his follow-up operation, Toshra looked at him more in pity than in anger.

'Go to your quarters and review your actions after the derailing, then come and see me and tell me what went wrong with your plan. It's the only way to learn.' A rather shame-faced young man saluted his superior and thankfully made his way to the sanctuary of his room.

Mick Martin's group made camp just before 1600 hours. They quickly constructed their shelters and prepared a meal. Joy gave Jan's ankle another look, and suggested Jim Muir carried her to the small stream and let her soak it for a while. Blake went with them to keep guard. After fifteen minutes they returned to the camp and settled down for the night. About midnight, it rained heavily for an hour, then when that stopped the mosquitoes started. They were all grateful when dawn came and after breakfast they cleaned their weapons ready to resume their march to the supply dump.

They made good progress, despite Jim Muir having to carry Jan. She said her ankle felt more comfortable now, but putting any weight on it was out of the question.

The major thought they were only a few hours from the food dump, and should reach it by about 1600 hours. They were finding the terrain more to their liking. Up on the ridge it was cooler and in the absence of thick undergrowth they kept up a good pace.

Just after 1500 hours the major and Blake went ahead, and within minutes they were at the food cache. The colonel's group had already been there. Attached to one of the boxes was a note, which read 'See you in a week's time'.

They took enough rations to get them back to the cave, re-covered the site and made camp about two hundred yards away. Jan's ankle, though all the colours of the rainbow, was not as swollen as it had been that morning. As she and Jim Muir lay in their shelter later that night, she gave him a kiss.

'That's for everything', she said.

Muir looked at her in the growing darkness, 'I feel really fucked', he said.

'I know the feeling', said Jan, and they both gave a quiet laugh.

They spent a quiet night, which was punctuated by some heavy showers, but by the time they made breakfast the sky was clear. They then cleared the site of all traces of their stay, and at about 0800 hours they resumed their march.

At first Jan tried to walk with the aid of a crutch, but the ankle was not ready for that so she resumed her place on Jim's back. They recrossed the Sungei Kinta about an hour after their start. It was flowing quite quickly and care had to be taken while crossing as it would have been quite easy to have been swept away.

The soaking they all received in the crossing was refreshing. Within twenty minutes their wet clothes were dry, though they were soon wet again from sweat. They took an hour's break at lunchtime, made some tea and had American cream cheese and biscuits. They were not that keen on the American rations. Some items were okay, but in general there was too much sugary food.

By late afternoon, Mick Martin thought they were only a day away from their cave. They made camp a little early as he thought that if they made an early start the next day they could reach the cave by midday.

Back at the cave, Hari and Mai Peng had enjoyed being on their own. To Mai Peng's surprise Hari was an accomplished lover. He was also well endowed, and Mai Peng had reached the 'towering heights' in most of their frequent encounters. They were both very much in love. Just before noon, Mai heard the voice of the major calling along the rear cave passage. She answered, and shortly afterwards, their friends were all back in the cave.

Hari gave his expert medical attention to Jan. He was sure it was not broken, just a very bad sprain. He gave Jim Muir a look of pure admiration when told he had carried Jan for the last five days.

Hari's wound was now well healed and he and Mai Peng insisted on cooking a special meal for their friends. The first priority was to clean their weapons and then have a good wash and a change of clothes. Then they settled down to a fine meal and, with full stomachs and a mug of tea, they all sat in the cave's entrance and watched a magnificent sunset.

At Japanese Headquarters in Ipoh, Col Tora Toshra was in full flow. His junior officers listened attentively as he ran through the lengthy list of ambushes on road and railway targets.

'You cannot achieve the results these people have had without good planning and first-class leadership. This is not the work of a few Communist Chinese. The British military are involved.'

He looked at his attentive audience, and went on.

'I want ideas on how to deal with this problem. Go away and put some thoughts on paper. We meet again after dinner.'

As his officers left the room, Toshra sat and allowed his brain to churn out a few ideas of its own. He knew, despite his reputation, that Kuala Lumpur wanted results and his future depended on it.

Mick Martin had decided on a two-week break from operations. He was tired and so were his team, and their luck would not last forever. An airdrop was planned to take place in two nights' time and that would keep them busy recovering the supplies and storing them in the cave.

Hari Khah and Mai Peng were making good use of all the parachute silk. They were making knickers for all the women. He had not realised it, but the two nurses had worn out their underclothes months ago. What the Chinese girls wore under their traditional black trousers was a mystery to him, though in Soo Lin's case it was very little. Morale was very good, and judging by the after-dark noises so was their love life. The major still found it hard to accept 'the goings on', though of course he was part of it. Good job he did not keep a diary.

The airdrop took place on time. As they watched the Liberator bomber disappear in the darkness they did not envy the crew's long dangerous flight back to Ceylon. It took them four hours to recover all the supplies, and all the next day to sort them out and store them. In the medical supplies were a large box of French letters, and an even larger box of sanitary towels. Mick Martin had let Joy make up and code the stores demand. Sensible girl, he thought, but what did they think back in Ceylon. There were no American rations in the resupply, but some new British ones, even some tinned salmon and sardines in oil, an improvement on herrings in tomato sauce.

Tora Toshra was pleased. Some of the ideas were excellent. One of his junior officers had suggested that small permanent camps be set up along the main road, and the railway line. The general feeling was they should be staffed by a minimum of ten men for a week at a time. Also, the obvious dislike the population felt for its invaders could be changed by gentler handling.

Toshra had enquired of the young officer who had suggested a softer approach to the inhabitants of Ipoh, 'And at Christmas I could appear as Santa Claus?'

The room erupted into laughter and the young officer went scarlet.

Toshra smiled, 'Your idea has merit. If we can maintain control of the population with a gentler hand, we will save on manpower. Put your idea on paper.'

As he dismissed them, and acknowledged their respectful bows, he was aware of the affection they had for him. They were good men, but so young.

Peter Blake returned from his two-hour watch, and snuggled up to Joy. As he lay there trying to get to sleep, he thought, 'We have been together for eighteen months. It's like being married.'

They still tuned into the radio each day, and Soo Lin wrote down a message for Royal from 'Tileman', which was Ralph Slater's call sign. It said he would call in the next two days.

Two days later the colonel appeared on his own. He had left his group near the tin mine. He told them four young Chinese had joined them, so he now had ten men all together. After dinner that night he told Mick Martin that one of the new recruits was very impressive. His name was Yong Hoy and he was highly intelligent and a born leader. Yong Hoy had said to him, 'When we have freed our country of the Japanese, we will ask the British to leave. We know you will not go, so we will drive you out, but until then we can be friends.'

Mick Martin laughed, 'The cheeky young bastard. What did you say?'

Ralph Slater smiled, 'Oh, I just listened and nodded, but you know I think he may be right.'

Later that night Blake and Joy had a very enjoyable encounter. As they lay in one another's arms getting their breath back, Blake said, 'Will you marry me?'

Joy kissed his cheek.

'Of course I will. Are we now engaged then?'

She slipped her hand down onto his flaccid penis. 'Well, show some enthusiasm then!'

'Christ!' said Blake. 'I'll never last the pace of this engagement.'

The next morning Blake asked the major if he was empowered to perform marriages.

'You know, Sir, like a ship's captain.'

Maj. Martin smiled, 'No, I regret I'm not. You will have to wait young Blake. I hope the young lady is not in any trouble?'

'No Sir', said Blake. 'She got the idea of marriage from Soo Lin.'

Over the next ten days they resupplied the food dump up the Kinta Valley. On the way back they saw a light aircraft flying parallel to the river. It flew up and down for an hour then turned and headed west. The aircraft gave Mick Martin some concern. He and Ralph Slater had thought for some time that the biggest threat to their security was a chance spotting from the air. The fact that Japanese interest seemed to be concentrated on the Kinta Valley was of some consolation; at least Gunung Jasar had escaped their attention. Another matter that was of some concern to Martin was the request from Blake to get married, and his remark that the idea had come from Soo Lin. The major thought Blake was just being cheeky, the young marine was like that, but he thought he would talk to Soo Lin, just in case it had been her idea.

Chapter 20

Col Tora Toshra had waded through the ideas his young officers had submitted. One of the problems now was manpower. He had four hundred men under his command and about one hundred of these were veterans who had been wounded in Burma. He decided to establish small fortified posts manned by ten soldiers, two on the railway line between Ipoh and Tanjung Rambutan, and three on the road between Ipoh and Tapah. In each of these posts he would put at least two veterans. That should give the eight inexperienced soldiers some backbone. He had also decided to lead a twenty-man patrol up the Kinta Valley and then on day two swing south and work his way to the Sungei Raia. At the end of three days he would finish the patrol at the tin mine near the Sungei Raia Gorge. When Col Toshra's orders were published, he was inundated with requests to be part of the Kinta patrol.

He thought to himself, 'They won't be so keen after two days in the jungle', and then sat down with his sergeant major to select his men.

Jan's ankle was now almost recovered from the severe sprain. She had walked on it without support through the cave passages and down the western slope of Gunung Jasar. Mick Martin considered he now had a fully fit team once again, but would leave Jim Muir and Jan behind when they next went out on patrol.

It was now mid-June 1943. Some of the information that Ralph Slater had gleaned from the Japanese radio traffic was encouraging. The Americans were certainly winning the sea war in the Pacific, and were even making land gains by retaking some of the islands lost to the Japanese in the first months of the war. The major had asked Soo Lin if she had spoken to Blake about marrying Joy. Soo Lin had given him that sweet smile and nodded her head. She had then asked Mick Martin a direct question.

'If you were free to, would you marry me, or am I just a good jungle fuck?'

Martin had pulled Soo Lin close to him.

'When the war is over, if I have to, I will resign my commission and spend the rest of my life here with you.'

The Japanese patrol made its way slowly along the bank of the Sungei Kinta. Tora Toshra was quite pleased with their performance. They still tended to bunch up, but were much quieter than when they had started. He gave them a ten-minute break every hour, and made sure his NCOs imposed a strict control on their food and water intake.

At 1500 hours on the first day he stopped and made camp. His small number of veterans quickly showed the young soldiers how to construct a decent shelter for the night. Rice and dried fish were the staple diet of the Japanese soldier in the field, and did not take much preparing. As night fell the colonel made sure his sentries were fully briefed. The last thing he wanted was an undisciplined outburst of firing at imagined intruders. During the night it rained heavily. When the rain stopped the mosquitoes began a determined assault on the young Japanese flesh. The veterans among them had urinated on their hands and rubbed the result on their exposed flesh; they thought the ammonia deterred the insect hordes.

127

Col Toshra had thought of splitting his patrol in two to cover more ground, but in the interests of safety decided to keep them all together. By noon they had almost reached the halfway point. He gave them a half-hour break, then pushed on. Mid-afternoon, he changed the direction of his march to the south, and at 1630 hours stopped and made camp for the night.

He invited his two young officers to show him on the map where they thought they were. Their estimated positions were disappointing. One was at least three miles out, the other five. He patiently explained where they were and how he had calculated this. They were both shamefaced.

The next day he gave them the task of leading them back to the tin mine at the Gunung Rapat Gorge. By noon he knew they were too far west, but he let them carry on; it would be a salutary lesson for them all. The terrain became more difficult; they were descending into deep ravines and struggling to climb back out. At 1600 hours they could see, about a mile away, a huge limestone gunung. One of the young officers said, 'That is Gunung Rapat, Sir. We are not far off now.'

Toshra called the two officers to him.

'That, my young friends, is Gunung Jasar. We will camp here tonight. Tomorrow you will head east-southeast. It will take us all tomorrow to reach Gunung Rapat.'

The rest of the patrol were not too pleased to find that their two young officers had almost got them lost, especially as they were almost out of food. That night it rained so hard that the shelters they had constructed were unable to cope with the downpour and they all got soaked. It seemed to get very cold. Dawn came bringing some relief. At least by nightfall they should be back in their more comfortable surroundings with some half decent food to look forward to.

As with most inexperienced troops, accidents will happen. In this case, a soldier, as he was cleaning some mud from his rifle, fired a round which went through the foot of another soldier standing nearby. Col Toshra had seen all this before. He had the culprit brought before him. As the young man stood shaking in front of his colonel, Toshra spoke quietly to him.

'You will learn the hard way. Your punishment is you will carry your wounded comrade and his equipment for the rest of this patrol, with no assistance from anyone.'

As the sound of the shot reached them in their cave on Gunung Jasar, they all took up their emergency positions. Maj. Martin knew there were no friendly forces nearby; it had to be the Japanese. Had they been found at last? After an hour and with no sign of movement, he decided to take his two marines and have a look around in the area from which the shot had come.

They slipped quickly out of the back exit of the cave and moved through the jungle towards the suspect area. After an hour they came across some evidence of a temporary camp, half a dozen crudely constructed shelters, and some uncovered mounds of shit. If this was the Japanese they were not top-line troops.

The track leaving the camp was easy to follow and the major thought the enemy patrol consisted of at least fifteen men.

'We will follow their track for an hour, and if it continues away from our cave we will go back to our friends', said Mick Martin.

Twenty minutes into their pursuit they heard voices ahead. With great caution the three marines crept closer. Below them was a small stream, and sitting on the far bank was a group of Japanese soldiers. Slowly crossing the stream to join them was a pathetic figure carrying another soldier.

Pte Cipso was exhausted.

'Why couldn't I have shot someone skinny, instead of this fat bastard?' Cipso thought. 'And he's shit himself, the smell is awful.'

The colonel was waiting for him to catch up.

'We are going on ahead. You must try and keep up, but we will leave you an easy track to follow.'

And with that the colonel walked away with the rest of the patrol following on. Within a minute they were out of sight.

Cipso sat down and let his wounded companion fall to the ground with a cry of pain.

'Shut up you fat slug. I'm sorry I shot you, but I can't carry you all the way. When I have rested you can lean on me.'

Unaware that three Royal Marines were within ten yards of him, Cipso washed his face and hands in the stream, then helped his wounded comrade to his feet and started off along the track.

The three marines watched the two figures slowly move out of sight. They looked at one another in amusement. Jim Muir was the first to speak.

'I think we have just witnessed some Japanese field punishment, the shooter carrying the shot, not original but effective.'

Mick Martin agreed, 'I almost felt sorry for him, the poor bastard.'

'We could have killed them both', said Blake. His two companions looked at him in horror.

'He was once such a nice lad', said Jim Muir. They all laughed.

It took them two hours to get back to the cave and rejoin their anxious friends. They were all relieved that the situation had been resolved.

Chapter 21

The main body of the Japanese patrol had reached the tin mine, and one of the officers went and phoned their main camp for a truck to come and collect them. It took almost two hours before a vehicle arrived. There was still no sign of their two comrades.

'We will give them thirty minutes then we will leave', said the colonel. Just as the thirty minutes elapsed, the two figures came into sight. They were helped aboard and the truck slowly made its way to Ipoh. Pte Cipso lay exhausted. His wounded companion sat in one corner of the truck, his smell keeping his comrades at a distance. The colonel sat next to the driver dwelling over the last few days.

'Well', he thought. 'They must have learned something.'

When Joy completed her watch that night Blake was still awake. As she settled down beside him he took her hand and placed it on his erect penis. She gently squeezed it, while his hand was busy down between her legs. She gave a gasp of pleasure as his finger caressed her. He moved over on top of her and as her legs parted slid his penis into her. Slowly at first, then, as their passion mounted, faster and more frantic, their bodies thrust at each other. Blake shuddered as he reached his climax, Joy just a split second behind. They collapsed together, her lips finding his.

After a few minutes their breathing returned to normal and they went to sleep close in each other's arms. Mick Martin was still awake, Soo Lin quietly sleeping in the crook of his arm. They had made love earlier with great passion. He had heard Blake and Joy.

'What a command I've got', he thought. 'This must be unique. Our own place in history. Our flag should be a rampant penis.'

They had a visit from Ralph Slater the following week, who had some ideas for future operations. He told Mick Martin that the Japanese had constructed some strong points on the main Tapah to Ipoh road and the railway line. There had also been a suggestion from Headquarters in Ceylon that some additional British military personnel would be landed from a submarine on the west coast. They were to take charge of the small groups of Chinese and Malay freedom fighters. The politicians in London were concerned with the growing Communist influence on these groups; they were keeping an eye to the future.

The colonel also wanted a combined attack on the railway line at Tapah. This would mean a two-week operation for the major's group, and a food dump provisioned for the outward and return journeys. The following day, leaving Jan and Jim Muir in camp, the remainder of the group each carried a box of rations on a three-day trip to the site of the new food dump. It was slow going; even the men felt exhausted at the end of each day. Maj. Martin and Ralph Slater kept the working day short by starting at 0900 hours and making camp at 1500 hours.

Finally, they reached the selected site. It was about a mile from the Tapah road, and about halfway between the cave and the town of Tapah. They had to dig a pit to hide the boxes, but it was in an area of thick jungle and it was unlikely to be found by anyone.

They rested up for a day, then Ralph Slater went on his way, while the major's group started their return journey to the cave. Moving quickly now they were unburdened, they reached the cave just before dusk on the second day. Jim Muir had a message for the major that had been received the previous night. Muir had decoded it. Mick Martin read the message twice.

It read, 'Regret to inform you of the death of your wife in an air raid on London. Your children were staying with your parents in Cornwall and are in good health.'

Soo Lin saw the distress on his face. She kissed him on the cheek, then left him to his thoughts.

Col Toshra had received a visit from a senior officer from Kuala Lumpur, which had gone better than expected. Toshra's area was now quiet in respect of sabotage, although the anti-Japanese forces were becoming active all over Malaya.

The reason Japan had invaded Malaya in the first place was for its rubber and tin. It also had given them a springboard to invade Indonesia for its oil. The general told Toshra the Imperial navy were having problems with the American forces. The Japanese naval loses were not sustainable, and a rethink was underway.

After dinner that night the two officers consumed a bottle of whiskey. This led to a loosening of their tongues, and a surprised Toshra was told, 'If we do not stop this mad quest for more territory, we will be in a war we cannot win.'

Before he left for Kuala Lumpur the next morning the general smiled as he bade Toshra farewell.

'Our talk of last night stays here, old friend.'

'Of course', said Toshra, and saluted as the general's car drove away.

Maj. Martin was surprised that the loss of his wife had upset him so much. He knew the marriage had been over, but he had once loved her and she had borne him two children.

Soo Lin had moved her bedroll a yard from his. After two days he had moved it back. She did not speak of his loss.

Martin received a radio message informing him that Ralph Slater had to go to the west coast to meet two British officers. They were to form a group that would operate between Tanjung Rambutan and Sungei Siput.

The coast was fifty miles from Ipoh. Being landed from a submarine and managing to make their way undetected back past Ipoh, would be some achievement. Slater also wanted the major to meet with him and the two officers at the pipeline intake in a week's time. Slater asked him to bring some extra rations and wait three days before giving up on them.

When Mick Martin told Jim Muir of the plan, Muir's first reaction was to think they would never make it in that timescale. The major told them the colonel was going to pick them up in the 'shit lorry'. This lorry was driven by a Tamil who had the contract to empty the latrine buckets from army camps between Ipoh and the coastal town of Lumut.

Ralph Slater waited just off the beach on the night designated for the landing. Shortly after midnight, he made out two figures struggling through the surf. As he waited for them to reach the tree line he could just make out the small boat that had landed them heading back to the submarine.

Slater moved towards them. They saw him and raised their weapons. He quickly called out to them and the weapons were lowered. He introduced himself and they did the same. One was Capt. Julian Onsway, Welsh Guards, the other Lt Jim Bottle of the Buffs.

Slater was amused as he thought, 'Whoever paired these two together certainly had a sense of humour.' But more important, could they work together?

He led them to a spot where at dawn they would meet up with the shit lorry. They managed to get some sleep, despite the attentions of the mosquitoes.

Just after dawn the lorry appeared. The driver quickly introduced them to their personal shit drums. There were twelve drums aboard and nine were empty. They climbed into the back of the truck and were assisted into the three drums nearest the cab. As they settled down in the drums they noticed a hole, about an inch in diameter, which had been drilled to provide them with air. A lid, which had a rubber seal around it, was pushed on to each of their drums. The driver pushed each one down at least six inches until it just made contact with their heads. To complete the deception he then poured some contents from a latrine bucket into the tops of their drums. Immediately, some of the liquid began slowly leaking in and dripping over them. Slater had travelled this way before, but he was sure this was a 'first' for an officer from the Brigade of Guards! Just as the lorry started up he heard one of the officers being sick. He smiled to himself, thinking, 'That must be Mr Onsway.'

Later that day, after visiting several more Japanese army camps to empty their latrines, the driver pulled into a rubber plantation on the western side of Ipoh. He took the lids off the drums and three very relieved looking British officers climbed out of their stinking hell-holes. The driver quickly drove off, with a parting handshake from Ralph Slater.

The colonel then turned to a very sick looking Capt. Onsway, saying, 'As soon as it is dark we will follow this rubber plantation round to the south of Ipoh. By daybreak we must be in the jungle's edge east of the town.'

Slater and Jim Bottle managed to eat some cheese and biscuits. However, Onsway declined, although he did drink some water.

As soon as it was dark, Slater got them on the move. After each hour they stopped for five minutes. Bottle was coping quite well, but Onsway was far from fit and slowed them down. By cutting out the five-minute break over the last five hours they made up time, and by daybreak they were just short of the Tapah road. They would have to stay there all day, and enter the jungle at dusk.

The three slept most of the day, each taking a turn at a two-hour watch. When Slater woke, Onsway and Bottle were asleep. Slater knew it was Onsway who had let them down, so he woke him with a kick to the ribs. Onsway angrily got to his feet. Slater pushed him back down.

'You are not in some cosy London Officers' Mess now, you lazy bastard. You could have got us killed. I am not sure you are any use to us, Captain Fucking Onsway.'

Onsway mumbled an apology but gave Slater a look of pure hate.

Jim Bottle smiled. 'You better buck yourself up Julian, or you are for an early grave.'

They ate some rations in silence. Slater was concerned with the choice of Onsway as a group leader. The colonel thought he was just not up to it, while the junior of the two, Jim Bottle, certainly was.

That night they moved across the road and into the jungle. It was moonlight and they made good progress; Onsway was keeping up, despite being at the rear. After their second stop he started falling further behind, but Slater refused to cut their pace down, thinking, 'The bloody man would have to survive on his own if he couldn't keep up.'

At some point during the march, Capt. Julian Onsway decided he was too tired to go on, so he sat down and rested against a tree. He had not wanted to come on this stupid operation. He was enjoying the social scene in Cairo too much and enjoyed being on the general's staff. He thought to himself, 'That damned nurse has spoilt it all. It wasn't really rape. She said no, but I knew she didn't mean it. Her being the sister of that squadron leader really fucked it up.' The outcome was either a court martial, or volunteer for special operations, so here he was. Onsway suddenly woke up; it was daylight.

'Christ, I better catch those bastards up', he thought, and moved off northwest instead of northeast.

The Japanese officer visiting the tin mine with six soldiers sat in the shade of the manager's house. One of his soldiers came up and saluted. The soldier told him a white man was sitting on the pipeline two hundred yards away. The officer gave the soldier a look of pure disbelief, but looked in the indicated direction.

Within seconds, with a quiet order, he and his men were moving towards the sitting figure. Onsway was too busy changing his socks to hear the advancing Japanese, but when he did it was too late. His arms were seized from behind and he was dragged upright, where he saw the calm features of the Japanese officer looking at him with some amusement.

Onsway started to bluster, 'I am an officer of the Welsh Guards.'

The officer said something and Onsway took a crashing blow to the side of his head. He was dragged to a waiting lorry and pushed aboard, each of the soldiers taking the opportunity to punch or kick him. A word from their officer and the beating stopped. The lorry drove off with the trembling Onsway face down in the back.

Col Slater and Lt Bottle spent the rest of the day looking for the Guards' officer. At dusk they made camp. After a meal Slater asked Jim Bottle what he knew of Onsway.

'Not much, Sir. He joined the course late, didn't fit in, was a stuck-up bastard, and I drew the short straw. There was some suggestion that he was kicked out of Egypt.'

Ralph Slater thought they would spend half the next day looking for him, then that would be that. In the morning after breakfast they backtracked without any success. At noon they took a break then resumed their journey. By nightfall they were near the village of Juang; it would only take them an hour the next day to reach the rendezvous with Maj. Martin. They ate the rest of their rations and had a mug of hot sweet tea each. They had constructed a shelter just big enough for the two of them. During the night it rained heavily. Jim Bottle, who was on watch, was already fascinated by this country and was looking forward to doing some operations against the Japanese.

Julian Onsway was terrified. He was naked and chained to the wall of his cell. He had been given water but no food and he could not sleep because the chains held him upright. Col Toshra had been surprised by the capture of this officer. The man's appearance did not suggest he had been in the jungle at all. He was tanned to a copper colour, and when his clothes were removed the only white parts of his body suggested he had spent most of the last few months in a swimming costume. The man had told them under gentle questioning that he was an officer in the Welsh Guards and his rank was that of a captain. Toshra had ordered that he be kept naked and chained in his cell. Nobody was to question him for twenty-four hours. That time had now elapsed and Toshra went to the interrogation room and ordered the prisoner be brought before him.

Ralph Slater had only been at the pipeline intake for an hour when Maj. Martin and Marine Blake arrived. He introduced Lt Jim Bottle to them both. Bottle was surprised to encounter two Royal Marines, who looked so at home in their surroundings. He mentioned this and both the marines laughed.

'Well, we have been here eighteen months, and you do adjust.'

The colonel explained about the missing captain. Mick Martin thought perhaps they were better off without him.

'From what you say of him, he could be a danger to us all. But if the Japs have got him how much does he know?'

Ralph Slater looked pensive.

'Only the method of transport from the coast. I hope he keeps his mouth shut about that, or the driver will be for it.'

The major and Blake handed over the extra rations they had brought with them. The colonel explained he would take Jim Bottle to the six men waiting at Tanjung Rambutan. He would stay with them for two weeks and then Bottle would take command of that group. His call sign would be 'Ten Green'.

Slater then left for the Kinta Valley with the eager Jim Bottle, while Mick Martin and Blake made their way back to the cave on Gunung Jasar.

Onsway was confused. He had been allowed to sit down in front of a seated Col Toshra. He had been asked, in the colonel's excellent English, some polite questions about himself.

'Are you hungry?'
'Yes Sir.'
'Are you tired?'
'Yes Sir.'
'Are you married?'

'No Sir.'

'Do you prefer sex with men or women?'

'Oh, women, Sir'

'I am told some of your officers are homosexual?'

'I have never met any, Sir.'

Toshra looked intently at Onsway, who was looking more confident.

'Capt. Onsway, you have one opportunity to tell me what I wish to know. If you fail to satisfy my curiosity you will be taken back to your cell and two of my NCOs, who prefer young men to women, will amuse themselves with you for the rest of the night. Is that clear?'

Onsway was almost fainting with fear. He spoke rapidly.

'My name is Julian Onsway. I was landed on the west coast from a submarine four nights ago, with another officer. We were to take command of a group of freedom fighters somewhere in Perak. A colonel met us on the beach and took us around Ipoh to the south. We then entered the jungle by the Tapah road. The next day I lost contact with my two companions and walked up the pipeline where your soldiers found me.'

Toshra looked into Onsway's eyes.

'I think there is more to tell. We will talk again in an hour. My two NCOs will take you back to your cell.'

Back in his cell Onsway's wrists were secured to the wall again. The two Japanese sergeants ran their hands over his back and his buttocks. One pressed himself up against the officer's bottom. To Onsway's dismay a hand grabbed his penis, and to his shame he began to get an erection. The two NCOs laughed, and left the cell.

An hour later he was taken again to Col Toshra.

'You lied. You are homosexual. Don't deny it, my men are experts. They are looking forward to the evening's entertainment, unless you tell me more.'

Onsway was destroyed. He told how they had been driven to the outskirts of Ipoh in the shit lorry. How he had been forced to join the Special Forces because of the allegation of rape.

Toshra was satisfied he had the complete story. He whispered to the sergeant to treat the man as a prisoner of war. Onsway misread the whispered instruction and as he was led out of the office he broke free of his captors and ran. He had gone ten yards when two bullets struck him in the back and head. He was dead before his body hit the ground.

The next day, as the lorry entered the camp to empty the latrine buckets, the driver was seized, severely beaten and flung in a cell. He was questioned for eight hours, said nothing and died later under interrogation.

Chapter 22

It was a week later that Col Slater got to hear of the driver's death. He told Jim Bottle it would take them months to repair the damage to their communications and find another way from the coast.

It took another week for the information to reach Ceylon, and then Cairo. A nurse, when told of Onsway's death said, 'I hope it was painful, and not too quick.'

Mick Martin and Soo Lin were now back together in more ways than one. One night he told her, if she wanted to, they would marry at the first opportunity, and if she did not want to leave Malaya after the war they would stay and make their home here.

They heard that the tin mine was back in production. Ralph Slater, who was still up in the Kinta hills with Jim Bottle, told them to pay it a visit. The major, Soo Lin, Jim Muir and Peter Blake made their way through the jungle to the pipeline overlooking the mine. It was decided to blow up the generator, then head southeast to their supply dump. After a day's march due east they would swing north and back to the cave, in order to confuse any pursuing Japanese.

They spent a day observing the mine, but there was no sign of Japanese troops, so they worked out a plan for their safe entry and exit. As soon as it was dark they carefully edged nearer to the mine. It took them almost two hours to get into position. They knew that at midnight the generator was switched off. They would lay the charges at 0100 hours and set the fuses for thirty minutes later.

At midnight the generator was turned off. As the sound of the engine died away, they could see oil-lamps were being lit; maintenance was being carried out.

It was 0300 hours before they saw the engineers depart. After another thirty minutes they moved forward and the major and Soo Lin set the charges, while Jim Muir and Blake kept watch. At last the charges were set and they made their way back to the jungle's edge. When the explosion occurred, it was spectacular. The whole structure was lifted out of the ground and then the fuel completed the 'fireworks'.

They stayed in position until dawn, when they made their way southeast. At 1600 hours they reached the food dump, took three days' supplies, then made camp two hundred yards further on. During the night they heard some explosions to the north, which they all agreed was mortar fire as it was not heavy enough for artillery. The Japanese were trying something new.

The two Japanese officers looked at the wrecked generator with dismay. It would take weeks to replace and repair was out of the question. As an emergency replacement the colonel had asked for a searchlight unit to bring their generator, but it would take five days to bring it up from Singapore. They had sent for their mortar section to spray a few bombs around. Their maximum range was only two thousand yards, but they might get lucky.

The mortar team arrived just as the light was failing. At 2300 hours they fired five rounds, then decided to wait for daylight and a spotter aircraft. The next day they were told the aircraft was not available, so every hour on the hour they fired two bombs in an arc, hoping for a lucky hit.

As the major and his party moved due east they heard more explosions, quite a way behind them and definitely mortar rounds.

That night they made camp in the pouring rain. The storm continued for most of the night, but they managed to stay largely dry. After breakfast it was still raining, so they delayed their departure for an hour. Then they made good progress, despite the continuing bad weather. They tried to avoid leaving evidence of their trek, but their usual ploy of following a streambed was made difficult because most of the streams were in flood.

By the time they made camp for the night Mick Martin anticipated they were about four hours from the cave, so they satisfied their hunger with a corned beef curry and a mug of tea, then settled down for the night. The night was dry, quite cool and almost mosquito free, and they all managed a good night's sleep.

After breakfast they tidied the campsite, then left for the last leg of their journey. After two hours they could see the eastern side of Gunung Jasar, and just before noon they entered the small cave passage leading to the main cave. They called out a warning as they neared the edge of the passage. An answering call came and they were then being warmly greeted by their friends.

Ralph Slater was pleased with the progress Jim Bottle had made. He was popular with the other members of the group, and they seemed happy to accept him as their leader. The loss of Onsway was now seen as a blessing in disguise. Slater dreaded to think what a week of Onsway in command would have produced.

Lt Bottle was anxious for the colonel to depart and leave him in command. He had developed a good rapport with the

Chinese in his group, and though he did not take part in the political discussions, on the colonel's advice, he was interested and had some sympathy with their aims.

At last, the colonel indicated he was ready to leave. He explained the radio procedure and the other group's call signs. Before he left, he made sure that Bottle knew that if anything happened to him, Mick Martin would take command of all the operations in Perak.

As the colonel left the camp and began to make his way back through the Kinta hills, he decided he would break his journey and spend a couple of days with Mick Martin, and catch up on their news. It would take him two full days to reach Gunung Jasar. His first problem would be crossing the Sungei Kinta, which would be in flood after the recent heavy rain.

Col Toshra read the report on the sabotage at the tin mine. He spent some time looking at the map of the area. All of the ambushes in the last twelve months were shown on the map, as well as the routes that the saboteurs had taken after the incident. He knew that there were several groups operating in Perak, and they were all in separate camps. It was doubtful that the groups knew of each other's location, but somebody did.

He suspected that all the groups moved around on a regular basis, and he was aware that airdrops had taken place at several points in Malaya. He planned to send out more patrols. His young officers needed the experience, but they should not go too far into the jungle, never more than a mile from the jungle's edge.

The calibre of his men was a major stumbling block, and the latest intake from Japan was disappointing. He had been forced to instigate a training course to raise their standards to an acceptable level. He sent for his sergeant major. They had served together in Indo-China. He would discuss his plans with him and see if he thought the men were up to it, then take it from there.

Ralph Slater looked at the rapidly flowing river with some unease. He had planned to cross and camp on the other side by the end of the first day. He decided to wait for morning, and hope the level of water would have fallen. He made himself a shelter and cooked a meal. As it began to get dark he knew he must get some rest, so he would sleep with his gun in his hand. He awoke twice during the night. It was dry and a pleasant breeze was blowing through the trees.

At dawn he awoke quite refreshed. It was still dry and the sound of the river was less obvious. Before he had breakfast he had a look at the river. It was still running quite fast, but not as bad as yesterday. After breakfast, he packed his kit and tidied up his campsite, then he cut himself a bamboo stake and made his way down to the river. He was halfway across when he got into trouble. His feet slipped sideways and he could not use his stake to check his fall. The current pulled him under and his nose and mouth filled with water. He tried to breathe, but only succeeded in taking water into his lungs. His mind amazingly enough stayed clear; he was drowning. His head struck a submerged rock and his world went dark and he lost consciousness.

The Sakai family had wanted to cross the Sungei Kinta and move further into the hills. As they sat by the river they saw a man's body drifting into the bank. Three of them pulled the man from the river. He was white and he looked dead, but still strapped to his wrist was a gun.

Slater coughed up the remainder of the Sungei Kinta, or so it seemed to him, and tried to focus on his rescuers. As he began to rally his scattered senses, he saw in front of him a small Sakai family, two women, one old, one young, a youngish man and three small children. He managed to sit up and tried to thank them. They looked very nervous, and glanced at the Thompson sub-machine gun still clenched in his hand. Slater put the gun down and took off his haversack, which had stayed on his shoulders throughout his drama. He opened a sealed tin and took out some chocolate and gave it to the children. They snatched it and broke the bar into pieces. They all put it into their mouths and, as the flavour came to them, they smiled, then the whole family was smiling.

Later that afternoon the family caught some fish from the river and lit a small fire to cook it. They gave a portion to Slater who shared some of his rations with them. He felt so tired he covered himself with his groundsheet and fell asleep. It was morning when he awoke. He was alone; his rescuers had gone.

Slater was not surprised, the Sakai were a shy people. They lived deep in the jungle and avoided contact with anyone except fellow tribesmen. He was not feeling too clever, so he decided to make for the cave on Gunung Jasar. By noon his head was beginning to ache and his limbs felt stiff. He made camp at 1600 hours and used up the rest of his rations. After he had eaten and had a mug of tea he felt a little better, but as it got dark it began to rain, and he fell asleep with the sound of rain beating on his shelter.

It was daylight when he awoke. He packed his kit away and started off to complete his trek to the cave, which he antici-pated would take most of the day. At noon he allowed himself a short rest. He had developed a cough and was prone to fits of dizziness. He continued his march, twice losing his balance and falling heavily. He had a loud buzzing in his ears and he wanted to dump his weapon and pack, but he resisted this.

At last he saw Gunung Jasar. He concentrated on a speck in
the distance which he knew was the mouth of the cave, but it
did not seem to get any closer. His legs did not want to
support him and he felt he was spinning round like a top. He
staggered on for a few more yards, then a hole appeared in
front of him and he fell headlong into it.

Peter Blake was on watch when he saw the figure climbing
slowly up the slope towards them. It was Col Slater. He called
out to Maj. Martin as the figure sank to the ground, and rolled
a few feet back down the slope and lay still. Jim Muir, Blake
and Joy reached the prostrate figure in two minutes, Muir
carried Ralph Slater over his shoulder and Blake and Joy
carried his gun and equipment.

Back in the cave they lay the colonel on a blanket and Hari
Khah and the two nurses attended to him. They stripped him
and washed his feverish body, then took his temperature.
Hari listened to his chest.

He announced, 'I think he has pneumonia.'

They dosed him with the medication they had, wrapped
him in a blanket and, with one of the nurses at his side, let
him sleep. Mick Martin was concerned. Slater looked awful.
He seemed to be shrinking and was awash with sweat. Hari
told him that within twelve hours they would know the
outcome.

The next morning there was a slight improvement, and by
noon the colonel was sleeping peacefully. His fever had gone
and his appearance had improved. When they had their meal
that night he was able to eat some food and drink some tea,
then he fell asleep again.

To their surprise he was on his feet at breakfast, and
demanding his clothes. They were all delighted with his
recovery. By lunchtime he was able to tell them of his rescue
from the Sungei Kinta by the Sakai family, and of Jim Bottle's

promotion to lead the northern group. Ralph Slater decided to stay a few more days with them; he liked their company and it would give him time to regain his strength.

Chapter 23

In Ipoh, Tora Toshra was planning a sweep of the jungle from the tin mine down to the Tapah road as far as milestone six. He intended to use sixty men and penetrate a mile into the jungle before beginning the sweep. It was planned to begin the operation the next day at 0600 hours. He would accompany them with the two young officers, and let them take command in turn.

At 0600 hours Col Toshra and his men left Ipoh to begin their planned patrol. The men were in good spirits. They held the colonel in high regard and trusted him completely. Toshra had briefed his two young officers that they each would command the patrol one day at a time. He had also told them he would only intercede if he thought they were putting the lives of their men at risk.

Their transport carried them as far as the tin mine. When they had de-bussed, they quickly formed up in their sections ready to commence the patrol. Toshra indicated to the officer of the day that they could start and the patrol moved off into the jungle. It quickly became apparent the young soldiers had learnt from their previous experience as they moved with much more confidence and in silence.

Back at the cave, Mick Martin had persuaded Ralph Slater to extend his stay with them. The colonel was much stronger and looked almost his old self, but a few more days would not do him any harm. Jim Muir, Blake and the two nurses were spending the day having a look over the ground nearer the pipeline to see if there was any Japanese activity. They had left at first light and were well on their way by now. They were all armed with Thompson sub-machine guns and one day's rations. Maj. Martin felt he was lucky to have men like Muir and Blake, perfect marines if there was such a thing, strong, brave, good-humoured and totally reliable.

Peter Blake was leading the small patrol. Muir was behind him and the two girls followed on behind. It was a pleasant day, dry and with a slight breeze, almost perfect weather. The route the two marines had chosen was almost due west. They had decided to spend five hours on the outward leg then swing round and return to the cave, but just slightly south of their outward track.

About 1000 hours they heard the sound of a light plane. As they reached the crest of a ridge they caught a glimpse of it. It was several miles away as they watched it turn and fly back the way it had come. Jim Muir thought there was something strange about the plane's behaviour. Then it came to him. It must be over-flying some troops on the ground, spotting for them. He told the others, and they watched as the plane did another run, this time waggling its wings.

Col Toshra was not best pleased and thought to himself, 'What does the fucking idiot think he is doing. The fool is telling interested parties that "My friends are down there".'

He told his radio operator to try and raise the pilot.

'And tell him to bugger off, or we will shoot him down.'

The radio operator managed to contact the pilot at his first attempt. Having received the message the pilot turned and flew back to the delights of Ipoh's military airstrip, and hopefully an early visit to the Eurasian girl he had met.

The marines and the two girls decided to move closer to the Japanese patrol. Blake was now at least ten yards ahead of the others, as this would give them more time to withdraw if the Japanese troops got too close. Two hours later he heard some movement to his front. He stopped and told Sgt Muir. All four of them sank to the ground and waited for things to develop. After a few minutes they could see movement in the dense jungle about twenty yards away. Whoever it was they were not getting closer, but moving across Blake's front.

The young officer, conscious of the colonel watching every move he made, had decided they had penetrated far enough into the jungle and he would now swing his patrol south. Toshra thought they had gone nearer two miles into the jungle than one but decided not to interfere. He did not want to destroy the young man's confidence.

As the patrol swung round and started to move south, Toshra indicated to the officer to give the men a five-minute break, and let them take the opportunity to fill up their water bottles in the nearby stream. The inexperienced soldiers started to talk and joke with each other, but two abrupt words from the sergeant major restored the patrol to its previous good discipline.

Not more than twenty yards away the marines and the girls watched with a cautious fascination as their deadly enemies filled their water bottles and did what soldiers do when they are given a rest. One soldier decided to empty his bowels rather noisily, others merely urinated and farted. Blake thought, 'We are all very much alike, only we wash more.'

The two nurses were aware of the danger they were in, but were nonetheless interested in the Japanese troops' behaviour.

Joy whispered to Jan, 'They are quite small men in more ways than one.'

Jan stifled a giggle. At last they heard an order given and the troops swiftly got back into their section formations and moved off. The two marines conferred, and decided there had been around fifty men in the patrol. They stayed put until the Japanese were well away, then started to make their way back to the cave.

At 1600 hours Col Toshra decided to make camp for the night. The men had done better than he had expected, so he would give them time to construct some decent shelters. He asked the young officer who had been in charge for the day to indicate their position on the map.

The officer pointed to a spot.

'Here Sir.'

Toshra smiled, 'I think you may be a shade out. Take two men, find a tall tree, put a man up it with your compass, and take a bearing on the two gunungs to the east and to the southwest.'

The officer did as he had been instructed. When he found a suitable tree he told one of his men to climb up and take the bearings as suggested. He made the soldier take two bearings, calling out the reading as he did so. He then instructed the man to take them again. His second reading was so close to his first that the officer was satisfied that they were as accurate as he would get. He converted the figures to a back bearing, and plotted the position on the map.

It was some distance from his original calculation. He told Col Toshra where he thought they were and Tora Toshra asked him if he was confident he had now got it right.

'Yes Sir', said the young officer. The colonel looked at the map.

'Yes', he said. 'That looks good enough. Well done.'

The young officer smiled with pleasure, at least his day had ended well.

When Sgt Muir had told him of their encounter with the large Japanese patrol, Mick Martin had thought that the Japanese could be on to them, but the subsequent direction the enemy had taken restored his conviction that they were still safe. Ralph Slater agreed. Apart from those who lived in the cave, he was the only person who knew of its existence, but the activity so near was a concern.

Later that evening the two British officers discussed the problem. Mick Martin thought it might be time to construct another camp, one they could use about a mile northeast of the cave. The colonel thought it was a good idea. It would keep them occupied for the best part of two weeks, but at least this might frustrate the Japanese efforts to find them.

The next morning, leaving Ralph Slater, Hari Khah and Mai Peng at the cave, the remainder set off, taking with them a box of rations each. By noon they had found a likely site for their camp on a small hill. A stream ran across its base and would provide all the fresh water they would need. From a security aspect, the stream was not big enough to mask the noise of an enemy approach. The top of the hill was about forty feet above the stream and apart from some large trees was quite flat.

They set about constructing some shelters, using bamboo and Atap palm. The three girls made good progress in weaving the palm, with Soo Lin being the quickest. By late afternoon they had made four substantial bashas.

It was time to prepare a meal and settle down for the night. They all decided on a rice curry but had three different ingredients. Blake and Joy had corned beef, Jim Muir and Jan chose chopped tongue and the major and Soo Lin preferred sardines.

As they began to settle for the night it started to rain heavily. It was a perfect test for their new shelters, and apart from one or two leaks they were fine. They each did an hour's watch, so they managed five hours' rest between duties.

They spent the next day improving the camp and eliminating the small leaks. They dug a latrine and rubbish pit, and a hiding place for the rations they had brought with them. The ration dump was located about thirty yards away from the camp in the centre of a bamboo thicket. The living and dead bamboo provided excellent cover. The major and Blake did a careful recce around their alternative camp, going out as far as half a mile to check the terrain and possible escape routes. On their return they were satisfied they had chosen well.

As they settled in their camp for the second and last night, Joy whispered in Peter Blake's ear, 'How about christening the new basha? Jan did last night.'

'OK', said Blake. 'But it's girls on top night.'

Col Toshra was pleased with his men's performance. They were not yet up to the standard of the battalion he had commanded in Indo-China and Burma, but the signs were promising.

They were now only about half a mile from the Tapah road. He had told the officer who was in charge for the day to try and take them out onto the road as near to milestone six as possible. He had already instructed the radio operator to ask for transport to meet them at 1600 hours and he did not want to keep the trucks waiting. A smiling and relieved young officer came back and informed him the road was a hundred yards away.

'I hope for your sake it's milestone six', Toshra growled.

The worried officer moved off to find out. As he returned the expression on his face told Toshra all was well.

'We have reached the road, Sir, only fifty yards from the sixth milestone.'

'As far out as that then?' said Toshra, but smiled and gave him a friendly slap on the shoulder.

The major and his party returned to the cave just before 1700 hours. He told Ralph Slater it was a good site and was about four hours away. The two officers decided that the next food drop, which was still a fortnight off, would be split between the cave and the standby camp.

There was a message on the radio that night for 'Tileman'. It was from 'Junior Tileman' and it merely stated 'Return soonest'.

'That's Mr Yong Hoy', said the colonel. 'It did not take him long to get his feet under the table. I better get back to them tomorrow.'

Ralph Slater left the cave early the next day. They were all sorry to see him go, but the rest had done him good and he was now his old self. Sgt Muir suggested that he, Blake and the two nurses make another trip to the new camp and carry out some more improvements. Mick Martin agreed, and the next day they made an early start, taking Hari and Mai Peng with them.

Soo Lin was pleased to get Mick Martin to herself for three days; she enjoyed the lovemaking much more when they were the only ones in camp.

Jim Muir's party only took three boxes of rations with them, and as they shared the load they made good progress, arriving at the new camp about noon. Peter Blake went ahead and made sure it was still unoccupied before he called the others in. The strands of vine they had placed at the entrance and the two exits were unbroken and the food dump was undisturbed. The two marines thought three slit trenches would be a useful addition to their defence, so they all started to dig. At 1600 hours they finished one trench and decided that was enough for the day.

Mai Peng had spent the afternoon preparing a meal for them all, It was one of her special curries. They did not ask what was in it as all her meals were good and this one was no exception.

As it got dark they settled down to their nightly routine. At 2200 hours Blake relieved Hari Khah. Shortly afterwards, he could hear certain noises coming from Hari and Mai Peng's basha; it was obvious what they were up to. Blake found it hard to concentrate, as gasps and groans assailed his ears. It seemed to go forever.

'Christ', thought Blake. 'No wonder they are always smiling.'

Ralph Slater, on his return, had received a warm welcome. His group all seemed pleased to see him, even Yong Hoy. The camp was tidy, and a rota of sentries had been organised. This was a vast improvement on how things had been. This was the influence of Mr Hoy. Yong told him four more Chinese wanted to join their group, two men and two young women. Slater asked him if he would like to have his own group. Yong Hoy looked pleased.

'Of course, it would be an honour.'

The colonel told him eight was a good number for a group; it made them mobile and with enough firepower to do damage. They talked long into the night. Slater suggested Yong Hoy take over the Tapah district. With the four new recruits he only needed three more to become operational.

The next day Yong Hoy left for his new command. He intended to make his base camp in the Chikus Forest, a few miles from Tapah. The colonel had given him the spare radio, and the call sign, 'Newman'. He would get an airdrop of food, weapons and ammunition the next week and would soon build his group up to eight.

Jim Muir's group had spent three days improving the camp and they now had three good slit trenches, which he reckoned would be easy to defend against a force of up to thirty attackers. They covered the trenches with Atap palm, putting out the vine threads as before, and just before noon on the third day started back to the cave.

The major was pleased to see them. He was impressed with their efforts to fortify their alternative camp and suggested that in future they approached the new camp by the streambed to avoid leaving an obvious track.

They started to prepare for the next airdrop, which was only a couple of days away. Mick Martin looked at the date of the drop.

'Christ, the 1st of October 1943. In two months we will have been here two years!'

Chapter 24

Yong Hoy was in his element. Despite the colonel's suggestion, he had increased his group to ten, four of them women. He had made sure they were all committed Communists, and all had been at the University of Ipoh before the war. He had already carried out two ambushes, killing ten Japanese soldiers and burning two lorries, and had three camps in the Chikus Forest, never spending more than a week in each. He had received his first airdrop and had supplies which would last him two months. He did not allow any improper conduct between the sexes, but once a fortnight he permitted his men to visit some willing women in the small town of Bidor. Col Slater knew Yong Hoy was a 'loose cannon', but knew if he tried to control him too tightly, the man would just operate on his own and add to his growing reputation.

At the Japanese Headquarters in Ipoh, Col Toshra was a troubled man. Despite his best efforts there had been some bad ambushes on his men in the Tapah area. He concluded that there must be a new group of these so-called 'freedom fighters'.

He decided to mount an operation in that area and had even managed to have the use of two artillery guns, which would give his men some added firepower. He had wanted to control the operation himself but his young officers needed to be let off the leash, so he would observe from a distance.

The fifty-man Japanese force moved to the outskirts of Tapah at dawn, and within two hours was in the Chikus Forest. The senior officer in charge ordered a limited barrage of two rounds from each gun, eight hundred yards in front of his men. He had not the slightest idea that the first of the four rounds had fallen within fifty yards of one of Yong Hoy's camps. Yong Hoy was resting when the shell exploded. Pieces of metal shards ripped through the air, cutting one of the young women almost in half. To his credit his group were always ready to move quickly, and taking all their equipment with them they hurriedly left the camp, leaving the young girl in her death throes.

Thirty minutes later the first Japanese troops entered the deserted camp. Already the bloodied body of the girl was covered in flies. One or two of the soldiers stuck their bayonets into the corpse, for no other reason than they wanted to see what it felt like to bayonet a person. They carried out a careful search of the camp, but found nothing of consequence; Yong Hoy's food supplies were hidden elsewhere.

The officer in charge reported the one 'kill' to his colonel, and asked for another four-round burst eight hundred yards ahead of the last strike. As the soldiers heard the shells go over their position and then explode a few seconds later, they moved forward to see if their luck still held.

Yong Hoy was out for revenge. He had gathered his eight remaining group members together and had them in an ambush position four hundred yards from his old camp. His plan was simple. He would let the Japanese pass his position then fire into them from behind. He knew this would cause absolute chaos, because it was not what they would expect. The Japanese advanced in three extended lines of sixteen men, about ten yards between each line. Yong Hoy let the first two lines pass, then, as the third line moved in front of his position, his group opened fire.

He knew he could stay for less than half a minute before the Japanese recovered from the shock of this sudden attack and organised fire came his way. He could in fact have stayed longer, as the sudden surprise ambush threw the troops into confusion and almost panic. Only the experience of the sergeants prevented a total disaster. As Yong Hoy's group moved further into the Chikus Forest and safety, the Japanese strove to restore their discipline. It took only a few minutes but by then the ambushers were well away.

Col Toshra heard of the ambush with dismay. He ordered the artillery to fire the remainder of their ammunition in a fan pattern in the direction he had been told the ambushers had headed. Only one of the sixteen rounds fired came anywhere near Hoy's group, and that caused just a slight flesh wound in the arm of one of the men. The Japanese had suffered three killed and six wounded, but the biggest casualty was their morale. All the confidence carefully built up over the last few weeks had gone.

As the troops returned to where the colonel was waiting, their faces betrayed the shock they had received. Toshra knew a gesture was called for. As each man passed him he put his arm out and made physical contact with every soldier, and said just a couple of words; they needed to know he cared. The men already held their colonel in high regard and with his gesture this now became genuine affection.

The news of the action in the Tapah district reached Ralph Slater over the next two days. While this was good news as far as upsetting the Japanese was concerned, it showed how independent Yong Hoy had become. Col Slater knew it was time for him to exert his authority. He arranged to meet with Hoy in a safe house on the outskirts of Bidor.

The meeting took place about a week after the Chikus Forest incident. Slater congratulated Yong Hoy on his success, but then told him he should not act without clearance from him or Maj. Martin; there must be some control.

Yong Hoy smiled, 'Why of course, Colonel. Do we not have the same objective, eject the Japanese and make Malaya free?'

Slater laughed, 'You are a glib bugger Yong. I'll go along with ejecting the Japanese, but what follows that is not in my hands.'

Hoy put his hand on the colonel's shoulder, and said softly, 'No, Colonel, but it will be in mine.'

Maj. Martin carried out the move of half of their food from the latest airdrop to their new 'standby' camp, while Hari and Mai Peng stayed back at the cave. It was the first time the major had seen the improvements that had been made. He liked the idea of the three slit trenches and thought their position was just right. They put the boxes they had carried into another dump about fifty yards from the first, again selecting a site in a clump of bamboo. Digging the pit for the rations would disturb the roots of the bamboo, but they knew the tree would recover so quickly that in a week all sign of freshly dug earth would be gone.

After their hard work they all had a bathe in the stream. Joy, Jan, Blake and Jim Muir went first, with the major and Soo Lin keeping watch. As the two marines knelt naked in the water, the two nurses looked on in admiration at the two well-muscled bodies.

Joy whispered to Jan, 'Look at them, hung like bull elephants!' Giggling, the two nurses took off their clothes and joined them. Soo Lin watched them as she stood guard with the major.

'I regret my breasts are not as big as theirs.'

Mick Martin kissed her, 'Your breasts are wonderful; they are a joy.'

Soo Lin sighed with pleasure. What a man he was.

In the last airdrop rum had been included for the first time. The two marines had been used to their daily tot when part of a ship's detachment. Mick Martin decided to issue a small tot each evening after dinner, ensuring it was drunk there and then and not hoarded. The last thing he wanted was any of his group becoming drunk. In their position they needed to be alert at all times, and not befuddled by strong drink.

Hari Khah did not drink of course, but the women seemed to like the taste of strong rum. It was their second Christmas in the cave and, despite their different religions, Hari, Soo Lin and Mai Peng all enjoyed this festival. It was decided to invite Ralph Slater to spend Christmas with them. He was delighted to accept, and had already decided to make those days operation free.

Peter Blake told Joy he had a special surprise for her at Christmas, and he hoped she would like it.

Joy thought for a moment, then said, 'I suppose it's like a large sausage all hard and hot?'

Blake gave her his 'hurt feelings' look. 'It's not that, but you'll have to wait for Christmas Day.'

On Christmas morning, he gave her a small parcel. When she opened it she found a dressing gown made out of parachute silk, and her name embroidered on it. Hari Khah had done most of the sewing but Blake had done the initials. Joy was delighted and gave the embarrassed Blake a kiss. As they settled down on their blankets that night, she laid her head on his chest and whispered in his ear, 'I really fancy a hard hot sausage tonight, just the thing to make me sleep.'

In the first week of 1944, Col Slater wanted all his groups to become very active, with Jim Bottle's group attacking the railway line and Mick Martin's group doing a couple of road ambushes near Gunung Rapat. Further south, Ralph Slater would ambush the road between Ipoh and Tapah, and Yong Hoy was going to attack and burn a Japanese army lorry park.

The major's group made their way south through the jungle until they were opposite Gunung Rapat. They stayed in the jungle's edge until it was dark and then moved out and over to the main Ipoh to Tapah road. For the first time no one had been left at the cave. The major wanted his group to split into two for the ambush; half would ambush any trucks that passed, the others would ambush any relieving force that came from Ipoh. They had brought a Bren gun for each of the two parties, and the remainder carried Thompson sub-machine guns. Blake was with the major, Joy and Soo Lin. Jim Muir and Jan had teamed up with Mai Peng and Hari, who was the Bren gunner.

As they settled into their ambush positions about half a mile apart, it began to rain heavily. There was no point in trying to shelter; they just had to lie there and put up with it, being acutely aware sudden movement would betray their position.

They had been there about an hour when four trucks came down the road from Ipoh. The major watched them go by and a few minutes later heard Sgt Muir's group open up. The firing went on for about three minutes and then they could see flames leaping into the night sky. Ten minutes had gone by when they heard some lorries coming very fast from Ipoh.

Two trucks, probably containing troops but it was too dark to see, suddenly came into view.

They opened fire just as the trucks drew level. Blake put a burst straight into the cab of the leading truck and it went off the road and turned over, with the occupants crying out in terror. He continued to fire into the overturned truck. Soo Lin threw a grenade, which exploded as it rolled under the vehicle. Maj. Martin and Joy had emptied two magazines into the second lorry with devastating results.

It was time to go. They knew Jim Muir would already be halfway back to the jungle's edge. They were taking a longer but less obvious way back through the Sungei Raia Gorge. Blake's group moved very fast for the first ten minutes then slowed down. It was important to initially put distance between yourself and the enemy. The rain had stopped and every now and then the clouds would part and the moon, which was almost full, shone through.

Back on the road, the first trucks to be ambushed were burning fiercely. The survivors stood by the roadside. Their officer and sergeant had been killed. Two corporals tried to motivate the soldiers to assist their wounded comrades. Slowly they began to transform the chaos into some form of order. There had been ten soldiers in each of the trucks. Six were dead and about the same number wounded. The relieving two vehicles, containing the same number of troops, had suffered even greater harm. Ten were dead and eight wounded.

It took four hours for the wounded to get attention back in Ipoh. Col Toshra looked on in disbelief as his men were brought back into camp. He issued a string of orders. It was now 0200 hours. At 0500 hours he would lead forty of his best men in pursuit of these bastards.

165

'I want a spotter plane up at first light to cover the open ground near the tin mine and the jungle's edge', he said. 'This time they shall pay.'

Sgt Muir and his party reached the jungle's edge in advance of dawn. They made their way to the rendezvous point and waited for the major's group.

As soon as they could, the major's party moved away from the side of the gunung and made their way quickly through the cover of the head-high lalang, while it was still dark. They could just make out the edge of the jungle about half a mile away. In the distance they could hear the sound of lorries and then they saw them; four trucks crammed full of Japanese soldiers. They watched as the lorries reached the tin mine and discharged their loads. The soldiers quickly formed up and made they way towards the jungle's edge. Within minutes the troops had disappeared. Mick Martin knew the Japanese were now between him and safety. He was also concerned for Sgt Muir and the others. The Japanese could walk right into them.

Tora Toshra had positioned himself near the front of his men. He wanted to be able to control events if they contacted the terrorists. Jim Muir heard the sound of people moving through the jungle. At first he thought it was the major, but this was far more people than four. It must be the Japanese. With Hari Khah leading, they headed quickly due east. After ten minutes they paused and listened for sounds of pursuit. The sound was still there but there was more distance than before. For the moment they were safe.

Col Toshra had instructed his best men to head east for about a mile and then they would sweep south in line abreast. The leading soldier, a veteran of the invasion of China, noticed the footprints in the mud. He stopped and informed his sergeant and together they examined the fresh marks. Both agreed four people had been moving quickly east. Col Toshra was delighted. A fresh track and easy to follow. He urged his leading soldiers to move as quickly as they could.

'Don't let these bastards get away, we have our comrades to avenge.'

Mick Martin had decided to follow a different route than the one planned. He headed north up the pipeline then east so he could approach Gunung Jasar from that direction.

Meanwhile, Jim Muir knew he had to borrow some time. Sending the two girls on ahead, he and Hari prepared to ambush the front of the pursuing Japanese column. Muir decided to fire half a magazine each, then race after the girls. It would take the Japanese a few minutes to get organised, but that was all the time they needed to get well away. As they lay waiting for the leading Japanese to appear, both Hari and Muir knew they had been very lucky so far. How long would it last?

The leading Japanese came into sight. Hari and Muir took careful aim and fired. The China veteran took at least five rounds of .45 in the chest. The man behind was hit in the upper legs and arm. The sudden shootings caused chaos. Having done the damage Jim Muir and Hari sped after the girls, to put considerable distance between themselves and their pursuers.

It took at least ten minutes to regain control of his men, and continue the chase. Toshra was furious. His men had not fired one round at the ambushers and they had suffered one dead and one wounded. Mick Martin heard the sound of gunfire and guessed what had happened; at least they had put some distance between themselves and the Japanese.

Muir was delighted that his plan had worked so well. They were now making good time up a small streambed and they could afford to swing further north now. By tomorrow teatime they should reach the cave. By nightfall they had already made camp, just one basha for the four of them. They quickly prepared a meal and settled down for the night. Col Toshra did not realise it, but his quarry was now north of his position not east.

As the Japanese made shelters and rested for the night Col Toshra reviewed the day's events. The spotter plane had been pretty useless and the pilot not over enthusiastic, so the colonel was already planning to take this pilot on a future jungle patrol, this time on foot.

Back in Ipoh, the pilot in question, Lt Shimu, was already showered and changed and planning a night of passion with his new Eurasian girl friend. Suki had already charmed her way into his heart with her healthy sexual appetite.

Maj. Martin had managed to reach the pipeline and had moved further into the jungle. They had made camp at about 1600 hours, had a meal and were now settling down for the night.

It began to rain heavily around midnight, and the Japanese spent a miserable night. They had made inadequate shelters, which were unable to sustain the onslaught of the storm, and they had only just sufficient time to eat before night fell.

Earlier Toshra had been forced to send his wounded man back to the tin mine. With four men in the escorting party, he had lost six men from his patrol. As soon as it was light enough, the Japanese snatched a quick meal and continued their pursuit.

The spotter pilot, much to his annoyance, was required again. His mind was still on the previous night's pleasures as he followed the colonel's instructions over the radio. He was told to circle Gunung Jasar then head southwest to the edge of Gunung Rapat, and report if he spotted any movement.

He had just circled Gunung Jasar, when he thought he saw movement in the jungle below. He was about to report this, but decided to confirm his sighting. He turned his aircraft, but his mind was elsewhere. He was too low and had lost airspeed when his starboard wingtip clipped the top of a tree and he plunged into the jungle. As his aircraft hit the ground the engine was forced back into the cockpit by the impact, killing the pilot instantly.

Mick Martin's party had seen the spotter plane pass low over their heads. They had instantly 'frozen', hoping they had not been seen. But, as the plane banked sharply back towards them, they assumed they had been observed. The major was considering whether to open fire or not, when the plane's wingtip caught the top of the tree and spun into the ground less than eighty yards from where they stood. There was no explosion, just a dull crunch. They moved quickly to the crashed plane to detain the pilot if he had survived. It was obvious that the pilot had died as the plane's engine had crushed him to the rear of the cockpit.

As they forced open the door to see if there was anything worth salvaging, a photo of a pretty Eurasian girl fluttered to the ground. Peter Blake picked it up and placed it in the jacket pocket of the dead Japanese pilot. They quickly left the scene just in case the Japanese had witnessed the plane's last moments.

Col Toshra was puzzled by the plane's disappearance. They had not heard it crash, but it was not responding to their transmissions. He decided to take half of his patrol and look in the direction that the plane had last been seen. It meant going further north than he intended, but a plane just does not vanish into thin air.

It was just after noon when the leading section of the Japanese patrol came across the crashed plane. When Tora Toshra got to the scene his men had already pulled the dead pilot from the wreckage. One of the soldiers went through the dead officer's pockets and quickly hid the occupation money the officer had and the girl's photo in his tunic. He handed the pilot's pay-book to the colonel saying, 'That's all he had on him, Sir.'

Toshra then ordered the pilot be buried near his plane; they certainly were not going to carry the body back to Ipoh. He then ordered his men to head south and follow the tracks of the rest of his patrol.

Jim Muir reached the cave just after 1700 hours. Thankfully it was just as they had left it; the black threads they had stretched across the entrance and the exits were undisturbed. Jan went on watch while Hari and Mai Peng prepared a meal. Jim Muir listened in to their radio at 1800 hours, but there were no messages.

Muir thought the major would not make it back until about noon the next day. It was quite dark after they had their meal, cloudy and with no moon to light up the hill slopes. They were all tired and, apart from their turn on watch, they all slept soundly, their dreams littered with the events of the last few days. As soon as it was light, they ate breakfast. Jim Muir kept a close watch from the mouth of the cave, leaving the others to make sure everything was tidy for the major's return.

Maj. Martin had decided his group would enter the cave from the east, just in case they were being followed, and that they would hold up for two hours before completing their journey. The two hours went quickly. Peter Blake had positioned himself one hundred yards down the track from the rest of the group, just in case any pursuing Japanese were close behind them.

Satisfied they were not being followed, they made for the cave's eastern entrance, and within the hour were reunited with their friends. Of course, Jim Muir's group knew nothing of the spotter plane's fate, but were relieved that it had ended with them remaining undiscovered. They had all begun to realise that the colonel in charge of the Ipoh area was no Asana and that he was clearly a determined and experienced soldier. In planning all future operations, they would need to bear this in mind. Mick Martin knew he must discuss this with Ralph Slater at the earliest opportunity.

Unaware that his enemy was thinking about him, Col Toshra was calling off his pursuit. The Japanese had consumed the last of their food and were heading back to the tin mine. His men were at last beginning to think like real Japanese soldiers, and their patrol discipline was good. Last night he had watched the men construct their shelters for the night, correctly placing them facing in the right direction without a word from their NCOs.

As the tin mine came into sight, Toshra was pleased to see their transport already there, waiting to return them to their barracks. Standing by the trucks was his adjutant, who saluted, bowed and smiled a greeting.

'Welcome back, Colonel. HQ KL want you there tonight. They say it's urgent.'

Two hours later Col Toshra, having showered and changed, was speeding south under heavy escort. It was 2100 hours before he entered the gates of the Japanese Headquarters. He was escorted to the general's quarters.

'I thought you would be late arriving, so we will have a meal here in my quarters', said the general. He added, 'I hear that you have been out on patrol. I wouldn't do too much of that or the bastards will send you back to Burma.'

After they had eaten, the general explained the reason he had wanted to see the colonel urgently. He told Toshra that all over Malaya their men and vehicles were being ambushed, railway lines being blown up and that Singapore had said it had got to stop, neglecting, of course, to say how.

'I have spoken to all the commanding officers. You are the last. My decision is that at dusk all of our vehicle and troop movements stop until dawn. Then the only opportunity to attack us will be in daylight, and I don't think these freedom fighters will fancy that.'

The two old friends talked well into the night, and depleted more of the general's dwindling whiskey supply. As at last he went to his bed, Toshra thought on what the general had said. His idea was sound, if somewhat humiliating, but it could work.

Chapter 25

Ralph Slater informed his group commanders that he would visit them in the next three weeks. Slater thought it was essential that he should be the only one who knew the location of all the groups' camps. He started with Yong Hoy, and explained what he had learnt of the new Japanese strategy regarding the ceasing of all movements at night.

Yong Hoy, still euphoric over his attack on the lorry park and fuel dump, saw this as the first signs of the Japanese preparing to leave Malaya. Slater disagreed, telling him that the only way the Japanese would leave Malaya would be if superior forces drove them out, and that was not yet a possibility.

He also advised Yong Hoy that if he decided to carry out any daylight ambushes he should be sure to have a foolproof plan for withdrawal. The colonel then made his way north to the cave on Gunung Jasar. It took him five days to make the journey, but it was, without question, his favourite place. He always felt comfortable and welcome there and envied the harmonious lifestyle of Mick Martin and the people in his group. Mai Peng and Hari prepared a special meal, a triumph of army field rations and Mai and Hari's ingenuity.

After three days with Mick Martin, Slater had to go north to see Jim Bottle. Jim Muir and Peter Blake went north with him as far as the Sungei Kinta. They made sure he was safely across the river before they started to make their way back to the cave. It only took them a day and a half to make the return journey, which prompted Maj. Martin to say, 'Obviously hormone driven.'

That night, in their respective sleeping areas, both marines put on a performance that left Joy and Jan breathless, both girls telling their partners, 'You should go away more often.'

Mai Peng, on watch at the time, could tell what was going on, and when she was relieved by Soo Lin she found Hari waiting eagerly to make love to her, much to her delight.

That night there was a tremendous storm. The rain was torrential and lasted for five hours. Mick Martin was concerned about Ralph Slater crossing the Sungei Kinta, bearing in mind what had happened the last time. That evening he raised Jim Bottle's group and enquired if 'Tileman' had left.

'Negative', was the reply. 'Tomorrow a.m. planned departure.'

Martin then said, 'Tileman should wait for friends at previous accident point.'

'Agreed', was the reply.

Mick Martin and Blake left early the next morning, heading north to the Kinta Valley. Every small stream they crossed was twice its normal size, and it had started to rain again. They made camp at 1700 hours and quickly constructed a waterproof shelter before having a hot meal.

They managed to sleep quite well, despite their watches of two hours on and two off, and by 0730 hours they were on their way to the Sungei Kinta.

They could hear the roar of the flooded river while they were still an hour away. When at last they reached its banks it presented a terrifying sight. Brown water was rushing past at breakneck speed and the noise was awesome. It was impossible to cross. Large branches and sometimes complete trees rushed by; they would have to wait for the river to subside.

They had been there for about three hours when they saw the figure of Ralph Slater on the far bank. He saw them and gave a friendly wave. Grinning, he spread his arms wide in a gesture of helplessness.

It was noon the next day before he could make an attempt to cross the river. The major and Blake had pulled some vines, each about an inch thick, from the trunks of some of the trees and joined them together with parachute cord. Blake removed the detonator from a hand grenade and tied a long piece of parachute cord to the grenade. With this fastened to the vine he managed to throw the grenade across the river, a distance of almost thirty yards.

Col Slater recovered the grenade before it could roll back into the river and carefully pulled the vine across. Securing it around his body, he entered the river, confident his friends could pull him across. Almost immediately he was swept off his feet by the force of the water and his head went below the surface.

'Oh, for fuck's sake not again', he thought, as he swallowed some muddied water. Then he was being pulled clear into the riverbank. He saw Blake with his hand outstretched and the major hanging on to Blake's belt. As he grabbed the hand he was pulled clear of the water and all three men lay on the riverbank laughing, more in relief than humour.

They untied the vine from the colonel's waist and recovered the parachute cord. Blake asked for his grenade back.

'Sorry old son, it's at the bottom of the river', said the colonel.

'Don't worry', said Mick Martin. 'I'll stop its replacement value out of his pay. Marines get too much as it is.'

'Well,' said Blake with a smile, 'considering I haven't been paid for two years, it won't break the bank.'

It took the marines and Ralph Slater two days to get back to the cave. They always tried to avoid the same track twice, but the terrain often prevented this. Their considerable experience of jungle trekking gave them enormous confidence and an almost infallible sense of direction, even without the aid of map and compass.

On their return a meal was quickly provided for them. As they sat together enjoying one of Hari and Mai Peng's specials, Ralph Slater counted himself lucky that he had such a fine group of people to serve with. And they were good friends as well.

That evening, a coded message was received for Col Slater. After decoding it, he passed it over to Mick Martin to read. It was from Headquarters in Ceylon. It informed them that future replacements would be parachuted directly into the area they were to operate in.

Slater confided in Mick Martin that Ceylon had not lost sight of the fact they had three trained nurses in one group, and had suggested that two of them be transferred to two of the other groups.

Seeing the major raise his eyebrows at the suggestion, Slater added that he had vetoed it. He had explained that, as two of the nurses were female and had formed strong attachments within the group, it would adversely affect the group's morale.

He then went on to say he would ask for a doctor to be sent to join them. They could then provide a mobile medical team to visit other groups if the need arose. Maj. Martin thought this was an excellent idea, as at the moment anyone seriously wounded would never survive with the limited care available.

That night the colonel transmitted his suggestion to Ceylon and, much to their surprise, within two days the idea had been approved. They were informed the new medical officer would parachute in with their resupply in a week's time.

At the main base military hospital in Ceylon, Maj. Phillip Park sat in the Officers' Club pondering his future. He was just about over the death of his wife, who had been killed in an air raid on the Bristol hospital where she had worked. They had met twenty years ago while training to be surgeons, and had been married for eighteen years. Her death two months ago had devastated him, but at least there had been no children for him to consider.

He was now forty-two years of age.

'Perhaps', he thought, 'when this war is over I will give Australia a go. It's a big country and I can start a new life.'

His thoughts were disturbed by the arrival of his friend and commanding officer, Col Hugh Price-Manners.

'Got a job for you old boy. Right up your street. Area Medical Officer. It's a jungle location.'

Park smiled. Perhaps this was what he needed, a move to up-country Ceylon.

'Wherever it is, I'll take it, Sir.'

'Good', said Price-Manners. 'I'll arrange tomorrow for you to learn the rudiments of parachuting.'

As the Liberator bomber slowly made its way towards its destination, the new medical officer for the Perak area of Malaya tried to make himself comfortable in the noisy vibrating fuselage. The American loadmaster had explained they would only be making one run over the dropping zone.

'You will jump first, Sir, and two seconds later out go out the supplies. They, being heavier than you, will land first. Try not to get tangled up with them, Sir, as it could be messy. We have about an hour to go.'

Park tried to remember all the RAF instructor had told him.

'Tuck your fucking head in, Sir, right down on your chest. Fold your arms across your chest as you exit the plane.

Remember your static line will operate your parachute and land loose.'

Park had asked the instructor how many practice jumps he would do.

'Oh, none, Sir, it's too fucking dangerous.'

The three marines had laid out the triangle of torches, and were waiting to switch them on. They were now very experienced in receiving airdrops, but tonight would be a bit different. Their new medical officer was about to arrive.

It was a still night. Suddenly they could hear the unmistakable dull roar of the Liberator bomber. They quickly switched on the torches and moved to one side of the drop zone.

Maj. Park stood in the open doorway of the aircraft. He was terrified. The dispatcher stood alongside him ready to push the officer out if he did not jump.

'Go', said the dispatcher and Park took a blind leap into space. He screamed as he thought his parachute was not going to open, but received a tremendous jolt as it did.

He swung in the still night air as three large objects rushed by him. Then he saw the ground a split second before he hit it.

He lay still. The impact had been horrendous. He was sure he must have broken something. His head spun, but he slowly gathered his senses and noticed someone standing over him. The figure knelt beside him and began to free him from his parachute harness. A young voice said, 'Welcome to Royal Marines' barracks, Gunung Jasar.'

Maj. Park was taken through the eastern entrance to the cave with his mind still in a whirl. His escort was a young Chinese girl who said her name was Mai Peng. They sat him down and gave him a mug of tea. A Malay, who said he was a medical orderly, showed him where he would sleep. He found them all very friendly.

One large crate was brought into him from the drop zone. It was his surgical instruments and a large quantity of medical supplies. It took them two hours to recover all the supplies that had been dropped. The last items to arrive were the parachutes.

Mick Martin introduced himself and the rest of the group. He told the new doctor it was pretty informal in their cave and they had all lived there for just over two years. Everyone had a role to play, and everyone stood watches.

They all settled down for the night; one of the marines was on watch for two hours. As Phillip Park settled down in his bed space, he realised that all the men were paired off with the females. Only one girl was on her own, her partner must be the marine on watch. As he settled down to sleep, he heard some unmistakable sounds coming from several places in the cave. Park smiled to himself. Suddenly he felt very much at home.

Over the next few days the doctor began to understand the situation they were in. They all called him 'Doc'. He liked that and he called them all by their Christian names, but he noticed that Mick Martin was always called Major or Sir.

He took his turn at keeping watch, as did the major. For the first time in months he felt content and very much at home. He was shown how to use a Thompson sub-machine gun, and went out with Jim Muir and Peter Blake on a tour of the area. They showed him the different entries and exits from the cave and took him on a three-day trek as far as the Kinta Valley. He learnt how to make a basha out of Atap palm, and how to cook rice and make the most of his rations. Within a short time he was accepted. But up to now he had not seen a single Japanese soldier.

Chapter 26

One evening they had a message from 'Ten Green', which was Jim Bottle's call sign. One of his group had suffered a badly broken ankle, so Doc's assistance was being requested. Phillip Park was only too pleased to get involved and left early the next morning with Peter Blake and Joy.

They headed for the Kinta Valley with three days' rations and some selected medical supplies. Doc Park found the going hard and was grateful for any break in their march. Blake was anxious to get to the Sungei Kinta as quickly as possible in case there was heavy rain, which would make the river crossing impossible. They made good time and reached the river late in the afternoon of the second day. Blake decided to cross straight away, while the weather remained dry. He crossed first, then covered Joy and the Doc as they made their way over. Once they were safely across, Blake decided to make camp for the night about a hundred yards from the river. With their experience, he and Joy were able to quickly construct a basha using their rubber groundsheets and some Atap palm. Only just in time for it began to rain heavily as they finished.

Joy did the cooking, while Blake used the map to show Doc Park where they would meet with Jim Bottle's group. Apart from the rain, they spent a quiet night, each of them standing the usual two-hour watch. During his watch Doc Park looked at the sleeping figures of his two friends. Joy was a very attractive girl and Blake clearly adored her. When dawn came it was still raining, but after their breakfast, they broke camp and resumed their journey.

At about 1500 hours Blake told them to wait where they were, while he went ahead and checked the rendezvous point. After twenty minutes he returned and told them Jim Bottle and his group had not arrived yet. They made their way to the meeting place and set up camp, building an additional shelter for their friends. Shortly after, Jim Bottle arrived with two others carrying their injured comrade.

The Doc and Joy examined the man immediately. He was a thirty-year-old Chinese who had sustained the injury climbing to a lookout post. While the others prepared some food, they treated the damaged ankle. Doc Park told Jim Bottle that it would be best if the man stayed immobile for at least five days, giving them the chance to put his ankle in a plaster cast once the massive swelling had gone down. He reluctantly agreed, and said he would leave in the morning and return to collect his man in four days or so.

Blake was not too happy about this. He would need to get some more rations from their emergency supply dump, which was the other side of the river, and he didn't fancy leaving Joy behind, even though the Doc seemed a decent bloke. After breakfast the next day Jim Bottle and his two men left. Shortly after, Blake started back to cross the river to collect the additional rations.

He got back to the Sungei Kinta in the early afternoon. It was not in flood but the volume of water was quite high. He crossed straight away and in just over an hour got to their food dump, where he selected a box of rations, before making his way back to the river. By now it was almost dark.

The level of water in the river had fallen slightly and he managed to struggle across without too much trouble, despite his added burden. It was too dark to go any further, so he made a rough shelter for himself and ate some biscuits and cheese, which he finished it off with a mug of tea.

He slept with his gun close to hand, confident there were no Japanese about and as soon as it was light he made some tea, cleared up any trace of his night's stay and resumed his journey back to Joy and the Doc.

The going was hard and it was almost dark when he finally got back to his friends. Joy was delighted to see him and greeted him with a hug and a kiss. She then cooked a meal while Blake made the tea. The Doc was full of admiration over Blake's ability to carry a box of rations and make such quick time back, and told him so.

He laughed, and said, 'I don't trust officers where my girl is concerned, not even a nice guy like you, Doc.'

The swelling had gone down on the man's ankle, and they decided to put it in plaster. Blake was impressed with the ease at which Joy and the Doc did this. Once it had set, the man was clearly more comfortable.

Over the next few days Blake helped to carry the man to the toilet they had dug, much to the patient's amusement. Blake thought so too, but told the patient, 'You wipe your own arse mate, my duties don't include that.'

He made the patient a set of crutches, out of bamboo and parachute cord, and within two days he was almost fully mobile. When Jim Bottle returned, his man was ready, with care, to make the return trip with him. After one more day in camp Bottle left, with instructions from Doc Park on how to remove the plaster in six weeks' time.

'Keep it dry', he cautioned.

The casualty shook hands with them all before he left. It was obvious a doctor was going to be very useful.

The next day Blake, Joy and the Doc broke camp and started back to the cave. It had been dry for almost a week and on reaching the Sungei Kinta, they noticed the level was the lowest they had seen. It was therefore easy to cross and they made good time on their return journey.

By late afternoon on the third day they reached the cave, approaching it by the eastern entrance. Everyone was glad to see them. Nothing of note seemed to have happened, as the recent Japanese strategy of not moving anything at night had curtailed the group's aggressive activities.

The problem this caused them was one of timing. Moving into an ambush position was not the difficulty, as this could still be done under cover of darkness. However, they would have to spring the ambush in daylight, which meant their immediate escape would be in broad daylight.

Col Slater was loath to risk the lives of his people, until this problem had been thought through. Maj. Martin was expecting the colonel to visit shortly to discuss this. Until then they were staying at home.

Chapter 27

Col Toshra had been surprised by the inactivity of the freedom fighters in his area. So far troop and supply movements during the day had gone unmolested. He did not expect that situation to last; these people were dedicated and tenacious. It was just a matter of time. He now had just three manned posts between Ipoh and Tapah, each with ten soldiers, two corporals and one sergeant.

Each day they checked the road and telephone lines. Since the change in tactics they had not been attacked. However, he had on his desk a complaint from the manager of a rubber plantation, who said two of his female workers had been raped by Japanese soldiers two days ago.

The girls had been unable to work for a few days after the assaults and the production of rubber for the Japanese war effort had been slightly compromised. Toshra had sent one of his young officers to investigate with six of his men.

The post in question was only a few hundred yards from the rubber plantation and the occupants were the prime suspects. Late that evening the officer reported he had the four offenders in the camp cells; all had confessed. Toshra ordered they be given a severe beating and transferred to a front-line unit on the Indian border, where fierce fighting was taking place.

Ralph Slater paid his expected visit to the cave and had a long talk with Mick Martin. They decided that for the moment ambushes were out, but they would, on a date to be decided, launch four coordinated demolition attacks on the railway line. Two would be north of Ipoh and two to the south. The attacks would be six miles apart, two on road bridges and two on river bridges.

Mick Martin's group would return to the road bridge just south of Tanjung Rambutan, the scene of the marines' first encounter with the Japanese. This meant a three-day journey to get there, travelling mostly at night. After Ralph Slater departed to return to his group, the major discussed his plan with Sgt Muir and Blake. Over the next few days they made their preparations. Joy, Jan and Mai Peng would stay behind in the cave, but the Doc insisted on coming with them.

At first light, four days before the attacks were to take place, the group left the cave to make their way to the pipeline. This would be the only leg of the journey to be made in daylight.

With Jim Muir leading they made good progress. It was the 'dry' period in this part of Malaya, sometimes going a whole week without rain. They were each heavily laden with food and explosives, but despite their loads they reached the pipeline just north of the tin mine at 1600 hours.

They cooked a meal and rested up until it was dark, then they carefully made their way towards the Gunung Rapat Gorge. They kept very close together, as it would be easy to get separated in the darkness. Doc Park was finding it hard to keep up, thinking his fellow travellers were like 'fucking mountain goats'. With relief, the doctor noticed the first glimmer of dawn in the eastern sky. Shortly afterwards Sgt Muir led them into a small jungle-covered re-entrant at the end of the Gunung Rapat Gorge.

They cooked their breakfast and settled down to rest up for the day. It was cool in the shade of the gunung, but the marines knew that just fifty yards away in a small cave lay the body of QMS Rogers, their old sergeant major, who had died when they first retreated from Tambun. Despite all of them taking a turn on watch, they managed to get some much-needed sleep. At 1600 hours they cooked a meal and prepared to move as soon as it was dark.

Doc Park was fascinated by the relationship between Maj. Martin and Soo Lin. He knew that the major was a widower, but it would not have mattered if he had been still married, they were so right together.

As the light faded they moved out away from the gunung and headed for the village of Tambun, where, before it got light, they would hide in some caves in the limestone outcrops that overlooked the village. Peter Blake now led, keeping a few yards ahead of the others. If he met with any Japanese troops he would provide the others with some warning of danger before the firing started. The doctor could not believe they were walking through Japanese-held Malaya. He had expected to find enemy troops everywhere, but, as Mick Martin had told him, the Japanese were overstretched. As they made their way towards Tambun, Blake remembered a previous encounter on this track with wild pig. These animals were common in this area, the lalang or elephant grass being the attraction.

As they got nearer to Tambun they could make out the lights in the village. Blake kept as close to the rocky outcrops as he could and just before dawn they found a good hiding place for the day. As they made themselves comfortable the sun appeared. Within minutes the cool of the night was replaced by the sticky heat of a typical Malay day.

They prepared a meal, then settled down to get some rest. Doc Park had the first watch. He was amazed how quickly they all fell asleep, totally trusting him to keep them safe. Towards the end of his two-hour stint, Park could see some activity outside the large house that Mick Martin had told him was a Japanese rest centre. He watched as some Japanese officers carrying towels made their way towards a large cave about two hundred yards from where he was watching.

Mick Martin was next on watch, so Park shook him a few minutes early and told him of the nearness of the Japanese. The major told him not to worry, the officers were using the hot springs in the cave as a bathing centre; it was a well-known local facility.

As the day went on and each person took over the sentry duty, they were told of the presence of the Japanese. The hot springs were very popular and, as the last of the officers left at about 1600 hours, about thirty men from the rest centre paid a visit.

As soon as the activity had died down the major's group prepared a meal and got ready to move once it was dark. As they left their hiding place they could hear music coming from the rest centre, and the sound of laughter. Mick Martin was tempted to pay them a visit and shoot the place up, but that would have to wait. They had to stick to the colonel's plan.

By 0400 hours they had reached the road bridge over the railway line. Within two hours the charges were laid and the fuses set for 0800 hours, the time all four attacks were due to take place. They withdrew to the northeast just as the sun came up, using the cover of an old overgrown rubber plantation to hide them.

By 0745 hours they were moving past the rocky limestone outcrops not far from Tanjung Rambutan, almost three miles from the road bridge. A few seconds after 0800 hours they heard their charges explode. The sound reverberated around the hills. They also detected another explosion further north and wondered if this was Jim Bottle's team at work or an echo of their own. Feeling pleased with themselves, they carried on in daylight, heading for the safety of the Kinta Valley and a resting up area for the night.

Chapter 28

The news of the four coordinated acts of sabotage reached Col Toshra at Headquarters by 0815 hours. It was not unexpected and he had made plans for a blocking operation sometime ago. Within minutes he and eighty men were on their way to the tin mine. He intended to put eight ten-man patrols out to cover the pipeline and the jungle beyond, to a depth of two miles. He would make his headquarters at the tin mine, along with four men. He could control his patrols from there and be conveniently out of the way when Kuala Lumpur started to demand explanations.

He was proved right when an irate brigadier tried to contact him demanding to know what was going on, the railway line now being severely damaged in four places. When told the colonel was in pursuit of the terrorists, the brigadier informed the commanding general that Toshra had taken to the jungle, and could not be contacted. The general, who was an old friend of Toshra, laughed, 'Best place for the wily old fox. I wish I was with him.'

Mick Martin's group were well into the jungle by late afternoon, and they made camp for the night near a small stream. They constructed three small shelters with Soo Lin and the major, Doc Park and Hari Khah and Blake and Muir 'messing' together. After they had prepared a meal they settled down for the night.

Jim Muir asked Blake what he thought of Soo Lin.

'Oh, she is lovely. If I didn't have Joy I'd be after her.'

There was a pause, then Muir said, 'I feel the same. Jan's great but there is something about Soo Lin. It's that sweet smile and that lovely arse.'

Unaware she was the subject of the two marines' thoughts, Soo Lin snuggled up to Mick Martin, at peace with the world.

At about midnight the dry spell was broken by a tremendous thunderstorm; lightning lit up the sky for miles. The rain poured down, turning the slowly running streams and rivers into torrents. By dawn the storm had moved on and the major's group had stayed dry. They enjoyed the cool air the storm had brought.

After breakfast they broke camp and left the site clean of their stay. The next target was their food store, as they had used up their rations. They all took a turn in the lead, even the Doc. He noticed young Blake was close behind him though, which he found reassuring.

Just after noon they came to their store. It was just as Blake had left it on his last visit. They all took two days' rations and re-covered the site. Only two boxes were left now, and Mick Martin mentioned to Jim Muir that they should add to that store from their next airdrop.

Sgt Hosan was in charge of the most northerly of Col Toshra's eight sections. He was a veteran of the invasion of China and had been in the army for twelve years. A large man by Japanese standards, he was a firm disciplinarian and had a strong grip on his men. He tended to position himself about a third of the way into his patrol formation. From there he felt best able to control the direction of the patrol.

They had reached the intake of the pipeline about noon, and following his orders had then moved a further mile up the river before turning east. The jungle was quite thick at this point. They had crossed over what could have been some-body else's track, but which Hosan thought could have been wild pig as there were many in this area.

He decided to make camp at 1630 hours and he told his radio operator to inform the colonel of their position, while he watched his men construct their night shelters. As dark-ness fell it started to rain. After a few minutes the sergeant could hear some of his men complaining their shelters were leaking; an abrupt word from him and all was quiet.

Maj. Martin felt uneasy. He had felt this way since noon and when they camped for the night, at around 1600 hours, he confided this unease to Jim Muir and young Blake. The two marines told the major they would have a scout round before it got dark. Moving about eighty yards from their camp, they worked their way around the major's position in a rough circle.

Almost immediately, they nearly walked into the Japanese patrol who, at that moment, were busy constructing their night shelters. They assessed the Japanese patrol strength as being about ten, and slipped away to inform the major that they had close neighbours for the night. When they reported this, Mick Martin decided to remain where they were for most of the night. They would move off at 0500 hours without waiting for breakfast or full daylight.

The next morning the major's party quietly slipped away, moving due east. After two hours they stopped and had break-fast, confident there was some distance between them and the Japanese patrol.

At 0730 hours Sgt Hosan had his men on the move. They would travel east for an hour then turn south. After a few minutes they came across a flattened area of undergrowth.

They made a careful check of the area and found some tins buried just below the surface. They informed Col Toshra on their 0800 hours transmission, and were told to try and follow the terrorists' trail. This they did with great care, as it would be easy in this terrain to walk into an ambush.

As they made their way east after stopping for breakfast, Mick Martin told Blake to drop back at least fifty yards to give them an early warning should the Japanese catch them up. At 1100 hours Blake could hear some movement behind him. He paused for a minute, and caught sight of a movement in the undergrowth some twenty yards away. He quickly moved forward and caught up with the rest of the group, informing them that the Japanese were getting close.

Mick Martin decided to set an ambush on a slightly higher piece of ground, just above a small stream. The six of them lay about a yard apart waiting for the Japanese to appear. A few minutes later the first of the enemy patrol came into sight. Doc Park was in a dilemma. As a doctor he was a non-combatant, but he was also a member of a sabotage team. When he heard the major say 'fire', the doctor pressed the trigger of the Thompson and announced himself.

Sgt Hosan was about to stop his patrol when they suddenly came under gunfire. The two men in front of him fell to the ground in the first blast of fire.

Hosan screamed out, 'Down, move and return fire.'

The next few minutes were total chaos. Some of his men did manage to engage the enemy, but Hosan knew he must disengage. Slowly the Japanese fell back to some worthwhile cover and regrouped. Three of his men had been killed and two were wounded. The sergeant knew the terrorists would not hang about and would be making their getaway in the thick jungle. He told his radio operator to contact the colonel and report what had happened. He was told by Col Toshra to follow the terrorists, but not to engage them, as two sections were on their way to his position. Leaving his two wounded men behind to guide the reinforcements, Hosan started to follow the trail of the major's group. He was fully aware he could be walking into another ambush.

Maj. Martin was acutely aware he must not guide the pursuing Japanese back towards the cave, so they would have to keep heading east until the pursuit stopped. The doctor was still in shock after his first taste of combat, and sadly troubled by his conscience. He was amazed how the rest of the group seemed totally unaffected by the action; they had seen death in its most brutal form, while he had only seen it in a hospital bed.

They made good progress and were soon well away from the Japanese. They followed a streambed that ran northeast for an hour then turned east, only stopping briefly for some food before moving off again. They put even more distance between themselves and the Japanese. Just before 1700 hours the major decided to make camp for the night, but two would be on watch instead of the usual one, and the sentry post would now be about fifteen yards from the camp.

The reinforced Japanese patrol lost the track of the major's group in the streambed. Sgt Hosan was no longer in charge as Lt Hiro had now taken command. He told Hosan that the terrorists would head north for the Kinta Valley, and thus they would move north until it got dark. Sgt Hosan was not in a position to disagree. In his eyes the Emperor was a god and officers were smaller gods. So the Japanese headed north and the distance between them and the major's group widened with each step they took. Leaving themselves no time to make camp, they slept in a half circle just covered with their groundsheets.

At first light they reported their position to Col Toshra. He asked if they were lost, to which Lt Hiro replied, 'No Sir, I am convinced the terrorists intend to head for the Kinta hills.'

Toshra exploded, 'If you want to achieve the rank of captain, Mr Hiro, head southeast fast. They are getting away from you. Call me at noon.'

Mick Martin's group were now heading southeast, and were not that far from the new camp they had constructed. The major decided to make for the camp as it would be easy to defend and it was doubtful that the Japanese had picked up their trail anyway.

They reached the new camp at about 1500 hours and settled in. Sgt Muir and Blake went a hundred yards back down their track, to give early warning should the Japanese come their way. The major and Soo Lin relieved them when they had finished their meal. They just had time to cook themselves something before darkness fell. The night passed quietly and even the mosquitoes were subdued. There had been no sign of the Japanese. Maj. Martin decided to spend the day where they were and, if the coast was clear, make for the cave the next day.

Lt Hiro had pushed his men hard the previous day. Once again he had driven them on until it was dark. One or two of them were secretly hoping they would be ambushed again so they could shoot the officer in the arse during the confusion, and have good reason to return to base.

Hiro moved his men off as soon as it was light. As they came to the top of a ridge he could see a gunung about a mile away. He checked his map. It was Gunung Jasar. He directed his leading men to head for the limestone feature.

It was time to report to the colonel. His radio operator contacted Headquarters and informed the colonel that Lt Hiro was heading for Gunung Jasar. A weary sounding Toshra came on the radio and told the operator to tell Mr Hiro to make for the tin mine with all speed, they were returning to barracks. When the men in the patrol heard this they were delighted, and suddenly recovered the energy they previously had lacked. By noon they had got halfway to the tin mine, and by 1700 hours they gratefully boarded the lorries waiting for them.

Col Toshra had been issued with a new directive for dealing with terrorist attacks. Singapore Command had decided that pursuing the terrorists into the jungle, unless they were in very close contact, should cease. Day patrolling of roads and the railway line was considered a more efficient use of their limited resources. When Toshra informed his junior officers of this tactical change, it was not received with any great enthusiasm. In their eyes action meant promotion. His old friend in Kuala Lumpur had also told him that his future as Commanding Officer Ipoh District was under discussion. There was a vacancy in Penang for a Military Governor, and he had been shortlisted.

Chapter 29

Maj. Martin and his group arrived back at the cave just before 1600 hours. Joy, Jan and Mai Peng were delighted to see them. As the returnees cleaned their weapons and themselves, the three girls cooked the evening meal of curried rice, with a choice of tinned tongue or corned beef. Later that evening, when they settled down in their blankets, Mai Peng, Joy and Jan showed their partners how much they had missed them. Doc Park, who was on watch, listened to the very obvious sounds with some amusement and also with some envy.

At the end of his two-hour watch the doctor should have woken Mai Peng but, aware of what had gone on earlier, he did her two-hour watch as well. He could not sleep anyway. His role on the recent patrol still troubled him. Was he in breach of his Hippocratic oath? He thought he probably was.

He woke Peter Blake to take over as sentry.

'You don't look much like Mai Peng, Doc. Couldn't you sleep?'

The doctor unburdened himself to the young marine, something that a few months ago he would not have dreamed of doing.

Blake listened intently, then said, 'If a Japanese soldier was about to shoot me as I was lying there wounded and unable to protect myself, would you just allow it to happen? I think not. You are a good man, Doc. Stop worrying.'

Doc Park returned to his sleeping place, thinking to himself that young Blake was of course right. He fell asleep, his conscience suddenly untroubled.

Mick Martin had decided to give his group some rest. There would be no operations for at least a week, after which they would resupply a couple of their food dumps.

In the late afternoon of the first day of rest, Blake and Jim Muir had spent the day cleaning all the weapons and refilling magazines. They were sitting in the entrance to the cave with Joy and Jan. The topic of conversation was about first sexual experiences. Jim Muir as usual was leading the conversation.

He told his audience, 'Peter told me he had his first sexual encounter at seventeen and do you know, that vicar is now a bishop.'

The girls burst out laughing, much to Blake's embarrassment.

Muir hastened to add, 'I'm only joking.'

Maj. Martin and Doc Park looked in the direction of laughter.

'You have got some great people in your group, Mick', said the doctor.

'I know', said Martin. 'And long may it continue.'

That night they received a radio message saying 'Tileman is on his way'.

Mick Martin knew that if Ralph Slater was coming their rest would be brief.

Col Toshra was unhappy. He was all but confirmed as the new Military Governor of Penang, yet deep down he knew he would rather stay where he was. Toshra did not like politics or politicians, and the job in Penang would be awash with them. Well, he would make sure he got at least one more jungle patrol under his belt, despite what Singapore had said.

The colonel's intelligence officer had suggested that the area southeast of Gunung Jasar was worth looking at. It was here that they thought the freedom fighters took their airdrops. Toshra decided he would take a small patrol and spend a couple of days checking this ground over.

The following day he assembled a ten-man patrol and, with three days' rations, set off from the tin mine. He had insisted Lt Hiro would be his junior officer and the experienced Sgt Hosan his senior NCO. They headed straight for Gunung Jasar for the first four hours, then swung southeast for the rest of the day, making camp just before 1700 hours. Sgt Hosan positioned the shelters in a defensive arc and, as they prepared their evening meal, it began to rain.

At the same time, unaware of the Japanese activity, Mick Martin was making plans to meet Col Slater the next day, southwest of the cave. Slater had indicated that he wanted a good look at the tin mine before moving north to visit Jim Bottle's group. The cause of his interest was the tin mine resuming full production now the new generator was in place.

At dawn the next day Maj. Martin, Sgt Muir and Marine Blake left the cave with three days' rations, heading southwest. Just before noon they stopped at the junction of two small streams and waited for the colonel to reach them. It was just after 1500 hours when Ralph Slater appeared and greeted them warmly. They made him a mug of tea, and sat quietly talking about forthcoming activities, including a fresh attack on the tin mine. Blake, who was some yards from the rest of the patrol, suddenly heard some movement about sixty yards to their front. He quickly returned and warned the others and within seconds they had ranged themselves on the slightly higher ground at the point where the two streams met.

Tora Toshra was pleased with the patrol's progress. He was third from the front, at his insistence, with Sgt Hosan just to his rear. They had covered a fair area that day and he was considering stopping shortly to make camp for the night.

Suddenly, a savage blast of gunfire smashed into their ranks. The two men in front of Toshra were hurled to the ground, their bodies riddled with bullets. Toshra was hit in the leg. Sgt Hosan, still quick on his feet, was unharmed.

'Tell Lt Hiro to get back to the tin mine, they are too many for us', said Toshra, disguising the fact that he was wounded.

Hosan hesitated.

'Move, Sergeant, now!' said Toshra. 'I will cover you then join you later.'

Hosan slipped away taking the rest of the patrol with him, and passed on the colonel's instructions to Lt Hiro.

As the rest of the Japanese patrol slipped away, Mick Martin was about to order his own men to withdraw, when he saw one of the downed Japanese try to stand up, then fall to the ground.

He and Blake were about to move forward when Ralph Slater told them he thought there was movement to their left and the Japanese might be trying to outflank them. They quickly gathered their equipment and swiftly moved away east. They stopped after a few minutes and listened, but there were no sounds of pursuit.

Tora Toshra was in some pain. He had seen the terrorists start to move towards him, then turn away and leave the scene. He tried again to get to his feet but his leg would not support him. He had a wound dressing in his pack and he applied it, tying it tightly around his wounded thigh.

Sgt Hosan, by now almost half a mile away, was concerned that there was no sign of his colonel.

'Sir, shall I go back and find him?' he suggested to Lt Hiro.

Hiro, who was anxious to be seen doing the right thing, agreed.

'Take one of the men with you, we will wait at the tin mine.'

Hosan selected the one man in the patrol who had first aid training and retraced his footsteps. Two hours later they came across the colonel. He had lost a lot of blood and was only just conscious.

'Ah,' said Toshra, 'my faithful Hosan. You took your time my friend, I thought Lt Hiro had taken you all back to Ipoh.'

They gave the colonel something to drink while they re-bandaged his wound.

'We will stay here tonight, Sir, and get you back to the tin mine tomorrow.'

They then constructed a shelter for the night, anxiously keeping an eye on their wounded colonel.

At first light Sgt Hosan prepared some food for them all, while the first aider put a fresh dressing on the colonel's wound. It appeared clean, but the bullet was still in there.

After some food, Sgt Hosan constructed a stretcher out of bamboo and their groundsheets and, making the colonel as comfortable as possible, they started out for the pipeline.

They took a break every fifteen minutes, each man taking a turn in the front. It was hard work, but gradually the going got easier. Tora Toshra gave them constant encouragement. He knew other officers would not have been so lucky and most likely left to die or even helped on their way.

At 1700 hours they reached the pipeline and thirty minutes later the tin mine. A 15-cwt truck was waiting there, with a bored looking driver and his escort.

As soon as they caught sight of the stretcher party they ran towards them and helped carry the colonel the last few yards.

Within minutes the truck was speeding towards Ipoh, the two stretcher-bearers lying exhausted in the back.

A worried looking adjutant, who had just finished giving Lt Hiro the bollocking of his life, greeted them at the barracks.

After a brief examination by the medical officer, Toshra was transferred to an ambulance and, with Hosan by his side, headed for the military hospital at Taiping. They rushed through the Malayan countryside in the darkness and arrived in Taiping just before 2200 hours. Within thirty minutes the colonel was in the operating theatre, the bullet was removed and the wound cleaned. Sgt Hosan was given a bed in the male nurses' barrack room, but he did not sleep until the colonel was taken to the recovery ward.

Tora Toshra regained consciousness just after 0800 hours. He could not believe he was lying in a clean bed with crisp white sheets and a cooling fan rustling above his head.

A female nurse smiled and said, 'Welcome back, Colonel. You had us all worried.'

She then gave Toshra a cool drink.

Toshra croaked, 'Where is my sergeant?'

The nurse wrinkled her nose. 'He smelt disgusting, so I have sent him to have a bath and get some clean clothes before I will allow him to see you.'

Toshra flared into anger.

'I am a colonel in the Imperial army. I see who and when I wish!'

The young nurse gave Toshra a cold look and said softly, 'Do not try to bully me, Colonel, or I will recommend you are given an enema.'

Toshra knew when to give in to overwhelming force.

'I am in your capable hands my dear, but I would like to see my sergeant.' The nurse smiled.

'In that case, Colonel, he will be here in ten minutes.'

Chapter 30

Back at the cave, Ralph Slater was bringing Mick Martin up to date with the Pacific war. The Americans were beginning to retake islands they had initially lost to the Japanese, and the US navy was inflicting major damage on the depleted Japanese navy.

'You may laugh old boy, but in a year this war could be over.'

Mick Martin grinned.

'I hope you are right, but I'm going to miss all this; it's been the best part of my life.'

Ralph Slater looked over to where Soo Lin was chatting to Joy, Jan and Mai Peng.

'And what happens to the lovely Soo Lin?' he enquired.

Mick Martin looked across to the girls.

'She is an important part of my life, and will remain so. Our future is together, not apart.'

Blake and Jim Muir were sitting in the cave entrance. They were getting the ration inventory up to date, and working out how much food needed to be transferred to their emergency food dumps. The next airdrop would be in two weeks and the planning needed to be made now.

Sgt Hosan sat next to the colonel's bed. He was pleased that the wound was not as severe as first feared. Toshra had quietly thanked his loyal sergeant; they had now known one another for almost five years.

'You are aware they want me to become Military Governor of Penang?'

Hosan nodded.

'Would you like to come with me?'

The sergeant nodded again and bowed.

'It would be an honour, my Colonel.'

Toshra smiled.

'And one other thing, my nurse is too bossy. She needs fucking.'

Sgt Hosan laughed.

'She would not give me a second glance, but you, Colonel, are a war hero. She could hardly refuse.'

When the sergeant had left to go back to his temporary quarters, Toshra thought on what the sergeant had said.

'Of course he is right. As soon as I am able I will try my luck.'

The nurse in question, unaware that she had been the subject of the two men's conversation, was off duty and writing to her parents, telling them she had the honour to be nursing a national hero.

After spending five days with them in the cave on Gunung Jasar, Ralph Slater left to return to his own group, who were currently located between Ipoh and Tapah. He was still concerned about Yong Hoy, who had now increased the size of his group to twenty and was very much going his own way.

The colonel had also heard that Yong Hoy had murdered two village elders who had advised some of the young men in the village not to join his gang. A showdown between himself and Yong Hoy was on the cards. He knew it would now be a risky option to walk into Yong's camp unescorted. He planned to take four of his own group as an escort when he went for the meeting, a sad reflection on the now fragile relationship. As Slater made his way south on the two-day return journey to his men, another idea crossed his mind. Perhaps he should escalate things and kill Yong Hoy himself.

Yong Hoy had constructed a substantial camp in the Chikus Forest. He now had twenty men and women in his group, and had a request from five others to join. He also had a female companion, who attended to his every physical need. She clearly adored him, but his commitment to her was not as strong. Her name was Suzy Han. She came from a wealthy family. Her father's transport business was now in Japanese hands and he had to work for the invaders as transport manager. Hoy knew that Col Slater would try and break up his enlarged group, but he would not allow this to happen; a tragic 'accident' would solve the problem.

Yong Hoy was planning an attack in daylight on the railway line at Bidor, where two trains passed one another at noon each day. The railway line in Malaya was single track. Most railway stations had a siding where one train would wait to allow the other through. His plan was to launch an attack as the trains met at the station.

Col Toshra was feeling much better. His wound was healing nicely and he was getting on very well with his nurse, whose name was Anna Masu. He had now been informed that as soon as he was able to leave hospital he should proceed to Penang and take up his new post. He had been promoted to brigadier, and now had his own room at the hospital. He was making progress in his planned seduction of Nurse Anna. She had given him a bed bath the previous day and as she had washed his private parts he allowed himself the luxury of an erection. As he watched her reaction to a senior officer with a hard-on, he felt a pang of guilt when he saw her cheeks redden. That night, as she bent forward to change the dressing on his wound, he slid his hand under her skirt and caressed her bottom. She finished redressing his wound and as she left he saw she was crying. Toshra felt ashamed of himself; he had not behaved with honour.

Anna Masu told one of her close friends at the hospital of the brigadier's advances. Her friend laughed.

'Why Anna, these officers are always trying to fuck us. Better them than a smelly private soldier.'

Anna thought on what her friend had said. She liked the brigadier. Under his stern exterior was a softer, nicer side. She would see how things developed. If he was too coarse she would ask the matron to move her to another ward.

When she bathed her patient the next day, she deliberately allowed her hands to linger on his privates, and was fascinated as she watched his penis harden rapidly. She heard him groan, and he turned his head away. Without thinking she allowed her hands to gently move up and down his erect penis; she had never done this before. She was conscious that his hand had moved up between her legs. A finger slipped inside her panties and teased her. She felt her body was on fire, and she enjoyed the sensation his finger caused. She felt Toshra's body jerk; the towel she had placed on his stomach dealt with the eruption. She heard him sigh. She turned to look at him.

'Thank you', he said. 'You are most kind.'

She leaned over him and kissed him, then she left the room.

Chapter 31

Yong Hoy's group had been in position for two hours on a jungle-covered hill slope overlooking the station. One train had arrived from the south and was waiting in the siding. They could hear in the distance another engine approaching from the north. As the northern train came to a halt in the station, Yong Hoy gave the order to fire and a murderous hail of destruction ripped into the stationary carriages and their occupants.

For two minutes chaos reigned, then the fifty or so soldiers in the two trains started to fire back. It was time to go. Pausing to throw a grenade each, the twenty men and women withdrew deeper into the jungle and made haste to gain the thicker cover of the Chikus Forest.

Behind them at the railway station the survivors of the attack helped one another from the now burning carriages. Twenty-five soldiers and nurses were dead, and twice that number injured. It had been a hospital train that had felt the full force of Yong Hoy's attack. The Japanese had no available men to pursue the freedom fighters and Yong Hoy's gang made good their escape to their camp and an evening's celebrations.

Ralph Slater heard of Yong Hoy's attack on the radio. The Japanese were describing it as an atrocity. Slater thought that was a bit rich coming from the Japanese, but he was furious he had not been consulted. The time had come for a showdown with the Yong Hoy terror gang. He knew he dare not go to

Hoy's camp without some protection, but was concerned that his own men seemed to see Yong Hoy as some legendary hero.

He did not wish to put the loyalty of his men to the test, they might decide to join Hoy. The answer was to borrow the two Royal Marines from Mick Martin. He could rely on them and they would make Yong Hoy think twice about any assassination attempt. That night he sent a message to Maj. Martin saying he would visit in the next few days. He would take his own group with him, but at the halfway point he would leave them with instructions to construct a new campsite. That would keep them occupied and perhaps stop them thinking of the 'heroic Yong Hoy'.

When Ralph Slater arrived at the cave he took Mick Martin into his confidence, explaining his problem with Yong Hoy. The major agreed immediately to lend him Sgt Muir and Blake, but insisted they were told the full story. Slater agreed and told the two marines the extent of his dilemma.

They left the next day with three days' rations. It would take them that time to reach the area under the control of Yong Hoy. Slater had informed Yong Hoy that he was on his way, but neglected to say he would have two marines as his escort.

Yong Hoy, now aware of the impending visit, was planning to arrange a fatal accident for the colonel when he left the camp on his return journey. On the afternoon of the fourth day of their journey, Ralph Slater and the two marines made contact with one of Yong Hoy's men. He was surprised to see the escort the colonel had brought with him, but said nothing. It took them three hours to reach the camp, which impressed Ralph Slater by its strategic location and the defences surrounding it. He was less impressed with the realization that Hoy's group now numbered forty, ten of whom were women, all quite young.

Yong Hoy masked his annoyance when he saw the two marines and made a good show of genuine pleasure as he greeted them. After they had eaten, Slater got down to business, speaking alone with Yong Hoy. He made it quite clear that either he cooperated or he would no longer receive supplies from the air.

'I thought the object of our operations was to make life unpleasant for the Japanese and I am doing just that', said Yong Hoy.

Slater agreed with the objective but said, 'These anti-Japanese operations must be coordinated and planned to cause maximum disruption. We can not afford to act independently.'

Yong Hoy grew angry.

'You are jealous of my success and my ability to recruit more men than you.'

'Bollocks!' said Slater. 'You, my friend, are becoming a pain in the arse. Either toe the line or you will have to operate on your own and you will not receive any more food, weapons or ammunition from Ceylon.'

Barely in control of himself, Yong Hoy rose to his feet.

'We will talk again in the morning, Colonel.'

Ralph Slater made his way to the basha allocated to him. The two marines were sitting by the entrance.

'We heard most of that', said Jim Muir. 'He's turned into a poisonous little shit, hasn't he?'

Slater agreed.

'We need to stay alert tonight my friends. I fear he may have plans.'

During that night they took it in turns to keep watch, but the hours passed without incident.

After breakfast Slater met with Yong Hoy again. This time Hoy was oozing charm.

'You are quite right, Colonel. We should work together. United we can weaken the Japanese for when the Allies help free Malaya.'

Slater nodded his approval, but was not taken in by Yong Hoy's apparent change of heart. 'I am glad you agree. So, in future submit your plans as before for approval.'

Hoy agreed. Slater then told him they would leave later that morning as they had some distance to cover. Hoy asked them what route they would take, and Slater told him. Two hours later they left the camp, Yong Hoy shaking their hands as they left.

Once they were clear of the camp, Jim Muir said, 'Where do you think they will hit us? I saw those six leave the camp ten minutes before us.'

Ralph Slater thought for a few minutes then said, 'I think they will have a go as we leave the rubber plantation and cross the river.'

The three of them took extra care as they reached the suspect spot, then took cover and observed for a few minutes. Jim Muir told Ralph Slater he would have a scout around, and quietly slipped away. Muir moved slowly towards a slight rise in the ground, which overlooked the river crossing. As he crept forward he heard a metallic click, then he saw the six figures lying just below him.

He made his way back to his companions and told them what he had seen. Ralph Slater decided they would cross the river half a mile up stream. There was no point in getting into a firefight with what should have been their fellow freedom fighters. By nightfall they were well clear of the area and made camp with some relief. They all knew that if the colonel had been on his own he would now be dead.

Early the next morning they had breakfast and made a start. Ralph Slater wanted to return to his group as soon as possible.

By that evening they were just a few hours away from the camp where the colonel's group had been left. They had completed constructing their shelters for the night when it started to rain heavily. As they ate their meal it was accompanied by thunder and lightning.

At noon the next day they arrived at the camp. Slater's team was pleased to see them. They knew the threat Yong Hoy posed and greeted their colonel with obvious relief. It was clear Yong Hoy's reputation was not seen as helping their cause. One or two of the colonel's group even favoured going into Hoy's camp and killing him.

Jim Muir and Peter Blake were persuaded to stay the night, before moving on back to the cave. After a good night's sleep and some breakfast they set off, with Ralph Slater's thanks and good wishes.

They made the last leg of their journey in record time and just before 1600 hours entered the south entrance to the cave. They received a warm welcome from Mick Martin and the others, with Jan and Joy showing them how much they had been missed. The two recounted the events and the atmosphere they had sensed in Hoy's camp, and the foiled plan to ambush them on their way out.

The major was appalled and said, 'Sooner or later we will have to deal with that bastard. Slater must be very worried.'

'I think the colonel is hoping that given enough rope, Hoy will hang himself', said Jim Muir.

As soon as it was dark, and once in their bed spaces, the two returning marines were treated to a very personal and passionate welcome back. In the morning when Blake saw Jim Muir, they both grinned and agreed they should go away more often.

Tora Toshra was now able to spend most of the day out of bed. He had let his relationship with Nurse Anna develop slowly, a kiss here and there, a discreet fondle of her breasts and bottom. Just before lights out in the main building, Anna came to his room with a cold beer for him. On the tray next to the bottle and glass was a packet of contraceptives. Toshra needed no further encouragement. He kissed Anna, bent her over the bed and dropped his pyjamas to the floor. He lifted her skirt. She had come prepared and was not wearing her underclothes. He slid on a contraceptive and slowly entered her. She gave a little cry. He gave in to his passion and thrust vigorously into her body. She pushed back into him with equal vigour. Finally, he climaxed and fell breathless onto her. Afterwards they sat together on the bed and kissed, while their breathing slowly returned to normal.

'Say you will come to Penang with me. I can arrange it after all, I am the new Governor', pleaded Toshra.

Anna touched the side of his face with her delicate hands.

'Would I go as your nurse or something else?' she said.

'As a start as my nurse; I am still only just able to walk', said Toshra. 'Then let us see what develops. Until now I have been married to the army, but things are now changing, for ever.'

Over the next few days Brig. Tora Toshra called in a few favours. As a result, Nurse Anna would accompany him to Penang with the possibility of a permanent posting. This satisfied everyone. The one dissenting voice was the Senior Medical Officer, who exclaimed, 'I'm not running a "knocking shop", you know.'

When it was suggested that a man of his seniority should be running a field hospital in the front line, his stance changed and he agreed that the brigadier would benefit from further nursing.

The following Monday, Brig. Toshra, Nurse Anna and Sgt Hosan travelled under escort to Penang. The Governor's house was just outside Georgetown, the major town on the island of Penang. He was also allocated a villa on the top of Penang Hill, the highest point on the island. This villa was reached by cable car, and it provided a cool haven in which to escape the tropical heat of the city.

Tora Toshra made an immediate impact by calling all the local politicians, senior police officers and the headmen from the many villages on the island to a meeting. There had not been any acts of sabotage on Penang and Toshra was determined it should stay that way. He surprised them by asking them all if they had any matters that were causing them concern. They looked uneasily at one another. They all had complaints but these had never before been aired at a meeting with the Military Governor.

Toshra saw the unease in their faces, so he asked each one in turn to explain their role in running the island. As soon as this started the ice was broken. The floodgates opened and they complained about everything. Toshra listened, letting most of it roll over his head. When he had given them all full rein, he held up his hand.

'Gentlemen, let us take refreshments before we continue.'

As they drank the cold soft drinks that were offered, they viewed the new Governor with a friendlier eye. This was the feared Tora Toshra, a legend in the Japanese army, but it would seem he was human.

Over the next two hours genuine progress was made. The dusk to dawn curfew was suspended for two weeks with the offer of its complete removal if the truce was not abused. The ban on sports meetings was lifted, and the main weekday market could be held each day instead of once a week. Toshra ended the meeting after four hours, telling them that in future he would see them all together once a month, but if they had a matter of urgency to raise they were to phone his office for an appointment.

As he and Anna lay in bed together that evening, she asked how his day had been.

'I have made a start, and I intend to be an active Governor. I will speak to anyone. I'm not here to sit on my arse.'

Anna kissed him and ran her hands over his lower body. The effect was immediate. Anna smiled.

'I see you still have some energy left, my Tora. May I ride the "Tiger" tonight?'

She straddled his body, while Toshra kissed her breasts and fondled her bottom. As the movement became more urgent their lips met, their tongues touched and stayed entwined till they climaxed together.

They lay inches apart after their frantic encounter. It was then that Toshra knew this girl was not just a fleeting thing. This was meant to be a long-term arrangement, a thought which pleased him.

Chapter 32

Back in mainland Malaya, Yong Hoy was becoming a serious problem for the local Japanese commander. The latest outrage was another attack on the army lorry park, which had caused significant damage. However, a local man had given the officer some interesting information. The man's wife had left him and joined the Yong Hoy group and he wanted two things. Firstly, he wanted his wife back and secondly, no charges to be made against her.

The Japanese officer agreed to both conditions, not intending to honour either. If he could be led to the gang's camp he would, given the opportunity, kill everyone in it, including the wife.

Satisfied that his spouse would be saved, the man led a Japanese force of sixty men to within two hundred yards of the camp. He was told to wait there and his wife would be sent back to him, after which he was to leave the scene with his lady as quickly as possible.

The Japanese got to within twenty yards before they were detected. It was too late. They swept into the camp with a blaze of fire. Yong Hoy was asleep, having had a passionate encounter with his latest female companion, who just happened to be the wife of the informer.

He grabbed his machine-gun and ran out through the back of the camp, leaving his men and latest girlfriend to fend for themselves. Fifteen of his men managed to follow him.

The encounter back in the camp was bloody and short-lived. No prisoners were taken; nearly twenty of Yong Hoy's group were killed. Two of his females were wounded and provided some amusement for the victorious Japanese soldiers as they were raped, then bayoneted to death. The informer's wife had fought to the end and died riddled with bullets.

Two Japanese had died and two were wounded.

'A small price to pay', thought the victorious officer.

As they left the camp, having burned everything including the bodies, the tearful informer asked where his wife was.

'Dead', was the reply.

A week later Yong Hoy visited the informer late at night. When he left, the man's head was stuck on a post outside his house as a warning to all.

Col Slater heard about the attack on Yong Hoy's camp within twenty-four hours of it taking place. He was not exactly heart-broken by the news; perhaps this would curb the man's activities for a while. One of Slater's men was quite ill with severe stomach pains. Doc Park was on his way with his usual escort of the two marines and Hari Khah. Making good time, the medical party took just two days to reach a rendezvous point with the colonel. Keeping to his policy of limiting the location of each camp to only one or two people, the patient had been carried with great care to a small camp a mile or so from the main complex.

Doc Park carried out an immediate examination. It was, as he had suspected from Ralph Slater's description, a case of appendicitis. With the skilled assistance of Hari Khah, the operation was carried out in the far from sterile jungle camp. Doc Park had performed this operation hundreds of times, but never under these conditions. However, there were no complications and they waited for their patient to recover from the effects of the anaesthetic.

While they waited for the man to recover consciousness, Jim Muir and Peter Blake improved the temporary camp, as they would have to spend at least five days there. By late afternoon the patient was awake. Apart from the usual soreness, the operation had been a success. Over the next few days the improvement was maintained, and after four days Ralph Slater arranged for the man to be returned to his main camp.

Doc Park and his party started their return journey the following day. They decided to make a slight diversion to see what activity there was at the tin mine. The mine buildings came into view as they crept closer to the jungle's edge.

The main buildings and the generator were fenced in by three coils of barbed wire, which made the Japanese army presence obvious. There appeared to be at least fifteen soldiers in post to protect the buildings from sabotage.

From this they could see that the new Japanese colonel in charge of the Ipoh district had made some changes. They observed the Japanese soldiers for about thirty minutes, after which they continued on their way to the cave on Gunung Jasar.

Mick Martin was glad to see his men when they arrived late in the afternoon. He told the Doc that he had heard from Ralph Slater that his patient was improving rapidly, and would soon be fit to resume his full duties. Sgt Muir told the major about the Japanese presence at the tin mine and about the barbed wire. He also suggested it could be a task for their 2-inch mortars. The major agreed. The mortars had not yet been used, and with a range of six hundred yards would be a tactical option. Later that night the three returning men's partners showed how much they had missed them. Doc Park lay in his bed space listening to the telltale sounds, feeling very much left out, and thinking how unfair life was.

The new Japanese colonel was very much a new broom. Newly promoted, he was determined to make a name for himself. Now all the road and rail bridges had a permanent guard, as well as the three tin mines in his area. He was not a cruel man but had little time for the suggested softer line. Like many Japanese officers, he thought the war could not be won, but that most of their gains could be retained if the British and the Americans wanted peace.

His name was Tihoka, a single man from southern Japan. A tall, well-built figure, he had one weakness, women. He had been sent up from Singapore to replace Tora Toshra, but his two Eurasian mistresses were unable to accompany him. This privilege was reserved for generals. He had, however, met a charming Eurasian girl who, until she had met Tihoka, still mourned a pilot who had died in a plane crash.

He spent most of his nights with her. She was a sexual athlete. She needed to be to match his sexual appetite. He thought she was sensational. He planned to take her to the Tambun rest camp that weekend. The hot springs opposite the camp were a big attraction, and he would use his rank to make sure they had them to themselves for an hour or so.

Yong Hoy sat in his main camp in the Chikus Forest. His ego had been badly dented by the Japanese attack on another of his camps. Luckily his radio and most of his stores and ammunition were kept here at his main camp. The strength of his group was now twenty-five. He had recruited four more young Chinese men to replace some of his losses in the recent encounter.

His swift revenge on the informer was a lesson for other likely traitors and his security was thus enhanced. The local population were not totally behind Yong Hoy, but most accepted they wanted their country free of the Japanese.

However, they were suspicious that Hoy's ambitions went beyond the removal of the current invaders.

Col Slater had been in touch with him since the shattering attack on his camp. Slater had suggested he took time to regroup, and not undertake any hostile operations for a week or so. This could suggest to the Japanese that his unit had virtually been destroyed and they might drop their guard, giving Yong Hoy the opportunity to take his revenge. Hoy could see the sense in this argument, though it went against his nature to remain passive for long.

Mick Martin discussed the use of his 2-inch mortars with Ralph Slater, who agreed it would be a useful exercise. It had the advantage of avoiding a close-quarter encounter with the Japanese troops. Martin discussed the plan with his two marines. Some form of observation would be necessary to ensure the accuracy of the mortaring. They had two small radios ('eighty-eight' sets), which the spotter could use to communicate the fall of shot. They decided the attack would take place in three days' time, after which they would withdraw north as far as the Sungei Kinta, to draw any pursuit away from Gunung Jasar. The raiding party would consist of the three marines, Joy, Jan and Soo Lin. The Doc, Hari Khah and Mai Peng would remain at the cave.

The following day, the raiding party left and started off towards the tin mine via the pipeline. It took them two days to move into position. The major and Soo Lin would move forward to the jungle's edge to report the fall of the mortar bombs and suggest adjustments to the range. Sgt Muir and Blake had found a clearing in which to fire the mortars. They would fire at a high angle with the two nurses loading the bombs. The marines had briefed them on how to do this.

'Tail first, and don't try and put another bomb in until we have fired the one in the mortar, or we will finish up in bits hanging from the trees.'

With the spotters in position, the two marines prepared to fire on the agreed compass bearing. They fired a bomb each, and a few seconds later heard the explosions.

The major came on the radio immediately, 'Eighty yards long and a touch left, fire two more.' They did.

'Spot on. Complete the barrage', was the reply.

The marines fired the rest of their mortar bombs. The explosions reverberated around the hills in an almost continuous thunder of sound. They secured all their equipment and waited for the major and Soo Lin to join them. Ten minutes later they arrived and the completed party moved off towards the Sungei Kinta to lay the false trail.

The sergeant in charge of the army unit at the tin mine tried to clear his head and gather his scattered wits together. He was sure he had been deafened by the exploding bombs. Two buildings were alight and the generator shed was a tangled mass of twisted metal and burning oil. He saw some of his soldiers walking around with shocked and dazed expressions. He shouted to them, his voice sounding distant and not his own. It took twenty minutes to muster his remaining soldiers; three were dead and four were wounded. The mine's deputy manager was also dead and the manager missing.

The phone in the house was still working and he rang Headquarters in Ipoh to report the attack. The officer he spoke to wanted to know why he was not pursuing the attackers. The partly deafened sergeant tried to explain they had been bombed.

'Were they American aircraft?' screamed the officer.

The sergeant tried to control his temper.

'Not planes, you prick, mortar bombs.'

There was a pause.

The officer said quietly, 'I am bringing out half a platoon to pursue your attackers. We should be with you in about twenty minutes.'

Lt Hiro was in charge of the pursuing force. He looked at the damaged tin mine and its wrecked buildings. The manager had been found and was inspecting the ruined generator.

The sergeant stood nearby, waiting for the full fury of Lt Hiro to descend on him. Hiro looked at him. Blood was still trickling from the man's damaged ears. He had heard the sergeant call him a prick and had intended beating him, then removing his rank, but the officer had been influenced by his contact with Tora Toshra, now regrettably in Penang.

'Sergeant, return to Ipoh with your wounded men, your ears need attention. We will speak when I return.'

Lt Hiro then turned away and moved his men off to find the track of the bombers, which led them into the jungle. After three hundred yards they began a careful search for the mortar firing position. It took them thirty minutes to find the site, a flattened area of grass, and two threaded bomb caps that Joy had dropped in the rush to get away. The Japanese troops eagerly followed the trail, Lt Hiro making sure his men had a ten-yard gap between the two front men and the rest of the patrol. All afternoon they headed north, and as it began to get dark, Hiro called a halt and gave the order to set up camp for the night.

Maj. Martin was halfway to the Sungei Kinta before he decided to give the same instructions. Their shelters were built with the ease of much practice, leaving ample time to cook a meal.

The last few days had been dry, and this would keep the level of the Sungei Kinta low. Mick Martin wanted to leave a trail the Japanese could follow, and the ability to cross the Kinta with ease was part of that plan. After a quiet night, they ate an early breakfast and resumed their journey to the river. The major needed to cross the river and then recross it if he was to fool the Japanese.

At about 1600 hours they arrived at the river. As expected, the level was quite low, which allowed them to cross without difficulty. They then walked for a hundred yards down an old woodcutters' track, after which they retraced their footsteps back to and into the river. Stepping out from the bank they waded up river for a good hundred yards.

Mick Martin spotted a rocky outcrop, which spilled into the river, a good place to exit without leaving a trail. Soon they were back on the southern side of the Kinta. With any luck their false trail would fool the Japanese. It would have been foolish to wait and see if the plan was successful, so the party continued east along the bank, hoping to put more distance between themselves and their pursuers.

Lt Hiro pushed his men hard all day. He was aware they could be walking into an ambush, but it was important to get as close to the terrorists as he could by nightfall. At last, in the remaining minutes of daylight, they reached the Sungei Kinta. Should he cross or wait till daylight? The thought of being ambushed crossing the river in almost darkness made him err on the side of caution.

The Japanese erected their shelters and cooked a meal. Then, with two men on guard, they settled down for the night. At midnight it started to rain heavily. The downpour woke Hiro and he cursed his luck. The track on the other side of the river would be washed away.

At first light and without stopping for breakfast, Lt Hiro sent the first of his men across the river. The level had risen and his men had difficulty in keeping their feet. As the first two scrambled up the bank on the other side, He waited to hear if the track was still visible. His men reported that it was. With relief Hiro and the rest of his men crossed the river, getting a through soaking in the process. It was obvious their enemy had followed the old woodcutters' track, and the Japanese gladly followed this easier path.

Mick Martin's group had spent a comfortable night, despite the heavy rain. They had constructed one shelter instead of the usual three, as it had been dark when they had stopped for the night. They ate a good breakfast with plenty of hot sweet tea, to make up for the cold fare of the previous evening.

On resuming their march they headed southeast; their food dump was not far away and they were out of rations. Just before noon Peter Blake, who was leading, found their cache of rations. It would need restocking from the next airdrop, but there was still plenty there to supply them on the final leg of their journey to the cave on Gunung Jasar. They rested up nearby for an hour. Mick Martin and Jim Muir retraced their footsteps for ten minutes or so, listening for any sounds of pursuit. Apart from the usual jungle sounds all was well. They knew that providing further diversions was unnecessary, so they would expect to reach the cave by noon the next day.

By mid-afternoon Lt Hiro knew he had been outfoxed. There was now no sign of the track having been recently used. The bastards had given him and his men the slip. He decided to set up camp for the night early and get some hot food prepared. This decision pleased his men, who in common with all soldiers liked a good meal. It was a strange situation for the Japanese. Their food in the barracks at Ipoh was poor, but out on patrol they were issued with the British Far Eastern rations, tons of which had been captured just outside Kuala

Lumpur. These rations were much appreciated by Lt Hiro's men, and allayed the discomfort of a jungle patrol. With full bellies the Japanese settled down for the night. It turned out to be anything but peaceful, with thunder and lightning and a torrential downpour descending on them.

By morning the storm had passed, though it was still raining. Lt Hiro ordered the camp to be struck, and they prepared to start their return journey. It was noon when they reached the Sungei Kinta. They had heard the sound of the river a good hour before reaching it.

When Lt Hiro eventually reached the riverbank, he was shocked by what he saw. The level of the river was almost up to the top of the bank, a good six feet higher than when they had crossed the previous day. Uprooted trees rushed past at a tremendous pace, and the river's colour was that of mud. It was obvious that it was impossible to cross. With his anger rising with the frustration of it all, Lt Hiro ordered they set up camp for the night.

Chapter 33

The storm that had prevented the Japanese recrossing the river had little effect on Maj. Martin's party. In fact, it totally washed away any track they had made. They reached the cave just after noon. They were warmly greeted by Doc Park, Hari Khah and Mai Peng. After the usual cleaning of weapons and equipment, their friends cooked a meal, and told them they would do all the watches that night. This offer was not accepted. The three who had stayed behind had been doing two hours on and two hours off for almost a week. A compromise was agreed, with the Doc, Hari and Mai Peng covering the watches till midnight, then the others taking their turn.

Peter Blake and Joy took advantage of the comfort of their bed space to make love. They were not alone. Whispering and the rustle of clothing being removed came from several areas of the cave, accompanied by gasps, sighs and then more whispering. This was all very frustrating for Doc Park, who partly solved the problem by putting some cotton wool in his ears.

As dawn came Lt Hiro took the short walk from their camp to the river's edge. The level had fallen but only by a foot or so. It was still too dangerous to cross. He decided to head west on the northern bank of the river; this would eventually bring him out on the southern outskirts of Tanjung Rambutan. If he made his way back to the main road this way it would take almost two days. If he could get across the Sungei Kinta it would save half a day.

He spoke to his platoon sergeant and told him they would make another attempt to cross at 1600 hours. As soon as they had breakfast and cleared the area of their rubbish, the Japanese started off along the riverbank. Hiro kept a careful eye open for any easier crossing points, but the level was still too high.

At noon they stopped for twenty minutes, then continued their journey. Shortly before 1600 hours Lt Hiro decided they would attempt to cross and camp for the night on the other side of the river. Only two of the patrol could swim and he decided to send them across first. He instructed all of his riflemen to remove their rifle slings. These could be fastened together to make a substitute rope, which his swimmers could take across and secure on the other side.

The first of his two swimmers slipped into the still fast-flowing river, the makeshift rope secured to his waist. The other man followed, holding on to the line a yard behind his colleague. The current carried them quickly away from the bank and into the middle of the river, which was about thirty yards from bank to bank. The rifle slings measured forty yards in total. All of this was carefully let out and the last yard secured to a tree.

The stronger swimmer of the two was almost across, when his colleague lost his grip on the line and was swept away down stream. His panic-stricken cries ceased as his white face was lost from view and he disappeared under the water. The men waiting on the riverbank stood helpless and shocked, the thought of what might befall them clear in their faces.

The first man slowly crawled up the bank on the opposite side, clearly exhausted. It took him some minutes to secure the rope of rifle slings before he stood ready to receive the first man to cross. Lt Hiro decided the sergeant should go first and himself last. The news did not seem to be welcomed by his sergeant, but he entered the water and pulled himself across on the rope. It took almost thirty minutes for the patrol to make their way over, leaving Lt Hiro to untie the rope and follow on.

Having untied the slings from the tree he fastened it round his waist and entered the water. His men enthusiastically pulled him across, which meant most of the time he was under the water before he emerged on the other side, like a drowned rat. He had never seen so many smiles on his men's faces. His semi-drowning was obviously much appreciated.

After they had sorted themselves and their equipment out, they made camp for the night and cooked the last of their rations. As they sat eating in the comfort of their bashas, they heard a cry and into the camp came their 'drowned' comrade, wearing just a shirt and his boots. The current had carried him a hundred yards down the river and swept him into the bank, where he had managed to grab hold of a hanging branch of a tree and pull himself to safety. Lt Hiro was glad the man was safe and made sure they all gave up some of their food to provide the returnee with a meal. Then they settled down for the night.

Col Tihoka had enjoyed his weekend at the Tambun rest camp. His new mistress was perfect. She was the first woman who had not wilted under his sexual demands. She had even pleasured him at the hot springs. What a find she was. He was determined to keep her.

On his return to camp the attack on the tin mine somewhat took the edge of his weekend's pleasure, but the news that Lt Hiro was in close pursuit of the perpetrators would satisfy Headquarters in Kuala Lumpur.

Tihoka had installed his mistress in a pleasant house not far from the main army compound. He had established a routine with her. He would visit her each evening and stay till midnight. He would also call most lunchtimes. She knew what he wanted and was always ready to comply.

Her name was Marie Tooma. Her mother had been Chinese and her father a French tin mine manager. Both were dead, killed in the bombing of Ipoh. She accepted her fate. She knew she was beautiful and her first lover, the pilot, and her latest, the colonel, gave her a comfortable life. The colonel's sexual excesses had frightened her at first, but she was not without experience and, if the truth were told, she enjoyed his attentions. Clearly he was much taken with her.

On his return to the barracks at Ipoh Lt Hiro lost no time in reporting to Col Tihoka. It was an uncomfortable fifteen minutes. As he was dismissed by the colonel, whose face was dark with anger, Hiro was in no doubt that he was being held totally responsible for the attack on the tin mine. With his career prospects at present in tatters, he had volunteered to take out another patrol at dawn.

The colonel readily accepted his offer, commenting, 'Another failure would be a personal disaster for you.'

That night Lt Hiro carefully selected fifteen men, plus the sergeant from his previous patrol. He told the sergeant that the colonel held them both responsible for the previous failure to catch the terrorists. This was not true, but Hiro found the suggestion a useful motivator as far as the sergeant was concerned. At dawn Lt Hiro and a very enthusiastic sergeant took their men to the tin mine. By midday they were well into the jungle, heading northeast. The terrain was hard, thick jungle and occasional rocky ravines, which at times took them an hour to cover two hundred yards. At 1700 hours Lt Hiro decided they had done enough for the day and ordered the patrol to make camp. They just had enough time to prepare a meal when darkness fell.

At that moment, Maj. Martin had decided to replenish the supply dump, which was halfway between the cave and the Sungei Kinta.

Just after first light Sgt Muir, Marine Blake, Hari Khah, Joy, Jan and Mai Peng left the cave with a box of rations each. It would take them almost two days to reach the food dump with their heavy loads, but the return journey would be made in almost a day.

With the Japanese now also on the move, both patrols were travelling parallel to each other, neither aware of the other's presence, and at times no more than a few hundred yards apart.

Sgt Muir called a halt every fifty minutes, giving his team a ten-minute break before moving on. During the stops they sat next to one another saying very little, the girls needing the break more than the men.

At 1600 hours they made camp for the night. Within ten minutes they had made their shelters and were preparing their food. The Japanese patrol had moved faster and further and they were a mile ahead of the resupply party.

By 0900 hours both patrols were on the move again. Sgt Muir's party was moving north, while the Japanese were now heading east. The distance between them was increasing by the minute.

Jim Muir and his party reached the food dump just before 1700 hours. While the girls sat recovering from the tiring journey the men put up their shelters. The girls then cooked a meal. As they sat in their bashas eating, the rain came down heavily. The downpour lasted an hour by which time it was dark, after which the group got what sleep they could.

After they had eaten their breakfast, they opened up the food dump and inserted the new rations. They spent the next hour re-covering the dump and removing any trace of their visit. By 1000 hours they had started out on their return journey, moving fast now they were free of their heavy loads.

The Japanese had started their trek some two hours earlier and were now heading southwest, both parties moving closer to each other again with each minute that passed.

Hari Khah was at the head of the patrol when, just before 1500 hours, the two groups met. It was the practice of Mick Martin's men to have a gap of at least five yards between the leading man and the rest of the patrol. The Japanese seldom exercised this discipline. Therefore, Hari Khah was suddenly confronted by a group of Japanese soldiers emerging from a track just a few yards in front of him.

Hari managed to fire first. His burst of tommy-gun fire hitting the two leading Japanese soldiers. The third soldier, who was carrying a light machine-gun, fired a long burst. Four bullets hit Hari Khah across his upper body.

Both patrols went to ground firing speculative bursts of fire, hoping to find a target. The Japanese soldier who had fired the light machine-gun made a wild and inaccurate guess as to the enemy strength.

'There are least twenty of them, Sir', he informed the shocked Lt Hiro. 'They have killed our front two men.'

Hiro ordered his men to fall back. Seeing the Japanese withdrawing, Jim Muir ordered that a concentration of fire be directed at the retreating enemy. This caused the Japanese to withdraw even quicker, two of them being hit by the hail of bullets. Peter Blake moved over to where Hari Khah had fallen. As he gently turned his friend over, the severity of his wounds became apparent. Blake used two field dressings to stem the decreasing flow of blood from the two massive wounds in his chest and abdomen. Hari was dying.

With the Japanese thankfully moving further away with each minute that passed, Muir's group quickly constructed a stretcher. With great care they placed their friend on it and made for the cave on Gunung Jasar. Mai Peng was in shock. The man she loved was slowly being taken from her.

About a mile from the cave Blake and Jan stopped and guarded the track in case the Japanese should recover from their surprise and start to pursue them. Muir, Joy and Mai Peng continued on to the cave with their wounded friend. Doc Park had seen them coming, and started to give what help he could. But there was nothing he could do. Mai Peng held her loved one's hand and felt a final tight squeeze of her hand as Hari Khah died.

Mai Peng fell across his body, tears streaming down her face. After a while, Doc Park took her into his arms and tried to comfort her. For the first time since they had been there, the cave suddenly became a place of sadness.

Early the next morning they took Hari Khah on his final journey. In a shroud made of parachute silk he was buried on the eastern slopes of Gunung Jasar. The place of burial had been chosen by Mai Peng. Hari's grave would receive the first rays of sunshine as each new day was born.

Lt Hiro and his patrol made their way back to the tin mine, still convinced they had tangled with an enemy patrol vastly superior in numbers to their own. It was dark when a lorry arrived to collect them. They had two wounded men to look after. They had left their dead where they had fallen. Col Tihoka called Hiro to his office, and listened as he described the encounter with the terrorists.

'Well,' Tihoka said, 'you did your best, and did them some damage, but I tend to agree with Singapore. We do not have the resources to go wandering around the jungle. We will stick to static guard posts and daylight road patrols.'

As Lt Hiro left Tihoka's office for his quarters, he felt relieved he had not been roasted by his colonel. Perhaps the gossip was right. The colonel was obsessed by his Chinese tart and army matters were not his first priority.

Chapter 34

Col Slater received the news of Hari's death with sadness. It brought home the ever-present danger they all were in. They had been lucky in the past and it was unrealistic to think their luck would last forever.

But he had other matters on his mind. That bastard Yong Hoy was still recruiting. Word had it that he had two groups in the Chikus Forest, each about twenty strong, and that Hoy's mistress commanded one group when Hoy was absent. Her name was Suzy Han. She knew Yong Hoy had another woman, and had been delighted when she had died in the Japanese attack. Slater thought that would be how Yong Hoy's life would end, murdered by a jealous lover.

The subject of Slater's thoughts was at that moment planning to burn down a rubber plantation's store sheds. The destruction of rubber trees was frowned upon because the owners wanted their estates back in production as soon as the Japanese were defeated. The only damage allowed in the plantations was the slashing of the trees, a temporary inconvenience.

The buildings which Yong Hoy had set his sights on were a mile from Tapah on the Bidor road. He was planning the attack for the next Sunday night. Afterwards he would spend the night with Suzy Han and celebrate the success of the operation. He did not intend to tell 'that fucker Slater', who would only try and stop him with some pathetic excuse.

On the Saturday evening Yong Hoy made his way with an escort of two men to join his second group. They arrived at the camp just before dawn. He explained his plan to Suzy Han, who was enthusiastic. She was also looking forward to having Hoy to herself that night after the operation.

They arrived near the rubber plantation just as it was getting dark and moved quietly into position to observe the store sheds. They appeared to be deserted, so Hoy's men moved up to them. Using the oil from the rubber presses they started a fire. It spread rapidly and soon the buildings were consumed by the fierce flames. It was time to leave. Three hours later they were back in their camp, elated with their success.

Later that night, in the privacy and darkness of her shelter, Suzy Han enjoyed a passionate encounter with her lover. Hoy took her twice during the night and again at dawn. They then both slept till noon.

Back in the cave on Gunung Jasar, it was now a week since Hari's death. Soo Lin had spent the first few nights in Mai Peng's bed space. They were great friends and she knew Mai Peng should not be left alone. Mick Martin accepted the absence of Soo Lin but missed her terribly. Fortunately, it was only a temporary arrangement. Doc Park had admired Mai Peng for some time, but was conscious he must not make his feelings too obvious, not for some time anyway.

The major had kept them all busy. It was pointless them all sitting around moping, and they appreciated the activity. They were due an airdrop in two days' time, so they tidied up the store space to make ready for the new rations. Mai Peng had been given the job of updating their stores. She was meticulous, recording everything, even the French letters.

On the night of the drop, Mai Peng asked if she could join the three marines in lighting the drop zone. Mick Martin agreed, putting her with Peter Blake. As they heard the Liberator approach they switched on the torches and moved to one side. Flying low over their heads, the supply plane released its load. They could see the parachutes open and the rapid descent of the stores.

Blake was suddenly aware Mai Peng had moved out into the path of the descending boxes. He ran towards her and dived, grabbing her out of the way of the heavy loads. As they rolled clear, he could see she was crying.

She sobbed, 'You should have left me, Peter. I would have been with Hari forever.'

Blake was stunned. He pulled her to him.

'Hari would not want you to harm yourself. He would want you to go on and lead a full life, even without him.'

He pulled her to her feet.

'Come on, we have these stores to collect.'

Mai Peng wiped her tears away and joined him in removing the parachutes from the boxes.

Mick Martin had seen the incident with Mai Peng. He had watched helpless as Blake had made a desperate dive to pull her away from the descending loads. He would speak to Blake, but not to Mai Peng. If she was suicidal she would be a risk to them all.

When all the stores had been moved into the cave with the parachutes he called Blake over to him and asked him for an explanation. Blake told him what had happened and what Mai Peng had said.

'I think it's out of her system now, Sir. Can we not just put her actions down to shock, and forget it?'

The major reflected on what the young marine had said and agreed to take no further action. Over the next few days

Mai Peng gradually returned to her normal self. She removed all trace of Hari from her bed space, and thanking Soo Lin for her kindness insisted she returned to Mick Martin. Doc Park watched all this from a discreet distance. He wanted to make some show of affection, but thought it too soon. He decided to bide his time.

Yong Hoy was feeling very pleased with himself. The attack on the rubber plantation had further enhanced his standing with the younger element of Chinese and Malays in the surrounding villages. He had decided to keep his two groups at least five miles apart in the dense Chikus Forest. He could now increase their size to twenty-five, and he had decided to call one group 'Batu', meaning stone or rock, and the other 'Ayer', meaning water.

He had also decided to make Suzy Han leader of 'Ayer' group. She would be a good leader. She was brave and determined and, apart from being his lover, she was popular with the others.

He would lead 'Batu' group. He resolved he would see Suzy about once a week, but would allow himself the freedom to impose himself on one or two of the young women in his group. Despite his own sexual freedom, Hoy did not allow his men the same opportunities. They were restricted to a weekly visit to Tapah or Bidor to seek the pleasures of the flesh. Strangely, this did not seem to harm morale at all. His men admired him and did not begrudge him his affairs.

Tora Toshra was beginning to enjoy his new role. Most of the time he wore civilian clothes. His lifting of the curfew was extremely popular, as was the reintroduction of the daily market. He had made it clear that any acts of sabotage would mean an instant return to the more restrictive regime, and nobody wanted that. There was only one small group of freedom fighters on the island and they were in no doubt that if their activities upset the present harmony, the Japanese would be told who and where they were.

Sgt Hosan had never been happier. He was infatuated with a young girl who worked at the Governor's house and they were both enjoying a frantic sexual affair. Anna had watched the relationship develop between Hosan and Tia, the young secretary. She liked Hosan and knew he was intensely loyal to her Tora.

She had asked Tia if Hosan was a good lover. The young girl had blushed, then laughed.

'He always pleases me. He is not rough and though his thing is big he is so gentle. I think I love him.'

Anna knew she loved her Tora and their relationship was wonderful, even though the future looked uncertain.

Toshra was reading the up-to-date news from the battlefronts. It was bad. They were losing ground everywhere. Soon the advancing Americans would be threatening Japan itself. If the enemy ever landed on Japan the fighting would be so fierce, any invaders would be thrown back into the sea. Everyone would fight to the death. He did not think it would ever come to that. Some understanding would be reached; no other solution would be acceptable.

There was a knock and Anna poked her head round the door.

'Come in my dear, and put the bolt on the door.'

Toshra grabbed hold of Anna and kissed her. His hands dropped to her bottom and pulled her close. She felt his growing erection through her thin silk dress. Within seconds her dress was up round her hips and her panties on the floor. Her legs were around his waist as he thrust into her. Their passion increased. They both lost control until Toshra exploded into her.

As they regained their breath, Anna kissed him and smiled. 'You are wonderful, my Tora.'

Toshra handed Anna's panties to her.

'And you, my sweet, are just perfect.'

Chapter 35

Ralph Slater was on one of his visits to Gunung Jasar. As usual he had been made very welcome. He had taken the opportunity to have a few words with Mai Peng, telling her how sorry he was about her loss, and asked if she would prefer to move to one of the other groups.

She had given him a wan smile. 'Thank you, Colonel, but I wish to remain here. These are my friends and I cannot leave them. There is no other place for me to go, please don't make me.'

Slater assured her she could stay where she was. She thanked him and rejoined the others. Doc Park had part heard the conversation and her answer with some relief. Perhaps he stood a chance, only time would tell.

Mick Martin and Col Slater had a long conversation about future operations. With most road and railway bridges now having a permanent guard and road convoys only moving in daylight, these targets were a high-risk venture. The use of the 2-inch mortars had given them more scope and they could be aggressive' without getting too close to the Japanese. Ralph Slater thought a mortar attack on the main Japanese camp in Ipoh, from the south, was an option. They could move into position in the dark, fire twenty mortar bombs and escape under the cover of darkness. Mick Martin agreed and asked when he should mount the attack.

'We could move into position over two days, launch the attack on the third night and be back here in about six days' time.'

'Good', said Slater. 'We will start tomorrow at dawn.'

At first light the next day they set out, leaving Doc Park, Soo Lin and Mai Peng behind. They were heavily laden with the mortars, two dozen bombs, three days' rations and their personal weapons. They made good progress and by nightfall were almost halfway there. They made camp and prepared a meal, intending to make an early start the next day.

In their shelter that night, as they lay there listening to the rain, Blake asked Joy about Mai Peng. Joy surprised him by saying.

'Don't worry about Mai Peng, Peter. She doesn't know it yet, but the Doc is very much smitten by her.'

After an early breakfast, they set off, moving south of Gunung Rapat and heading for the Tapah road, It was late in the afternoon when they reached the road. They observed the area for thirty minutes and, seeing no sign of any movement, quickly crossed into the safety of the overgrown rubber plantation.

As it was approaching dusk they made camp for the night. They intended to carry out a reconnaissance the next morning to find a suitable firing site for the mortars, which needed to be placed about five hundred yards from the Japanese camp.

As they had on the previous night, they erected three shelters. The colonel and the major shared one, while Jan and Jim Muir occupied the second and Joy and Peter Blake the third.

After their turn on watch, Blake and Joy settled down to sleep. Blake was surprised at feeling Joy's hand sliding down inside his trousers. Not one to complain, he felt the cool night air on his erect penis as it was freed from the confines of his trousers. Joy suddenly moved astride him and his hands encountered her bare bottom. She paused briefly to slide a French letter over his now very alert member and then settled down on him with a contented sigh. She moved slowly up and down. Gradually her movement grew quicker. Blake pulled her down on him as he came. She shuddered and shared his climax.

As they replaced their clothing Joy said, 'That hurt.'

He muttered an apology.

'No, not you, Peter. A mosquito bit my bum.'

He offered to kiss it better. His offer was accepted and the spot was indicated. Blake kissed the soft warm cheek several times before he was asked to stop.

As soon as it was light they had breakfast, cleared their campsite and with great care slowly moved the mile or so to a likely firing site.

They came to a dirt track from which they could see, about four hundred yards away, the barbed wire of the camp perimeter. With no one in sight they set up the two mortars and prepared the bombs. Setting the weapons for high angle, they fired two bombs. Judging by the plume of smoke the range was about right, so they fired the rest of their bombs.

As the sound of the explosions rolled around the hills, they took the luxury of a quick glance, then quickly packed up their equipment and moved back into cover, It was important to get as far away from the scene as possible. The colonel and Mick Martin stayed and observed the rising clouds of smoke for a few minutes then raced after the others.

Col Tihoka was returning from a delightful night with Marie. He was a few hundred yards from the camp when he heard the first explosions. He instructed the driver to stop, and getting out of the car he watched the smoke rising from his camp. There were more explosions in rapid succession and a pall of black smoke rose over the camp.

Tihoka cursed.

'Mortars, fucking mortars, how dare they! Someone will suffer for this.'

Screaming at his driver to hurry, he headed for the smoking army camp.

Later that afternoon the damage reports were on his desk. It was not as bad as imagined. Two soldiers killed and eight wounded, two of them seriously. All the casualties had been caused in the direct hit by two bombs on the wash-places and the latrines. Three lorries had been destroyed, one packed with new tyres. One unexploded mortar bomb was awaiting a volunteer to move it. As usual Lt Hiro and twenty men had been ordered to pursue the attackers, but Tihoka sent them north instead of south.

Mick Martin's group made good time in reaching the cover of the disused rubber plantation. They were anticipating a furious pursuit by the Japanese and in view of this decided not to hold up for the night but to keep going. Just before dawn they reached the Tapah road. With no sign of any Japanese troops, they lost no time in crossing the road and reaching the comparative safety of the thick jungle beyond.

After an hour the colonel decided they could rest up for a few hours. Mick Martin agreed and they prepared a meal and rested till 1400 hours. Ralph Slater decided to make his way back to his own group, who were only about three hours away. As soon as the colonel had left, Mick Martin's party resumed their journey, with Peter Blake leading. The first objective was their southern food store, for they had no rations left. About 1700 hours Blake led them to the bamboo clump at the junction of the two streams. They helped themselves to a couple of days' food, then made camp for the night about two hundred yards from the food dump.

Lt Hiro and his men returned to the still smoking army camp twenty-four hours later. Col Tihoka listened in silence as Hiro reported his lack of success. The colonel told Hiro that some empty mortar bomb containers had been found five hundred yards south of the camp.

'You went in the wrong bloody direction you fool. I give you every opportunity to impress me, and you fail me every time. Dismiss.'

Hiro bowed, saluted and left the colonel's office, fuming. Once in his quarters he said out loud what he had dared not to say in Tihoka's presence.

'You useless lump of shit. You instructed me to go north. The trouble with you is your obsession with sticking your cock up that Chinese girl's fanny. I hear she has syphilis. It must already be affecting your brain.'

Feeling better for the harmless outburst, Hiro showered and went to the Officers' Mess for some food. He was convinced he would shortly be transferred to the front line and the fierce fighting on the Burma/India border.

With Jim Muir in the lead and Mick Martin bringing up the rear, they arrived at the southern entrance to the cave just before 1500 hours. They had been away six days.

All was well at the cave and the returnees received a warm welcome. Soo Lin made obvious her relief at seeing Mick Martin returning unharmed. The recent tragic end of Hari Khah had brought home to them all how vulnerable they were.

The news they picked up on the radio meant more bad news for the Japanese. The war had turned against them with a vengeance, with another naval defeat by the Americans.

Doc Park had managed to have a few words with Mai Peng, but Soo Lin had always been close to her friend's side. The

Doc was aware he could not let his admiration for Mai become too obvious.

Mick Martin had decided to give his team a week off from patrol activity, but he kept them busy around the cave. Jim Muir and Blake had found another cave entrance high up on the eastern side of the gunung and asked for permission to climb up and explore it. The major decided to join them and the three marines started their exploration just after breakfast.

The climb up was far from easy and was steeper than anticipated. All three were having second thoughts. Jim Muir expressed graphically what they were all thinking.

'Whose fucking bright idea was this? We could break our necks.'

But they pressed on and at last reached the entrance to the cave. It was smaller than it looked and at first did not appear to go anywhere. However, once through the narrow entrance, it widened and the passage led upwards and to the right.

Once inside it was possible to stand upright and after twenty yards it split into two passages, one descending and one staying at the same level. They stayed together as they explored the one that stayed level, but this ended abruptly and they could go no further.

They retraced their steps and followed the other passage. It descended for about twenty yards, then it began to climb steeply. It then split into two. The right-hand one was quite narrow, so they followed the wider of the two and saw a glimmer of light in the distance.

The passage ended at the source of the light, a vertical crack in the rock face just a few inches wide. They retraced their footsteps, and worked their way along the narrow passage. It grew wider after about fifty yards then climbed steeply. Mick Martin thought they must be in the centre of the gunung.

After ten minutes of climbing steeply, they could see a glimmer of light. The passage turned sharply to the right and the light increased. Now they were in the open, almost at the gunung's peak, standing on a flattish piece of rock and with a view for miles.

The three of them sat dumbfounded by the sheer beauty of the country around them. It was a clear sunny day, with all the shades of jungle green on display. They had a good view of Gunung Rapat and the Sungei Raia Gorge. They could not quite see the tin mine, but could make out the jungle's edge and the road leading to the mine. A hill obscured the mine itself.

They spent thirty minutes on the peak, then slowly made their way back along the passage and the less enjoyable decent down the rock face. It took them another hour to get back to the others in the main cave, and tell them of their find and the magnificent view. However, their friends' enthusiasm waned when they heard of the frightening climb to the cave entrance.

That night as Blake and Joy lay in their bed space, he told her more about the view and how high up it was. She ended the conversation by kissing him hard on the lips. They both slowly led each other to a state of high sexual excitement, as they removed each other's clothing. Their naked bodies came together. Blake spread Joy's legs apart and thrust himself into her. She began to move against him, the pace of their love-making increasing until they both climaxed and their bodies were bathed in sweat.

Theirs was not the only activity going on in the cave. Mai Peng, now alone in her bed space, heard the same sighs and missed her Hari even more. Doc Park groaned in frustration, put more cotton wool in his ears and longed for the opportunity to hold Mai Peng.

Chapter 36

In Penang, the new Governor had read the latest war reports with dismay. Toshra could see the end for Japan would soon be in sight unless they could somehow turn the tide. It was obvious to most of the Japanese High Command that they had made the fatal mistake of overextending themselves.

As a practical man, Toshra knew that if the war ended with a Japanese surrender, he needed to avoid capture. He also knew the Allies would want their pound of flesh, but he was determined it would not be his.

He had friends in Siam. When they had landed there, the Japanese army had been careful not to upset the population, it merely being a route into Malaya. Perhaps he would be safe there. Money would certainly improve the prospect.

He would take Anna of course, she was his life, and Sgt Hosan with his pretty girl friend. They too were almost inseparable. Toshra decided he would speak to Hosan and see if he felt the same. As for money, the banks in Penang must have some gold.

That afternoon, he and Anna had gone to bed for an hour. She had become a wonderful lover and they gave each other great pleasure. When he returned to his office, he sent for Sgt Hosan and shared his thoughts with him.

Hosan smiled.

'I too have been concerned for our future. Tell me what you want me to do, and it will be done.'

Toshra explained that, for their escape to be successful, they would need gold, silver or precious stones. Occupation money would be useless. Hosan asked how he was to obtain the stones and precious metals. What could he trade?

Toshra smiled.

'While we are still in charge, the locals want rations, passes, contracts and petrol. You will be in charge of granting these requests. The fee will provide our treasure chest.'

Hosan left the office elated. This kind of business was his forte.

That night, Tia and Hosan gave in to their frantic passion. As they lay sated after a prolonged and strenuous encounter, Hosan mentioned the need to start a treasure chest to provide for their future. Tia was full of ideas. She knew many of the local merchants through her secretarial duties and was able to tell Hosan which of them traded in precious stones and metals. She also knew some of the young girls at the Governor's residence and they had been keen to share with her the source of their rewards, small rubies in return for sexual favours. The next day Tia provided her Hosan with a list of these merchants and what they would want in return.

Within a matter of days Sgt Hosan had a price list, and the items the merchants wanted. To his surprise, weapons and ammunition were high on the list. This did not worry Hosan. The armoury on the island of Penang was full of weapons and ammunition, most of it left by the British.

He met with some of the leading merchants. They were surprised to be dealing with a mere sergeant, but Hosan was an intimidating figure and had the authority of the Governor behind him. One of the corporals at the residence had worked in his father's jewellery business before the war. He was quite competent in judging whether stones were genuine or not and assessing their quality.

One merchant who had paid for his goods in poor quality stones was greeted at the top of the residency stairs by Hosan. The sergeant kicked him all the way to the bottom. The next day the stones were replaced by ones of top quality. Word got around, and traded goods were always paid for promptly in quality gems or precious metal.

The 'treasure chest' was kept in Toshra's office safe. Each item of value was carefully recorded in the payment book and each week they all checked it, each signing to its accuracy.

Ralph Slater paid another visit to the cave. When he arrived he greeted them all with the words, 'Pin back your ears, I have news of promotions for you all.'

Mick Martin was now a colonel, Jim Muir a colour sergeant and Peter Blake a corporal. Joy and Jan were now senior nurses.

'I am now a brigadier', said Slater and they all bowed.

'Also, all promotions have been backdated six months for pay purposes.'

Their new colonel ordered the issue of a special tot of rum to mark the occasion.

As they sipped the strong spirit Doc Park complained, 'I'm the only one not promoted.'

Ralph Slater laughed.

'You can call yourself the Senior Medical Officer, but I'm afraid there's no extra pay.'

Soo Lin and Mai Peng smiled, but found the laughter hard to understand.

Brig. Slater saw their bewilderment.

'I have left out our two loyal friends here. That is unforgivable. You have both been promoted to "Freedom Fighters First Class", and will wear a red circle on the right arm of your tunics.'

Both the girls looked pleased and they were all embraced in turn by their friends, Doc Park taking the opportunity to kiss Mai Peng on both cheeks.

Later that evening they all sat talking after their evening meal. Ralph Slater said, 'It may have escaped your notice my friends, but in two weeks' time it will be Christmas. We have been here three years.'

Col Tihoka lay next to Marie unable to sleep. The year was coming to an end. 1944 had not been good for the Japanese and 1945 promised no better. He lay looking at his lovely Marie. Her chest rose and fell as she slept, her firm breasts beginning to reawaken the heat in his loins. She turned onto her stomach, showing Tihoka her firm bottom and legs. Fully aroused now, he moved over on top of her and entered her from behind. Marie woke up feeling her lover thrusting hard into her. She responded and Tihoka grunted his appreciation as she pushed her bottom back hard into his groin.

Afterwards she got out of bed and fetched Tihoka a cold drink. He kissed her and stroked her face in a rare show of tenderness. He then lay back and instantly fell asleep, leaving Marie now wide awake to ponder the future.

Lt Hiro received a summons to the colonel's office, fully expecting that the 'bastard' would smirk and inform him of his transfer to the front line in Burma. He was surprised to find he was offered coffee and a chair.

'I have decided to recommend you for promotion to captain. You are not without merit, and as you know we have a vacancy in this command. You will assume that rank in an acting capacity as from now. That is all.'

Acting Capt. Hiro walked back to his quarters in a daze. He had expected to be boarding a train for the north, instead he was sewing on the extra pip. 'That bastard's up to something', he thought, then took out his needle and thread.

The next morning Col Tihoka sent for Hiro again.

'I have a task for you. Take one of the small trucks, a driver and a two-man escort, plus four days' rations. I want you to drive non-stop to the Thai border. Keep your speed to a steady thirty miles an hour. You are required to make a note of all bridges over the railway line or river, also note which bridges have a guard on them. On your return journey you can go as fast as you like. Have you any questions? Good. The mission is confidential. You may make your preparations and leave by midday. Good luck.'

Hiro left the colonel's office and made the arrangements. He instructed the driver to take extra cans of petrol sufficient for the whole journey. At 1130 hours, as instructed, he left the camp with two puzzled soldiers as escort and an equally puzzled driver.

They drove all day. As it began to get dark, Acting Capt. Hiro took over the driving. The escorting soldiers did their best to provide some food in the back of the swaying truck. At midnight they reached the border. Hiro thought they had covered close to two hundred miles. As the mile indicator was broken there was no way he could be more accurate, and at times they were reduced to ten miles an hour because of the damaged roads.

They parked the truck by the side of the road, put up a shelter for the night and tried to get some rest. At dawn, after a substantial breakfast, they began the return journey. Hiro instructed the driver to drive at a comfortable speed, while he checked his notes on bridges and river crossings. After a two-hour break for lunch, they arrived back at the camp at 0200 hours. Hiro swore the men to secrecy and dismissed them to their barracks.

In the morning he completed his report, with fuel consumption included, and went to find Col Tihoka, who was in a good mood. Marie had surpassed herself that night and had left the colonel drained and very satisfied.

He looked at his acting captain's detailed report, and read in silence. He raised his eyebrows a couple of times and looked at a large-scale map. At last he put down the report and spoke.

'Well my friend, you have done an excellent job. One question. The journey was completed in dry conditions. What would be your estimate for a journey in heavy rain?'

Hiro thought for a moment.

'I would think you should allow another three hours. Perhaps half that in a covered saloon car, Sir.'

Tihoka looked down at the map, tapped his fingers on the table and looked back up into Hiro's face.

'Good. I am taking you out to lunch at my cottage. You have done well.'

It was the first time Hiro had seen the colonel's mistress. She really was beautiful, and charming with it. She fussed around them both, serving drinks then bringing in their food, fresh crab and lobster salad. After an hour he was captivated by this wonderful creature. After coffee, the colonel sent for his car. He then told Hiro he would stay a little longer and that Hiro should send the car back for him in an hour.

Acting Capt. Hiro thanked Marie. Was it his imagination or did she press his fingers just a moment longer than was necessary? As he was driven back to the camp he knew what his colonel was doing and a wave of envy consumed him.

Back at the cottage, Tihoka lost no time in taking Marie into the bedroom. He took her roughly, but she responded in evident pleasure. Both were bathed in sweat as they reached a climax. Two hours later the colonel was back in his office, just

in time to take a phone call from Headquarters in Kuala
Lumpur. It was an urgent summons to attend a meeting the
next day. He asked if he could bring his companion. The
answer was a blunt 'No', and a further blow. The meeting
would last three days.

The newly promoted brigadier and colonel were planning
an end of year operation, using the mortars again on the
railway sidings just outside Ipoh. They had received information that large supply trains were staying in the sidings
during the hours of darkness before resuming their journey
north.

They decided to launch the attack about the middle of
December. Jim Bottle's group would attack an army camp
just outside Sungei Siput at the same time. This gave them
two weeks to complete the plan and move into position. The
journey to and from the target would take five days.

Mai Peng had come to terms with the loss of Hari. It was
now almost three months since his death, and time is the great
healer. She was also aware of Doc Park. She knew he was
interested in her by the looks he gave her. She was not sure.
He was a decent man, but she did not intend being a safety
valve for his frustrations. The subject of her thoughts was not
in the best of moods. He was required to travel to a point near
Ralph Slater's camp to treat two of his Chinese who had
developed venereal disease.

Early the next day, with Peter Blake and Joy, Doc Park
started off to the rendezvous with Slater's men. It was a miserable journey made in almost continuous rain. They made
camp as the light began to fail and after a meal they settled
down to sleep in their wet clothes. Joy slept between the two
men, unaware her close presence was aggravating the Doc's
frustration.

At first light, after a quick breakfast, they resumed their trek, reaching the rendezvous just after midday. The two rather shamefaced Chinese arrived about an hour later. Doc Park embarrassed them further by insisting Joy had a look at their 'condition'. She confirmed his diagnosis. Both men had been with the same woman, who had also sold her favours to the Japanese soldiers. Doc Park gave them some medication, with instructions to drink plenty of fluids and avoid any sexual intercourse for three weeks, then to use a French letter in the future.

Having done their duty, they made camp for the night and made a filling corned beef curry, Joy doing the cooking. She was not too impressed when Blake asked, 'You did wash your hands, after inspecting their cocks?' Joy's retaliation came that night when she insisted that the Doc slept in the middle.

Chapter 37

Col Tihoka left for Kuala Lumpur at first light. He told his acting captain that he was in charge until his return. Hiro was not planning any patrols, but thought he would pay a visit to the tin mine the next day.

At 1600 hours there was a phone call from Marie. The lights would not work, what could she do? Hiro told her he would call round and see what the problem was. With his imagination working overtime, he was at the small house within thirty minutes, greeted by an anxious Marie.

He quickly solved the problem; one of the fuses had blown. Taking a great deal more time than was necessary, he replaced the damaged fuse. When he switched the lights back on Marie's face showed her gratitude. She insisted in giving him a cold drink, and they sat talking on the small balcony.

Hiro could not take his eyes off her as she lay back in the chair showing off her splendid legs. Her skirt seemed, in his eyes, to be moving further up her legs. He knew he must get away, before he made a complete fool of himself.

Making the excuse that he was the duty officer, he managed to make his escape, but not before agreeing to return for lunch the next day. Marie kissed him on the cheek as he left, promising something special for lunch. When he reached the barracks his mind was in turmoil, visions of he and Marie naked, their bodies thrashing passionately on the bed.

Peter J. Foot

As Hiro sat in the colonel's office the next morning, filing reports from the outlying units, the phone rang. It was Col Tihoka.

'I shall be stuck in this bloody place for another three days. Call round and make sure Marie is OK. If you are lucky she may give you lunch. Tell her I'll see her soon.'

Tihoka asked if there were any urgent matters to discuss. Hiro said, 'No', and the colonel rang off.

He left for Marie's cottage shortly before midday. He had taken great pains with his appearance. He had showered and changed into a clean uniform.

Marie greeted him at the door. She was wearing a white dress, which showed off her figure and tanned skin to perfection. Hiro felt a painful pang of lust consume him. She gave him some chilled wine. 'Tao loves this, It's Australian. He managed to get two dozen bottles from Singapore.'

'Tao, so that's his fucking name', thought Hiro.

Marie led him to the dining table. Lunch was superb, and Hiro was fascinated as Marie dominated the conversation. They had coffee, then sat on the balcony. As they chatted, he again noticed that Marie's dress was moving up to show more and more leg. His throat was dry and his face flushed. Suddenly she stood up and held out her hand. He took it and she led him into the bedroom.

He stood awkwardly by the bed as Marie stepped out of her dress. She was naked apart from a small pair of panties. She began to undo the buttons of his tunic. In a short time he stood naked, his erect penis betraying his desire. Then they were both on the bed, her hands and mouth bringing him to the brink. Just managing to control himself, Hiro spread Marie's legs and thrust himself fully into her. She was incredible. Her legs came up around his waist, her mouth claiming his tongue. He climaxed, but still her body wanted more.

Then they both lay exhausted on the bed, gasping for breath, their bodies covered in a sheen of perspiration. An hour later Hiro was back at the barracks, having promised to return that evening. He was worried at what he was becoming involved with.

Three days later Hiro was in his office when Tihoka returned. He saluted the colonel and reported all was well.

Tihoka looked pleased.

'Did you call on Marie as I asked?' he enquired.

'Yes Sir, she was fine, I repaired a fuse while I was there.'

He wanted to wipe the smug smile off the colonel's face by saying, 'And incidentally, we have been fucking one another senseless in your absence', but that would remain his and Marie's secret.

Tihoka gave a smirk.

'I won't be back tonight, I shall stay over with Marie. You can deal with anything in my absence. See you tomorrow.'

Hiro watched the colonel depart, with some envy. Marie had told him to come round whenever Tihoka was away. From what Hiro had heard, that would be quite often.

On the 9th of December 1944, Mick Martin led his mortar party on the three-day journey to attack the railway sidings just to the north of Ipoh town centre. They had left the Doc, Soo Lin, who had a slight temperature, and Mai Peng back in the cave. Soo Lin had wanted to come with them, but in Malaya a slight temperature can turn overnight into a raging fever.

With Peter Blake and Jim Muir taking it in turns to lead, they made good time reaching the pipeline intake in time to make camp for the night. The dry day was followed by a very wet night, but such was their expertise in constructing their night shelters they stayed dry.

By the end of day two they wanted to be in a position to cross into the Gunung Rapat complex and find a safe place to lay up for the day. There was no sign of any pipeline workers or Japanese soldiers as they worked their way carefully to their chosen point. As soon as it was dark they made their way across the open ground and just before dawn took shelter in a jungle-covered ravine on Gunung Rapat.

They rested there all the next day. A truck containing six bored looking Japanese soldiers passed below them on its way to the tin mine. An hour later it returned with six different soldiers, all chatting away and looking forward to enjoying the flesh pots of Ipoh.

As soon as it was dark they resumed their journey. They headed for the south of Tambun village with the intention of reaching the rubber plantation before dawn. It was less than half a mile from the plantation to the railway sidings, from where they would launch their attack the following evening.

They arrived at the rubber plantation well before dawn, and made their way into the thicker and somewhat overgrown centre. Mick Martin decided to rest up for a few hours, then move to the edge of the plantation before deciding on the best spot to locate their mortars for the night's attack.

After a good breakfast they took turns to rest, two on watch and four sleeping. At 1500 hours Mick Martin with Blake and Jim Muir, carefully made their way to the boundary of the plantation. Reaching the edge, they peered towards the railway sidings almost half a mile away. To find the best firing position they needed to get much closer.

Using some undergrowth as cover the three marines gradually worked their way to a point some three hundred yards from their target. They found an ideal position. It would enable them to fire the mortars from a low angle, which meant the bombs would be in the air for a shorter period of time than aiming them higher. When they returned to this position after dark, they could pace out the distance to their target to find the precise range.

Ralph Slater had coordinated three of his groups for the night's attack, with Jim Bottle to the north, Col Martin in the centre and Slater himself to attack Tapah station.

He had contacted Yong Hoy, inviting him to take part. Hoy said he might participate, with targets of his choosing. This was as much as Ralph Slater could expect. All the attacks were due to take place at midnight, giving the attackers the rest of the night to make good their escape.

By 2300 hours the marines and the two nurses were in position. They had brought two dozen bombs with them, twelve for each mortar. Peter Blake had checked the range by pacing out the distance to the target. They were five yards under three hundred.

The girls unscrewed all the protective caps from the bombs and sat by the mortars patiently waiting for the time to fire. At two minutes to midnight Blake and Jim Muir set the mortars at a low angle, judging the required degrees below forty-five. At one minute to midnight the girls loaded a bomb in each mortar, and at midnight Mick Martin quietly said, 'Fire.'

The six Japanese soldiers guarding the sidings heard their relief coming towards them. At the same time, they all heard a cough-like noise some way away. They all turned in the direction of the strange noise. The sergeant in charge was a veteran and recognised the noise.

'Get down, it's a mortar attack', he screamed.

As they hurled themselves to the ground the first two bombs exploded. The marines fired all the bombs in less than a minute, and then started to withdraw. They had five hours to reach the safety of the gunungs to the east of Tambun village.

The railway sidings were ablaze. Three tanks of oil and two of aviation fuel had received direct hits. This damage had been caused by six bombs; most of the others had missed vital targets. The resulting fierce fire had caused a chain reaction, involving an ammunition wagon deliberately parked some distance from the other wagons. It ignited with a stunning explosion, breaking every window within half a mile of the railway siding.

None of the Japanese soldiers guarding the complex had been killed, but all had suffered some injuries from the explosion, mostly burst eardrums.

Tao Tihoka and Marie had just fallen asleep after an exhaustive sexual encounter. Despite being nearly a mile away, the blast of sound almost threw them from their bed.

Capt. Hiro was reading in his bed when the explosion occurred. He phoned the guardroom and told the guard commander to get together twenty men and two trucks. He was at the guardroom in five minutes and was about to leave with the hastily assembled men, when the colonel rang from Marie's house.

Hiro explained what he was about to do. Tihoka, to his surprise, wished him luck, and said he was returning to the barracks immediately. He also asked Hiro which direction he would search in.

'Tambun area', said Hiro. 'I think they will try and get back to the jungle through there.'

With the light from the blazing goods yard behind them, the mortar party made good time through the rubber plantation. Within thirty minutes they were clear of the rubber and could see a few lights from Tambun village about a mile away.

As they made their way through the scrub only the darkness provided any cover. The Tambun road was now less than half a mile away. At this rate, in another twenty minutes they would be safe.

Mick Martin had taken the lead. They were only about fifty yards from the road when they all heard the sound of vehicles approaching at a high speed. There were two lorries. One stopped almost opposite their position and the other went further up the road before stopping.

They heard the sound of orders being given and of running feet. They could just make out the shape of Japanese soldiers lining up on the road facing them. They lay perfectly still waiting for the soldiers' next move. It soon became clear that the troops were being deployed in pairs about eighty yards apart. Capt. Hiro wanted to cover as much of the road as he could, but his troops were untried and he was forced to place them in pairs, covering in total about half a mile of the road where he judged the terrorists would try to cross.

Col Martin knew their best chance of escape was to cross the road under cover of darkness. If they stayed where they were discovery was certain as soon as it was light. Quietly and with great care they moved to a spot between the pairs of soldiers. It began to rain and, as the heavy downpour beat a tattoo on the trees bordering the road, they began to cross one at a time.

Blake was the last across. A flash of lightning illuminated him, but the bright flash had temporarily lost the Japanese soldiers their night vision. Within minutes they had put at least a hundred yards between themselves and the searching troops.

By dawn they were able to seek refuge for the day in one of the many covered ravines in the chain of gunungs. They made camp halfway up a steep gully and prepared breakfast with what remained of their rations. Then, with one of their number keeping watch, they tried to get some sleep before the heat of the day made them too uncomfortable.

At 0900 hours Blake took his turn on watch while the rest of the group slept quietly. He looked across at Joy. She lay asleep on her stomach, out to the world. The road was about a mile away and he could see some troops moving on it. About half a dozen were searching the undergrowth by the side of the road. He thought to himself, 'Just stay where you are chaps, don't come this way.' As he watched, more soldiers made their way from the road towards the gunungs, though not directly towards the gully they were hiding in.

With some reluctance Blake shook his sleeping colonel.

'You better take a look, Sir. They could be on to us.'

Mick Martin said nothing. Moving to the lookout post, he turned to Blake.

'Wake up the others, Corporal, we need to move.'

With Blake leading, and all of them now very much awake, they climbed further up the gully. As they neared the top the jungle cover all but disappeared. One by one they moved to the crest of the gunung. Then began the descent, at first frighteningly steep, but as the jungle began to give more cover it became easier. It was sheltered and cool on this side of the huge limestone feature, but they were covered in scratches from the thick undergrowth.

Well out of sight of the prying Japanese soldiers, they carried on, reaching the bottom of the gunung and moving with ease through the jungle at its base. They took a ten-minute break then continued their trek, now heading for safety in an unintended direction.

Chapter 38

Capt. Hiro knew he had lost track of the terrorists. He kept his men searching the undergrowth on both sides of the road, but knew it was pointless. At noon Col Tihoka appeared on the scene with a face like thunder. Hiro braced himself for the expected furious outburst, but it did not come.

Instead Tihoka looked at him and said, 'Take the men back to camp, Captain, you have done your best. HQ KL have ordered all troops to standby in barracks. There have been terrorist attacks all over Malaya.'

An hour later, and with all the soldiers back in camp, a visibly shaken Tihoka told Hiro, 'For the first time in four years of fighting I fear we are going to lose this war, and we need to plan for that eventuality.'

The two officers sat talking, neither liking what the future appeared to hold. Tihoka told Hiro.

'They want me back in Singapore next Monday, for five days. You will never believe this but we are making plans to repel a British invasion during the coming year.'

Later, as they drank coffee, Tihoka asked Hiro to keep an eye on Marie.

'She trusts you. She thinks you are very shy, but you remind her of her brother.'

Hiro nearly choked on his coffee, but managed to say, 'It would be an honour, my Colonel. You can rely on me to see she is safe.'

Hiro wanted to add 'and well fucked in your absence', but kept that thought to himself.

Mick Martin had decided that as they had been forced well north of their intended route back to the cave, they should make for the food dump just south of the Sungei Kinta. With any luck they would get to the location by late afternoon. With little food left, their empty stomachs would be urging them on.

Despite heavy rain, which at least kept them cool, they arrived just before 1700 hours. They extracted sufficient rations to get them back to Gunung Jasar and then made camp for the night. They erected just one shelter for all five of them and with full bellies settled down for the night.

As Blake finished his watch and settled down next to Joy, she squeezed his hand. Peter Blake suddenly realized what great comfort that gave him; it didn't need to be any more physical than a touch. He was definitely in love.

At dawn they ate a leisurely breakfast, before starting to remove all trace of their stay. They were about to resume their trek when they heard movement to their right in the direction of their food cache. Mick Martin led them quietly forward in extended line, ready for anything. They saw two figures removing food from their store. Raising their weapons and with fingers tightening on the triggers, they were about to fire when Jim Muir recognised the figures as the Doc and Mai Peng.

'They are friendly', he cried, his voice reflecting the urgency of the situation. With relief, they moved forward to greet their friends.

'What the hell are you two doing here?' said the colonel. 'And where is Soo Lin?'

The Doc explained all. They had received a radio message from Jim Bottle to say two of his men had been wounded, one quite seriously, and he needed medical help. One of Bottle's men would meet them at the regular Kinta crossing point and take them to Bottle's camp.

Soo Lin had told them to go and that she would stay behind and guard the camp until the others returned. After Mick Martin had digested this information, he told Blake and Joy to join up with the Doc and Mai Peng. He and Jim and Jan would head back to the cave with all speed.

Topping up their rations, and with Blake leading, the medical party headed for the Sungei Kinta. Doc Park, though he welcomed the added security of Blake and Joy, was disappointed he now no longer had the lovely Mai Peng to himself.

Mick Martin and his group reached Gunung Jasar in record time and just as the light was beginning to fade. Soo Lin was delighted to see them, in particular Mick Martin. She did not fancy another night on her own in the cave, where the wind created strange and disturbing noises in the honeycomb of passages.

After they had eaten they settled down for the night, Soo Lin showing Mick Martin how glad she was for his safe return. Standing watch, Jim Muir heard the unmistakable sounds of gasps and sighs and longed for his two-hour watch to finish so he could get back to his Jan.

The medical party reached the Kinta just before the light failed and crossed immediately. Waiting for them was one of Jim Bottle's men. Unable to go any further that night they settled down in one large shelter. There was a strong body smell in the shelter to keep them company. It was obvious that Jim's men did not put washing high on their list of priorities. The person in question slept soundly, unaware of the effect his presence had.

They made an early start the next day, conscious of the urgency of their mission. They reached Jim's camp just before 1500 hours, Doc Park losing no time in examining the two wounded men. The abdominal wound was the most serious and, with Joy's help, he operated straight away. It took him nearly two hours to complete the task. He thought the man's prospects were not good.

The other operation was more straightforward, with two bullets to be extracted from the man's thigh but luckily no damage to the bone. As he finished the second operation, his first patient was coming out of the anaesthetic.

Both the patients were kept in one shelter away from the others, Joy and Mai Peng taking it in turns to sit with them. Mai Peng had brought some of their mosquito netting with her and it was draped over the hospital shelter, making it almost insect free.

To the doctor's surprise and delight, both patients showed signs of making a good recovery. Jim Bottle was full of praise for his skill, but Doc Park cautioned optimism.

'This is not a hygienic place, it's alive with bugs, but the signs are encouraging.'

Peter Blake and Joy, despite her involvement with the two wounded men, wanted to get back to the cave. After ten days, the Doc thought he could leave his two patients and they could return to Gunung Jasar. With the thanks of Jim Bottle and the two wounded men, they started their return journey to their friends. As they left, Bottle wished them a Merry Christmas, which made them suddenly realise it was Christmas Day.

They reached the Sungei Kinta in the early evening. As it was still light enough, they crossed straight away, realising that if it rained during the night they may not have been able to cross in the morning.

They camped for the night a few hundred yards from the river. In the morning they raided their food dump again, taking enough food to last them for their journey to the cave.

Joy and Peter Blake had watched with interest the growing friendship between Mai Peng and the Doc.

Blake confided to Joy, 'Do you think he's slipped her a crippler yet?'

Joy laughed.

'Hardly a romantic expression, Peter, but I know what you mean. No, I don't think the "crippler" has been slipped yet, but it's just a matter of time.'

At noon the next day they came in sight of the cave, and two hours later were greeted warmly by their friends. They enjoyed a belated Christmas meal that evening, and to celebrate the occasion they had a double tot of rum each. Later that night they settled down to sleep and, with the exception of Mai Peng and the Doc, they all enjoyed a physical encounter.

Mai Peng could not sleep. She had heard the other couples making love, and her body ached for the same. She knew how Phil Park felt about her. Perhaps the time was right to begin a new relationship? She quietly moved across to where he slept and lay by his side. His arms drew her close. As his cheek brushed hers, he felt her tears on his face. He gently kissed them away.

Her hands were busy with her clothing and he felt her bare flesh against his. Slowly and with great tenderness they began to make love, then their movements grew more urgent. She met his passion with that of her own and they finally climaxed together in a frenzy of thrusting bodies.

There was a contented atmosphere in the cave now. The final coming together of the Doc and Mai Peng had restored the harmony that had existed before the death of Hari Khah.

For the Doc, life had changed completely. For him this was not a temporary romance. He was deeply in love with Mai Peng and had been for some time. He was even thinking of the future. Once the war was over he would stay in Malaya. He was a skilled surgeon and would be welcome in any hospital. This was something he would discuss with Mai as soon as the opportunity arose.

A message had been received from Jim Bottle concerning the two wounded men. Both continued to make good progress, with no apparent problems. Ralph Slater had also been in touch and advised that no further operations should take place until the Japanese relaxed their guard; all Japanese units were still on high alert following the pre Christmas attacks.

At the cave they spent their time cleaning the weapons and getting their stores lists up to date. Jim Muir, Blake and the two nurses had taken some more ration boxes up to the food dump near the Sungei Kinta, as the stocks there were getting low.

Col Tihoka had tasked Capt. Hiro to survey fifteen miles of west coast beaches to see if a seaborne assault would be possible in their area. Tihoka would need this information for his next visit to Singapore. Hiro approached this task with his customary thoroughness. Taking an experienced sergeant and ten men they spent a week checking the beaches. At times using a boat, but mostly by wading and swimming, they charted rocks and other obstacles. They also paid particular attention to the proximity of roads and ground firm enough to bear the weight of tanks and large trucks.

His men enjoyed the task they had been given and the rations they had taken with them. The ration packs were better fare than the barrack food, which consisted of fish and rice or, for a change, rice and fish. Either way they were sick of the repetitiveness.

They extended the week by three days, and when they returned to barracks Hiro had compiled a remarkably detailed map. The colonel was impressed. He had not expected anything so detailed and, without doubt, when he presented this to the top brass in Singapore his stock would rise.

'This is most impressive, Captain. You have surpassed yourself and justified the faith I have shown in you. Tomorrow I will take you to lunch as a reward.'

Lunch the next day was a disappointment. Hiro had anticipated being taken to the cottage with another chance to enjoy Marie's cooking. Instead lunch was at a local restaurant in Ipoh, but the food was good, as was the wine. As they were about to leave the colonel asked him to pay a visit to Marie whilst he was in Singapore.

'I shall be away for a week. Make sure everything is OK. She may even give you lunch.'

Two days later the colonel left for Singapore with Hiro's maps and detailed notes. As Tihoka was driven out of the barracks, Hiro breathed a sigh of relief. At 1300 hours he made his way to the cottage. Marie was pleased to see him and poured him a glass of chilled wine. After lunch they sat together, hands entwined. They kissed and Hiro's hands began to explore Marie's ample curves. In a short time her clothes were lying on the floor, mixed up with his. He carried her to the bedroom, lay her on the bed and began to kiss her all over. Then their bodies were joined in a frantic race for satisfaction.

As he left two hours later, she asked him to return that evening. He kissed her and promised he would.

That evening, as he was about to leave for Marie's, the colonel rang, asking if he had managed to see her. Hiro said he had called briefly, and she was fine and he would call in every other day.

Tihoka said, 'No, call every day. I worry about her and I can trust you to make sure she is alright.' He then rang off.

As he made his way to spend the night with Marie, Hiro felt a pang of guilt, but the thought of enjoying that beautiful body quickly eased his conscience.

Col Tihoka was half asleep. It was the third day of the conference, and as yet he had not been called to make his presentation. He had listened to the other colonels as they presented their assessments. Nearly all had a rough time from the senior officers present, who in general did not seem too impressed with their efforts.

At last the current performance ended. The Commander-in-Chief Land Forces tore the unfortunate officer to pieces.

'Rubbish! Lacks detail. You have failed totally to comprehend what we require. Return to your unit and this time, do a proper report. We will take refreshments now and when we return Col Tihoka will make his presentation.'

During the fifteen-minute break Tihoka prepared his maps and notes, reading them again to make sure he had missed nothing. As all the officers trooped back into the room, he was invited forward and, with a nod from the senior officer, began his presentation.

He spoke for thirty minutes, gaining confidence as he progressed, going to great detail to describe the areas where a successful assault could be mounted. When he finished he dealt with the numerous questions that were hurled at him. Some were quite technical, but thanks to Hiro's excellent notes he answered them all.

As he finished the room fell silent, waiting for the general to rip into the latest victim.

The general rose, looked around the room, and said, 'I am most impressed. Please join me for dinner this evening in my quarters; my aide will collect you at 2000 hours.'

All stood as the general left the room. Tihoka was dumbstruck. He was congratulated by the other officers; some even meant it. Eventually the colonel's breathing returned to normal. He lost no time in ringing Ipoh, to find out how Marie was. He spoke to Capt. Hiro, who enquired how the presentation had gone.

'It went well. I am invited to dine with the general tonight. Can you visit Marie?- She worries about me.'

Hiro explained he was duty officer and could not call on Marie until the next day.

'Detail someone to cover your duties and visit Marie tonight. She may even give you dinner.'

Hiro appeared to agree reluctantly and the colonel rang off. Hiro smiled to himself. He was already invited to Marie's that evening. He decided to give her a special shagging on the colonel's behalf.

Dinner with the general was very enjoyable. The food was excellent, as was the wine. There were only three of them, the third being the general's aide. After coffee, three rather attractive girls joined them; they were nurses from the local hospital. They sat talking and drinking till midnight.

Then the general rose and left the room with one of the girls. The aide explained that the colonel should stay the night. A room had been prepared for him and his companion and they would all take breakfast with the general at 0830 hours the next day.

The girl led Tihoka to their room, where she quickly removed her clothes to reveal a stunning body. She helped him undress, then treated him to a night of sexual delight that even Marie could not have equalled.

Tihoka was totally drained by morning. As the girl left his room at dawn he was quite relieved, but he was fascinated by her.

He joined the general for breakfast and was asked if he had slept well.

Tihoka smiled.

'Only when I was allowed to, Sir.'

The general gave a great bellow of laughter. After breakfast Tihoka was driven back to the conference building.

That evening, as the meeting finally finished, the general's aide handed him an envelope. Inside were his orders. He was to hand over his command in Ipoh to his next senior officer and return to Singapore unaccompanied. He was promoted to brigadier and would be on the general's staff, in charge of planning. His companion of the previous evening would move into his quarters with him. Tihoka was stunned.

When the colonel arrived back in Ipoh the next day, he immediately sent for Hiro and explained his new orders. He told him, 'You are now in charge here. I doubt if they will replace me and according to KL you will be moved up to acting major. This means, of course, that I must leave Marie behind. Look after her and in time she may accept you as her lover.'

Hiro could hardly disguise his joy. He enquired if the colonel intended to see Marie before he returned to Singapore.

'No', said Tihoka. 'It would upset her too much. I intend to leave for Singapore this evening. I want you to visit her tonight and break the news.'

That evening, as the colonel left for Singapore, he shook Hiro by the hand.

'You are a good man, Hiro. That report you compiled was first class, and I am grateful. I wish you well for the future.'

Hiro lifted his hand in a final salute as the colonel was driven away to his new post, then he made his way to the waiting Marie. When he arrived at the cottage Marie looked anxious.

'We must be careful, the colonel is coming back today. I don't want old "fat arse" to catch us.'

Hiro gently kissed her.

'My sweet, he's gone to take up a new post in Singapore. You are free of him.'

She looked stunned, then her face lit up.

'But will you want a colonel's cast-off?'

He smiled, 'Let's have dinner, then we will have an early night, and by the way please show me some respect. I am now an acting major.'

When Acting Maj. Hiro returned to the barracks the next morning, his mind still full of the wonderful night he had enjoyed with Marie, there was a message for him to contact Headquarters in Kuala Lumpur. The colonel he spoke to brought him down to earth with a bang. The Ipoh garrison was to be reduced to two companies, a total of two hundred men. He would remain in charge, but only in the rank of captain. His two junior officers would command the companies.

Hiro was not as disappointed as he thought he would be, at least he had Marie, and he could have found himself fighting for his life in Burma. The information that was filtering back from there was a succession of defeats, with the once invincible Imperial army in full retreat.

At lunchtime he visited Marie at the cottage, which in reality was a wooden bungalow. Its previous owner before the war, a rubber plantation manager from Dorset, had called it 'the cottage' in a moment of nostalgia and the name had stuck. Marie took the news of his demotion with a smile, saying, 'My dear Ro Ro, you have only recently been promoted to captain. Have some wine, and let's drink to our future.'

Chapter 39

The cave at Gunung Jasar was a hive of activity. Ralph Slater had visited to see in the New Year and had stayed for a fortnight. He had informed them that plans for the retaking of Malaya were well advanced. July or August were the favoured months, with landings on the west coast in at least two places. He was returning to Ceylon to discuss the plans, and was waiting for a date when he would be picked up by submarine.

The news of possible landings just a few months away was a great boost to their morale, as suddenly there appeared to be an end in sight of a war that had marooned them behind Japanese lines for so long. Ralph Slater also told them that the strength of their freedom fighters, or to give them their correct title, the Malayan People's Anti-Japanese Army, was now seven thousand. This figure surprised them all, but Malaya was a big place, and of course the changing fortunes of the Japanese forces had led to a rush of volunteers. The fact that the majority of these were Chinese, and politically Communist, was for the moment not important.

The day before the brigadier was due to leave, the date for his pick-up was received. It was to be in two weeks' time, so he left immediately to return to his group in Tapah. He needed to make sure his men were organised to operate in his absence. He told Martin's group he would return to them in one week and would appreciate an escort to the coast. Col Martin told him nothing would give them greater pleasure.

An airdrop was due and they made everything ready on the eastern slopes of Gunung Jasar. The three marines set up the torches and waited for the aircraft to appear. It was nearly two hours late and came in quite low from the south. They switched on the torches and a minute later the Liberator passed overhead. As it disappeared to the north the supplies crashed to the ground and they were all busy for at least two hours bringing them into the cave.

To their surprise, four new Sten guns were included, but unfortunately someone had forgotten to include the 9-mm ammunition. The rest of the stores were correct, more mortar bombs to replace those used, and everything else they had asked for, including red cloth to make the badges for their 'Senior Freedom Fighters'.

In Penang, things were going well for the Military Governor. The 'treasure chest' was expanding by the week. Tora Toshra and Anna had discussed with Sgt Hosan and Tia what they should do if the war came to a sudden end. Relocation to Thailand was their favoured option, by boat to the mainland then by car to the border via Butterworth and Alor Star. Toshra was counting on his friends in the Thai military to give them sanctuary. He could also grease their palms, providing they were not too greedy. He had toyed with the idea of making some contact with his old friends, but he judged it to be too early to make his plans known.

At weekends the four of them went to the old Governor's residence on Penang Hill. It was over a thousand feet above sea level, and cool in comparison to the Governor's house. All four were totally at ease with one another, despite the difference in rank. Toshra had asked Hosan if he intended to marry Tia.

'Of course. Why don't we make it a foursome?' replied his sergeant.

273

So the following weekend both couples were married, the bridegrooms' chests heavy with medals. The honeymoon was spent on the hill, the couples retiring early to bed to see if making love was different now they were married.

At breakfast the next morning both girls had a fit of the giggles. Tora Toshra demanded to know what was so amusing.

'Nothing, my Tora', said Anna. 'It's just that we are both so happy.'

Capt. Hiro had spent the last two days coming to terms with his depleted command. Now that he had only two companies he had halved the strength of each of his fortified outposts from ten men to five.

He spent every night with Marie; she had taught him a lot in the art of lovemaking. As a result their frequent encounters were not so frantic and lasted longer. She found Hiro a delight. Tihoka, though not an unpleasant man, had been rough with Marie in bed and had often hurt her. Hiro was so different, gentle and considerate.

Ro Ro, as she called him, was also beginning to think of the future. The unbelievable was happening; Japan's armies were being defeated in every sector. Hiro could see his country being beaten badly, unless some diplomatic avenue of escape could be found. He asked himself what would become of him and of Marie. The thought of being placed in a prisoner of war camp, while his Marie was raped by the Americans or British, whoever landed first, did not bear thinking about. He would devise a plan. Over the next week he applied his mind to an escape strategy. Thailand seemed to be the best option, but they would need money.

It was almost the end of January as Ralph Slater prepared to leave for the coast. Col Martin had decided that C/Sgt Muir and Cpl Blake would be his escort. The journey would take a week at least, and supplies would be left at the jungle's edge for part of the return journey. Joy and Jan made the two marines' last night at the cave a memorable one, and by dawn they were both thinking a few days away from the girls would give them a rest.

At 0900 hours the brigadier's party left. They made good time, reaching the pipeline just before dusk on the second day. They crossed the open ground in the dark and just before dawn sought shelter in one of Gunung Rapat's gullies. They cooked breakfast, then rested up for the remainder of the day.

As soon as it was dark they resumed their trek. They needed to be the other side of Ipoh before it got light. Despite being near to Ipoh, they saw no sign of any Japanese troops. Working their way round to the south, the group avoided any villages. The only moments of alarm occurred when they disturbed some dogs that lived among the small groups of huts on the edge of town. As soon as the dogs barked, someone inside the hut would shout and the dogs would then quieten down.

By dawn they were some five miles west of Ipoh, where they spent the day resting in a rubber plantation that was partly overgrown. That evening, after a meal, they resumed their journey. They walked by the side of the road, only diverting to avoid a village or a military post. When they were within a mile of the beach chosen as the pick-up point they hid in the undergrowth and waited for the rendezvous with the submarine.

It was a cloudy night with no moon as submarine HMS *Harpoon* surfaced three miles off the coast of Malaya. With the conning tower manned, it crept quietly towards the beach. At one mile out and in shallow waters it heaved to. Four Royal Marines, especially embarked for the mission, pushed their wood and canvas craft into the water and started to paddle for the beach. They had thirty minutes in which to cover the mile to the beach to arrive on time. When just two hundred yards out, two of the four left the paddling to the others and knelt in the bow, their weapons ready for action. Suddenly a green light flashed ahead of them. Dah Dah Dit Dah. Morse code for the letter 'Q', meaning 'beach here'.

Ralph Slater waded out to meet them, while Blake and Jim Muir watched from further up the beach. Slater was helped into the small boat. Then it quickly disappeared as the marines bent their backs and paddled hard back to where the submarine waited.

Within forty minutes, with the brigadier aboard, HMS *Harpoon* had reached deeper water and had submerged to begin its journey back to Ceylon and the Naval Base at Colombo. Ralph Slater thanked the marines who had picked him up. He told them about their colleagues who had escorted him to the beach and their base in the cave on Gunung Jasar.

When he told them they had been there three years, the marines to a man said, 'Poor bastards', but when he told them of their female companions, the expression was quickly changed to 'Lucky bastards!'

On the beach seeing their charge safely away, Jim Muir and Peter Blake made their way back to the safety of the undergrowth, and while it was still dark started on their return journey. Two nights later they reached the safety of the gully on Gunung Rapat, and spent the daylight hours there. As the light began to fail they ate what little remained of their food, then once it was dark they made for the jungle's edge south of the tin mine.

They reached the jungle well before daybreak and found their ration dump. As dawn broke they cooked a good breakfast and had their first mug of tea in two days. After taking a two-hour break they continued on their journey. Just before dark they made camp for the night. Tomorrow, by late afternoon, they should be back at the cave.

Joy and Jan had been sitting in the cave mouth since noon, expecting to see their men climbing up the steep slope towards them. Soo Lin relieved them at four and twenty minutes later she called out, as the two weary looking marines came into sight. As they were greeted warmly by the others, and in particular the two nurses, both marines admitted to being exhausted. Seeing the disappointed look on the girls' faces, they grinned and said a ten-minute rest and a cup of tea would see them ready for anything. As they drank their tea, they told Mick Martin of the journey and the pick-up on the beach. They also mentioned the total absence of any Japanese movement at night.

Later that night, as they settled down in their bed spaces, both girls showed how much they had missed them. Later, with their naked bodies still entwined, Blake and Joy decided on their long-term future. The next day Blake told Jim Muir he was going to marry Joy as soon as the war was over. Muir looked surprised.

'Strange, Jan and I decided to do that last night as well.'

They both looked in the direction of the two girls, who looked away, and started laughing.

Capt. Hiro and Marie lay naked on their bed, their bodies covered in a faint sheen of perspiration; it had been a strenuous encounter. Marie's hand gently stroked Hiro's penis, trying to persuade it to show some interest. The captain watched her efforts with some amusement.

277

He thought to himself, 'After what we have just done, it needs a rest.'

Marie played her trump card.

'Old fat arse was always ready again in ten minutes.'

Hiro's penis sprang to attention.

Marie smiled, 'But my Ro Ro is ready in five.'

Later the captain drove back to barracks, the ache in his balls a reminder of the afternoon's activities, thinking up an excuse to avoid visiting that evening.

When he arrived in barracks there was a message from Kuala Lumpur.

'Report here soonest.'

With some relief he rang Marie to give her the bad news, then left as instructed.

On arrival in Kuala Lumpur, Capt. Hiro was ushered into the office of the divisional commander. The old general greeted him cordially.

'Not good news, young Hiro. Our leaders have obtained some intelligence suggesting an Allied landing in force. The date is thought to be mid-July and the likely landing point the west coast at Lumut.'

Hiro swallowed hard.

'That's not too far from Ipoh, Sir. I did beach surveys there for Col Tihoka.'

'I know', said the general. 'The bastard is really stirring things up in Singapore, and the GOC thinks the sun shines out of his arse. We have been told to erect watchtowers thirty feet high along the coast, manned twenty-four hours a day. You will erect six in your area, a mile apart. Join me and the others for a meal tonight, then return to Ipoh in the morning.'

As Hiro left Headquarters the next morning for Ipoh, he had managed to extract another fifty men to help man the watchtowers. Engineers would arrive within the week to start the construction; the target was one tower a day, more if possible.

A few days later Capt. Hiro escorted a major in the Engineer Corps to the beaches at Lumut. After spending two hours inspecting the sites of the first two towers, the major took Hiro into his confidence.

'These towers are to be constructed of wood and are meant to be thirty feet high. Unfortunately the ground will not support that weight. The maximum height will only be twenty feet, and even then there may be some subsidence.'

After some further discussion both officers agreed to start the construction straight away, and by the end of the day the first two were almost finished. By the end of the week all of the towers in Hiro's area were completed. The flat platform at the top was five feet square and was protected from the elements by a canopy of wood and canvas. Each tower was equipped with a radio and binoculars, and halfway between the six towers a small military camp had been erected.

With their strength of fifty men, each tower had a team of six, working two hours on watch and ten hours off. When not on watch the men had certain duties in the camp to perform, but had plenty of free time. To entertain the Japanese soldiers a Brothel owner from Ipoh had opened a branch in Lumut; it was a great success.

Chapter 40

On arrival in Colombo, the submarine HMS *Harpoon* was met by a senior officer, who quickly drove Ralph Slater to Headquarters. After a shower and a change of clothes, he was ushered into the presence of the commanding general. He was warmly welcomed.

'You are doing a splendid job behind the lines. We are most grateful for your efforts.'

Over the next two hours Slater had the plan for the forthcoming invasion of Malaya explained to him. Only the date was not disclosed. The general emphasised the important role the Anti-Japanese Army was to play.

'In your area you must deprive the Japanese of easy access to the landing zone. Do not blow up the road bridges or the railway line. You must ambush all troop movements and delay them for as long as possible. This will enable us to get our men and tanks ashore.'

Over the next week Slater showed the general's staff the location of the Japanese troops and described their strength. He asked if the landing force would have air support. The officers looked embarrassed.

'We may get an aircraft carrier from the Royal Navy, but it's doubtful.'

Brig. Slater enjoyed his stay in Colombo, but he really wanted to get back to his men. He asked if he was to be returned by submarine.

'Not a chance old boy. The Japs have erected watchtowers along the west coast, so you'll be dropped back in by parachute.'

A far from happy Slater spent the next few days learning the basics of parachuting. His instructor had helped Doc Park. He was told not to worry, it would all be over very quickly.

'That's what is worrying me', said Slater.

A few days later he was sitting in the incredibly noisy fuselage of the four-engine Liberator, high above the Indian Ocean. The flight seemed to last forever. He tried to sleep, with little success, so he forced himself to eat a corned beef sandwich and drink some hot cocoa.

On the slopes of Gunung Jasar, the marines made ready to take their airdrop, and the VIP package. At last a faint drone from the south became a roar and the Liberator flew low overhead, trailing a line of parachutes. As the chutes reached the ground, the marines and the nurses ran out to secure their supplies. Peter Blake made for the figure still lying on the ground. As he reached him he could hear the string of oaths coming from their new comrade. To Blake's delight it proved to be Ralph Slater.

'Welcome back, Sir', he said.

'Thanks', said Slater. 'Get the Doc, I've broken my fucking leg.'

They carried their injured brigadier back to the cave, where Doc Park and the two nurses carried out a swift examination.

'Well,' said the Doc, 'I'm glad to say you have not broken your leg, just your ankle.'

With a circle of interested faces watching every move Doc Park placed the damaged ankle in a plaster cast, then elevated it on a pile of blankets. Ralph Slater was soon comfortable, with a mug of sweet tea in his hand, and telling them all of his adventures.

The brigadier had resigned himself for a stay of at least five weeks in the cave on Gunung Jasar. He and Mick Martin developed detailed plans for offensive operations against the Japanese when the Allied invasion came. This was not to be a hit and run operation, which was their normal *modus operandi*. This time they would have to stay and fight and deprive the Japanese of an easy passage to the coast. It was a sobering thought that, having avoided a stand-up fight for over three years, in the last few weeks of their stay in Malaya they might well all lose their lives. The two senior officers were determined to carry out the role that Headquarters in Ceylon had them in mind for, but would try to ensure a reduction in the risks involved.

They decided to take all of the personnel at the cave into their confidence. Most had already guessed what was in the air. They took the news of their role in the invasion quite calmly. They could see the danger that would face them, but they were all optimistic about their survival. The particular role for Mick Martin and his group was a moving ambush on the Ipoh to Lumut road.

Over the next few months they would need to move food and ammunition to various points along the road. Stage one would be the setting up of a large supply dump in the jungle's edge south of the tin mine. Stage two would require them to transfer all these stores to a point southwest of Ipoh. Stage three, moving the stores to various points along the Lumut road where they intended to mount their ambushes. With these substantial supplies of food and ammunition they hoped to delay the Japanese response to a seaborne invasion. Jim Bottle had been tasked with delaying rail reinforcements from the north, and with one or two road ambushes. Ralph

Slater's group would delay reinforcements coming from the south, and Yong Hoy's two large groups would hit the Japanese supply dumps in his area.

Of course they were not the only groups involved, with almost seven thousand freedom fighters under arms through the length and breadth of Malaya. They would all make life as difficult as they could for the Japanese when the invasion came. Ralph Slater confided to Mick Martin that certain senior officers in Ceylon thought the Japanese would not resist the invasion, but would stay in barracks and hope for a face-saving peace offer.

Mick Martin was not impressed.

'This sounds like the view of brass hats who have never fought the Japanese.'

Ralph Slater nodded his head.

'Don't worry Mick, the general at the top does not share that view.'

For the next week they all spent their time drawing up a list of the stores they would need to mount this operation. They were all surprised when they saw the massive amount they would have to move.

At the Japanese army base in Ipoh, Capt. Hiro had just returned from a visit to his new lookout towers. He was most impressed. The view from the towers was magnificent, despite being ten feet shorter than planned. He had climbed one to see for himself. In the bright sunshine and at that height you could even make out a dark smudge, which was the coast of Sumatra. Communications were good. Each post reported every thirty minutes, and the base camp reported to Ipoh every hour.

His relationship with Marie was a delight. He had made up his mind to make plans for their future. If there was an invasion he was not going to hang around and find himself a prisoner. Marie had told him her late mother had two sisters in Thailand. Both were married to quite wealthy Thais. Hiro suggested she contact them to see if they would be welcome.

Their love sessions were not as frantic as they had been. Both knew what the other enjoyed and, as a result, their sessions were not so frequent, but more satisfying. Despite taking precautions, Marie discovered she was pregnant. When she told Hiro he was delighted.

'You will have a son, who will be a great warrior', he said.

'Perhaps it will be a daughter, who will be a great beauty', said Marie.

'That', said Hiro, 'would also be very satisfactory.'

In Penang, Tora Toshra was most content. He and Anna were very happy, as were their friends Sgt Hosan and Tia. Already the treasure chest had grown far beyond their expectations. Toshra and the Thai government representative in Penang had formed a firm friendship, and Toshra in his direct manner had enquired if he would be welcome in Thailand.

The official had smiled.

'You are a wealthy man, my Tora. You would be welcome anywhere, and certainly in my country, as would your charming wife and your two friends.'

After this exchange, the envoy and his wife were frequent visitors to Government House. The envoy's wife confided in Anna that due to a medical condition her husband was unable to make love. He wanted her to take a discreet lover as he loved her dearly, and knew she had enjoyed the physical side of marriage. Anna said she would try to help, and passed on the information to Tora Toshra.

Toshra asked Sgt Hosan if he could suggest someone.

'Well Sir, she is an attractive lady. If I wasn't happily married I would take the job on myself. I'll make discreet enquiries.'

Two days later the sergeant went to Toshra's office.

'Problem solved. Pte Yama will do some gardening at the envoy's residence five afternoons a week.'

'Is he suitable?' asked Toshra.

'Yes Sir', said Sgt Hosan. 'He is hung like a bull elephant, with a sexual appetite to match.'

A few weeks later a smiling envoy and an equally happy wife had dinner at Government House.

'How are things?' enquired a curious Toshra.

The envoy gave a conspiratorial grin.

'The garden is looking wonderful and so is my wife. She is always smiling. That man you lent us seems very good at his job.'

As a result of her enquiries, Marie had two replies from her aunts in Thailand. One was not enthusiastic about Marie and her Japanese officer boyfriend visiting. However, the other, her Aunt Mona, said she and her husband would be pleased to see them and, with their large house, they could stay as long as they liked.

Capt. Hiro was delighted and suggested that Marie pay her aunt a visit. He would arrange transport and a pass. A week later an excited Marie was driven to the border by one of Hiro's drivers. Her pass was examined by a Japanese sergeant, who insisted on running his hands over her body. She complained angrily. He leered at her and said he was making sure she was not armed.

She walked across the border and paid for a taxi to her aunt's village. Thailand was not like Malaya, and had very few troops on the roads.

Peter J. Foot

She arrived at her aunt's in the late afternoon. It was clear by the size of the house that she had married well. Aunt Mona welcomed her warmly.

'I have not seen you for ten years. You have grown into a beautiful woman.'

Marie spent the next two hours telling her aunt about her mother and father's death, and about her friendship with Capt. Hiro. When Mona's husband came home, she had to explain everything again.

When she had finished, he smiled and said, 'You are welcome in our house any time. This includes your captain.'

After a week with her aunt and uncle, Marie thought it was time she returned to Ipoh. She contacted Capt. Hiro who told her he would send a car for her the next day. Promising to return, she made her way back to the border. The same obnoxious Japanese sergeant was waiting on the Malayan side. He took her by the arm, led her to his office and shut the door. Grinning, he ordered her to remove her clothes.

'I intend to conduct a proper search this time', he said.

At that moment the door opened and one of Capt. Hiro's young officers came in. He saw the fear on Marie's face.

'Please wait outside, Madam', he said.

As she left the office, she heard the officer's angry voice and the sound of fist hitting flesh.

The drive back to Ipoh was very pleasant. She thanked the young officer for saving her from the unwelcome attentions of the sergeant.

He smiled. 'You are my captain's lady, I have a duty to protect you. That sergeant needed to be taught a lesson.'

She was driven to her cottage, and an hour later a worried Hiro arrived on the scene. After they had a meal, she told him of her visit and the invitation for them both to visit or stay. She also told him of the unwelcome attentions of the border sergeant and the timely arrival of the young officer. Hiro was furious, but after he calmed down he said, 'I will thank Lt Anso tomorrow. As for the sergeant, his days are numbered.'

In bed that night, after a long and slow session of love-making, Hiro kissed her stomach.

'And how is our son?'

Marie laughed, 'If he was asleep, I think you have just woken him. He's very small. I am only two months' pregnant after all.'

Mick Martin and his group had started to move the supplies to the jungle's edge just south of the tin mine. They cleared an area of bamboo and hid two weeks' rations under a pile of Atap palm. It was hard work and they were all involved, except Ralph Slater who was still in plaster. It would be another couple of weeks before he would be mobile again.

They moved their entire stock of mortar bombs, sixty in number, over the next week, then started on the grenades and ammunition. After ten days, Mick Martin decided to give them all a five-day break. It was most welcome. All the girls were exhausted, and the men needed a break as well.

It was now the last week in February, but there was still no firm news of the invasion date, even though the Japanese were taking a beating in every area. There was news of some desertions in the Japanese army. Those caught were immediately executed, but it was apparent the rot was beginning to set in. The best of the Japanese troops were still fighting hard in Burma and the many islands they had held in the Pacific Ocean.

Chapter 41

In Penang, Tora Toshra could not believe how dramatically the war was changing. He had thought that the situation would be so bad by September, that would be the time to make for Thailand. But he had changed that date in his mind now to July or August. All was arranged: transport across to the mainland, and two cars for the journey up through Malaya to the Thai Border.

Through his friendship with the Thai envoy, Toshra had already purchased two substantial properties near Pattani, paying for them in rubies. The friendly envoy had provided a letter of introduction to one of the banks in the port of Pattani.

At one of their frequent dinner parties, the envoy's wife had asked Toshra if they could keep their gardener.

'He is such a treasure, our garden is a picture. I don't want to lose him.'

Toshra promised to do what he could. Sgt Hosan had told him that he had heard the envoy's wife couldn't keep her hands off their man.

Pte Yama had told Sgt Hosan, 'As soon as I arrive she wants to play with it. I fuck her at least twice a day; she wants it in every position you can imagine. I think I'm in love.'

Capt. Hiro had been summoned to Kuala Lumpur again. The old general who was in charge of all troops in Malaya was not in the best of health. He wearily greeted Hiro.

'I hear the watchtowers are a great success, but I am not sure we will appreciate their value. Singapore has had a change of heart.'

The general went on, 'It has been decided that we do not have the troops to defend in depth a seaborne assault. Word is we will fight hard to defend Singapore and Kuala Lumpur and attempt to obtain some honourable settlement. The British will not want to see either of them completely destroyed in a long siege, so we may achieve some compromise.'

Capt. Hiro thought on what he had said, then asked, 'Where does that leave me and my men as regards Ipoh?'

A faint smile played on the general's lips.

'Up shit creek without a paddle, my young hero. You will be expected to oppose an assault, but for how long will be up to you.'

Hiro was shocked. He could not believe that the huge Japanese war machine had reached such a weakened state. Seeing how the news had shocked the young officer, the general put his hand on Hiro's shoulder.

'Go back to your command and plan for the future. *Your future*, need I say more?'

Hiro thanked the sick old man and left. As he was driven back to Ipoh his mind was made up. He must get Marie to her aunt. Then he would think of his own situation.

Unaware of the limited Japanese plans to oppose an invasion, Brig. Slater was going ahead with the build-up of their supplies. All the groups under Slater's control were moving their military stores to their strategic positions.

Mick Martin and his group had spent the last week moving stores from the jungle's edge to a rubber plantation south of Ipoh. In one corner of the overgrown plantation there was a partly collapsed shed and they hid their stores there. It took them six nights to complete the transfer and it was exhausting work. They made their way back to the cave for some rest before their return the next week to complete the movement to their first defended position on the Ipoh to Lumut road.

Peter Blake and Jim Muir had discussed the plan to delay the Japanese response to an invasion. They were not too optimistic as to their ability to survive.

'After all this time taking risks and giving the Japanese the occasional bloody nose, in the final stages of this business we could all be killed', said Blake.

Jim Muir laughed, 'Hang on a minute, Peter. We could have all been killed in the final stand at Tambun. Because of Joy and Jan we have had the best three years of our lives, don't forget that.'

Blake was forced to agree, but insisted they shouldn't view what could be their final operation as a suicide mission.

Further south, Yong Hoy was completing his plans to support the invasion. He was thinking some way ahead. The attack he would make on the Japanese supply dumps would be to destroy the small garrison. He had long-term plans for the food and ammunition that the dumps held. His mind was already deciding where he could hide his booty. Suzy Han, his lover and commander of his second group, had suggested hiding all of their 'prizes' in the many caves in their area. Nobody would dare thieve what was Yong Hoy's.

A careful and discreet examination of these caves convinced Yong Hoy Suzy was right. They would be ideal, and he had enough men to leave a token guard on the sites. He slept with Suzy Han that night. She was a delight in bed, with an appetite for sex that matched his own. In the morning before he left, she asked him if he was faithful to her.

'I may have other women to ease the pressure of command, but I love only you.'

She kissed him. 'I am satisfied with that', she said.

As Yong Hoy left to rejoin his other group, he thought on what he had said to Suzy Han. He realised, with some surprise, that he had spoken the truth.

After a gentle bout of love making, Hiro put his arm around Marie as they lay in bed.

'I want you to arrange with your Aunt Mona for you to go and stay with them in Thailand. I will join you later. We will need to live there for at least a couple of years, until the after-effects of the war have subsided.'

Marie thought on what he said, and could see it to be the only solution to their problem.

'I will write to Aunt Mona tomorrow, my Ro Ro. You are right. That is where our future is, for all *three* of us.'

The next morning Capt. Hiro left for his barracks in a better frame of mind. His concern over Marie could soon be solved if her Aunt was cooperative, then he would only have himself to worry about.

There was not a great deal for him to do in the camp, so he decided to pay a visit to the tin mine with half a dozen men. The manager made him welcome and poured out all his troubles over coffee. He looked closely at the captain, wondering if he could speak frankly.

'May I share some news with you, Sir?' he asked.

Hiro nodded.

'My workforce seems to think you will be driven out of Malaya within six months. Of course I have said that will never happen, but could it be true?'

Hiro smiled, 'The war will not last forever and who knows what tomorrow will bring.'

The manager realised his questions were falling on stony ground, and tried another ploy.

'I recently have recruited two young girls to my workforce. We could have some fun with them if you wish; they are very pretty.'

Hiro stood up, 'I suggest you concentrate your energies on producing tin. If you cannot do that I will have you replaced.'

Tora Toshra was having a discussion with Sgt Hosan about their future.

'It will soon be time to send Anna and Tia to Thailand, and deposit most of our treasure chest there. The bank manager there will cooperate.'

The sergeant looked at his friend. 'Will we be apart for long? I will miss my Tia.'

Toshra sighed, 'That is why you are still a sergeant. Every decision you make is dictated by what dangles between your legs.'

Toshra went on, 'We now have plenty of money. When we get to Thailand we will open a business, as equal partners, but the girls need to go first. Trust me.'

Sgt Hosan gave a sigh of relief.

'You know I will follow you anywhere, and do anything you say. I trust you as a friend and leader. Please forgive my doubts.'

Toshra gave his friend a playful punch, 'And with Tia in Thailand, you can help poor old Yama, he's beginning to look quite exhausted.'

Ralph Slater was now fit to travel to his main group. Blake and Jim Muir offered to escort him most of the way. They left as soon as they had breakfasted. With Blake leading they took it easy, as it was Slater's first real trek since the Doc had removed his plaster cast. By noon the brigadier was looking a little worn, so they stopped for an hour.

By 1600 hours Jim Muir thought they had done enough for the day and they made camp for the night. After they had cooked a meal, they ate in silence, but when they made tea Ralph Slater asked them what they would do when the war was over. Both marines had decided to stay on in the marines for the pension, which was twenty-two years from the age of eighteen.

Slater said he was thinking of staying on in Malaya. There would be a post for him in either the police or military.

'You both could do a lot worse, and you have your girl friends to consider. Don't rule it completely out.'

Later, when he was on watch and the other two were sleeping, Blake thought about what the brigadier had said. He knew Col Martin and Soo Lin were going to stay on. He would discuss it with Joy.

By noon next day the weather, which was looking stormy, finally broke. They hurriedly made camp, just managing to get their shelter erected before the rain became torrential. It thundered and the lightning flashed all over the sky. In all the time they had been in Malaya, this was the worst storm yet. Several lightning strikes hit trees not far from them, and it went on for the rest of the day. Just after dark the storm eased, and the night passed almost peacefully, with just a gentle rain. At dawn they could hear the nearby Sungei Chenik in full flood. It had always seemed such a quiet little river, but today was different. It seemed angry and threatening. To complete their journey to Ralph Slater's camp they needed to cross the river, but at the moment that was out of the question.

They waited until the next day to cross. The river had fallen considerably, but it still required care in crossing it. Halfway across Ralph Slater slipped over. Blake grabbed him

293

and heaved him upright. Slater smiled his thanks and safely made it to the riverbank.

By mid-afternoon they reached the brigadier's camp. Most of his men were out moving supplies to their chosen positions, ready for the promised invasion. His men were pleased to see him, and Ralph Slater insisted the marines stayed the night. With the brigadier's men doing the night watches, Blake and Jim Muir had a good sleep. After breakfast, with the thanks of Ralph Slater still fresh in their ears, they started the return journey to Gunung Jasar.

It took them two full days to make their way back to the cave, reaching their friends just before it got dark. That night, after he and Joy had made love, he asked her if she fancied staying on in Malaya.

'I will if you will', she said.

Blake ran his finger around the nipple of her right breast. It hardened, and his penis reacted in empathy. Joy guided him between her legs.

'Twice in an hour', she said. 'And judging by the sounds from Jim and Jan we are not alone. What have you boys been eating?'

Brig. Tihoka was feeling well satisfied with life. He was now an established figure in the Singapore Headquarters' machine. What was of importance was his close relationship with the commanding general. Tihoka had spent the last week working on a defensive plan for Singapore and Indonesia. He was due to present it to the general after lunch. He no longer missed Marie. His present companion was more than an adequate substitute, and was quite happy to perform in any position his mood dictated. She had introduced him to what she called the 'love drug'. Its effect on Tihoka was dramatic, driving him to perform sexual acts he had never dreamed of. Last night they had surpassed themselves, both falling asleep exhausted in the early hours of the morning.

It had needed several cups of strong coffee before he was fit to go to Headquarters. His companion was still asleep, her naked body sprawled in an abandoned position on the bed, tempting Tihoka to have her again. He resisted the temptation. He needed to be fully alert for the afternoon planning meeting, hoping to impress the general even more. He spent the rest of his free time going over his plans and his notes, hoping he had covered all the expected questions.

Tihoka made his way to the conference room in good time for the meeting. The colonel from the Indonesian Command was already there. He and Tihoka had become friendly over the last week or so, and had dined together several times. Tihoka had also persuaded his female companion to bring a 'friend' on these occasions, and the colonel had been delighted.

As soon as the conference room was full the general indicated to Tihoka that he could begin. An hour later the general was congratulating him on the presentation.

'A first-class job, Tihoka, as I expected. I want you to fly over to Indonesia tomorrow and acquaint them with our plan. Well done.'

Tihoka thanked the general, and gathered up his notes. His friend the colonel asked if he could fly back to Indonesia with him.

'Of course', he said. 'I shall be glad of the company.'

Flying was not one of Tihoka's pleasures. In fact, he was terrified and he would have preferred to make the journey by sea.

That evening they went to Tihoka's quarters after dinner, the colonel once again provided with a companion by Tihoka's girl friend. After a few drinks they all took 'the love drug'. It led to a night of debauchery. At one point Tihoka and the colonel both had sex with the colonel's companion, with Tihoka's girl friend as an interested spectator.

In the morning there was a rush to get showered and changed and be at the military airfield at Changi by 1000 hours. The flight to Indonesia was to be in a converted bomber. It was not uncomfortable and there were only two other passengers. There was a slight delay when one of the two engines was reluctant to start, but after some frantic attention, and with both engines now running, they taxied to the end of the runway. Tihoka shut his eyes as the plane, engines roaring, rushed down the runway and, with some reluctance, left the ground and slowly climbed to its cruising height.

With the now throttled-back engines having a soporific effect, Tihoka and his fellow passengers fell into a comfortable sleep. One of the crew served some coffee from a thermos flask after an hour, and Tihoka, who was seated next to one of only two windows in the fuselage, looked down at the sea a few thousand feet below him. As he drank his coffee, he could see mirrored in the sea the reflection of their plane; then strangely he saw two more reflections.

He was about to draw his friend the colonel's attention to it when their plane gave a lurch, turned hard to port and went into a steep dive. Then they were almost thrown from their seats as, with both engines roaring at full power, they climbed steeply, this time turning hard to starboard. One of the crew shouted, 'American fighters! There are three of them.' Then the plane was diving for the sea again.

The flight of three American fighters had completed their patrol, some hundred miles south of their aircraft carrier, when they saw the Japanese bomber. With only a limited amount of fuel left they could only make one pass at the

Japanese aircraft before heading for home. As the doomed bomber desperately tried to avoid the fighters, the flight commander ordered his planes to make one attacking run. The first and second planes' machine-gun fire missed as the bomber slipped to one side. The flight commander anticipated the bomber's next manoeuvre and fired a long raking burst into its port engine and cockpit. It lurched to the right and began a twisting tumble to the sea, flames pouring from the port engine. As the three fighters left the scene they saw the plane hit the sea in a great spout of water and disappear from view.

With the crew dead, the passengers clung to one another in sheer terror as the plane tumbled out of the sky. Just a few seconds from impact Tihoka managed to have one last thought. It was of his beautiful Marie. He tried to say 'I loved you', but only managed 'I love … '. His body, and that of his companion, was pulverised as the plane struck the water.

The shattered pieces of human flesh provided a meal for a passing shark and other lesser fish. The heavier pieces of the bomber eventually reached the seabed, lost forever. The crew of a small Indonesian fishing boat had seen the aircraft crash. They made for the scene, not in an effort to see if there were any survivors, but to see if they could salvage anything of value to supplement their meagre wages. They were disappointed. The sum total of their finds was only a few items of torn bloodstained clothing and a briefcase. They took the briefcase with them; the Japanese might give them something for it.

It was a week later that news of Tihoka's death reached the ears of Capt. Hiro. He thought of telling Marie, then decided against it. It might cause her some distress and he didn't want that. She had heard from her Aunt Mona. She could go and live with them as soon as she liked. She and Hiro discussed a leaving date that night and, with some reluctance, Hiro persuaded her to leave at the end of April, just a couple of weeks away.

With Marie safe with her aunt in Thailand, Hiro felt he could do his duty in trying to repel an invasion, then, when defeat was obvious, he could join her in Thailand with a clear conscience. His major concern was money, or rather the lack of it. He needed to obtain some tradable goods of high value; silver or gold would do, of course, or precious stones.

The next day Capt. Hiro went to the offices of Ipoh's largest bank. The manager received him with typical bland politeness. Hiro decided he would put his cards on the table. Looking the manager in the eye, he said,

'If I arrived with ten armed men and forced you to open your strong room, what would we find?'

The manager paled and a rapid twitch assailed his left eye.

'It would be illegal for you to do that. The Japanese High Command have protected our banking system. You would be severely punished', said the manager, now regaining his confidence.

'Bollocks!' said Hiro. 'Who would report me? You would be dead.'

A look of pure horror came over the manager's face. He licked his lips.

'How can I be of assistance?' he said.

Chapter 42

Mick Martin and his group returned to the cave. They were tired after their week's exertions, but satisfied that everything was now in place to support the coming invasion. It had been hard and dangerous work moving their supplies to their selected defensive positions, sometimes even moving in daylight.

Martin had discussed with Soo Lin their future once the war was over. She had raised her eyebrows when he suggested he could join the Malay police or the Malayan army. But the idea of them staying together after the war clearly was important to her. He was not the only one thinking of the future. Doc Park's mind was almost made up, and a future in this beautiful country had great appeal.

Peter Blake returned to his bed space after his watch, hoping to persuade Joy into making love. He was disappointed; she appeared fast asleep. As he settled down beside her, a warm soft familiar hand slid down inside his trousers and captured his rapidly awakening penis. They settled into the exciting routine of making love, each determined to give the other pleasure. He gave her breasts a lick around, the nipples on each breast springing to attention. Slowly he entered her, her legs climbing up around his waist preventing a premature exit. At last they both climaxed, and settled back to sleep, their bodies still entwined.

Capt. Hiro was pleased with the visit to the bank manager. They had reached an understanding, which would benefit them both. At a given time Hiro would go to the bank and at gunpoint force the manager to open the strong room. He would force the rest of the bank staff, two men and two women, into a room and lock them in. He would then remove some silver, gold and some precious stones. The manager would take an equal amount, placing it in his private office.

Hiro would then tie up the manager and leave, driving straight to the Thai border to rejoin Marie. The manager would then claim that the Japanese officer had taken all that was missing, leaving them both richer and the manager blameless.

He told Marie of their plan. She was worried the manager would betray him, but knew the haul Hiro planned to take would provide handsomely for their future. Her pregnancy was just beginning to show. Those not in the know would think she had just put on some weight. She was still stunningly attractive and Hiro counted himself a lucky man.

In Penang, Tora Toshra was making his plans for a rapid exit for himself and Hosan should the need arise. Plans for Anna and Tia to go on ahead were already in place. They wanted to leave the girls' departure until the last minute.

The Thai envoy and his wife both knew of Toshra's plan and would assist their friends once they were they in Thailand. Pte Yama was now living at the Thai Embassy and Toshra was releasing him from the army on medical grounds. The exact medical condition was unspecified. The envoy and his wife were delighted to have Yama's services on a permanent basis. It was a strange relationship. Yama was a crude, uncultivated man, but he made the envoy's wife smile and that made the envoy happy. Yama thought life was wonderful and was in love with Shan, who, though she loved her husband, had strong feelings for Yama as well.

In the United States of America, decisions were being made that would have a dramatic effect on all the Japanese-occupied territories. Few people were privy to these plans, least of all the commanding generals on the British and American side. The American Pacific Command had already prepared a plan for the invasion of Japan, with projected figures for the casualties that the invading force would suffer. When the American President and his advisors saw these figures they were horrified, and began to put in train their secret alternative to speedily end the war.

Totally unaware of these plans, Brig. Slater was finalising his arrangements to support a British invasion. Ceylon had put on standby the necessary naval and military units required to secure a bridgehead in the Lumut area of Malaya, while in Singapore and Kuala Lumpur, Japanese Headquarters were finalising their plans for a limited defence of the larger cities in the Malayan Area.

On the 28th of April, Capt. Hiro drove Marie to the Thai Border. The sergeant who had upset Marie on the previous occasion saw them, but he remained in his office. Marie's Aunt Mona was waiting for her on the Thai side. Hiro was embraced by Mona who told him Marie would be safe with them. After saying their goodbyes, a tearful Marie was driven away by her aunt, leaving Hiro devastated.

The Japanese sergeant was about to leave his hut and speak to the captain, but the expression on Hiro's face suggested he should stay where he was. It was a long and lonely journey back to Ipoh. The two soldiers acting as escort to Hiro kept silent, aware of their captain's feelings. Later that night he slept alone in the cottage. The sheets still carried a faint trace of Marie's perfume and this added to his sense of loss.

Now that Marie was safely in Thailand, Capt. Hiro was free to concentrate on his military duties. His arrangement with the local bank manager seemed to have solved the position of their long-term finances.

Every military communiqué seemed to bring more bad news. The morale of his garrison was low and there had been several acts of indiscipline by the younger soldiers. One thing in Hiro's favour was his popularity; he was seen as a fair man. The sergeant who was at the tin mine when it was mortared, and who had called the then Lt Hiro 'a stupid prick', was now one of his greatest admirers. He was aware of the trust this particular senior NCO had in him and had decided to use him in the bank operation.

The captain's daily routine involved visiting his static posts on the roads and railway line, and the lookout towers which would give them some warning of an attack from the sea. In a recent briefing in Kuala Lumpur, all the officers present had been warned of the danger of a combined attack from the Anti-Japanese Army acting in support of the expected landings from the sea.

Col Martin and his group at Gunung Jasar were growing impatient with the lack of a firm date from Headquarters in Ceylon. They needed at least two weeks' notice to be able to move to their chosen positions. Ralph Slater had pressed Ceylon for more information, but had been told to be patient.

Mick Martin had toyed with idea of not using the women in the coming operation and had mentioned it casually to Soo Lin. She was horrified at the idea, and warned him he would face a mutiny if he tried to break up the couples after all this time.

All four couples had now discussed their future if they survived the war. Staying in Malaya seemed a popular choice. Doc Park and Mai Peng still paid the occasional visit to Hari Khah's grave. Both realised once they left Gunung Jasar they would never return. It was a sad thought.

In Penang, Tora Toshra's plans were in place for the girls to leave. He and Sgt Hosan would follow as soon as the situation allowed. Both could not afford to be captured, as this would jeopardize the safety of Anna and Tia.

The support of the Thai envoy was crucial. Toshra had asked if there was any service he could provide. The envoy had thought for a few minutes.

'My friend, my wife is happier than she has ever been since my illness. That gives me joy, but of course one can always use more money. I have no private wealth. I am sure you understand, my Tora.'

Toshra did understand. In future, a percentage of their profits went into the envoy's account and everyone was happy. Sgt Hosan asked the former Pte Yama if he needed any help in entertaining the envoy's wife.

Yama laughed.

'I am no longer under your authority, you old bastard. Shan and I are very happy. You should be satisfied with your pretty Tia.'

Hosan was disappointed with Yama's response. He was thinking of his own physical needs once Tia left for Thailand, and the envoy's wife was very attractive.

The Indonesian fishermen who had found the briefcase of the late Brig. Tihoka were rewarded for returning the item to the

Japanese. The value of the reward allowed them to give up fishing for a week and spend their time drinking and using the pretty young girls who frequented the waterfront bars.

One of the men, who had opened the briefcase to see if it contained money, confided to one of the girls that the case had contained plans to stop the coming Allied invasion of Malaya and Sumatra. Later that same evening the girl passed this information to a local merchant, who gave her regular money for such intelligence. Two days later Ceylon was aware of the Japanese plans and put back the invasion to August.

Marie was very happy with Aunt Mona. She gladly helped her uncle in his office; it kept her mind off her Ro Ro. For the first time in years she was without regular sex and to her surprise it did not seem that important, though she did have a pang of regret when she heard her aunt and uncle groaning and gasping in their bedroom one night. She was surprised they still did it; after all they were nearly fifty years old. She had received two letters from her captain. Both referred to their financial position, with the welcome news that this was taken care of. She did not understand the implications but was happy just to receive the letters. Her aunt had taken her to the family doctor to make sure all was well with her pregnancy. The doctor said she was an extremely healthy young woman and would have a fine baby.

Mick Martin decided the lack of activity was a bad thing, so he took his two marines on a scouting trip to the tin mine. It took them two days to reach the jungle's edge, but Peter Blake and Jim Muir were glad of the exercise as they were getting bored, despite the attractions of Joy and Jan.

They watched five Japanese soldiers wandering around the area of the mine. The original number of ten had clearly been reduced. The soldiers were more interested in two young girls who were now working there and the girls clearly enjoyed teasing the soldiers, but never got too close to them.

That night the marines moved out past the tin mine, almost into the Sungei Raia Gorge, with the intention of shooting up the relieving guards the next day. In the early hours of the morning, the marines were surprised to hear the noise of a truck leaving the tin mine at high speed. To their surprise, when it went past their position it contained the five soldiers from the tin mine, still getting dressed with their equipment strewn over the floor of the vehicle. Clearly some emergency had occurred.

'Surely the invasion hasn't started?' thought Col Martin. He decided to find out.

The three marines boldly made their way back to the tin mine and entered the manager's office. The manager almost fell off his chair at the sight of the British marines.

'How did you get here so quickly?' he babbled. 'The invasion fleet was only spotted an hour ago.'

Two hours earlier, one of the lookouts in the towers near Lumut had spotted some lights flashing about ten miles out to sea. He had reported this to the duty sergeant, who asked if there were many ships out there. Confused, the man said there could be. The sergeant, not wishing to act in haste, informed the duty officer in the beach camp that some unidentified ships were off the coast. The officer, who was still half asleep, informed Ipoh and Capt. Hiro that the invasion was about to begin.

Hiro informed Kuala Lumpur he was about to investigate a possible Allied landing at Lumut, and left for the beach area with almost his entire garrison. Four medium-sized guns took up position five miles west of Ipoh ready to shell the landing area.

On arrival at the beach, Capt. Hiro deployed his two hundred men, instructing their two young officers and senior NCOs to make sure the men quickly dug in ready to try and repel an attack.

Hiro climbed one of the towers and questioned the soldier who had reported the armada. The man said he had merely reported strange lights at sea. It was now almost 0500 hours and nearly dawn. Hiro scanned the sea in the direction the man had indicated through the powerful binoculars and he could make out five small fishing boats.

He gave a sigh of relief. It was clearly no invasion. He turned to the soldier standing beside him. The man flinched, expecting a rain of blows or worse.

Hiro smiled, 'You did your duty, you will never be punished for that.'

He left the soldier and climbed down from the tower, quickly issuing his instructions.

'Inform KL it was a false alarm.'

He turned to his young company commanders.

'When you are satisfied with your men's defensive positions return to Ipoh.'

Hiro then left for Ipoh with his loyal Sgt Manu. On their way back they informed the artillery officer he could stand down and return to barracks. When Hiro arrived back at camp, he told Sgt Manu that they would be calling at the main bank in Ipoh later that morning, and to bring a canvas holdall.

The manager of the tin mine sat at his desk, the marines covering him with their weapons. The phone rang. Col Martin indicated that the manager should answer it, but warned that he should not betray their presence. The manager listened then hung up.

'Who was it?' said Col Martin.

'It was the army camp in Ipoh. There is no invasion; it was a false alarm. My five guards will return this afternoon.'

Mick Martin was relieved.

'You will not speak of this visit. In a few months the Japanese will be beaten. If you inform on us you will die, is that understood?'

The terrified manager promised he would keep silent, and the three marines left. Twenty minutes later they were in the safety of the jungle and on their way back to their friends on Gunung Jasar.

The manager of the bank was surprised by the arrival of Capt. Hiro and his sergeant.

'The plan has changed', said Hiro. 'We need to remove some valuables now. Rest assured you will be well rewarded in due course.'

The manager, with some reluctance, led them to the strong room, and out of sight of his curious staff.

Hiro was amazed with the contents of vault. They took some gold and silver and a considerable quantity of precious stones, which they placed in the canvas bag.

'Some of these are for you,' said Hiro, 'but I will keep them for you for the time being providing you keep your mouth shut.'

As they left the bank, a curious Sgt Manu asked if they could trust the manager.

'Of course', said Hiro. 'If he opens his mouth he gets a bullet. Keeping it shut earns him a small fortune.'

Together, the two Japanese soldiers returned to the main camp. Their futures were now secure, if they survived the war.

A week later Capt. Hiro and Sgt Manu drove to the Thai border where they handed the canvas bag over to Marie and her uncle. As Hiro said his goodbyes to a tearful Marie, her uncle took his hand.

'You can trust us, Captain. When the time comes your nest egg will be here waiting for you.'

Hiro indicated Sgt Manu.

'Some of it is his.'

'Of course', said the uncle. 'It will be here for you both.'

A relieved Capt. Hiro and a somewhat bemused Sgt Manu made their way back to Ipoh, the sergeant doing most of the driving. Manu looked across at the sleeping captain as the car bounced along the road.

'And to think, I once called this man a "stupid prick"', he said to himself.

Chapter 43

When Tora Toshra heard of the invasion false alarm he decided it was time for Anna and Tia to go to Thailand. From the intelligence briefs he was privy to as Governor of Penang he knew that an invasion could not be far off. It was now mid-May. On a Saturday afternoon, Toshra, the faithful Hosan and their wives started their journey to the Thai border. They had an escort of ten soldiers who followed in a separate lorry.

The soldiers rather enjoyed a break from the boring garrison duties they performed in Penang. By nightfall they were almost at the border. The officers and their wives spent the night at a small hotel, while the soldiers enjoyed the comfort of a smaller establishment nearby. As this doubled as the local brothel, and with some extra money provided by their Governor, they spent an enjoyable evening.

Toshra and Hosan took advantage of their last night with their wives to indulge in a frantic night of passion. In the morning the girls, now firm friends, exchanged knowing glances and smiles. The two husbands looked somewhat drawn, the girls radiant.

With their escort in tow, they reached the border at noon. As arranged, a friend of the Thai envoy was there. He would drive their wives to Pattani, where they would be installed in the property they had purchased there.

After a tearful farewell and with the girls out of earshot in the car, Toshra asked if their wives would be looked after in their new home. The envoy's friend smiled.

'Have no fear, your wives will be safe. I give you my word. My wife and I will see them every day, and we will pass their letters to you through the Thai envoy in Penang.'

He then drove off, with the two girls waving from the rear window of the car.

A somewhat subdued Toshra and Hosan drove back to Butterworth, a large town on the Malay mainland, where they boarded the ferry to Penang with their escort. They arrived back later that night to the strangely quiet Governor's residence.

Two days later they were both handed letters from the Thai envoy. Anna was full of praise at the treatment she and Tia had received from the envoy's friend and his wife. Their house was large and well equipped, with three servants and two gardeners. The other property was still being decorated, but it was nearby and when it was finished Tia would move in.

The local bank manager had opened cash accounts for them both, but the bulk of their wealth was secure in the bank's strong room. The news relieved Toshra and Hosan, who were still adding to the haul they intended to transfer to Pattani through the envoy, less his percentage handling fee.

In a telephone conversation with the commanding general in Kuala Lumpur, the general, an old friend, had asked him if he had his future secured. Toshra said he had. His friend then indicated he was too old and sick to bother himself, and wished Toshra and his wife a long and happy life. After the conversation had ended, a somewhat saddened Toshra sat thinking of all the friends he had lost and would lose before the war reached its close.

Mick Martin decoded the latest message from Ceylon with acute disappointment. There would be no invasion of

Malaya until August at the earliest. This news would dampen morale, and he needed to get his group active. He contacted Ralph Slater, who of course was facing the same problem, and they jointly decided to carry out a couple of daylight ambushes.

Col Martin decided to ambush the Tapah road just east of Gunung Rapat. They could hide up for twenty-four hours in one of the gunung's many gullies after the attack.

The following day, Martin, with his two fellow marines, made for the jungle's edge south of the tin mine. It took them a day and a half to get there, and after resting up for four hours they made for the Tapah road under cover of darkness. By dawn they were in position, and waited for a suitable target to appear. They were on the Gunung Rapat side of the road and would have less than a mile to travel to reach the safety of the huge limestone outcrops.

Two lorries passed them during the morning but were not a tempting enough target, being almost empty. The three marines were having difficulty staying awake in the hot sun, until the sound of several lorries approaching brought them to a high state of alert.

The three lorries came into sight, travelling at a slow speed. The second lorry was towing the third. Now ready to spring their ambush they waited for the first lorry to pass, before opening fire into the second and third, with devastating results. The towed lorry must have been carrying explosives, as it just blew apart. The lorry towing it was caught in the intense ball of fire and tipped onto its side, blazing fiercely. The driver and escort leapt from the doomed vehicle, their clothing burning intensely. The marines blasted them from the road in a burst of fire, almost as an act of mercy.

The leading lorry accelerated away from the ambush. Blake managed one five-round burst from his Bren gun as it did so. It swerved across the road, suggesting the driver had been hit, then straightened and headed for Ipoh.

The job done, the marines quickly left the scene and made for the sanctuary of Gunung Rapat. Within the hour they were near the top of one of its many gullies, hidden by the dense undergrowth.

On hearing of the attack, Capt. Hiro decided on a limited response. He did not intend to rush into a second ambush. He led twenty men to the scene, where they spent an hour searching for the ambushers' escape route. One of his men spotted a few damaged clumps of lalang and a muddy imprint at the base of one of the many gullies along the foot of Gunung Rapat.

Hiro was not keen to subject his men to the potential danger of a close encounter on the steep and jungle-covered gully. He had a grenade launcher with him and instructed the soldier carrying the weapon to fire three grenades at the top of the gully. The results were quite impressive, and disturbed a troop of monkeys living high up on the gunung's sides. The animals' shrieks and rapid departure to a safer area provided some amusement to the watching Japanese troops.

As there was no response to the grenades, other than the monkeys, Capt. Hiro led his men further round the gunung's base. They spent another four hours in a fruitless search, then they returned to their camp in Ipoh.

Peter Blake winced with pain as a shard of shrapnel sliced across his right buttock. The other two grenades exploded slightly below them, the first, being the closest, only ten yards to their right.

Not wishing to betray their position the marines stayed motionless, until the Japanese moved away from the base of the gully. Mick Martin and Jim Muir had heard Blake give a faint cry of pain, and carefully moved over to where he lay.

'Where have you been hit?' asked an anxious Col Martin.

'In the arse, Sir', said Blake and waited for the expected wisecrack.

He was not disappointed. Both of his fellow marines took a close look at the damaged area. Jim Muir was the first to respond.

'What a beautiful bottom you have, Peter. Not a hair to be seen, just a nasty gash. I'll kiss it better.'

'Piss off you pervert', said Blake.

Mick Martin put a stop to this exchange by applying a field dressing.

'You will survive, young Blake. Just another scar to add to your collection.'

With no further sign of the Japanese troops, the marines moved to the top of the gully, and carefully made their way along the ridge. After about eighty yards they descended down a steep and narrow ravine, stopping about twenty yards from the bottom. They lay up there for the rest of the day, eating some cheese and biscuits.

Blake's wound was sore and his leg felt very stiff and numb. As soon as it was dark they completed their descent and made their way through the Sungei Raia Gorge. They gave the tin mine a wide berth and just before daylight they reached the safety of the jungle's edge.

The marines rested up for four hours. Blake had the dressing on his wound changed. It was still sore and was quite inflamed. They needed to get some rations from one of their food dumps. Once they had done this, they moved on for another couple of hours. They then made camp for the night and cooked a good meal, followed by some hot sweet tea.

It started to rain just after dark and Blake felt quite feverish. He was sweating profusely, and managed little sleep. By dawn he was feeling quite ill. His two companions were concerned at his worsening condition, so when they resumed their march after breakfast, they carried most of his equipment.

By midday it was obvious he could go no further, and with the cave on Gunung Jasar only a few hours away, Mick Martin went on ahead to get some help. Jim Muir constructed a shelter and made his friend as comfortable as he could, Blake drifting into an uneasy sleep. Just before dark, help arrived in the shape of the returning Mick Martin, Doc Park and an anxious Joy.

By the light of a torch, the wound was cleaned and some medication applied. Blake was given some tablets to reduce the fever. With Joy lying next to him he slept soundly, and by dawn he was feeling much better.

They left the camp at 1000 hours and slowly made for the cave, arriving at 1600 hours. Joy put Blake to bed, and gave him a wash down in cold water.

She confessed to Jan later. 'Peter must have been quite ill. That's the first time I have touched his groin area without him getting a hard-on.'

Over the next three days, with the wound stitched and healthy and with Joy's nursing, Blake made a rapid recovery, to everyone's delight. Proof of his return to full health was a hand encircling Joy's right breast on the fourth night back at the cave, and a frantic plea, 'Christ, love, I'm as hard as a chocolate frog!'

After twenty minutes of careful passion, she was satisfied that Peter Blake's recovery was complete.

The Ipoh bank manager was surprised when one of his female clerks knocked on his office door one evening as the rest of his staff left. She was an attractive girl in her twenties.

'We have locked up, Sir, and the rest of the staff has left. I am concerned that those Japanese soldiers are forcing you to give them money from the strong room.'

The manager's mouth dropped open.

'Miss Chan, I assure you there is nothing to worry about, but thank you for your concern.'

The girl smiled, said goodnight and left the bank. The manager watched her leave, suddenly aware what an attractive girl she was. The manager was in his early thirties; his wife had died in childbirth, just before the Japanese invasion. Most Sundays he visited their graves in the cemetery just outside Ipoh.

David Wei, on his appointment, had been one of the youngest managers in the Barclay DCO system. Despite his assurances to Suki Chan, he was desperately concerned about his involvement with the Japanese officer. He had always been scrupulous in his banking career, and had even managed to derive some profit for his bank following the Japanese invasion.

Many people whose houses had been bombed had no recourse to insurance because it had been an act of war, leaving them destitute. David Wei had stepped in when the rest of the banks had offered nothing. He had bought the land the houses had stood on, giving the previous occupants at least some money. The deeds of these sites were now in the strong room, alongside valuables belonging to people Wei knew had died in the bombing.

One of the richest men in Ipoh had been a moneylender called Li Li Wong. His personal box in the strong room contained a fortune in diamonds and rubies. Wong's body had

315

been found near his house after an air raid; he had been stabbed to death. Clearly one of his desperate former clients had taken the opportunity to erase their debt.

David Wei had previously tried to get Li Li Wong to make a will, Wong's response being, 'Why? I have no family. If I should die give a hundred dollars each to the two tarts who visit once a week to give me pleasure.'

Following Wong's death, David Wei had paid a visit to the 'Happy World Dance Hall' and paid the two surprised women the money Wong had bequeathed. The delighted girls had offered David Wei an hour of their personal service as a thank you, but he had declined their offer with a shy smile.

Following a disturbed night, a worried David Wei decided to share his problems with the concerned Suki Chan. At closing time that day he called her to his office, just as the rest of the staff were leaving. Making sure the bank was now secure, Wei told Miss Chan of the arrangement he had reached with Capt. Hiro.

He was touched by her concern, which was quite obviously genuine.

'Mr Wei, you are the most honest man I have ever met. I can understand why you are so worried', she said.

They talked for an hour. She made several suggestions as to how he could solve the problem, but all meant breaking his word to the Japanese officer. Finally, they both accepted he had to keep quiet about the theft of the valuables, knowing the wealth of the late Li Li Wong would more than offset any loss to the bank.

David Wei was grateful for the help Suki Chan had given and invited her out for a meal at the Ipoh Golf Club that Saturday evening. The club had recently reopened after being shut for two years. Capt. Hiro had decided the gesture would be seen as a step in the right direction. Suki Chan could not wait for Saturday to come. She had secretly admired David Wei for a long time.

Chapter 44

Toshra was finding life in Penang somewhat lonely. Most evenings he and Hosan sat drinking beer on the terrace of Government House. The news that was being received from Headquarters was deeply disturbing. Air raids were now a daily occurrence on the Japanese mainland and Tokyo had received a daily visit from American carrier-based aircraft for the last week, with considerable damage being inflicted.

What was a major cause of concern was the split in the Japanese War Cabinet, half wanting to fight for every inch of Japan, the other favouring a peace treaty with the Americans. Already some overtures had been made through neutral countries to see what the American terms might be. The news was not good. America would insist on an unconditional surrender and nothing less. This revelation strengthened the position of the hawkish element of the War Cabinet and dismayed the others.

Toshra knew the end for his country was not far off. With Anna and Tia safely in Thailand and their financial future assured, he had only the troops under his command to worry about. Over the last few months he had progressively eased the yoke of occupation. His men maintained law and order with a very gentle hand, compared to what had gone on before.

Sgt Hosan had once again offered to assist his former private in providing comfort to the wife of the Thai envoy.

Yama, now released from the army, had laughed and told Hosan to 'bugger off'.

'My Shan, is very happy with my performance, and certainly does not need the feeble efforts of an old married man.'

Hosan was outraged. He walked away trying to preserve some dignity, wishing a severe case of venereal disease on the smiling Yama.

In total secrecy, in a remote area of the United States, the key to end the war with Japan was being prepared. In its advanced state of readiness it needed only the President to authorise its use. It would change forever the concept of war. When used it would cause all nations to shudder at the terrible force unleashed.

The choice for the American President to make had been simple. Both options involved a large and potentially unacceptable loss of life.

Should they be American or Japanese lives?

The answer was obvious and, with a crucial election looming, the decision was made.

The date for the use of the new weapon was the last week in July. Several bomber crews had begun training, carrying a dummy bomb of the same weight and dimensions as the real thing. They flew across the United States the exact mileage the operation would entail, dropping the dummy bomb with pinpoint accuracy. The crews were sworn to complete secrecy. One crew member, who confided to a friend that he was on a special mission, was removed to a remote area of Alaska for the remainder of the war.

Ralph Slater was uneasy. He had been informed that the invasion of Malaya might not take place, as hopes were high for a

Japanese surrender. It had also been suggested that certain Japanese officers were prepared to accept a ceasefire, but not a surrender. What disturbed him further was a suggestion that he should make some kind of contact with the Japanese, to test out this theory.

He turned up at the cave one morning to everyone's surprise and went into a deep discussion with Mick Martin. With the rest of the group trying unsuccessfully to listen in, their curiosity was further roused by Mick Martin saying, 'Don't they appreciate the risks involved, or perhaps they don't care.'

The conversation went on for another twenty minutes, then they were all called together for a briefing. Brig. Slater explained the position, and asked for comments. Joy asked him who would be selected to meet up with the Japanese.

'Oh, no problem there', said Slater. 'That's my job.'

After some discussion on arranging a meeting, Jim Muir suggested using the tin mine manager as a go-between.

'We could create a small diversion to draw the five soldiers away, then talk to the manager, and arrange a meeting at the mine.'

'I like the sound of that. When can we do it?' said Ralph Slater.

Mick Martin looked around, 'I suggest we leave in the morning.'

At first light the next day, the three marines and Ralph Slater left the cave. The girls watched them go with anxious waves.

Making good time, they reached the jungle's edge by the mine just after 1400 hours the following day. They observed the mine for thirty minutes and saw the manager leave and return to his office. Jim Muir and Peter Blake moved north of the mine and along the pipeline for half a mile. They then moved clear of the jungle and fired two bursts over the mine. The five Japanese soldiers rushed out of their hut and into view. The marines fired two more bursts. The Japanese soldiers moved quickly in their direction. When they were two hundred yards away, the marines moved back into the jungle.

As soon as the soldiers had left the mine, Ralph Slater and Mick Martin made their way to the manager's office. As they walked through the door, the manager almost collapsed with fear. A tell-tale puddle of urine spreading under his desk showed the extent of his surprise.

In a few brief sentences the two officers explained what they wanted. The manager, by now recovering some composure, said, 'The commanding officer in Ipoh is a Capt. Hiro. You want me to get him here so you can kill him?'

'No,' said Ralph Slater, 'merely to talk with him. We will return here tomorrow at this time. The soldiers are to move half a mile down the road. Any funny business and you die. Understand?'

The manager said he would do what he could. The officers left and made their way back into the jungle, just in time to see the soldiers returning empty-handed.

Capt. Hiro listened to the tin mine manager with disbelief. He looked at the phone, wishing he could see the man's face.

'They want to talk to me?' he said. 'Are you fucking pissed, you useless bastard.'

'No Sir', cried the panic stricken manager. 'They want to discuss something with you. Perhaps they want to surrender.'

Capt. Hiro listened for a few more minutes, then told the manager he would ring him back in an hour. He sat thinking for a while. He wanted advice. He made a decision, and dialled his Headquarters in Kuala Lumpur.

Two minutes later he was explaining all to the old general. When he finished, there was a pause from the other end of the phone, before the general replied.

'Fuck me, young Hiro you lead an exciting life. Go and see them. You can trust them; they are not like us. Then tell me what they want.'

Just after lunch the next day, Capt. Hiro and his faithful Sgt Manu drove out to the tin mine. The garrison of five soldiers was dispatched half a mile down the road, their faces a picture of curiosity. Hiro and his sergeant sat in the porch of the manager's office, Sgt Manu with a sub-machine gun in his hands.

A few minutes later four men suddenly appeared. They viewed each other with mutual dislike and suspicion. Capt. Hiro spoke first, in quite good English.

'I have only agreed to meet you as my commanding general in KL is curious as to your motives.'

Ralph Slater suggested they go into the manager's office and sit down. Sgt Manu, Blake and Jim Muir remained outside, watching each other like hawks.

Hiro listened to the British officers with a growing anger. At last he spoke, his voice an angry hiss.

'You want me to surrender? Never. We Japanese know how to die, unlike you British. When we entered Malaya there were white flags everywhere. You disgraced your uniforms.'

Slater swallowed hard.

'*We* didn't surrender. We have fought you from the depths of the jungle, with considerable success, as you well know.'

The brigadier and the captain stared at one another, neither looking away. Mick Martin broke the impasse.

'May I suggest we consider the situation if both our superiors decide on a ceasefire prior to an official end to hostilities?'

Slater nodded.

'Perhaps Capt. Hiro would consult with his general over that?'

Hiro stood up.

'I agree to that. We could meet again in a week's time. Until then the war continues.'

Hiro left the office and he and Sgt Manu walked away with not a backward glance.

Ralph Slater and his party left the tin mine and quickly reached the safety of the jungle's edge. After an hour they stopped, and over a mug of tea Jim Muir and Peter Blake were brought up to date which what had transpired. This led to further discussion, by the end of which they sensed that the war for them had not that long to run.

They could not get back to the cave that day, so they made camp at 1700 hours. After a meal it began to rain heavily. All four sat quietly, their minds still turning over the events of the day.

After breakfast they started back to the cave, reaching their friends just before noon. Ralph Slater and Mick Martin briefed the others on the events of the previous day. They listened enthralled, hardly believing what they were told. Later that evening the two officers composed a coded signal for Headquarters in Ceylon, and transmitted it at 2100 hours.

Capt. Hiro had also been busy. A brief phone call to the general in Kuala Lumpur was suddenly cut short, the general insisting the subject was too sensitive for an open line. Hiro was instructed to report the next day.

'Get here by noon, young Hiro. Someone is flying up from Singapore to listen to your report', said the old general.

That night Hiro wrote to Marie, careful not to say anything that might worry her unduly. He still slept at the cottage and when he closed his eyes he could imagine she was still there.

At first light the next day, he left for Kuala Lumpur with the faithful Manu as his escort. It was an uneventful journey and they arrived just before 1100 hours.

Hiro had spent the time on the journey rehearsing what he would say. He was shocked when he was shown into the general's office. The old man seemed to have shrunk and his skin was the colour of slate. Another senior officer sat beside him.

'Let's hear your news then, young Hiro. Tell us of your meeting with the enemy', said the old man.

Hiro spoke for twenty minutes. He was not interrupted. He told them about the British soldiers and then corrected himself, one soldier, a brigadier. The others were Royal Marines, a colonel, a senior sergeant and a corporal.

'They asked if we would surrender. I said no. They then asked if we would participate in a ceasefire, pending a formal end to hostilities. I told them I would pass their request on to my general, and see them again in a week's time.'

Hiro continued, and described the condition of the men, how they were armed and dressed, and that they had told him they had been in the jungle since December 1941.

When Capt. Hiro finished, he was questioned for another twenty minutes, mainly by the senior officer from Singapore. He was then told to wait outside, so he sat down on a chair just outside the door. He heard the phone inside being used several times.

After an hour he was called back in. The old general gave him an encouraging smile, but it was the senior officer from Singapore who did all the talking.

'Capt. Hiro, we have a delicate mission for you. Make contact with these people again, and meet with them at the same place. Only discuss a ceasefire, and find out what else they have to offer and where this offer is coming from. We need to know what level of authority they have to back up this suggestion. If we accepted the offer, we would need to know who would control these freedom fighters? We would insist on retaining our weaponry.'

At last the old general spoke.

'You are now promoted to major. Only an officer of field rank could discuss these matters. Dine with us tonight, then return to Ipoh tomorrow and arrange to see your new "friends". Then come and see us again.'

The next morning, Hiro made his way back to Ipoh, with Sgt Manu admiring the major's new badges of rank.

Suki Chan had never been happier. Since the dinner with David Wei at the Ipoh Club they had been out together five times. At the bank their relationship had not changed, but outside banking hours they had become very close. Tonight they were going dancing at the City Lights Cabaret, which the Japanese allowed to open twice a week till ten o'clock. After this they were having supper at his flat. He had kissed her several times, and on their last evening out he had briefly touched her breast. Her body ached for him to go further, but she was content to wait.

They met at eight o'clock. He pinned a flower to her dress and kissed her lightly on the lips. They both were good dancers, and Suki noticed that after their second dance he held her body closer to him. By the end of the evening's dancing she could feel all of his body pressed firmly against her.

They went to his flat and sat down to a light supper with some wine. Afterwards, they sat on his sofa and drank their coffee. He leaned over and kissed her. She responded. His hand cupped her breast, his fingers tracing the outline of her nipple. His hand slid down to the top of her leg, gently squeezing her thigh. He became bolder and slid his hand under her dress, his hand moving up the inside of her thigh.

Suki slightly parted her legs, allowing his hand to move between them. His fingers moved rapidly inside her panties, then inside her. She was melting. She placed her hand on the top of his legs and moved upwards. She quickly encountered his swollen penis. It seemed massive. He paused and freed his erect penis from the confines of his trousers. She saw him slide a contraceptive over its length. She removed her panties, moved over onto her back and guided him into her.

His body was like a coiled spring suddenly released. He thrust deeply in and out. Her body screamed its pleasure, not wanting him ever to stop, then he gave a massive shudder and climaxed. She joined him. They lay side by side regaining their composure. He leaned across and kissed her.

'Marry me, Suki Chan', he said.

She smiled. 'Of course', she replied, and kissed him hard on the lips.

Chapter 45

Ralph Slater, Mick Martin and the two other marines peered through the dense foliage at the jungle's edge. They had been there two days making sure the Japanese had not hidden extra troops in the vicinity of the mine.

It was almost noon and near the time of their arranged meeting. They could see a cloud of dust moving along the road from Gunung Rapat. It must be the Japanese officer; at least he was punctual.

The garrison of five soldiers was waiting at the entrance to the manager's office. As Ralph Slater and the heavily armed marines came into sight, the Japanese soldiers raised their weapons.

The Japanese officer alighted from his car with his sergeant. He gave a brief instruction to the five soldiers and they moved off down the road. He then indicated that they should go into the manager's office. The manager stood as the Japanese and British officers entered.

'Leave us', commanded Maj. Hiro.

The manager gladly fled the scene, quite rightly fearing the enemies could open fire at one another at any time.

'Congratulations on your promotion, Major', said Ralph Slater.

'Thank you', said Hiro. 'Let us get on. The Japanese army will not surrender to you or your bunch of trained monkeys. Should your forces invade Malaya, we will drive those who get ashore back into the sea. However, should your leaders wish for a ceasefire, we would be prepared to listen to what they have to say. Our forces would cease active operations against your so-called freedom fighters, provided they ceased operations against us.'

Hiro paused to allow the implications of what he had said to sink in. He went on.

'During this ceasefire our troops would remain in barracks, except to transport essential supplies. Your forces should also adopt a passive role. Any breach of this agreement by your people would be met with awesome force, and we would target the civilian population for particularly harsh treatment.'

Hiro sat down, having delivered the words composed by his senior officers.

Ralph Slater looked at Mick Martin. What they had heard was what they had expected to hear. Slater looked at Hiro and smiled.

'Major, I don't think our superiors are too far apart on the method of implementing a ceasefire. You may also be interested to hear that Germany has agreed to surrender unconditionally to the Allied forces. This was signed three weeks ago on the 8th of May. As I am sure your High Command is aware, all the massive forces which have been engaged against Germany are now free to turn their attentions on you.'

Hiro paled. He had not been told about Germany's surrender, but his generals must have known. He should have been told.

'I have no interest in what happens in Europe', said Hiro. 'The German cause was different to ours. As I understand you, should our High Command agree, you would be prepared to adopt a ceasefire stance. This would not allow any additional forces to enter Malaya, unless we agreed.'

Ralph Slater stood up.

'Yes, Major, that's it. I think you should now consult with your general. If you wish to speak to us again, raise a blue flag over the manager's office. We will respond to that in twenty-four hours.'

They all stood, then left the room, both parties turning their backs on one another and walking away.

As soon as he was back in his Ipoh office, Hiro rang his Headquarters in Kuala Lumpur. The general was not available, but a colonel who seemed aware of their meetings told him to come to Headquarters the next day.

There had been a letter from Marie, which he had read several times. She was well, and had heard on the radio that the war in Europe was over. She hoped he would come to her soon as she missed him terribly.

He wrote her a letter. It came easily to him. He told her he was sure the war in the Far East had only a short course to run and they would soon be together again, this time forever.

He decided not to sleep in the cottage anymore, but to keep to his quarters. He also decided that the deeds of ownership of the cottage, given to Marie by Col Tihoka, would be transferred to the young manager at the bank; it would repay the service he had rendered.

After a troubled night's sleep, Hiro drove down to Kuala Lumpur. Sgt Manu, who was the major's escort, could see how worried his officer was. Matters did not improve when Hiro found that his general was in hospital. The old man was seriously ill, and unlikely to take part in the meeting.

The meeting took place at 1100 hours. The senior officer was there, as well as the colonel who Hiro had spoken to the previous day. Maj. Hiro explained what had transpired, and the threat that had been made regarding the freeing of forces from the European war. The two officers listened to him grim faced, the colonel making a few notes. When Hiro had finished, they questioned him for some time, then they adjourned for lunch.

They resumed at 1400 hours. Clearly the senior officer from Singapore had been in touch with his superiors. He gave Hiro clear instructions.

'Maj. Hiro, it has been decided that no further contact will be made for the time being with this brigadier. However, you should be prepared to instigate at short notice a further meeting should you be so instructed. Is this clear?'

Hiro said it was, and that he could arrange a meeting at twenty-four hours notice. He was then told to return to his duties at Ipoh.

He took the opportunity to visit the general before he started his journey back. The old man smiled when he walked on to the ward.

'Come and sit down, and tell me all the latest news', he said.

Hiro talked with him at length. At the end, the general, whose voice was now almost a whisper, leaned over and said, 'We won't meet again, young Hiro. My time is nearly up, so remember what I said to you before. I hope you have planned for your future?'

Hiro assured him that he had.

'Good', said the old man. 'Now bugger off back to Ipoh.'

Hiro shook the old man's hand as he left. He knew he would not see him again.

Mick Martin had set up a camp a mile from the tin mine. He and the two marines would keep watch on the mine during the day in case a blue flag was raised. Ralph Slater was back in the cave on Gunung Jasar keeping in touch with Headquarters in Ceylon.

They had brought plenty of supplies to the camp and could stay there for another week if necessary. The marines missed their partners, and wished they were all together; the uncertainty of their situation did not help matters. Col Martin had decided to change things if they were to stay there longer than a week. He would bring Soo Lin and the two nurses to the camp and extend the shelters. It would give them all just a little more privacy.

David Wei was surprised by a visit from Maj. Hiro. He invited the officer to sit down, his expression prompting the major to speak.

'Don't worry, I have not come to rob the bank. We have sufficient funds now. I have brought you a small gift, as a thank you for your help.'

He handed to David Wei the deeds to the cottage. Wei was dumbstruck. The deeds were in order, as was the transfer to himself, all legal and above board.

'This is a very generous gift, Major. I am to be married and this will solve our housing problem, thank you.'

Hiro shook hands with the delighted manager and left, his conscience now clear and honour satisfied.

As soon as the major had left, David Wei called Suki Chan into the office. They had kept their forthcoming marriage a secret from the rest of the staff, and had behaved with great restraint when at work. He showed Suki the deeds to the cottage.

'It's ours, all legal, signed, sealed and delivered. We will go and have a look round this evening.'

He grabbed Suki and held her tight, and for the first time kissed her while they were at work. She was delighted.

'Perhaps there is a bed there. If there is, we could try it out tonight; it would be better than your sofa.'

In the United States, the bomber crews had completed their training and were just waiting for the final orders to be given. They had been put on standby to move to an airfield in the Pacific area. This order would be activated in three days. At the highest level, the date of the mission and its target had been approved. It would be the 6th of August, and the unfortunate city, Hiroshima. This would be an event that would change the world forever.

The following week the flight of heavy bombers left for their new base in the Pacific, the crews aware their mission might end the war quickly, but unaware of the level of destruction they were about to unleash.

The two naked lovers moved slowly apart to allow their perspiring bodies to cool. Suki could not believe the pleasure David had given her. They had only intended to visit their new home to see what it was like, but the bedroom, with its large double bed and crisp white sheets, had proved too much of a temptation.

The cottage had two bedrooms, both double, and was fully furnished, the contents being of good quality. Suki Chan knew it would be a happy home for them both, and in time, for their children as well.

She glanced across at David Wei. He looked a picture of contentment. She moved her hand onto his lower stomach, and then onto his sleeping penis. Her gentle caress stirred it into life and it began to harden, then finally to rear up. She leaned over and allowed her firm breasts to tease it further. Its owner gave a grunt and his lips traced a pattern of moisture along her throat down to include her breasts, and further down along the inside of her thighs, completing their journey between her legs.

She squirmed with pleasure, not wanting him to stop. He pulled away, his erection only inches from her face. The temptation was too great, and she took him into her mouth. This proved too much for David Wei's control and he only just managed to pull away from her face, his juice spurting over Suki's breasts.

Ralph Slater had left Gunung Jasar and had returned to his group near Tapah. He had been told the invasion of Malaya had been postponed, and in all probability would not take place. Events were beginning to move to a conclusion. A chain of key moves was already in train, and the end was in sight.

Mick Martin had left Jim Muir, Jan, Peter Blake and Joy in the camp near the tin mine, but maintained a radio link with him at the cave, in case the Japanese wished to talk further. It had been quite a change to have Soo Lin almost to himself. Doc Park and Mai Peng were almost joined at the hip, their future clearly decided.

It was almost the end of July, and the awaited invasion of Japan would be the final supreme effort of the Allies to end the war. All attempts to persuade the Japanese to surrender had failed. They seemed determined to fight to the death.

Governor Toshra and Sgt Hosan were ready to move. The colonel in charge of the garrison had asked Toshra's permission to move his men to the mainland, so that if the war came to a sudden end they had the choice to escape or surrender. Toshra had given his permission and the men were now in a camp at Butterworth, awaiting developments.

With his garrison troops off the island, Toshra called a meeting of the political heads, senior police officers and village elders. He recalled his first meeting with these same people when he had been appointed as Military Governor. The atmosphere then and now was quite different. Over the course of time he had gained their respect for the fair way he had dealt with their problems.

When they had assembled, he explained his situation to them frankly. They were aware that almost all the Japanese soldiers had left the island, leaving not more than a dozen guarding Government House.

'I have ordered my soldiers to leave the Island of Penang in case of an Allied landing. If we had stayed it would have meant a pre-landing bombardment, with considerable loss of life and damage. I am sure you did not want that. I will leave soon. Therefore, the responsibility for law and order and the smooth running of the island's affairs will be in your hands. As of now I relinquish the power of Governor. I wish you luck and good fortune, and perhaps in time I may return to this beautiful island as a friend.'

Toshra waited for the abuse to start, perhaps even violence. His faithful Hosan was by his side, ready to protect him.

The room went quiet. Then as a man they stood and applauded. When the applause died down their spokesman stood and faced the surprised Toshra.

'We are pleased that the Japanese are going and delighted the war appears to be ending, but we shall miss you. You have been like a father to us. You have been fair and always ready to listen to our problems. We cannot forgive your country for invading us under force of arms. However, you have shown us nothing but kindness. You, Tora Toshra, have been a good friend and we wish you a safe journey wherever you decide to go. You will be welcome here any time.'

After they had all left, Toshra turned to Sgt Hosan.

'Well what did you think of that?'

Hosan smiled, 'I think that means we can get off this island in one piece, and that's a welcome surprise.'

Later that day Toshra and the rest of his men left Penang and took up residence with his garrison in Butterworth, to await developments.

•

Chapter 46

On the 4th of August, Ralph Slater arrived back at Gunung Jasar.

'We need to contact the Japanese immediately. Can you arrange it?'

Mick Martin contacted C/Sgt Muir at his camp opposite the tin mine. Within fifteen minutes, watched by the five Japanese soldiers guarding the mine, they were in contact with Maj. Hiro.

As Jim Muir and Peter Blake approached the mine, one of the soldiers guarding it called his comrades out. They watched as the two marines approached, ready to fire, their sergeant holding them in check. When the marines had passed on the message to Maj. Hiro, via the mine manager, the soldiers turned their backs on them as though they were not there.

A meeting was arranged for noon the next day. On hearing this, Ralph Slater and Mick Martin left for the tin mine straight away. Maj. Hiro contacted his Headquarters in Kuala Lumpur and was told, 'Go and see what they want.' He was also told the old general had died the previous day.

It was 1100 hours on the 5th of August before Ralph Slater and Mick Martin arrived at the camp near the mine. Just before noon they moved out into the open and approached the mine.

A plume of dust on the road from Gunung Rapat heralded the arrival of Maj. Hiro. There were no formal greetings, Hiro merely saying, 'What do you have to tell me?'

Ralph Slater looked grave and almost apologetic.

'Tomorrow there will be a significant development. I think it will end the war. You should contact your Headquarters and obtain permission to act with complete authority in this area. When you have this we must talk again.'

Hiro stood and made to leave.

'Will you be close by?'

'Yes', said Slater. 'If you return here I will know.'

Hiro left straight away for Ipoh, his mind in a whirl. What was going to happen?

As soon as he was back in his office, he rang Headquarters and reported the conversation he had had. The senior officer there said he would contact Singapore, and would ring him back in due course. Hiro spent the next twelve hours waiting by the telephone.

Several thousand miles away, a lone American bomber at maximum height approached its target. Ten minutes earlier the captain had issued safety goggles to his crew, with instructions not to watch their bomb impact but to face away from their target after releasing their weapon.

Below them lay the sleeping city of Hiroshima, unaware that within a few minutes it would cease to exist. As the bomb aimer released his single bomb, the captain turned his plane to starboard and had completed a complete reversal of their course when the weapon detonated. The crew had followed their instructions and were looking away from the target with their safety goggles in place, when a blinding flash lit the sky for miles.

On the ground, Hiroshima received a visit from hell. Thousands died instantly, with not a word on their lips. These were the lucky ones. Thousands of others were incinerated, some at once, some slowly. The crew of the bomber looked back at the huge mushroom cloud slowly rising from what, a few moments before, had been a major city. They would never forget this day for the rest of their lives, and they would all wish they had not been there.

It was midday before the news reached the Japanese Headquarters in Singapore, and a message was flashed instantly to all Japanese units. Maj. Hiro was shattered.

'How could an entire city literally disappear, and just one bomb?'

If there were any doubts about Japan coming out of this conflict with an acceptable peace deal those doubts were now gone. Kuala Lumpur rang a few minutes later and a very shaken senior officer told Hiro to make contact with the British brigadier and find out what was on offer.

Maj. Hiro made his way to the tin mine and waited in the manager's office. The manager, seeing the expression on the major's face, excused himself and left him to his thoughts.

About an hour later Ralph Slater entered the office with Mick Martin, Blake and Jim Muir staying outside. Slater told Hiro he should keep his troops in barracks. The men under Brig. Slater's control would not enter the large towns, but would come out of the jungle and make camps by the roadside. A ceasefire would exist as from now and until a formal declaration was made that hostilities had ceased.

It was a bitter pill for Hiro to swallow, but reluctantly he accepted it, at least until he received further instructions. Slater also told him he would make his headquarters in Tambun House, the former Japanese rest centre. Hiro merely nodded and left, taking the five Japanese soldiers with him.

When he was back in Ipoh, Maj. Hiro phoned Kuala Lumpur and reported the conversation. He expected to be savaged for exceeding his authority, but the subdued senior officer said he would contact him at noon the next day. Hiro had all his men assemble in the dining hall. He explained they were to remain in camp for the time being, and to behave in a proper manner. He was asked if the rumours about a devastating bomb were true. He nodded, and a hiss of anger ran through the ranks of men. He spoke to his two junior officers and told them to work closely with the senior NCOs to keep the men occupied in the camp.

Mick Martin, on his return to the cave, told them all they were moving into Tambun House and would leave the cave for the last time next day, taking a full quantity of rations with them.

On the next day a somewhat reluctant departure took place. In one of the cave passages they sealed all the rations and ammunition they could not carry. Doc Park and Mai Peng paid a last visit to Hari Khah's grave, then they all started on the three-day journey to Tambun. Ralph Slater and Peter Blake made a small detour to the site of the crashed Dakota, making good their promise to bury the crew's remains.

The weather remained fine and not a drop of rain fell for the entire journey. Just after noon on the third day they arrived at Tambun House, tired, but eagerly anticipating how quickly the war would end. To their surprise, three elderly women from the village were still keeping the house clean. When the last Japanese officers had left a week previously, the women had carried on with their work. There were enough bedrooms for them all. Ralph Slater occupied a single room on the ground floor. That night the four couples slept together in a bed for the first time. They all took the opportunity to make love, leaving a somewhat frustrated Slater listening to the creaking springs and mattresses above him.

All of the groups under Slater's control had left their jungle camps. Jim Bottle had his group in part of the mental hospital in Tanjung Rambutan. Slater's group, in his absence, was camped by the Tapah road. Only Yong Hoy was not completely cooperating, his two groups being camped in Tapah Station.

Ralph Slater had managed to obtain a 15-cwt truck, which had been left behind in Tambun village with a blocked fuel pump. He could now drive under escort into Ipoh, and also recover the large stock of food and ammunition they had buried on the side of the Ipoh to Lumut road.

In Japan, the War Cabinet were totally split, some of the more hawkish members still wishing to fight for every inch of Japan. The Emperor was thought to favour a ceasefire. It took a second bomb to convince the majority that further resistance was pointless.

The destruction of the city of Nagasaki shocked the War Cabinet into beginning peace talks with the Americans. To their horror, the Americans insisted on an unconditional surrender and nothing less, no face saving ceasefire. It was to be a total humiliation for the Japanese.

With no alternative, they surrendered unconditionally on 2nd September 1945. The war was over.

Chapter 47

In Malaya, as with other occupied territories, chaos ensued. Japanese forces largely remained in camp. In some parts, including the Ipoh region, things never got out of hand. Ralph Slater and Mick Martin met Maj. Hiro on many occasions, and a working relationship developed.

Members of the Malayan People's Anti-Japanese Army walked the streets of Ipoh and other towns and cities ignoring the Japanese soldiers, who still carried their weapons.

Maj. Hiro received only limited information from Kuala Lumpur, and was desperate to join Marie over the border in Thailand.

Tora Toshra and the loyal Hosan were already in Pattani, reunited with their wives, and waiting for the dust of surrender to settle.

Yong Hoy had already murdered some of his own countrymen, who he said had helped the Japanese, though the proof did not exist. His reputation as a brutal thug was established. Ralph Slater knew the man was beyond control. He had become too powerful and was a serious threat to the future peace of Malaya.

Peter Blake and Joy were enjoying the luxury of Tambun House, as were the others. Clean beds and the unlimited use of the showers were something they had never dreamed of. In some respects they missed the informality of their old cave home. After all, it had been their sanctuary for three and a half years.

Doc Park had visited the hospital in Ipoh. His skills were needed there, as were those of the two nurses. Once the routine was established, Doc Park, Joy and Jan, with either Peter Blake or Jim Muir acting as escort, would drive into Ipoh for the day, returning about 1800 hours.

For Joy and Jan it was a strange feeling to return to the hospital they had been lucky to escape from during the Japanese invasion. Mai Peng had installed herself as Dr Park's secretary and in a very short time, by dint of her genuine ability, became the hospital's administrator. Most of their patients were Japanese soldiers, wounded either locally or in Burma, who were grateful for the services of a skilled surgeon.

As the days went by, some Allied prisoners of war began to arrive from Burma, where they had worked under appalling conditions constructing roads or the railway. Taiping hospital took most of the former prisoners, many of whom needed good food and treatment for neglected fever or leg ulcers. Doc Park spent a couple of days a week operating at Taiping, doing mostly amputations.

Ralph Slater and Mick Martin were responsible for the whole of Perak, in respect of Japanese troops and maintaining law and order. Maj. Hiro and Mick Martin had become quite friendly. Hiro had told Col Martin of his wish to join Marie in Thailand. Mick Martin saw no reason why he should not, once the Ipoh garrison of Japanese soldiers was officially taken into custody.

A battalion of British troops finally arrived by train from Singapore. There was some unease at first, but once Mick Martin had concluded a lengthy meeting with their commanding officer and Maj. Hiro, the Japanese troops handed in their weapons and were escorted to Singapore to begin their journey home to Japan.

The day after their departure, Mick Martin drove Maj. Hiro and Sgt Manu to the Thai border. It was Hiro's reward for his full cooperation. At the border, the three former enemies shook hands and wished each other luck. Then Hiro and Manu crossed the border to the waiting Marie and Aunt Mona and, with a final wave to Mick Martin, drove away.

A month after the war had ended, Ipoh seemed to be little changed. The population quickly realised they had exchanged one occupying army for another, although, of course, the British and Australians were more acceptable. Soldiers do what soldiers do. The brothels and bars continued to do a good trade, and the numerous prostitutes plying their profession in the dark could not tell the difference between their old and new clients.

Mick Martin's group still resided at Tambun House. An attempt by an army company to take it over was resisted, first by Blake and Muir, who told a very young army officer to 'Fuck off! This is the Royal Marines' barracks.' Then Col Martin put the refusal more politely but just as bluntly.

The young officer reported to his company commander that he had been abused by two Royal Marine NCOs. The company commander, who was aware of the marines' long stay behind the Japanese lines, listened to the aggrieved young officer, then explained to the young man how long the marines had been in Malaya. When he finished the young officer said, 'Gosh, how exciting.'

The company commander smiled. 'Yes, I expect it was.'

The main church in Ipoh was the venue for a large wedding. Ralph Slater, now a major general, gave away all four brides, and a visiting bishop conducted the service. Col Michael Martin and Soo Lin, Dr Phillip Park and Mai Peng, C/Sgt James Muir and Janet Riley, Cpl Peter Blake and Joyce

Hammond were married in one combined service. Tears and wine flowed in equal measure. They all honeymooned at Tambun House. Later that night, as a naked Blake lay on their bed with an equally naked Joy, he whispered in her ear.

'Will it be different now we are married?'

'Oh yes', said Joy. 'I think we can dispense with the French letters.'

Over the following twelve months Jim Muir and Jan, Peter Blake and Joy returned to the United Kingdom, the marines to continue in their corps. The two former nurses were now mothers, and had resigned from the nursing service. Mick Martin and Soo Lin remained in Malaya; he was serving a three-year secondment to the Malayan Armed Forces. Doc Park was senior surgeon at the Taiping hospital, Mai Peng being deputy administrator. They all kept in touch.

Maj. Gen. Ralph Slater had stayed in the Far East, on the War Crimes Tribunal. All of the men had been decorated. Slater and Martin were both awarded the DSO, Capt. Jim Bottle the MC, Doc Park the CBE. The two marines both received the MM, while the girls had not been forgotten, all receiving the BEM.

In Thailand, a new trading company emerged. It was the Tiger Import and Export Company. Its directors were Tora Toshra, Hosan, Hiro and Marie. Over the next five years it became a major business in Pattani. All of the partners became rich men, as did their wives.

The only other shareholder was David Wei, a respected senior bank manager in Ipoh. His dividend was paid twice yearly to him and his charming wife Suki.

Marie had presented Hiro with a son. Both agreed he should not pursue a military career.

'Perhaps a doctor?' said Marie.

'That would be most acceptable', Hiro replied.

The political situation in Malaya never really settled down after the war. The largely Communist Anti-Japanese Army, which had done so much to assist in the defeat of Japan, failed to gain enough support in the elections to further their ambitions.

This left them feeling bitter and frustrated. In 1948, they returned to the jungle, carrying out murders and destruction on people and property of those who opposed them. Yong Hoy became one of the leaders of the now retitled Malayan Races Liberation Army. Yong Hoy's words to the then Col Slater, when Slater suggested Hoy had a hidden agenda, were coming true.

'When we have ejected the Japanese, we may have to start on the British.'

In view of the situation, a state of emergency was declared and British and Malay troops entered the jungle to seek out the Communist terrorists.

In 1950, the Royal Marine Commando Brigade was transferred to Malaya from Hong Kong. The brigade consisted of three Commando Units, 40, 42 and 45 Commandos. Serving in 'A' Troop 42 Commando were Sgt Maj. Muir and Sgt Blake. Their troop was based at Tambun House, and their area of operations included Gunung Rapat and the jungle beyond. It was like returning home for the two marines. Joy and Jan, back in England, were not so happy, and would be glad when their husbands' two-year tour in Malaya was over.

One evening, after returning from a two-week patrol, the two friends were having a cold beer in their mess. They both agreed that Malaya had been good to them. They had met and married their wives there. Blake looked at his friend.

'You know, Jim, I'd like to do it all again, and I wouldn't change a thing.'

Muir smiled.

'You are right, Peter. We had the time of our lives here, and didn't that Soo Lin have a lovely arse?'